# Intertwined

## Jerilee Kaye

# Acknowledgements

Lots of hugs and kisses and big thanks to the following wonderful people who made this journey an even more memorable experience:

Angel and Norma, the best parents a person could be blessed with. Without you, I wouldn't be me and I thank God every day for that.

Alfredo and Linda, my parents-in-law, thank you for accepting me into your family.

Yolanda and Bertier, and all my aunts and uncles: thank you for always believing in me.

Kathie, KC, Karen, Roland, Ronald and Kelly: with you, I am blessed to have not just brothers and sisters, I am also blessed with friends.

Joe, my oldest friend, my BFF: words are not enough to express how thankful I am for your friendship and loyalty. You're the reason why every book I write has a fab BFF in it!

Ralph and Mai: you are not just friends, you are family.

Roze, Criz, Leña, Claire, Helen, Ella, Debbie, Agie, Jacq and Cathy: friends who took time to walk inside my head. That meant a lot to me.

MarQ and KeOn, my little angels: you keep me young every day.

Sam my inspiration, my pillar, the love of my life: I thank God every day that my life is intertwined with yours. Thank you too for the dreamy book cover!

Morgan Childs: thank you for the wonderful editing job.

Dariia Sonoga: thank you for your creative eye and inspiration.

Credits also go to OneinaMillion for the cover shot.

Kristen Switzer of SwitzerEdits.com, my agent, my editor and my adviser: I wouldn't be able to pull this off without you. Every author should be blessed with an editor/agent like you!

And finally, to all Wattpad fans of Intertwined. Thank you for loving Travis and Brianne as much as I do. You guys totally rock!

# Prologue: Tradition

All families have a tradition. Sometimes it goes all the way back to their ancestors in the eighteenth century. Some families only started one in the twentieth century.

I don't know when my family tradition started. But one thing is for sure: This tradition doesn't make a single bit of sense.

But one cannot choose the family he or she will belong to. And you cannot choose which family traditions you will end up honoring in your life.

My family has close ties. While some people can sit together at parties not even knowing they are related, I had to know each and every one of my cousins, aunts, and uncles. We have family reunions about twice a year. In between those reunions, my family engages in gossip about each other. They have the chance to confirm that gossip during the reunions.

They especially like the women in our family who are approaching their thirties. It's the finish line for them.

According to my family tradition, we have a curse. If one of our women is not married before she turns thirty-one, she is doomed to be single for life.

I thought this was complete bull. But I've got Aunt Rosalie, who sits at family reunions alone. She had her heart broken when she was thirty. The guy left her at the altar. Ten years later, she's still single with no hopes of ever marching down the aisle.

We also have Aunt Mildy. Full of love, this one. So full of love, she passed from lover to lover and none of them ever wanted to put a ring on her finger. Now, rumor has it, she's the mistress of a rich Sultan, who comes to see her once every two months. She lives a luxurious life, though. But she's still a mistress in the eyes of her family.

There was also Theresa; she was one of my older cousins. Pretty and successful. But it was her choice to be single. She's a lesbian and has no desire to be married to a man. So I guess that was not really the workings of a curse.

One of our older aunts got married at thirty-two, giving the women in our family hope that the curse was just the lore our ancestors passed down to ensure the elders would always have grandchildren to dote on. But a week after she got married, her husband died. And she has remained a widow since then.

There are many stories of aunts and cousins who disregarded the tradition. I don't know whether it was just coincidence, but somehow they are in the family's *Hall of Shame*—the unwritten list of women in our family who had tragedy or bad luck fall upon them because they disregarded the family's deadline of thirty-one.

And so ever since I was young, I have been a hopeless romantic. I read all sorts of fairy tales and love stories, hoping someday one of those love stories would come true for me. That my knight in shining armor would come to rescue me, sweep me off my feet, and rush me to the altar. I intend to marry at the age of thirty, at least one year earlier so I'm sure I'm saved.

Apart from the fear of living my life alone, childless, or husband-less, I refuse to be the subject of my family's conversation and gossip at the reunion table. I hate it whenever the table is all abuzz and then suddenly falls silent when Aunt Rosalie or Aunt Mildy join in, and every single person at the table picks a different topic to talk about off the top of their heads.

By hook or by crook, I vowed: I would be married before the deadline! It would be a plus if my prince were handsome and capable of giving me the life I deserved. But I guess compared to the chitchat and the impending curse that would be bestowed upon me, I would much rather marry an ogre.

I have years to complete my quest. Two decades to plan my "forever" is a lot of time.

# Chapter One

## *The Other Member of the Family*

My parents are going to kill me! My best friend Cindy asked me to come with her to some kid's party. I didn't want to go, but she sort of begged me. I told my parents I was just going to hang out with some kids from school. Since I've always been a good, responsible kid, they said yes the first time I asked.

"But be home before eleven, okay?" my mom reminded me.

"I'm sure I won't be long," I said to her. And I had every intention of keeping that promise.

Little did I know that Cindy had plans of her own. When we got there, she drank almost every glass of alcohol that was shoved into her hands. She danced to her heart's desire and flirted with the older guys.

I was babysitting her. We were only fifteen and I was pretty certain we shouldn't be even be partying at all; least of all, drinking.

I was aching to leave. But I couldn't abandon my best friend in a sea full of sharks looking for fresh meat. I kept glancing at the clock. It was past midnight and Cindy had no intention of going home just yet.

"My parents are going to kill me!" I said to her. "And you've already had too much to drink."

"Chill out, Miss Prudy!" she said to me with a giggle. "We'll go home soon. Give me a few more minutes."

Yeah, right! Her minutes became hours. When the clock struck three, I mustered all my courage to call Cindy's brother.

Thirty minutes later, he was dropping me off in front of my house.

"Thanks for looking out for her," Josh said. "You're a good friend."

I nodded and then went to my front porch. Nervously, I opened the door. The whole house was quiet. Everybody was sleeping. I had never broken my parents' rules before. That's why they trusted me so much. My older brother was a responsible kid, too. Now I really hated Cindy for putting me through this.

I removed my shoes and tiptoed to the stairs. I didn't want to wake anybody up. I could deal with my parents the next morning. But

I didn't want to be caught red-handed. Moreover, I didn't want them to think that Cindy wasn't a good influence on me.

Our house had four bedrooms. My brother's room was the first one when you reached the top of the stairs, opposite the guest bedroom. Mine was across my parents' further down the hall.

The corridor was dark so I walked carefully toward my room.

Just then, I heard a clicking of locks and the twisting of a doorknob. It took me a moment to realize that it was coming from my parents' bedroom.

*Shit! I'm doomed for sure!*

It could be my mom, I thought, on her way to get milk or water from the kitchen.

I froze, thinking of reasons why I would be standing in the middle of the corridor at three in the morning when I promised her I would be home by eleven.

All of a sudden, I felt the door to my right open. It was the guestroom. Then I felt something wrap around my waist forcefully. Something clasped against my mouth before I could manage a scream. Then I was leaning against a hard wall and something hard and heavy was pressing against me.

I took deep breaths and found the courage to open my eyes. I saw a tall, slender figure leaning against me. I could make out the contours of his devilishly handsome face.

Instantly, I glared at him. He saw this even though the room was dark. I heard him chuckle softly.

There was a knock on the door.

"Travis?" my mom asked on the other side of the door. "Are you okay?"

He had winked at me before he replied. "Yes. Everything is fine."

"Is Brianne home already?" she asked.

Travis raised a brow and smiled at me mischievously. I reached up for his hand and struggled to remove it from my mouth but *damn!* He was strong. His eyes were dancing, and I knew he could say whatever he wanted to my mother and I would be helpless to stop him. If I spoke up, my mother would ask what I was doing in his room at three in the morning.

"Yes," he said. "I think she got in before midnight," he lied.

I glared at him. I didn't lie to my parents and he knew that.

"Oh, good. I didn't hear her come in," my mother said. "Okay. Goodnight, Travis."

"Goodnight." Travis's eyes never left mine.

I heard my mother's footsteps on the stairs. When we were sure she was out of earshot, I pushed Travis away from me.

"I don't lie to my mom!" I hissed at him.

He chuckled humorlessly. "You didn't," he said. "What are you? Deaf? I was the one who lied. So don't worry. You're still going to heaven." He put his hands together as if he were praying.

"I hate you!" I hissed. I pushed him again, and this time, he caught my hands in his.

He raised a brow at me. "Funny you say that, because you can't seem to stop touching me!"

I struggled to pull my hands away from his, but he held them tighter. "Let go, Travis!"

We heard footsteps coming from the stairs, indicating that my mother was going back to her room.

I stopped struggling. I kept my mouth shut and held my breath.

Travis pulled me closer to him. Suddenly, I felt his hot breath against my neck. I froze.

*What the fuck is he doing?*

I felt him run the tip of his nose against the base of my neck, sending shivers down my spine and making my knees go weak. Good thing he was holding my hands—otherwise, I think I would have fallen to the floor.

But I realized I knew exactly what Travis was doing. He was daring me to make a sound. He was daring me to fight him, curse at him, and hit him. But he knew I wouldn't dare. *Damn!*

I bit my lip to keep from making a noise. My mother was walking in the corridor. Then I heard her stop by my bedroom and turn the knob.

I felt panic grip me. She would see that I was not yet in my room! She would know that Travis lied. But after a few seconds, she was still turning the knob. My door was locked, even though I didn't remember locking it.

I felt Travis's smile as he buried his face in my hair. He must have done it. He must have locked my room. And thank God he did!

Finally, my mother went inside her room. As soon as I heard her door close, I pushed Travis away from me.

11

He was laughing.

"Damn you!" I cursed at him.

"You should have felt how shaken you were!" he said.

I got hold of my messenger bag and started hitting him with it. He shielded his face against it, but he still didn't stop laughing.

"For somebody who hates me so much, you sure tremble a lot against my touch, sweetheart," he said.

I gave him one last hit and then I headed toward his door.

"Bad idea," he said.

I turned to him. "What, you moron?"

"I don't know what's worse. You coming home at three in the morning, or you going out of my bedroom at four. I would rethink going out that door if I were you."

"For somebody who hates me so much, you sure find ways to trap me in your bedroom!"

"I don't hate you, Brianne." I could see the gleam in his devilish eyes. Then he took a step closer to me. "In fact, I think you're hot…and…"

I glared at him and then I took my bag and hit him with it again. He didn't bother to shield himself.

"I hate you!" I said to him.

"I know," he said, laughing hard. Then he managed to take hold of my hands to stop me from hitting him. He stared down at my still-angry face. "You smell good, by the way."

I gave him one hard push. "And you stink!"

"Liar!" he chuckled. He was right, actually. Travis smelled like fresh soap and aftershave. He showered at least three times a day and he never went to bed without taking one. I would know because it seemed like I'd been sharing a bathroom with him for the last four years. He pointed to the bathroom on the right side of his room. "I locked your bedroom door. So the bathroom is the only way you can go in. Unless…you'd rather sleep here with me." He winked.

I wrinkled my nose in disgust. Then I went through the bathroom.

"You owe me, princess!" he called out, but I shut the door without a backward glance.

*That*, ladies and gentlemen, was Travis James Cross! Like a son to my parents. Best friend to my brother. And Dennis the Menace to me!

***

I hated Travis. I really did. I cursed the day four years earlier when my brother had brought him home like some stray dog. In fact, a stray dog would have been a hundred times better.

My brother had a good heart—truly an angel in disguise. How he could be best friends with Travis was beyond my understanding. Travis was really...the devil incarnate!

When we were younger, his pranks included pulling my hair, stealing my lunch, and reading my diary. But this year, I decided to take the high road and just ignore him, tune him out. I guess he found more creative ways of making my life hell. Lately, he'd been putting me into uncomfortable situations. He flirted with me, not because he thought I was attractive, but because he knew I blushed the brightest shade of red whenever he touched me or threw a sexual joke my way.

After he and my brother had become best buds, he stayed in the guest bedroom at least three times a week for four years. And my parents just adored him—they felt the family was incomplete when Travis was not around.

One time, when I wanted to insult him and irritate him, I asked, "Why do you stay here all the time? Don't you have a house of your own?"

He smirked. "Of course, I do. Depends on which state or country you are referring to," he said in an arrogant tone.

My brother slightly shook his head and shot me a look that almost said, *Don't go down that lane. You won't win.*

I didn't get what my brother meant at the time. But one day, I saw a limo park in our driveway. I stared at it in awe. Then the driver got out and opened the passenger door. Travis stepped out of it.

The driver spoke in Spanish. The only words I understood from him were *Master Travis.*

*Master Travis? What is happening to the world?*

Travis saw me watching him and his driver with my mouth wide open. His eyes gleamed, and I didn't miss the cocky look he pasted on his face as he approached me.

Then he leaned forward and whispered to my ear. "Try not to look too amazed, sweetheart. It's called a limousine. *Limo* for short." Then he pushed my chin up to close my mouth. With a low chuckle, he went inside my house.

13

When Travis turned sixteen, I never saw the limo again. But a sleek red Porsche, or a white Bentley, or a yellow Corvette, or an orange Maserati would always be parked in front of my house, indicating his presence.

Okay, so Travis was not just rich. He was super rich! But I wondered why he spent more time in my house than he did in his many, many estates?

And why did he torture me a lot?

Since Travis told my mother I came home at eleven, I had to wake up early the next day to make sure I showed up for breakfast; although in truth, I'd only had about three hours of sleep.

"How was the party?" Tom, my brother, asked me.

"Okay, I guess," I replied curtly.

"Who brought you home?" my mother asked.

"Ah…Cindy's brother." That was not a lie. Immediately, I felt Travis's eyes watching me carefully, and I fought the urge to stick my tongue out at him.

We sat and ate breakfast.

"Jesus, what happened to your arms, Brianne?" Tom asked, reaching across the table to examine my wrists.

I looked at them and found some blue and purple spots on both my arms and wrists.

Instantly, I remembered how Travis and I played tug of war with my arms early this morning. I forgot that I bruised very easily and my skin complexion was just too white—any mark would be noticed almost immediately.

"Did somebody hurt you at the party?" my father asked, alarmed.

I pulled my arms away from Tom and hid them under the table.

"No," I said. Then my eyes shot up to Travis. "Not at the party."

Travis had a hard expression on his face, but I didn't know whether he was scared or sorry. Except when he was playing a trick on me, Travis was so good at hiding his emotions. Did he feel at all sorry that he had bruised me?

"Then where did you get those?" Tom asked.

I shrugged. "I don't know. I bruise easily, Tom. Somebody must have pulled me and caused this. I don't really remember. No big deal."

"Brianne, you know you can always tell me. Whoever leaves a mark on you, Travis and I…we'll beat him up!"

14

My eyes darted to Travis, who actually bit his lip with Tom's statement.

I smiled contentedly at Travis's guilt and discomfort. "Thanks, Tom. I'll hold on to your word. It's good to know you're ready to beat up anybody who hurts me." Then I looked at Travis meaningfully.

"Of course, I will. Nobody could hurt my little sister and get away with it."

I smiled widely at Tom, but it was more for Travis's benefit.

My father finished his breakfast. Then he kissed me and my mother goodbye.

"Where is he going?" I asked my mother.

"Golf." I finished my breakfast and then kissed my mom before running back to my room.

Before I could reach my bedroom, I felt somebody tug at my shoulder. I spun around and found Travis hot on my heels.

"What do you want now?" I asked.

He didn't reply. Instead, he reached down for my hands and examined my wrists. True enough, he saw faint bruises from the grip he had on me the night before.

I pulled my wrists away. "I bruise easily."

"I can tell," he said. Then he looked into my eyes. "I would never hurt you physically, Brianne. I'm...sorry." He sounded like he was in pain while he was saying that.

I laughed. I decided to enjoy this.

"What?" I asked.

"I'm sorry," he said a little louder.

"I can't hear you."

"I'm. Sorry."

"Still can't hear you," I pressed on.

He raised a brow at me. "I'm so sorry for bruising your arm, sweetheart." Then he added, "Do you still hurt? Come, show me your arms again. I would like to kiss them to make the pain go away," he said in a puppy-like tone.

I glared at him. "What am I, three?" And before I shut the bedroom door, I heard Travis's low chuckle behind me.

*** 

15

My parents were always busy with their work. But at least once a week we sat and had long dinners together. I cooked my famous meatloaf, which they all enjoyed. Even Travis was into it, though he didn't want to compliment me. But the contented look on his face and his second servings were enough to tell me how much he loved my cooking.

One night, I ate alone because both my parents were out of town. Tom was probably hanging out with Travis or on a date. Yes, there were days like that when we didn't even see each other at all.

Just as I was about to finish up my dessert, Tom walked in, followed by his devil of a best friend.

"You ate alone?" Tom asked.

"Yup."

"You should have called me," he said. "We could have picked you up and gone out."

"And eat with him?" I asked, pointing at Travis. "No, thanks! I'd rather eat alone."

"Of course! I'm sure you find my body more appetizing than food—you wouldn't be able to eat at all," Travis murmured, and I glared at him.

"Cut it out, you two," Tom said to both of us. Then he turned to me. "Next time, okay? Call me. I would come home no matter where I was or what I was doing. I don't want you to be alone."

Tears welled up in my eyes. I was so thankful that in spite of my parents' oblivion to their kids and their family, I had the best brother in the world. And I knew I would never be alone.

I leaned forward and hugged him. "I love you, Tom," I whispered.

He kissed the top of my head. "I love you too, princess."

Behind us, I saw Travis's mouth curve into a half-smile. I couldn't believe that he looked sort of touched at the sight of our familial bond. But then again, maybe the reason why he was close to Tom was because only an angel like Tom could stand a devil like him.

Early the next Friday, Tom barged into my room. "Pack your bags!" he said, waking me up.

"We're running away?" I asked lazily. "What did our parents do?"

"They're sending you back to the orphanage where they got you," Travis said with a smirk when he appeared by the door of my room.

"Is that the same orphanage where your parents got you? How come I didn't see you there before?" I shot back.

16

"Because I got adopted the first day I was there. Some of us are just too adorable. You…you stayed there for at least five years," Travis said seriously. *How could he insult and joke so convincingly?*

"And what happened then? Your parents realized it was a mistake to adopt you?" I asked, raising a brow at him.

His face hardened for a second, and then he disguised the hurt look on his face with another smirk. "No. I decided *I* didn't want *them*." His voice told me that I hit a nerve…something he was sensitive about. Come to think of it, why did Travis practically live with us?

"It must be a relief for them, huh," I said relentlessly.

He raised a brow at me. "Probably. But that's bad news for you, isn't it? Because every day I can't stand to be with my folks only means I'll be here to annoy you. And I prefer that any day." Then he winked at me and walked away, not giving me a chance to retaliate.

I turned to my brother, who wasted no time getting my luggage bag out of my cabinet and filling it with my clothes. "Tom, remind me again why you picked that punk to be your friend?"

I stood up from my bed and shoved Tom away from my cabinet. He had already packed half of my things for me.

"Travis is a good guy, Brianne. Actually, more than good. He's great," Tom said. "He has a troubled home. We're the only family he knows now. So please, it would mean a lot to me if you tried being nice to him."

I rolled my eyes. "And you don't ask him to be nice to me?"

"No," Tom shook his head.

"That's unfair!"

Tom sighed. "I have my reasons, little sister," he said. "I love you both. But no. I have seen the charming side of that guy, and you're the last girl I want to see it."

"I'm sure I cannot see what doesn't exist."

Tom chuckled. "It does exist. You would be surprised how soft-hearted Travis can be. But let's give it to him. He prefers to be a tough nut, and I think he'll need that more to survive in his world."

"Where are we going, anyway?" I asked.

"To Travis's grandparents' beach house."

"Why?"

"Because he invited us and we're all going."

"Mom and Dad, too?"

Tom nodded and I smiled. It had been a while since we all went away together on a family weekend. Suddenly, I got excited. After ten minutes, my bag was ready and Tom was carrying it down the stairs.

"It was really nice of you to invite us, son. We could use some time to unwind from work," my father was saying to Travis.

*Son?*

"You're welcome anytime," Travis said.

Then I saw my mother pull Travis into a hug and gave him a kiss on the forehead. I groaned. It's like he was a real son to them already. Travis stared up and saw me glaring from the top of the stairs. He smiled devilishly and winked at me.

*Oh, this is going to be a long weekend!*

I realized I'd left my phone in my room. I went back for it while everybody loaded our bags into the cars. When I came out, I saw my parents in our car with Tom behind the wheel.

"Brianne, your brother will drive for us. My leg has been cramping since this morning," my dad said.

"It's okay," I muttered and started to get in.

"No, sweetheart. You ride with Travis," my mom said.

"What?!" I asked in horror, and I knew Tom was biting his lip to keep from laughing. *Traitor!*

"It's not nice to make him drive alone, considering he's inviting us over, after all," my mother said.

"But Travis is a menace!" I complained. "I hate him!"

"Stop that, young lady! He's like a son to us and a brother to you. He's a part of this family, too," my mother scolded me, and I knew she was disappointed to know my real feelings toward Travis.

"Come on, sis." Tom smiled at me encouragingly. "You promised me you'd be nice to him."

"You forced me to promise," I muttered. I sighed and headed toward Travis's car.

As soon as he saw me approaching, he got out of his car and opened the passenger door for me, smiling like an angel, knowing that my whole family was watching.

"It's an hour and a half drive, sweetheart," he whispered so only I could hear. "Two, if I drive especially slow."

I glared at him.

"You're not scary when you glare. In fact, I think it's cute. It makes me want to you annoy you even more."

18

I groaned and stepped inside his beautiful car. If I wasn't too busy hating him or the fact that I would be riding with him, I would have stopped to admire his sleek two-seater Porsche.

The minute he stepped inside the car, I caught a whiff of his cologne. It smelled fresh and masculine. Not overwhelming, but rather refreshing. The inside of his car was almost dust-free. The interior was made of sleek leather and smelled like ocean air freshener. *What a surprise!* Travis was a neat freak, not just about his hygiene, but also about his belongings.

I leaned forward to turn up the volume of the music, letting him know that I was in no mood to talk to him during the ride.

But just as soon as the music got louder, it immediately became quiet in the car. I raised a brow at Travis. He didn't look at me. Then he pushed some button on his steering wheel and the volume turned up a little louder, and then a little lower. He looked at me and smiled.

"Sorry, *cherie*. I control everything in the car. Including the radio," he said smugly.

I sat back in my seat, quietly fuming. I was trying my best not to let Travis get to me.

He played rock ballad songs. Surprisingly, we had the same taste in music. I decided to hum to the tunes of the songs I knew. Just as I was lightening up, Travis switched to the next song midway. Then, just before the chorus played, he switched to the next song again. He did this for the next five minutes, not finishing an entire song, just switching from one to the next after a few seconds of playing each.

I knew he was trying to annoy me. I glared at him again. "You're very immature, you know!"

He grinned at me. "News flash! I'm sixteen, you know."

"I hate you!" I groaned.

He chuckled. "I know. And I love it."

I sat back in my seat and turned to look out the window again, trying to tune Travis out. He was quiet beside me. Thank God he decided to stop being an ass. He settled for a U2 song that I really loved. And soon, I was drifting off to sleep.

I felt a gentle tap on my cheek. When I opened my eyes, I saw Tom peering down at me.

"Wake up, princess." He grinned at me.

We had stopped. I turned to my left, but Travis was no longer sitting in the driver's seat.

"Are we here?"

"Yep," Tom said. "Come on! I wanna surf!"

I sat up straight in my seat and realized I was warm. A jacket was draped over me and the seat was reclined so I could lie back and sleep more comfortably.

I looked at the jacket I was wrapped in and knew it wasn't one of Tom's. There was embroidery on the back. *TJCross*. I knew the scent all over me was familiar. But wait—did Travis do this while I was sleeping? How? And more importantly, why?

I put his jacket aside and stepped out of the car.

My breath caught in my throat when I saw the huge house in front of me. It was a breathtaking three-story mansion. I could tell that even my parents were impressed.

"Who lives here?" my mother asked Travis.

"Maids, butlers," Travis responded, helping my brother unload our bags from the cars.

We were met by two men who immediately took the bags from Tom and Travis. They greeted Travis in Spanish and he spoke to them fluently, impressing—I mean, surprising—me. *I didn't know he could speak a language other than douchebag.*

The inside of the house was even more impressive. It had a huge staircase on the sides that led to the second floor. The front of the house faced the beach and was covered in glass. As soon as you stepped out, there was an infinity pool with a perfect view of the ocean.

I was speechless. I wondered why he spent most of his days in our modest home when he had all this?

A woman about the age of my mother greeted us.

"This is Mrs. Beets. She will take care of everything you need," Travis said to us. "Mrs. Beets, they're my family. You know Tom. These are his parents, Mark and Alicia. Please take them to their rooms."

I realized that Travis didn't even introduce me, which was really another one of his ways to annoy me. He was dismissing me as unimportant.

I looked up the lady shyly. She was smiling at me.

"Hi," I greeted her.

"Welcome, Miss Brianne," she said, which surprised me.

"How… how did you know my name?"

"I know everybody the young master cares about. It's my job," she whispered to me. She led me up the stairs, with my parents following behind us while Tom disappeared with Travis.

I shook my head. "He hates me. He doesn't care about me," I said to her, not letting my parents hear.

She smiled again. "He cares more than he shows. Be patient with him. The young master is a fine boy. He may be mischievous on most days, but he loves you and your family and cares about all of you a great deal. He wants you to feel right at home here."

She showed my parents their room, which seems to be the master bedroom. It was huge—they could hold a party there.

She led me to another room. It was beautiful. The bed was freshly made and covered by bright green matching bedcovers and pillows. The couches were also in different shades of green, as well as the paintings on the wall.

I smiled. I loved green. But nobody seemed to notice that. Tom always bought me pink stuff. And my mom would always get me pink duvets and pillows.

The huge bathroom was all white, with a huge Jacuzzi sitting beside the glass wall. I gasped because the bathroom didn't look private at all. I could see through to the beach, which meant anybody could see into the bathroom as well.

"It's one-way vision, just in case you were wondering," I heard Travis's familiar voice behind me say.

I turned around and found that Mrs. Beets was gone. I didn't hear Travis come up behind me.

Then he flicked a remote and the window suddenly turned dark, as if it were covered by wallpaper.

"Either way, it's private," he said.

"Where did you come from?"

"My room," he replied.

"Your room?"

I looked behind him and found that there was another door there that led to another bedroom, which meant we were sharing a bathroom again.

I glared at him. "Yeah! I feel right at home already," I muttered. I turned my back on him and closed the door behind me, but not before I heard Travis's laughter as he went to his room.

I must have fallen asleep because the next think I remembered, the other side of the bed sank as somebody sat on it.

"Wake up, princess," Tom said to me. "You're wasting the day. Come on! Put on your swimsuit and let's go. Even Mom and Dad are already having barbeque outside."

"Is Travis there?"

"Of course."

"Then I'll stay here all day, thank you!" I muttered.

Tom laughed. Then he stood up and pulled me.

"Come on, lazy head. Travis will always be Travis. He just teases a lot and makes fun of you. But he cares about you as much as I do. Just think that you have two brothers. One is nice, the other is naughty."

I groaned and headed to the bathroom with my swimsuit.

"I told Travis to make your room pink," Tom said, looking around. I bet Travis deliberately changed it to green to annoy me, not knowing that I really like green and not pink. *Ha!* The joke's on whom now!

I went to the beach with Tom. I wore a green and yellow floral dress over my two-piece suit and shorts.

Travis was laughing with my parents. When he looked up and saw me, his laughter died in his throat.

"You like nice, sweetheart," my mother said.

"Thanks, Mom."

When I looked up at Tom, his brow was raised and I saw the daggers he was shooting with his eyes…directed toward Travis. Travis immediately turned his back on us and went back to the grill to get some food.

What was that about? It was probably the first time I saw Tom act like that toward his best friend. Before, it was like that devil couldn't do anything wrong. Well, I can't say I wasn't happy to have him side with me for a change.

Tom and Travis surfed while I was left with my parents. Travis was a pro at surfing. It was like he actually lived there along with the waves. It was only recently that Tom tried surfing, too. He was good. But still not as good as his best friend.

I turned to my parents. They were eating barbecue. I noticed that they were barely speaking to each other. They were not even looking at each other.

"This is a nice house," I said.

"Yes, it is!" my mother agreed immediately.

"It was nice of Travis to invite us over," my dad said almost too eagerly. It was like the two of them were struggling to find a topic to speak about. Geez! What happened to my parents?

"How was your room, sweetheart?" my mother asked.

"Nice. All green."

"Well, it's only for the weekend. Green is a neutral color. I'm sure this house wouldn't have pink stuff since Travis doesn't have a sister."

*I like green!* I screamed in my head. It's as if even my own mother didn't know me.

"I'm glad Tom and Travis became friends," my dad said.

*I'm not!*

"That kid may have everything his heart desires, but he doesn't have family."

"Where are his parents?" I asked, not that I really cared, simply out of curiosity.

"His father is the head of Cross Magnates, one of the biggest companies in the country," my father explained. "His mother is the head of one of the biggest magazine chains in the country. They are very rich. You can tell from all this property and the cars that Travis drives. I guess they're out of the country most of the time. I think his mother lives in France more."

"Yay! That makes us lucky! We get to keep Travis!" I said sarcastically.

My mother sighed. "Sweetheart, I know you two don't get along well all the time. But over the years, we've learned to love Travis as our own. He needs a family. He needs us. Your brother adores him. I hope you try to get along and sort out your differences. I don't think this setup is going to change anytime soon."

I sighed in frustration. At that point, I didn't think my setup with Travis and my life was going to change, either. But I guess life can be a total bitch, huh?

# Chapter Two

He was young and responsible...the epitome of sunshine. If one said angels do not walk on earth, I would disagree. Because Tom was one of them. He was always positive, always considerate of the people around him.

One night, he didn't come home. We were waiting for him at dinner. His phone was off. And then we received a call from the hospital, informing us that he was rushed to the emergency room.

Tom had been racing when we didn't even know he could race.

It had been hazy, as if everything moved in fast forward. We rushed to the hospital and waited frantically as they operated on him.

I found myself praying so hard. I loved Tom. He couldn't die! He was only seventeen. He had so many things going for him. He was an angel. There were a lot more people in the world he could help, a lot more lives he could touch.

Like Travis's. Travis was a troubled kid when he met my brother. But then he was able to find a new family with us. Because Tom took him in.

When the doctor came out of the room, he told us that they did everything they could. He was alive, but we were told not to keep our hopes up. There were complications and we could not be guaranteed he would walk out of the hospital healthy again.

The first time that Tom opened his eyes, he asked for Travis.

Tom was driving Travis's Porsche. It had been totaled. The car's safety features were the only things that gave my brother a little chance at survival.

From the window, I saw Tom make an effort to raise his hand. Travis hooked his pinky with his and pulled it away to bump it with my brother's fist. That was their sign of brotherhood.

I'd never seen Travis cry before. But as I watched them from the window, I could tell that he was on the brink of breaking down. He was always so proud, always so cold and distant. He never really showed much emotion. But now I realized that Tom really was a brother to him. He really did care for us.

The next time Tom opened his eyes again, I was with him.

"I...love...you," he said with each precious breath he took.

Tears rolled down my cheeks. "I love you, too," I said in a broken voice.

"Promise me...you will always...be happy," he said.

I nodded. "And you will be there with me, Tom. You will see me live each day happily!" I said. "You're the best brother anybody could ever ask for."

"You will never be alone...baby sister," he struggled to say. "I promise you that. I love you...you won't be alone." He gave me one sad smile, and then closed his eyes.

Just then, I heard a sharp sound that froze me on my feet.

"Tom!" I shouted. The nurses and doctors rushed into the room. They pushed me away. I struggled to come closer to my brother. Just then, somebody wrapped an arm around my shoulders and pulled me away as they tried to perform CPR on Tom.

And then finally, I heard somebody say, "Time of death..."

I didn't hear the rest. "No!" I screamed. I didn't know who was holding me. But I was thankful for him because I was breaking down. I almost fell to the floor. I felt arms wrap around me to support my weight.

"It's going to be okay, Brianne," I heard Travis's familiar voice as he cuddled me against his chest. But I could hear the tears in his voice as he struggled to be strong.

"He can't die, Travis!" I cried against his chest.

"He will always be with us," he whispered against my ear and I wrapped my arms around Travis's waist. Right then, it didn't matter that I hated him or we never got along. Right then, I knew that if there was one person who understood exactly what I felt at this moment, it was him...because every pain I felt in my heart, he felt exactly the same. Tom was a brother to both of us.

I don't know how I survived the following days, trying to keep a brave face in front of our relatives and our friends. I tried to be strong. But whenever I was alone in my room, I hugged one of Tom's shirts and I cried my heart out.

My parents stopped talking to each other. It seemed that they were both blaming each other for what happened. Even Travis had been confined in his own world. I felt that he kept blaming himself for what happened to Tom because it was his car that Tom drove that night, and he had not been there to stop it.

I stared at Tom's grave, after his funeral when everybody had gone, including my parents. I didn't want to go yet. I was left all alone. I read the words written on his tombstone.

*Thomas Antoine Montgomery*
*Forever Young*

It began to rain, as if the heavens were crying with me. My parents seemed to have forgotten that they'd left their little girl behind. I stood there in the rain for at least an hour, and neither of my parents came to find me.

*You will never be alone, baby sister*, Tom promised me. But he was gone. And even my parents caved in to their own worlds to mourn on their own. Whom did I have now?

Suddenly, I felt an arm around my shoulder. I looked up and found Travis staring down at me. His eyes were teary, too.

He hugged me to him, and this surprised me again. Travis and I hated each other's guts. But the embrace he gave me was warm and sincere. More than that, it was needing, too. It was as if we suddenly felt so alone and now all we had was each other to hold on to.

"Ssshhh…" he hushed me. "Everything's going to be okay. I promise I will take care of you for as long as I live," he said. Then he turned toward Tom's grave. "I will protect her with my life, bro. You don't have to worry. She will never be alone for as long as I am alive."

And suddenly, I realized this was what Tom had asked Travis for in the hospital. He asked Travis to take care of me…because he would no longer be able to.

And even though I hated Travis in the past, I knew he meant what he promised Tom. And I knew Tom would not leave me in Travis's care if he didn't trust him with his life.

I buried my face in Travis's shoulder. I felt him kiss the top of my head and then he leaned his cheek against it. He was taking deep breaths once in a while and I knew he was crying, too. But as he held me in his arms, I knew he was trying to be strong for both of us.

***

"I was… I was…" I watched Peter Zonokkis stammer in front of me.

Because he was taking so much time saying what he wanted to say, it gave me more time to study him, up close. He was wearing khaki pants, his shirt buttoned all the way up to his neck, and he was wearing glasses.

Peter was one of the smartest kids in school. He was regarded as a geek most of the time. And it killed me to hear him stammer in front of me, knowing full well what he was going to ask me, and knowing full well, too, what my answer would be.

"So? Will you?" he asked.

I blinked back at him. *Did he already ask me something?*

"Sorry, Pete." *I'm not really going to ask him to repeat himself, am I?* "I'm not allowed to date…yet," I said. *I hope I was right in thinking he was asking me out.*

His mouth formed an O. "But…aren't you sixteen already?"

I shook my head. "Not yet. I'm three days shy."

"Some… some girls start dating earlier than fifteen."

I shrugged. "Not my parents," I lied. Actually I didn't think my parents cared anymore if I got pregnant!

"All right. Maybe I'll ask you next week?"

I shook my head. "Well…I'm not sure. I'm not in a hurry. Maybe much later."

He smiled at me. "All right. Well, see you around."

I nodded and turned around toward the exit.

"I hope you're not just letting him down easy," a male's voice said behind me.

I turned around to find Allan Gilmore walking behind me.

I raised a brow at him. Allan was two years my senior. He was captain of the debate team. Very smart, and very cute.

"No. That's the truth, actually."

"How can a gorgeous girl like you not be allowed to date at this age?"

I shrugged. "I'll ask my parents when I see them," I answered sarcastically.

He smiled. "So, if I asked you out, I'd probably get the same answer?"

"Yes."

28

"Why? Because I'm not your type?" he asked wistfully.

I shook my head. "Not that. Because I wasn't lying to Peter."

"Okay. Maybe I'll check up on you in a couple of months."

I nodded. "Maybe."

He walked past me and gave me a wink. "See you in a few months!" he yelled as he walked away.

I walked home and thought about Allan and Peter. Not that it wasn't true, but it wasn't a lie, either. I hadn't discussed dating with my parents. With all of us still mourning Tom's death, boys were the last thing I needed to worry about.

I remembered talking to Tom a couple of years back. I asked him about his first date, the rules and proper dating decorum if there was one.

He laughed and told me I was too young to be asking those questions.

"I promise, when you are allowed to date, I will be your first date!" he said to me. "I will take you out on a real date. I will tell you the *do's* and *don'ts*. Let you know what to expect. And hopefully, set the bar really high for your future dates…it's good to have high expectations, so your first boyfriend will be a cut above the rest," he said with the boyish grin on his face.

"Promise?"

He raised his right hand. "I promise."

And then Tom was gone even before my parents could give me a go ahead on dating. How could I go on my first date now without remembering that my brother should have been with me? He should have been alive.

I didn't know it, but tears were welling up in my eyes already. I missed Tom so much. It had only been a few months since I'd lost him. And it still felt exactly the same as that first day.

When I reached home, I saw a sleek new Porsche parked in front of my driveway. I thought one of my parents had a visitor.

As I approached the driveway, the door of the car opened. I watched a familiar figure step out of it.

My breath caught in my throat. Straight black hair, streaked with some dark blond strands and sleek, sporty sunglasses hiding his devilishly cold eyes.

I stopped in front of him.

"*Cherie*," he greeted me.

"Wow! Someone is still in Paris mode," I teased him.

I don't know how Travis had been making his classes. He'd been in and out of the country for the past couple of months after Tom died. One month he was home, and then after a few weeks, he went back to his home in Paris, with his mother.

"How are you?" he asked.

I shrugged. "Okay. Alone most of the time."

He pushed his sunglasses up his head to reveal his startling crystal blue eyes.

"Alone?" he echoed and something in his expression told me that he didn't like the sound of that. "What about your parents?"

I shrugged. "You would think that since they lost one child, they would care more for the other, right?" I shook my head sadly. "I think I lost them the day I lost Tom."

Tears suddenly slipped from my eyes. I tried to fan my hands in front of my face and disguise my sadness with a giggle. But when I looked up at Travis, I could tell that I hadn't fooled him.

He reached for my shoulder and pulled me to him. I rested my head against his shoulder, took a deep breath, and then for the first time in many months, I let all the tears fall.

\*\*\*

I sat on my seat and attacked my banana split as if I hadn't eaten ice cream in months. Well, I hadn't, actually.

"How's school?" Travis asked me. He was sitting opposite me, having a soda.

"Same old," I replied. "Except that today, I had two boys coming up to me, asking me out."

"And?" he asked with a raised brow.

I shook my head. "I told them I wasn't allowed to date yet."

"Aren't you?"

"I don't think my parents care anymore, to be honest," I replied sadly. "But that's not really the reason why I don't date yet."

"Then what is?" he asked.

I shrugged. *Because Tom promised me…*

Travis took another sip of his soda. He didn't ask me again. Instead, he waited for me to be ready to tell him.

I sighed. "Tom promised me..." I started. "He promised he would be my first date."

"Okay, that sounds weird...even for me," Travis said.

"Don't be absurd!" I said. "He promised to take me out on a real date, to tell me what to expect, to teach me what I should know about...the do's and the don'ts. And he was hoping to set the bar really high so I could set high standards for myself." I sighed. "I guess that's not going to happen now. And somehow, it held me back. Every time a guy asks me out, I think about how that first date should have been my educational date, you know. Now, I guess I'm up for...trial by fire. And I'm not very thrilled to do that just yet."

"Aren't you turning sixteen in three days?"

"Hey, you remembered!" I said. "I hope that was not the reason you cut your Paris trip short."

He took a deep breath. "It was, actually," he said in a low voice.

My head shot up at him. "Really? Because the Travis I know didn't really care about me."

He raised a brow at me and sighed. "I'm bound to care about you now, remember?"

I rolled my eyes. "A little sincerity would be nice."

"How do you know I wasn't sincere?"

"Because...you barely show...any sincerity."

"I barely show any emotion, period," he corrected me.

I sighed. There was no winning that argument. Travis Cross was cold and ruthless now. There was a time in the past that he was so playful and mischievous. But now that Tom wasn't around anymore, he had gotten worse. As if my brother's death taught him not to care too much, get attached too much. Because when these people went, he would get hurt over and over.

Now, he didn't care about the people around him. He was trained not to show how he really felt. Trained to cave in and shield himself from getting hurt. The only person he didn't shield himself from...was buried six feet under. It must have been quite ironic for him that the first person he opened up to was taken away from him. So I guess I shouldn't really have complained about his lack of feelings toward me.

I heard him release a breath. "But it doesn't always mean I don't...feel anything at all," he said.

I stared into his eyes. They were cold, but somehow I could see his soul there...hiding in the shadows.

31

"You should know this about me, Brianne," he said. "Because our lives are going to be intertwined for the years to come."

I sighed and nodded. "But you must know…" I said. "I tease and laugh a lot! Or at least, I used to."

"I know. If some girls are candies and bubble gums, you're a Tootsie Roll," he said, and somehow, I couldn't tell if he found that endearing or irritating.

I smiled and then I reached across the table for his hand. "We're going to be okay, Travis," I said. It wasn't just an assurance for him. It was more of a question for him to reassure *me*. Funny, because a few months before, I really loathed this guy. Now, I felt like he was the only thing I had left…the only thing I had to remind me of the happy family that I used to have.

He turned his hand over and gave mine a gentle squeeze. "Yes, *cherie*. I'll make sure we're going to be."

***

I couldn't have mistaken it. The locker with a rose tucked in the handle was mine. There was a note with it.

I nervously opened it. I didn't know what to expect. I was hoping it didn't come from Peter or Allan since I really wouldn't know what excuse to use this time around.

*Sweet Sixteen...*

*Tom was right. You need your educational date.*

*And since I'm filling in for him, the honor of becoming your first date has officially been transferred to me.*

*Real world. Real date.*

*Pick you up at seven tonight.*

I smiled to myself.

*Travis!*

"Happy birthday!" Cindy said behind me.

I quickly tucked the rose inside my locker.

I should probably have told Cindy everything. Except that in a way, I was also like Travis. I didn't always tell people about every single detail in my life. And right then, it was embarrassing to admit, even to her, that I needed an educational date from my brother's best friend before I really became confident about going out with boys.

"Thanks," I said.

"Anything planned?" she asked.

I shrugged. "I don't know. Maybe just a simple family get-together." That wasn't a lie. For years, Travis had been a part of my family, too. And right then, he was the only person who probably understood the pain I still felt on a daily basis after losing my brother.

"That's nice. I think you need that after…" Her words trailed off. "Well, I think it's nice to strengthen family ties. Especially on your birthday."

I nodded, and somehow, I wished my parents felt the same way. But I knew that Tom's death had crumbled their already failing marriage. For years, we had refused to see the elephant in the room. My parents were busier with work than with each other. Apart from the weekly family dinners, they didn't see much of each other at all. And with Tom gone, they chose to mourn apart. Unfortunately, they forced me to do it by myself, too.

# Chapter Three

I waited in my living room anxiously. I wore a pair of white capris and black halter top. I didn't know how to dress, but I was pretty sure I looked nice. Not that I wanted to impress Travis, but this was a practice date.

I tied my hair in a neat pony, and then put on powder and gloss.

The doorbell rang.

Maria, our maid, ran to get it.

"I'll get it!" I said to her.

She looked at my outfit and then smiled. "It's nice that you're going out on a date on your birthday."

I was going to correct her that it wasn't really a date, but then I asked her instead, "How do I look?"

She beamed at me. "Really lovely!" she replied. "Your date will not be able to take his eyes off you!"

I giggled nervously. I doubted that was true. If it was any other guy, maybe. But not Travis Cross, who saw me in pajamas and shirts with holes in the wee hours of the nights he slept over at our house.

I never imagined Travis would be my first date. A couple of months before, I would have vomited at the mere thought of it. But now, I felt like…better him than some guy I don't even know.

I opened the door. Travis was standing in front of me wearing jeans, a white shirt, and a black jacket.

"Hey!" I greeted him cheerily.

He nodded at me.

"Happy birthday," he said.

I smiled. "Thanks!" I closed the door behind me. "I suppose I should introduce my date to my parents first, but…first of all, they already know you. And second of all, they didn't even bother to come home on my birthday. So, that's out the window. Let's proceed to step number two."

To my surprise, Travis suppressed a chuckle at my attempt to joke about the fact that my parents weren't home on both my birthday and the first time I would be going out on a date.

Travis opened the door of his Porsche for me.

"Quite the gentleman, aren't we?" I teased.

"If the guy doesn't open the passenger door for you, don't proceed with the date at all," he said in a serious voice that really sounded like he was giving a lecture.

"Note taken. Does he have to have a Porsche, too? Because that really limits my choices."

He raised a brow at me. "Doesn't matter. As long as he doesn't make you walk all the way home."

He rounded the car and got into the driver's seat. He drove to a classy restaurant that was famous for steak and overlooking views.

"Wow!" I breathed. I stared at him. "Travis, this is setting the standard way up high!"

"Good! Maybe I'll have more peace if you never go out on a date at all," he said and then got out of the car. A second later, he was opening the passenger door for me.

"Hey, Tom would not be so strict!" I said.

"Well, he's the angel. I'm the devil incarnate, remember?" he asked in a cold voice.

"Do all my dates have to be sarcastic, cynical, and cold, too?" I asked back.

He stared at me for a while. Then he sighed. "You're right," he said. He tossed his keys to the valet. Then he reached for my hand and guided me inside the restaurant.

"Good evening, Mr. Cross," the receptionist greeted him. "This way to your table, sir."

We were led to a secure corner on the terrace. It had a perfect view of the city and offered just the right amount of privacy.

"Privacy," I said.

"That's not for you," he said. "I prefer that you date in public…where lots of people can see you…hear you scream if your date is a lunatic. This privacy…is for me."

I raised a brow. "You're ashamed to be seen with me in public, aren't you?"

"Accusations are to be saved for the end of the relationship," he said. "Not when you are hoping to start one."

He had a point. But then I remembered, I did, too. "You're avoiding my question."

"No. Being seen with you is the least of my worries," he said. "And if I were really a guy hoping to start a relationship with you, I would be proud to be seen with you in public. But enough with the compliments...the truth is...I don't want *you* to be seen with *me*. At least not tonight."

"Why?"

He sighed. "Because my father's in town."

"And?" I asked.

He stared at me for a moment. Then he said in a whisper, "Tom really could keep a secret." It took him a moment to speak again. "My father and I have a broken relationship. It is worse than I let you know."

"How bad?"

"Really bad," he replied. "He lost his right to ground me and so I could do whatever I wanted, whenever I wanted."

"How could a parent lose his right to ground his child?"

"The moment he stops doing his job of being a parent," Travis replied coldly.

I sat back on my seat and waited for him to continue.

"And so whenever he wanted to keep me at home, he resorted to...tactics that would make you want to call child services if you found out," Travis said. "I'm emancipated. I would sue his ass if it weren't for my mother."

"Travis..."

"He has bodyguards...hounds on the loose. Sometimes, I think they're watching me, studying who moves in my circle."

"Who you're close to?"

"Right now, there's only one," he said. He stared at me for a long while, and in a rueful voice, he said, "I don't want you to be involved in our war. I don't want to break my promise to your brother."

I smiled and reached out for his hand. "Thank you, Travis," I said. "And anytime you want to talk about your father...I'm here."

He pulled his hand away. "Thanks. But nope. I'm not going to waste your time talking about him." He motioned at the menu. "Order."

I ordered a New York steak and mashed potatoes. Travis ordered a ribeye and vegetables.

When the waitress was gone, we stared at each other.

"So, I suppose this is the part where I talk to my date about myself? And ask about him?"

He nodded. "Yes."

"Now, what could I possibly ask Travis Cross that I don't already know?"

"A lot," he replied. "But I don't necessarily need to answer every one of them."

"Aren't you interested to know anything about me?"

He stared at me for a while and then gave me a crooked smile. "I know you more than you think."

He said that with so much confidence I was actually surprised. "Really? You really think you know everything, don't you?"

He shrugged. "You're welcome to test that theory, *cherie*."

I narrowed my eyes at him. "My favorite color?"

"Green," he replied without blinking. Wow! I didn't know he knew that. My entire family thought it was pink.

"My favorite book?"

"*Romeo and Juliet*," he said, wrinkling his nose.

I was taken aback, surprised he knew that, too.

"Movie?" I knew I had a lot of favorites. *Only You, The Princess Bride, Some Kind of Wonderful*...the list went on. Even I couldn't answer that question easily. I would be shocked if Travis could.

He thought for a while. Then he said, *Ever After*.

I stared back at him. He raised a brow at me, as if he was challenging me to deny that. But then I realized—he was right. Out of all those movies, Drew's Cinderella story was the one I watched over and over. Sometimes, I just turned it on and played it until I fell asleep.

"Song?"

"'Walk On,'" he replied.

I couldn't believe it. It's like I replied to an interview and Travis spent hours memorizing my answers. "My secret crush."

"If I knew that, then it wouldn't be a secret, right?" he asked back.

*Ha!* There's a page in the interview he'd missed reading after all. And I smiled to myself proudly.

He took a sip of his soda.

"But isn't Ricky Martin gay?"

My mouth dropped. How could Travis know that much about me?

He was suppressing a laugh when he sipped his soda again.

Our food was served. I couldn't say anything. I was still wondering how he knew all those things about me. Travis and I were not exactly friends when Tom was alive. I remembered him for his snide remarks—mischievous pranks, even. But I didn't remember ever talking to him about anything regarding myself at all.

"You're not upset, are you?" he asked.

I sighed. "I'm not. I'm just...shocked!" I replied. "How could you know all those things?"

He shrugged. He sliced his ribeye and then took a bite of his food. He didn't speak for a long while.

I put my fork and knife down. "Would you tell me?"

"Tell you what?" he asked.

"How did you know my favorite color, or movies, or songs? Even my thing for Ricky Martin?"

He shrugged again.

"Travis!" I protested. "Did you read one of my diaries?"

"Do you have a diary that has all that information?" he asked back.

I shrugged. "I don't know. I can't remember."

He smiled at me as if I were being ridiculous.

"Even Tom thought my favorite was pink," I said.

"Well, he did get that wrong a lot," he said.

"But how could you know all those things?"

He sighed. "I don't know."

"My favorite color, for instance," I said. "How could you know that?"

"The ink of your pens are green. You have a lot of green shirts." Then he reached out across the table to touch my bracelet. It was a chain of green Swarovski crystals. "It's the color of your birthstone."

"So that day we went to your beach house...the room I stayed in was all green. Tom asked you to make it pink. Did you make it green on purpose? Did you already know I preferred that color?"

He stared at me for a while. Then he nodded. "I've always known you liked green."

I sighed guiltily. I remembered that that day, I thought he was playing a joke on me that backfired. And yet, all along, he actually did it because he knew I would like it. I guess Travis really wasn't as bad as I thought.

"What about the books I read?"

39

"Weren't you carrying a *Romeo and Juliet* and *Wuthering Heights* book around all the time?"

"The movie?"

"I slept next room to you about a hundred times. I could hear Drew Barrymore's voice through the walls," he replied.

"I suppose I play Menudo a lot, huh," I said.

He rolled his eyes. "And the portrait of Ricky Martin that you drew is stuck on your bedroom wall," he said.

"So you got all that by observing?"

"Now you can't say that nobody ever pays attention to you, *cherie*," he said. "You're...patriotic when it comes to the things you like. It's hard not to notice."

I sat back in my seat. "Funny. I didn't know anybody really cared before."

"I'm a very keen observer, particularly of the people around me."

"Well, since you already know so much about me, maybe we should talk about you."

He stared at me for a while. Then he took a bite of his ribeye.

"Can I ask the questions now?" I asked.

He shrugged.

"Favorite color."

He stared at me for a while and then asked back, "Looking at me, what do you think?"

"Black?"

He shrugged. "Black will do."

"Favorite movie?"

He sat back for a while, and then he said, "*The Good Son.*"

It was the way he said it that made me look at him carefully. There were sorrow and bitterness in his voice.

"Something about the movie you want to talk about?" I asked.

He shook his head. "Nope." He looked at me and grinned. "You won't trick me into telling you about my relationship with my parents, *cherie*. No matter how cute you try to be."

I sighed. "Fine. But I will get you to talk about your parents. Maybe not now. But we have our lives to wait until you're ready, Travis."

"Don't hold your breath," he said, and somehow, I knew he meant that.

We had dessert. Since it was only Travis, and I didn't need to pretend, I ordered their Mocha Lava specialty, which was a molten chocolate inside a chiffon cake with ice cream on top.

"Should I order dessert when I'm really out with a guy?" I asked. "I mean…will it turn guys off to know I don't count calories?"

He chuckled. "I find it cute, actually. I think…if I wasn't me, I have fallen in love with you already."

"Why?"

"I don't really like girls who are obsessed with their figures. I would rather they give in to the temptation of a nice Molten Lava cake. But that's just me. And I'm not into relationships, really. It still depends on your guy. So I suggest you go with what you feel. You want to be comfortable with your boyfriend. You wouldn't want to change just to fit his taste. He should fit yours."

I looked at him thoughtfully. "I hope most of the guys our age think like you."

"You have your whole life to look for him," he said. "Well…not your whole life. But a decade and a half."

I blinked back at him. "How could you know *that*?"

"Since I was twelve, I have been going to your family gatherings," he replied. "Tom told me all about the ridiculous 'curse' the females in your family believe in." He looked at me from under his lashes. "You don't really believe in that, do you?"

I shrugged. "I don't think it will hurt that much to believe," I replied. "I mean…in my family, if the curse does not happen to you, the others make it seem like it did. Like, for example, you don't get married by thirty-one, and they look for all sorts of things that are wrong with you and they only talk about *that* at family reunions.

"I mean, who's to say that it's not Aunt Rosalie's choice to be single for life, as supposed to marrying a man who would only break her heart? Or maybe Aunt Mildy's dream was really to become Princess Jasmine she just couldn't resist that proposal from a rich Sultan? But they talk about it at reunions and they give you a certain look, or they dish at every table that it looks like you're doomed after all!" I sighed. "And sometimes, I realize I don't want that. I prefer to be invisible compared to being so visible in the wrong sort of ways."

"And so you prefer to get married before you're thirty-one?"

I nodded. "Or be cursed for life? I think I prefer the lesser of two evils."

He chuckled humorlessly. "*Cherie*, some men are not the lesser of two evils. Let's just pray you don't marry one who is a curse in his own right...like my father."

I sighed. "Don't bring up topics you don't want to discuss further, Travis. Because I'm really getting curious about your father now."

He brought his fingers to his lips and made a zipping gesture.

After dessert, Travis got the bill.

I took my wallet and pulled out some bills. "How much is my share?"

He stared at me as if it offended him.

I rolled my eyes. "I know you're filthy rich, Travis Cross, but I'm not a free rider."

He chuckled. "You did half of it right, at least."

"Half of what right?"

I watched him place a platinum card in the folder and hand it to the waiter.

"Expect that the guy must always pay," he said. "For me, if you cannot pay for the entire date, then don't have the guts to ask a girl out. But it's good that you did the check dance. You got that right. It's impressive."

"What did I do wrong?"

"The rolling of the eyes, and the sarcastic remark that followed," he replied. "Offer to pay or split the bill, once, twice, or three times. Don't try to insult or tease to prove why you should pay. Because you really shouldn't. If the second or third time, he insists on paying, graciously thank him."

I smiled at him. "Okay." I took a deep breath. "Thank you, Travis...for such a lovely dinner."

He nodded back at me. "You're welcome, *cherie*."

He signed the bill and then fished through his wallet to leave a tip. It was huge. But since he paid, I wouldn't know how much the bill was.

"Can I..." I started.

"What?"

I shrugged. "If it was a real date, could I ask how much the bill is?"

He shook his head. "You must never ask how much the guy spent on your date...and this is a real date, *cherie*. So you can't ask me how much the bill was, either."

42

We stood up from our seats and he led me toward the exit.

"It was a lovely dinner, Travis," I said to him. "But shouldn't a normal teenage date usually involve going to the movies or something? Because I will be dating normal guys. And you're not really in that range, Travis." I stared up at him, my eyes laughing.

He narrowed his eyes at me. "Who said I wasn't planning on taking you to the movies?"

He drove to The One Hotel, which is one of the high-end hotels and shopping destinations in the city. He led me toward the back and we reached the entrance to a stadium.

He handed two tickets at the entrance, which meant that he'd already purchased them beforehand.

"Are we going to watch a game?" I asked him. "I thought you said you were going to take me to the movies."

"The purpose of first dates is usually to find something in common," he replied instead. "Now, I know that neither you or I have patience as one of our virtues."

I rolled my eyes.

"And refrain from rolling your eyes so much. It will intimidate the guy. Unless you're not aiming for a second date," he said.

I sighed. I didn't ask questions anymore. Travis would not answer any of them. He was taking this educational date seriously. *Maybe I should, too*, I thought. *This is for me anyway.*

It did look like we were going to a movie theater. Travis opened a door and motioned for me to go in first. But when I stepped in, I was surprised to find that I had stepped outside into an open area. There were knee-high tables with candles in the center and beanbags on each side of them with a large projector screen in the middle. It was like a restaurant, but instead of chairs, you had comfortable beanbags to sit on.

"I told you I was going to take you to the movies," he whispered into my ear. I could feel his breath against my neck, and I actually shivered.

"Movies Under the Stars," I breathed. I had heard about this, but not many of the kids my age actually went. Not many of us could actually afford it.

We were led to our table. I found the beanbags were more comfortable than they looked. It was very relaxing. A waiter approached us to take our orders.

"I'm still full," I said.

"A soda? Nuts? Popcorn?" Travis asked.

I smiled. "Pepsi and nuts will do."

"Macadamia nuts and two diet Pepsis," he told the waiter.

We waited for the movie to start.

"This is really nice," I said to him.

"I'm glad you like it," he said. "Enjoying your date so far?"

I nodded. "Although, if it wasn't you, I might feel intimidated."

The waiter served our orders and told us to press the button on the table if we needed more services.

"Why?" Travis asked after the waiter was gone.

I shrugged. "This is all too…surreal."

He gave me a crooked smile. "Then it's exactly how your first date is supposed to be," he whispered.

The lights dimmed suddenly, marking the start of the movie.

"What are we watching?" I asked him in a whisper.

He stared at me mischievously and said, "Ssshhh…"

It took me a moment to realize what movie is going to be shown.

My breath caught in my throat as I saw Drew Barrymore's name on the screen.

"*Ever After*," I whispered and I bit my lip to keep from crying. Because this gesture was far too touching. And it was the very last thing I expected from Travis Cross.

We watched the movie in silence. Even though I almost had every scene memorized, watching it under the full moon and stars only made it so much better for me. It was perfect!

"Do you like it?" he asked.

I stared up at him and nodded. "Yes." I reached out for his hand across the table and gave it a squeeze. "Thank you, Travis."

He nodded and turned his hand over to intertwine our fingers. Then he looked back at the screen. I smiled to myself. This was the first time I'd held hands with a guy. Travis may have been the guy I hated the most, but now I thought we were in a much better place than we had been in before. Because now he was the guy I knew would always mean well for me. And now, on my fifteenth birthday, he was the only family I had to celebrate with.

Travis was still holding my hand when he led me toward the exit. I didn't feel self-conscious. Instead, I felt comfortable and safe…assured that an ally was within reach.

I looked at our intertwined fingers. "So I guess it's okay to hold hands with my date."

"I leave that up to you," he said. "Although, next time, let him initiate the act."

I looked back at him. I realized I was the one who'd reached out for his hand. Immediately, I started to withdraw my hand from his.

He laughed, tightening his grip on my fingers and preventing me from letting go of his hand. "I know, *cherie*," he said. "Your initial intention for touching my hand was to thank me."

I glared at him. And I made a serious effort to withdraw my hand from his. Finally, he let go. But then he put an arm around my shoulder. "Now, I initiated this. Happy?" he asked, giving my shoulder a gentle squeeze.

I did feel better.

He chuckled. "Your temper is cute," he said, and then he kissed the top of my head.

He didn't release me until we got to his car. Before he opened the door for me, he said, "I seriously hope Tom didn't intend to give you a lesson on kissing, too. Because one, that would be *very* weird. And *two*, I'm not up to give you *that* lesson."

I raised a brow at him. "No. Because one, my brother and I weren't perverts. And two, I wouldn't ask you for that lesson even if you *were* up for it."

He chuckled. "Then it's good we got the air cleared."

He drove me home. It was ten minutes to midnight; he pointed at the digital clock on his dashboard. "Your parents may not always be around, but I hope you remember that twelve o'clock is your curfew."

"And who set that?"

He shrugged. "For the time being, me, your designated guardian."

"You're the same age as I am!" I protested.

"I'll be seventeen in a couple of months. I'm almost a year older than you," he argued.

I grunted in my seat.

He took something out of his pocket. "Happy birthday, *cherie*," he said, handing me a box with a ribbon tied around it.

"What's this?"

"Looks like a birthday gift to me," he said.

I raised my brow at him, and then untied the ribbon and opened the box. My mouth dropped when I saw the gleaming necklace with a large heart-shaped purplish-red pendant. The pendant was surrounded by clear diamonds.

"Wow," I breathed. "This is beautiful. What stone is this?"

"Alexandrite," he replied. "You'll probably prefer its color in daylight. It will turn emerald green."

I blinked back at him. "But...Travis, this is rare."

He shrugged.

"You shouldn't have!" I said. "You didn't care about my birthdays before!" That was true. In the past, Travis didn't even wish me happy birthday. Not even after I blew out the candles on my cake. And now, he was making everything perfect!

"Maybe the necklace is for all the other years I didn't wish you happy birthday," he said quietly. "Back then, I didn't have access to my own money. And I didn't want to spend my father's money on you or your family."

"You have money that didn't come from your parents?"

"Yes. My grandparents from my mother's side named me their heir," he replied. "Maybe Grandpa knew I would not sit well with my father's ways and decided to treat me like an adult three years earlier."

"Well, your Grandparents must have loved you."

"Love died in my life the moment they did," he said sadly.

I reached out to touch him in the cheek. "Hey...we were here."

He looked up at me. "Tom was. But not anymore."

"I'm still here," I said.

He smiled ruefully and nodded. "Yes, *cherie*. You're still here."

I looked at my necklace again. "This is beautiful," I said to him. "And so is everything else. Thank you for making this birthday count, Travis."

He nodded. "You're welcome. And I promise, I'll make all your birthdays count from now on."

And that promise warmed my heart for the first time in many months after Tom passed...

# Chapter Four

"How could I have my period now?" Cindy groaned as she dragged me along with her into a supermarket close to the beach.

We were headed toward a beach party that afternoon. I was a junior and dating a guy named Liam. He was the latest football star and had a strong chance of being captain when he turned senior.

"It's only your first day. It won't be that strong, so don't freak about it," I told her. "But let's go buy your tampons."

I was heading for the feminine hygiene section when Cindy stopped me.

"Don't be in such a hurry!" she hissed. "Be discreet! I don't want people to know I am having my period underneath my string bikini!"

I laughed. "Then I'll buy them for you. I only care about what Liam will say anyway. And I can always tell him the real story. He won't tell on you."

"But still...let's pretend we're looking at some other stuff," she said. She took me to the chocolate section and I took a bag of M&M's. "You're not seriously going to eat that, are you?" she asked.

"Why not?"

"Okay, that is just unfair! How could you manage to be so slim and yet attack chocolates and desserts?"

I shrugged. "I have no idea. It could be the emotional stress. I live alone, remember?"

"Anyway, how are you getting home tonight?" she asked. "I might go somewhere else with Ben."

"I'm sure Liam can give me a lift home," I replied.

"Nice to have steady boyfriends!" she giggled.

Finally, we went to the section where all sorts of feminine stuff were located. There was a couple there making out in front of the pregnancy kits. It took me a moment to realize that they were familiar to me.

"Liam?" I asked in disbelief.

They stopped kissing and looked up at me. Liam blinked back, and then he shoved the girl away from him.

47

"Ahh...Brianne...this...isn't what you think?"

"Oh, really!" I rolled my eyes.

"It was a spur of the moment—I don't know what's gotten into me."

"Oh, come on!" the girl behind him complained. She looked at me apologetically. "Don't believe him! We've been fooling around behind your back since last week!" She looked back at Liam. "Spur of the moment? You slept in my bed last night!" Then she gave him a push in the shoulder.

Liam looked at her. "Look, can we sort this out later? I need to talk to Brianne in private."

"So you can fill my head with more lies?" I asked sarcastically. I looked at the girl, whom I recognized as one of the cheerleaders. "He and I are over. Although, I suggest you don't stick around with a guy who denies you in front of people. You're too pretty for that." I turned to grab a box of tampons next to me, and then turned to Cindy. "Let's go."

But Liam wouldn't let it go. He ran after me, yanking me by the forearm. His grip was so strong I actually got hurt.

"I bruise easily, Liam!" I told him coldly, looking at his tight grip on my forearm. "And if you leave a mark on me, there's one person who will not be happy about it!" I looked at him haughtily. "And he would hunt you down and turn you black and blue!"

He took a step back and released my arm. "I...thought you weren't seeing anyone but me."

"I wasn't. But looks like you were! Now leave me alone!" And I turned on my heel with Cindy.

She ran to the counter to pay for her tampons quickly, not caring anymore who would see her with them.

Then we rushed out of the supermarket and hopped inside her brother's car.

"Whoa! What happened with you two?" Cindy's brother asked as he backed out of the parking space.

"Do you want to go home?" Cindy asked. "Because I'm cool. I'm worried about you."

I shook my head. "No. I won't spoil your fun." I looked back at her. "I'm upset because he was cheating on me. Not because I was head-over-heels in love with him and I'm heartbroken right now."

"Are you sure?"

I nodded. "I don't want Ben to be disappointed when you don't show up or if you show up late. I'll be fine."

Back at the party, I tried to mingle with the others, tried my best not to bother Cindy and Ben that much, although they were clearly sympathetic with me.

I giggled. "I'm okay, guys. I'm just pissed. But I'm fine."

By the end of the afternoon, I wasn't sure I was fine anymore. News had probably spread around already, and Liam came with the same girl he was making out with. They continued making out in plain view now. I could tell some people were looking at me and whispering behind my back. In the end, the curious looks on their faces were bothering me more than the sight of Liam and that girl making out, which made me want to vomit.

Apart from Liam's cheating escapade, I was worrying about how I would get home. I couldn't bother Cindy and Ben. I knew they wanted to enjoy the party. They'd been talking about it all week. Cindy's brother dropped us off and headed off somewhere else. Most of the other girls in attendance either had boyfriends or were flirting with some boys. Originally, I had planned to catch a ride with Liam because I knew Cindy and Ben had other plans later. Now, it was either I impose on them or go by foot and by myself. Both options were less than enticing.

I sat on a bench in a secluded area and watched the sunset.

*I'm not going to cry!* I told myself. *If I do, people might know it's because of Liam, and he's not worth any teardrops at all.*

I fished my cell phone from my beach bag.

*Please don't be in Paris! Please don't be in Paris!* I silently prayed as I dialed a number.

"*Cherie*," he answered after two rings.

"Travis!" I was glad to hear his voice. "God, I hope you're in town."

"Why?" he asked.

I sighed. "Because I need a ride home."

"What happened to your boyfriend? Lost his wheels?" he asked. That was not very encouraging. He knew I was dating Liam. I could tell he didn't like him.

"He...lost me, actually," I replied.

Travis didn't answer. But I could tell he was waiting for me to tell him more.

"I caught him...making out with some girl on my way to the beach party."

"Stay where you are," he said in low, quiet voice. And then, before I knew it, he had already hung up.

*What does he mean stay where I am? Is he coming to get me?* And I silently prayed he would.

I went back to the beach. It was dark already. The party organizers had lighted torches around the area and the smell of barbeque was everywhere, reminding me that I had not eaten anything since the morning. Some couples were dancing, including Cindy and Ben. My eyes drifted to one secluded corner and found Liam staring at me, with his other girl in his arms. The moment he caught my eye and saw me looking at him, he tightened his grip on her and nuzzled her neck.

"Was that for your benefit?" I heard somebody ask behind me.

I spun around and found Travis behind me, staring at Liam murderously.

I sighed. "I guess." I looked up at Travis. He was wearing a pair of black and red board shorts, a white shirt, and a cap over his head.

Slow music played. I felt him touch my waist and I looked up at him. "Dance with me," he whispered.

I smiled at him, tears starting to well up in my eyes.

"Don't," he whispered softly. "Not here, *cherie*. I will give you time to cry all you want later. When we're alone. But for now, you need to show everybody that you are delighted to be in my arms, instead of his."

I giggled humorlessly. I gave him a hug. "Travis..." I whispered. "Believe it or not, I am crying because I am delighted to be in your arms. Not his."

He hugged me to him and we swayed to the music silently. I didn't care anymore if Liam was still devouring that girl. I was really happy to let some of my defenses down and lean on Travis. Here with him, I could be weak for a little while. Because I knew he would always be strong for me.

He caressed my forearm, and I flinched at the little pressure he gave. I realized Liam's grip was too hard and rough. I did bruise a little.

I heard Travis's harsh intake of breath. I pulled away so I could look back at him.

"What's wrong?"

He closed his eyes for a while. He was turning a little red and I could tell he was trying to control his temper.

"Travis..." I whispered.

When he opened his eyes again, I could see that he was furious.

"He did this to you, didn't he?" he asked.

"What?"

"Your arm," he replied.

I bit my lip. I couldn't lie to Travis. He was good at reading my expressions. He narrowed his eyes and then he looked around, scanning the area for Liam.

"Travis...please," I whispered. "I don't want trouble here."

He looked back at me again. "He hurt you. There's not much I can do for the emotional pain, but...I can't let the physical one happen!" he said, his anger seething between his teeth.

"Travis..." I pleaded. "I bruise easily. He just grabbed my arm."

"Too roughly?"

"I don't want trouble here," I said in a desperate tone.

When Travis realized this, his expression softened a little. "Ssshhh..." he said. He pulled me to him and gave me a hug. I heard him sigh. "Okay, *cherie*. As you wish. Not here."

I pulled back from him. "What do you mean not here?"

He stared back at me. "That's the only bargain I can give you. *Not here*. Not in front of you."

"Travis, I don't want you to get in trouble, too," I said in a desperate voice.

He laughed humorlessly. "Your ex-boyfriend bruised you up and you're worried about *me*? I can take care of myself, Brianne," he said. "And don't worry. I'll make sure he lives to learn the lesson."

"Travis..." I started.

He shook his head. "Don't change my mind, Brianne," he said. "I promised your brother I would take care of you."

"And you are!" I argued.

He looked at my bruised forearm. "Not good enough."

"You can't look after me twenty-four seven."

"Maybe I should do that from now on," he said.

"You can't!"

"Sure I can...if only to make sure you're safe."

"I'm safe. A little bruise will not kill me."

51

"Nevertheless…he should have left you spotless," he said in a sober voice.

I smiled at him ruefully. I placed my hand on his cheek. "Travis…two years ago, you didn't even care about whether or not I tripped and fell on the stairs."

"Just because I didn't show it doesn't mean I didn't care at all," he said. "And your brother gave me a new reason to live for now."

"I can't be the only thing you care about in this life."

He sighed. "You are now," he said. "And I mean it. *Not here.* That's the only promise I can make you."

I gave up. "Travis…whatever you do, just please don't end up in a hospital bed, in jail, or worse, in the same place where Tom is! I still haven't recovered from his death. I would go mad if I were to lose you, too."

"That's touching. Two years ago you wouldn't even have cared if I got run over by a train."

"Well, Tom's given me a reason to live, too!" I muttered.

He finally laughed. "Touché." He pulled me into his arms again and we continued dancing.

I leaned my head on his shoulder. "I'm starving," I said to him.

He pulled away from me. "Come. Let's get out of here," he said. "Before I end up breaking my promise not to beat up your ex-boyfriend before your eyes."

The following Monday, Cindy came and met me in the hallway with some news.

"Ben told me that Liam got cornered by your guy yesterday after playing basketball with some of the guys. Travis Cross got out of his Bentley and went for Liam. He pushed him against the wall and told him that he had no right to hurt a hair on your body. Liam actually got scared. He went blank for a long while. Then Travis punched him and told him to never to come near you again." Cindy stared at me dreamily. "Wow! Travis Cross! Seeing you together sent shivers down my spine! You can't be that affectionate and just purely platonic."

"But we are," I sighed, remembering Liam again. "Dating is not a piece of cake, huh?"

"You can go through a chain of boyfriends and still find yourself marrying your safety guy at age forty." She looked at me. "Well, in your case, thirty. But the problem is, you don't have a safety guy."

"A what?" I echoed.

"Safety guy. You know, that guy who promises to marry you when you reach a certain age and you're nowhere close to getting married at all."

An idea played in my head. What if, just in case I didn't find my true love by the time I was thirty, I married somebody who was willing to marry me? A good friend, even a gay friend. We would be married only on paper.

I might or might not find the guy I would spend my 'forever' with by the time I was thirty, I realized. But it helped to know that whatever happened, I'd be married...I wouldn't be cursed for the rest of my life.

The next day, I asked Travis to meet me in front of my house. I'd given this a lot of thought the night before. It was the only thing that actually made sense. It was my insurance to take the pressure off and not chase guys or be desperate to fall in love all the time.

I stared up at Travis nervously after asking him the most difficult favor I would ever have to ask anybody.

"You said you'd look out for me," I told him. "Please?" I almost begged.

"You've got to be freaking kidding me!" he said in a frustrated tone. He usually didn't show emotion. But now, he made no effort to hide any of it. "Are you crazy?"

I sighed. "Maybe. But I'm desperate."

He looked at me with narrowed eyes. I thought he was mad at me, but what I saw in his eyes was actually...frustration. "You're a silly little girl!"

"I know! But I don't know what I'm going to do when that time comes."

"It's fourteen years down the line, Brianne!" he said. "You're crazy to think that you can't find a man by then!"

"I'm not saying I won't be able to. I'm saying...I need a reassurance that I will be married even if I don't find someone else."

He raised his chin to the sky and closed his eyes. "Of all the things to ask me, bro, why this?" he whispered more to himself, and I realized that he meant that for my brother.

Travis stared at me again. He didn't say a word. And then with an icy expression on his face, he stormed away.

I stood there alone and felt embarrassed. I knew I shouldn't have asked him that. When we first met each other, I didn't like him one bit. And now, I'd asked him to marry me!

I didn't see Travis for the next two days, and I was thankful. I was too embarrassed about the favor I had asked him. I couldn't believe that I was as brazen as that.

I was on my balcony one afternoon and I decided to draw. Whenever I felt bad, I channeled all those feelings onto my canvas. This time, I drew something dark, evil...and handsome. It was too late when I realized that the image that I drew of the demon clad in a leather jacket looked like Travis. His face was the same...but I'd given him fangs and fire eyeballs.

"You couldn't be that mad at me," I heard a familiar voice say behind me.

My heart skipped a beat as I realized that I'd been caught red-handed. I spun around and found Travis looking down at me.

I was surprised because this was probably the first time Travis had come inside my house again after my brother had died.

"I...forgot you used to come here." I knew I was blushing violently.

Immediately, I flipped over the canvas to remove the spitting image in front of him. He didn't say anything.

"What do you want?" I asked him.

"The last time I checked, it was you who wanted something from me," he replied.

I raised a brow. "Well, you could just forget I ever said anything to you!" I turned away from him to pick up my brushes and my pencils.

"I'll do it," he said quietly.

I turned to face him again. "What?"

"I said I'll do it," he repeated. "I'll be your safety guy." I was dumbfounded. He stepped closer to me. "In fourteen years, if you aren't married yet, or nowhere close to marching down the aisle, I'll marry you."

"Travis...you probably won't have to do it anyway," I said. "I mean...fourteen years is a lot of time, right?"

"Yes. But you can be a handful," he said evenly.

I sighed. "If it makes you feel better, I only meant that we're going to marry on paper. You can still go ahead, screw as many girls as you want. We'll only appear married in front of my relatives and then we'll divorce after two to five years. No pressure."

He stared at me for a while, studying me and absorbing what I had just said to him. "I didn't intend to marry at all, Brianne," he said quietly. "I don't have faith in marriage. You have to remember that my parents haven't been seeing each other for almost half of my life, and yet they remain married on paper...for money...for power, for political reasons. I'll marry you...but I'll just be a guy who will meet you at the altar. You cannot expect anything more from me."

I smiled. "Yes. That's all I wanted."

He nodded.

I felt relieved, quite thankful that he was willing to play this game with me. In truth, I knew it might not happen anyway. I could fall in love and marry right after college. Or I could find him at the last minute...on my thirtieth birthday.

But still, I was quite thankful that Travis had given in to my little request...if only just to give me peace of mind. I didn't really know how to thank him. So I leaned forward and gave him a peck on the cheek.

"Thank you, Travis," I said to him. "You're not such a bad guy."

He almost scowled and looked like I had just offended him.

I turned to fix my brushes and my pencils again. "You know...when I told you about this...you could have said no right away. Or you...could have said yes to me anyway. Who knows what could happen in fourteen years? Why did you have to wait two days to give me your answer?"

No answer. For a while, I thought he'd left without another word, but when I turned around, he was still there, standing in the same spot.

"I had to think about it," he said. "It's my life you're asking from me."

I giggled humorlessly. "Come on, Trav. You take things seriously. All I wanted was some peace of mind. Do you really think nobody's going to propose to me in fourteen years?"

He took a deep breath. "A lot of guys will fall at your feet and hope to be your husband," he said. "But nevertheless...I don't make promises I do not intend to keep." Then he turned on his heel and left.

# Chapter Five

It took a while after Liam before I dated seriously again. Senior year, I was in love with Trip Jacobs. He was the captain of the basketball team and one of the most popular guys on campus. He was cute with blond hair and hazel eyes. For months, my world revolved around basketball leagues. I never missed a game. I especially loved it when he shot three points, looked at the crowd at the bleachers where he knew I would be sitting, tapped his heart and then gave a thumbs-up sign. I knew that was meant for me.

After Liam, I dated another guy before Trip. David was head of the debate team. He was smart and funny as well as cute. I thought we had a connection. We went out for the whole year. Then he went to a ski trip with his family. I saw less of him after that. And then one night, he had a glum look on his face and told me that he hadn't been honest with me. He'd been seeing someone else behind my back. He ended it with her, but he wanted to be honest with me. He said that it was just all sex and nothing else, and it was over. But I couldn't take him back after that. I could not bring myself to kiss him knowing that he might have been kissing someone else or doing worse things with her.

"Now I'm dating the hottest guy in school."

"No offense, sweetie, but I do not think he's the hottest guy on campus," Cindy said. "He's hot, yes. But not really the hottest."

"He's the hottest of all my boyfriends," I said.

"I don't know. You have a thing for blond guys. I find them...a little meek." She giggled.

"Okay, if Trip is not the hottest guy in campus, then who is? I mean...he's the captain of the basketball team, he has a Porsche, he's a straight-A student, and he looks like Barbie's Ken with hazel eyes."

"Well, you know me. We've always had different tastes. I wonder why we're best friends."

I laughed. "All right. I wonder who you find worthy of being called the '*hottest*' guy in campus, then?"

She stared at the ceiling thoughtfully and then said, "Travis Cross."

"Amen!" Amanda Jones, who had her locker beside Cindy's, said. She beamed at us. "No offense, either, Brianne. Trip *is* hot. But Travis Cross? Out-of-this-world hot!" Then she walked away.

Well, I guess even I couldn't refute that. Travis was easily the hottest guy I'd met, but growing up with him and hating him from the beginning, and now thinking of him as a sort of replacement brother and guardian to me, made it difficult for me to look at him in a sexual way.

"If Travis Cross was my safety guy, honey, I'd do whatever it took to stay single until the deadline so he'd be honor-bound to marry me!" Cindy teased.

"Then I'll die a virgin!" I said, rolling my eyes.

"You're still a virgin?" Mich Jackson, who had her locker beside mine, asked.

I stared at her and then at Cindy. "Is it eavesdropping day today?"

Mich laughed. "It's eavesdropping day every day, sweetie." She laughed and then looked at me again. "So are you?"

"With all due respect, it's none of your business."

"Well, I hope nothing's wrong with you. No wonder David and Liam screwed around. Word of advice, honey: Don't stay a virgin for too long. Men these days prefer a vixen in bed, not a little girl at slumber parties." Then she strode off.

I looked at Cindy and she was eyeing me wearily. "What?" I asked.

"I hate to admit it, but she has a point. I lost mine two years ago. My brother's best friend was so hot and my parents' bed seemed so tempting."

"Cindy!"

She laughed. "It's no big deal, Brianne. Nowadays, if you haven't gone to bed with a guy, it may mean that there's something wrong with you. Either you don't have the capability of being aroused or you cannot seduce a guy to...do things to you."

"I didn't want to just give myself to a guy who would cheat on me the next day."

"I gave mine to someone who wasn't my boyfriend, so he couldn't really cheat on me."

"I don't want to give it to a random guy, either."

"Ouch!" Cindy feigned an offended look. "He's not some random guy! He's…a good friend. He won't disappear from my life overnight, and since we're not dating, he's not gonna cheat on me. Brilliant, isn't it?"

I rolled my eyes. Then Trip's handsome grin appeared in my mind, and suddenly I became excited. "Well, prom is just around the corner."

"You want your first time to be magical?"

"I want it to be special. I want to remember it someday, have a smile on my face and think…'Wow! That was good!' Even if I don't end up marrying the guy, at least I won't have regrets."

***

"Oh my God, Brianne, I think you're the talk of the town!" Cindy called me that evening. "I got a broadcast message in my mail. And I think it's about you."

I went to my laptop and checked my mail. True enough, our Campus Bulletin showed this broadcast message: *Virgin Mary. Guess whose virtue has no takers? Clue: Bubble Gum girl who sports a boy's nickname.*

"This bulletin is supposed to be for important stuff. Like dances, fairs, and competition schedules. Who the hell posts gossip like this?" I asked angrily.

"But this section is a hit! That's why they didn't abolish it. Kids at school probably only subscribe to the bulletin because of the gossip."

"Okay, so who cares if I'm still a virgin?" I turned off my laptop, not letting this further affect me.

"About a hundred other people," Cindy replied weakly.

"What?"

"Let's see. Three hundred hits and a hundred comments."

"What are they saying?"

"They're justifying why David and Liam cheated on you. And some others are betting on how long it will take for Trip to…slam dunk."

"Holy shit!"

I couldn't believe what was happening to me. "Kids can be so mean!" Cindy said sympathetically. "There's really nothing wrong with being a virgin at eighteen. So you're inexperienced. So what? That doesn't mean you're frigid or unwanted."

I was on the verge of crying. For a while, I had been proud that I remained untouched. But now I wished I'd given in to David's advances or even Trip's subtle hints at going to bed. Why was there so much pressure on this in the first place?

I could not believe I was the subject of such mean gossip. The whole campus could be a bunch of sluts and whores for all I care. Why did they have to curse me for trying to be different?

I didn't want my first time to be meaningless. I was curious about sex, but I wanted it to be with someone who had respect for me. Who would not use my body as just a means of pleasure and nothing more. I wanted it to mean something to him, too. And I wanted to share it with some guy who would always be dear to me whenever I thought of him.

Was I the only one on campus who was a virgin? Why did kids have to make so much of an issue out of this? Why did they care? And why did gossip have to be in print nowadays?

I felt like everybody had been talking about me in every conversation at the moment. And my lack of sex life was the center of attention. Whoever said that there was no pressure to lose their virginity nowadays could kiss my ass! It was happening now. Sure, they didn't tell you to do it. They just judged you or gossiped about you if you didn't. What's the freaking difference?

I got hold of my brush and painted a roomful of flowers and candles in perfect romantic hues. I didn't know why, but suddenly, inspiration came over me and I imagined a marbled room, a king-sized bed, flowers, and candles. I guess lovemaking was also on my mind. I was imagining how I wanted it to be. As I looked at it, I couldn't imagine how kids could bear to lose theirs in an attic or in the back of a car.

As I thought about it, I got angrier. Tears were rolling down my cheeks, and I wasn't even aware of it. The last thing I wanted was to be the talk of the town...especially when it came to being unwanted. My family had a lame tradition of marrying young and being wanted before the age of thirty. I just wanted to be invisible. I didn't want to be the center of attention or unwanted talk at all. But with my dating history, I'd provided everybody at school some juicy things to talk about.

I felt an arm around my shoulder, giving me a squeeze. I was startled to realize that I was no longer alone. I looked up and found Travis looking down at me wearily.

"I was staring at your painting and I don't get it. I don't get how you can cry over a...bed," he said.

I narrowed my eyes and gave him a playful jab in the stomach.

"Ouch!" he said, but he only squeezed my shoulder tighter. "So tell me. What is it about that bed that you found so utterly offensive it made you cry so hard?"

I stared at my painting, leaned my head in Travis's shoulder, and heaved a sigh. "The whole town is talking about me. It's embarrassing!"

He was thoughtful for a moment, and then he said, "What's embarrassing about not being a slut?"

I stared up at him. "*You* heard?" He didn't answer. I pulled away from him. "Then I'm truly dead! Travis Cross, the guy who cares the least about campus gossip, heard about my untouched virtue—then everybody must know! Trip must know!"

He snorted. "If I were Jacobs, I would be...proud. My hot girlfriend is not a slut."

Now I smiled. "Really?"

He shrugged. "If I were Jacobs. But I'm not. So I can't speak for the guy."

And somehow, I was positive that if Travis, who was a ruthless rake at the age of eighteen, could think that, then my gentler boyfriend would definitely think that way...maybe even more so.

"What are you doing here, anyway?" I asked him.

He shrugged. He walked over to the rails of my balcony and stared at the houses in front of mine. "This used to be my second home," he murmured. There was pain in his voice.

"You don't come here anymore."

"Your living room has less light than it used to have."

I nodded. "Yes. We don't have dinners together anymore. It's not like before."

"Where are your parents?"

I sighed. "Mom's opened a new branch in Manhattan. Dad's...probably with his mistress." Yes, my mother tried to play dumb about my father's conquests—I was less tolerant.

Travis stared at me for a moment and then asked, "Cook your famous meatloaf for me?"

When Tom was alive, we had Meatloaf Friday. I would cook and we would all sit and enjoy dinner together...as a complete family, including Travis.

I stared up at Travis. I knew we were thinking of the same thing. And I realized it was Friday today. Tears filled my eyes. The more I looked at Travis, the more I remembered Thomas...and how happy this family had been.

Travis's eyes were also teary. He reached out and wiped my cheeks with his fingers. Then he gave me a hug. I wound my arms around his waist and cried against his chest...for the happy family that I used to have...for the wonderful brother who left me.

"I'm sorry," he whispered to me. "I shouldn't have asked."

I shook my head and pulled away from him. "No. It's okay. Remembering him doesn't mean we haven't moved on. You promised him you'd take care of me. I'll do what I can to look out for you, too—not that you need it." I giggled humorlessly. "This will always be your second home, Travis. You can come and go as you like. Thomas would want that."

He smiled, then leaned forward and gave me a kiss on the forehead.

I took his hand in mine. "Come. Our dining table has been unoccupied for a very long time. And I haven't cooked meatloaf in years."

# Chapter Six

Prom was a month away and my relationship with Trip was getting deeper. He was making some moves to be more intimate, and I was becoming more open to his advances.

We were making out in his car one night. He nuzzled my neck and started to reach behind me to unhook my bra. I pushed him slightly.

"Trip...wait," I said gently. "Can we wait? Prom?"

He looked at me for a while and then he nodded. "You're right. I'm sorry. It's your...first time. It shouldn't be in the back of a car." He chuckled, then he leaned forward and gave me a smack on the lips.

"Thank you," I said.

He turned to start the car. He was quiet the rest of the way, and somehow I wasn't sure what he was thinking.

He stopped in front of my house. "Good night." He smiled at me. "So, I guess prom night's it for us?"

I smiled at him shyly and then I nodded. In my mind, I was thinking he'd rent a hotel suite where we could spend the night, candles and roses all over the place. It would be romantic. It would be a night I would remember for the rest of my life.

I was dreamy when I got home. I took a long bath in jasmine soap. I dreamt of how it was going to be for me and Trip. After Prom, nobody would accuse that something was wrong with me.

I dried my hair and put on purple pajama bottoms and a pink sleeveless top. *I should remember to stop by a lingerie shop before prom*, I thought. *Maybe a Victoria's Secret nightgown would come in handy for me in the future.*

I dialed Trip's number as I lay on my bed. It was busy. I tried about ten times, but it was still busy. I decided to wait ten more minutes, then I tried again, but he didn't pick up. I decided I was going to wait fifteen minutes more, but I dozed off.

In my dreams, I dreamt of candles and roses while Enya played in the background. He kissed me gently, thoroughly, and then he took my clothes off. I couldn't see his face, but I was pretty sure it was Trip. He'd been so gentle with me. He knew it was my first time. Then there

63

was a tearing pain. He held me in his arms gently. He told me he was sorry for hurting me. He was so sweet I couldn't help falling for him more and more.

Just then, I woke up. I found myself lying in my bed alone. I looked at the time. It was past midnight already. I looked at my phone to see if Trip had returned my calls, but he hadn't.

I caught a flash of movement in front of me. There was a figure on my couch. I turned on the lamp beside my bed and found Travis sitting on the couch at the foot of my bed, his eyes closed.

I got up from the bed and approached him. He had kicked off his rubber shoes and draped his jacket on the arm of the couch.

"Travis," I whispered. He let out a little moan but didn't wake up. "Travis," I said a little louder.

He moved a little and then finally he opened his eyes. He looked at me for a moment and then he said, "Hi."

"What are you doing here?"

"My father's home," he replied. "He wanted to talk to me about university options."

"And?"

"I've made up my mind where I'm going," he said. "I left the house. His bodyguards are out looking for me."

"And you came here?"

"This is the last place they would look. Since Thomas has been gone, they don't think I come here anymore. I hope you don't mind if I stay here until morning."

"Of course not," I said. "But why in my bedroom? You have a room in this house, Travis," I said, pointing toward the bathroom that connects my room to the guestroom—Travis's.

He smiled at me bitterly. "Nah! Too many memories, *cherie.* Your house reminds me of Tom a lot. Except for your room. We never hung out together here. And right now, I don't really want to feel like I have no one."

"You don't have no one, Travis. You have me," I said to him.

He nodded. "I know. That's why I'm here."

I went to my cabinet. I pulled thicker blankets out and handed them to him. "Here, use these."

"Thanks," he murmured.

"Won't they notice that your car is in the driveway?"

He shook his head. "I didn't bring a car. I walked."

I went back to my bed and checked once more if Trip had sent me anything. Still, there was nothing.

"Goodnight, Travis," I said.

"Goodnight. Thanks for letting me stay," he said. "I was almost afraid you would kick me out."

I giggled. "I would never do that. You can come here anytime you want. How did you get in, by the way?"

"I climbed up from your balcony. Your sliding door is unlocked. That's not right, Brianne. Anybody could have come here and broken in."

"You should be happy I forgot to lock up. Otherwise, you wouldn't have been able to come in."

"My refuge is not as important as your virtue, *cherie*," he murmured. "Please promise me you won't forget to lock your doors from now on?"

I smiled at him, and then I closed my eyes. "I promise."

When I woke up the next day, I found that Travis had gone. He neatly folded the blankets he used and placed them on the couch. On top of the blankets, I found a note saying, *"Thank you, cherie. But please remember what you promised me."*

I smiled, feeling the bond that I now shared with Travis. Right then, it was difficult to remember why I hadn't gotten along well with him when Thomas was still alive. I wished Thomas had been able to see us like this.

***

By the end of that week, I was looking for Travis in school. It was difficult since we barely saw each other on campus. In fact, not many people knew we were still speaking to each other. They knew Travis and Thomas were inseparable. But since Thomas had gone, Travis had been a loner. He did show up to a beach party a couple of years before to give my ex a shiner he deserved, but other than that, he was barely visible.

He came to attend his classes and he aced all of them. But he didn't hang out with anyone. He was almost anti-social. Except for some girls he 'casually' hung out with.

By the end of the day, there was still no sign of Travis, so I just decided to go to the counselor's office to ask where his locker was located.

"Travis? Travis Cross?" the student assistant asked with a blush on her face. I didn't have to be a genius to guess why she was blushing violently at the mention of his name.

"Yes," I said trying to keep my voice at level.

She flipped through her files and then gave me the locker number.

"Thank you."

I rushed with Cindy to where Travis's locker was, hoping to catch him there.

"Why don't you just call him?" Cindy asked.

"Tried. His phone is off," I replied.

Finally, I located his locker, but there was no sign of him. I decided to leave the keys I duplicated the day before in a small envelope and taped it to the front of his locker.

I wrote a note: *I'm keeping my promise.* :-)

I promised to keep all the doors locked from then on, but I also meant what I'd said to him that he could come to our house any time he pleased. Travis just appeared out of nowhere most of the time. Usually, it was the times he felt most alone or upset that he chose to come…to find some peace, some comfort, some… family. I wanted to do for him what Thomas would have done had he lived. Like the way Travis was looking out for me, the way that Thomas would have.

I waited by the parking lot for Trip. Cindy waited for her boyfriend, Allan, who was also a member of the basketball team.

"What was that you left at Travis's locker?"

"House keys," I replied. "To my front door, my room, and my balcony."

"Wow! Why would you do that? With a sweet note that you would keep your promise? You guys sound like you are having a secret affair or something." Cindy kept her tone very low. The last time we talked in public, my virginity was advertised on the Campus Bulletin Board.

"Don't be silly! Once in a while, he comes to my house," I said. "Last Friday, I found him sleeping on my couch when I woke up in the middle of the night."

"What?" Cindy asked. She couldn't believe what she was hearing. "Why? He just breaks in to your room?"

"I forgot to lock my balcony door. Anyway, he made me promise to lock up all the time, but that would also mean he wouldn't be able to come in any time he pleased. Travis has some issues with his dad. I'm the only family he has. He's looking out for me. That is the least I can do to make his life easy."

"Thomas could have been the one looking out for you," Cindy said sadly.

"Travis promised my brother that he'd take care of me. I'm not going to make it difficult for him."

"How cool is it to wake up and find Travis Cross sleeping on your bedroom couch?" When I looked at Cindy, she looked star-struck.

"Wipe off that drool, here comes your boyfriend!" I whispered to her, seeing her new boyfriend, Allan, approach us.

She scowled at me, and then she smiled sweetly at Allan.

"Where's Trip?" I asked.

Allan looked dumbfounded and looked behind him. "He…was with me and then…I lost him."

Cindy got on her tiptoes and gave him a thorough kiss. I looked away from them. I checked around for signs of Trip.

"How are you getting home, Brianne?" Allan asked.

"I'll wait for Trip. He usually meets me here," I replied.

"He might have scooted already," he said. "I was the last in the locker room."

I fished my phone from my pocket and dialed Trip's number. It was off.

"Nevertheless, I'll wait a while. He might turn up. He always does."

It was thirty minutes after Cindy left with Allan, and there was still no sign of Trip. The parking lot was almost empty now. I decided to take a walk home, still trying Trip's number.

When I rounded the corner, I found his car parked just outside the campus. I looked inside, but it was empty and his gym bag wasn't there, either, which meant he was still inside.

I walked back and headed toward the gym.

I stood by the entrance of the locker room, but it was quiet, which meant nobody was there anymore. I decided to head out, dialing Trip's number again. This time it rang. It took me a moment to realize that I could also hear his phone ringing from inside the girls' locker room.

My heart pounded in my chest as I tiptoed in.

"Don't answer it!" I heard a girl moaning. "Who is it, anyway?"

"Nobody," Trip's familiar voice said. "Now, where were we before we were rudely interrupted?"

"You were right on this spot." And then there was a giggle, followed by a series of moans.

I followed their voices, tiptoeing as quietly as I could. Then finally I reached the end of the row of lockers. I peeked and found Trip with a blonde whom I recognized to be one of the cheerleaders. They were naked. She was lying on a bench and he was on top of her.

The image was so vivid, so clear, it couldn't have been painted as anything else. They were having sex. And it was nothing like what I pictured in my mind. What they were doing was…rough…animalistic.

"What about your girlfriend? Have you successfully popped her?" the girl asked.

"Prom night is the night, baby."

She laughed. "Too bad for you, then. She'll want you to be gentle."

"Oh no," Trip said. "I'll teach her how to be rough the first time around!"

"Oh, poor girl. I'll bet she'll cry. "Where do you plan to do her anyway?"

"We're all going to Michael Hornby's place. His parents are away. I reserved a room in their servant's quarters for my precious Virgin Mary! Hang around Mikee's after prom. I'd like to have fun after I'm done with her."

At that point, I thought I'd seen and heard enough. But I refused to be the only person embarrassed to be in that room. So I showed myself to them.

"Don't worry. You can have all the fun you want with her! I don't want your filthy body ever touching mine!" I said angrily.

They were both startled as they realized I'd been watching them all that time.

"Oh my God, Brianne!" Trip said, blood draining from his face.

"You'll never get the chance to sleep with me, Trip Jacobs!" I said. "Goodbye!"

I stormed out. Because I was so mad, I broke the fire alarm window and pulled the plug down, setting off alarms across the whole campus. Problem kids did this all the time at our school and they went unpunished. At least I was breaking the alarm to report a violation happening inside the girls' locker room.

I couldn't believe what I had seen and heard. How could he? And I fancied myself in love with him! The words he said about me...they were degrading! Did he think I was low like those girls who snuck into the locker rooms to have sex with him? I thought he was the one! I thought this relationship would last forever.

When I looked back at the gym again, guards were running toward the entrance to the locker room. *Serves them right if they get caught in their underwear!*

I was blinded by tears as I walked out of the campus. I didn't expect Trip to follow me. I believed he was busy putting his pants on in front of the campus guards.

Suddenly, a car slowed down beside me and stopped a few feet ahead. It was a luxurious Bentley, and I wasn't sure if the driver was waiting until the car plate caught my eye:

TJCROSS

Suddenly, relief washed all over me. I ran toward the car. The passenger door opened from inside as soon as I reached it. I hopped in and found Travis staring at my tear-stricken face.

"When can I come and find you and you won't have tears on your face?" he asked quietly.

I giggled humorlessly and realized that lately, whenever I'd cried my heart out, Travis was the first person to find me.

"What is it this time?" he asked.

I shook my head. I couldn't help myself—I leaned forward and gave him a hug. I felt his arms wrap around me.

"Sshhh..." he whispered. "You're safe now."

It was a couple of minutes more when my tears subsided. I was resting my head on Travis's shoulder.

"I got your keys," he said quietly.

"I've been looking for you all day," I said. "Your phone is off."

"Sorry, *cherie*," he said. "My...father was calling me non-stop."

"College options?"

He nodded.

"Where are you going?" I asked.

"Have you decided where *you're* going?"

I shook my head.

"Then I'll tell you when you've decided," he said.

A car sped past us. It seemed that the driver was in such a hurry he almost hit the tree in front of us.

"Isn't that supposed to be your ride?" Travis asked me.

I sighed and remembered the pain in my chest again. "Not anymore," I whispered.

Travis looked at me wearily, his usual, cold, careless façade completely gone. Instead, he gave me a look of genuine concern and sympathy. I leaned my head on his shoulder again.

"You'll be fine," he whispered to me.

And I knew he was right…

# Chapter Seven

Trip and his girlfriend were almost expelled from school. It turned out they couldn't dress fast enough to hide the evidence. Rumor had it that Trip still had a condom on his thing when they were escorted to the principal's office. He was kicked off the basketball team.

I'll bet he was furious with me. I could see him throwing daggers at me whenever he saw me walk the corridors. I was devastated, but I refused to let people see how Trip broke me.

Prom was two weeks away. I was dateless and, needless to say, I'd still be a virgin by then. But then I thought Trip's plan to defile me at Prom was not something I should have been looking forward to anyway. I thought I should say goodbye to my daydreams and fantasies of losing myself in bed with a man in a romantic kind of way.

Maybe this time I should be cynical, I thought. Maybe I should take control so guys will not run me over. The problem with me is that I trust too much, too soon. Every boy I go out with will save me from the shame of being unmarriageable, as per my family's tradition. Every guy is a Prince Charming. Every single one of them a knight in shining armor.

"It's not a big deal," Cindy said to me. "Just have fun out there. I lost my virginity to my brother's best friend, in my parents' bed, and everything was just the way it was."

"I'm going to take control," I said. "I won't let these high school boys ruin me! I will go out, and if I like the guy and things get a little bit cozy, then I guess…that's it, huh? I think I over-fantasize things."

Cindy shrugged. "No biggie. Don't make such a big fuss over it. It's just sex. You gotta know what it's like, what to expect. Just do it and get it over with. Doesn't mean you'll end up marrying the first guy you've been with."

"Now I guess I only need to worry about who's taking me to prom," I said.

There were guys who tried to make conversation with me all of a sudden, knowing what happened with Trip and finding out that Trip and I were over. I was still heartbroken. I still felt that none of them was ever good enough to replace Trip. Well, the Trip that I fell in love with, anyway. Not the real Trip, who was hiding beneath the angelic disguise.

I was hurt by what Trip did, and I hated him so much I wanted to get back at him. I wanted to show him that he was wrong to do that to me. That he was wrong to think so lowly of me.

I dropped French class because I had it with him.

"You need to replace this subject with something that has the same credits, or you won't graduate," my adviser told me.

I nodded. She handed me the list of options that I had.

There was Spanish class, but I'd been enrolled in French for months and all I'd learned was *Oui*. Then there was poetry, but I was afraid I'd had too many false flowery words from Trip to last me a lifetime. There was music, but I was pretty sure I was tone deaf. The other option left was art. I guessed art would have to do.

"Are you sure?" my adviser asked me.

I nodded.

"Brianne, I have to warn you. Mr. Atkins is very strict, and his standards are very high. You're a straight-A student, and I don't want you to break that record," she said.

I smiled at her. "I think I can keep up with Mr. Atkins."

She looked at me reluctantly, and then she signed the form. "All right. Last period, Mondays and Fridays. Mr. Atkins loves to extend his hours, so expect to be home a little bit later than usual."

I nodded. Anything to get away from Trip would be fine.

Friday, I showed up for art class just in time.

"Miss Montgomery, I hope you understand that you have a lot of catching up to do," Mr. Atkins said. "And just so we understood each other, I see only art and talent in this class. Everything else is just doodling. I hope you have what it takes to stay in this class," he said. He motioned for me to take a seat.

His class was only half-full.

"This was a full house at the beginning of the year," he said. "See how many have fallen in just a few months?"

I scanned the room to pick a place. Suddenly, someone came into the room saying, "Sorry I'm late, Professor."

Mr. Atkins immediately smiled. "Not a problem at all, Mr. Cross. I was just introducing your new classmate, Miss Montgomery."

At the mention of my name, Travis's head snapped my way. I smiled at him. He raised a brow, clearly surprised that I was finally taking art class. He went to his seat and pointed at the empty seat beside him.

"You may take whatever seat you'd like, Miss Montgomery," Mr. Atkins said.

I immediately headed for the seat beside Travis. He was at the end of the row, and no one sat beside him.

"Aren't you the outcast?" I whispered to him.

"I can be very intimidating. They think I bite." He grinned.

"If they only knew how sweet you really are," I said sarcastically.

"Glad to see that you're finally taking art class."

"I had to drop French. I was taking that with Trip."

He raised a brow. "You won't be missing a thing. If you really want to learn French, I can tutor you."

"*Merci, Monsieur*," I said, smiling at him.

"Why are you only taking this class now?" he asked.

I narrowed my eyes at him. "Why aren't you taking French class?"

He grinned. "I see. You think you're already too good."

"Some of your talents are innate. You don't have to learn them," I whispered.

"Miss Montgomery, you will officially start on Monday. Today, you can just observe and take notes," Mr. Atkins said, and I nodded at him.

He reminded the class about their assignments, and then he asked them to work on their charcoal masterpieces.

To me, he said, "Look around you and draw anything that inspires you to take this class. You can draw a paintbrush, a canvas, you can look at the paintings around you and draw in your own way...I just want to see the level of skill you already have before you start my class."

I nodded.

Almost all the people in the class were introverts, as most artists usually are. I didn't think I liked Mr. Atkins that much yet. The paintings around me were amateur compared to the ones I'd seen in Mom's galleries. I knew the only thing that pushed me to take art class was that I didn't have a choice when I dropped my French class.

I couldn't think of anything else I liked about the class. But I needed it so I could graduate. I heaved a sigh and then I looked to my right. I found Travis engrossed with his painting. It was a tree with a swing moving with the winds.

"What's your topic?" I asked him.

"He asked us for a happy childhood memory," he replied without looking at me.

"That memory seems eons away," I told him as I recognized that swing from one of their estates, from when we were about twelve.

"Remember, he said, 'happy,'" he murmured.

I bit my lip. I couldn't help feeling sad for Travis. I remembered that he and I were just alike. We were two broken souls trying to look out for each other at best we could.

And then suddenly, I knew what I had to draw.

When I was done, my painting was just as good as any other student's charcoal painting, maybe even better than most. It was a very good painting of Travis's face, showing the same expression he wore when he first saw me in the class.

I didn't know that Mr. Atkins had been watching me. When I looked behind me, he was engrossed in his thoughts. Then he stared at me and smiled slowly.

"Mr. Cross is the one thing you liked in this class?" he asked.

The others looked at me. That should have embarrassed me, but I smiled instead.

"Travis is my childhood friend," I said. "It's nice to see a familiar face when you enter a room full of strangers."

Mr. Atkins nodded, clearly impressed. "Well, it looks like you have talent after all, Miss Montgomery. Welcome to my class." And he moved on to the next student.

Travis was looking at his portrait. Then he said, "I look nothing like that!"

I giggled. "Sure you do."

He stared at me for a while. "Well, since I was your inspiration to take this class, I guess I'll paint a portrait of you if he asks us to paint our inspiration to *stay* in this class."

I smiled at him. "Why? I thought you liked art."

"Maybe you're not the only one who has the talent." He winked at me, and I couldn't help giggling.

Mr. Atkins sent us home about an hour after the bell rang. No wonder Travis caught up with me that day I was walking home after finding Trip with his cheerleader. He had just gotten out from art class.

"How did you intend to get home?" Travis asked.

"I thought I could catch a ride with Cindy. I didn't know Mr. Atkins would send us off so late."

"You better get used to it," Travis said. "I'll drive you home. It's Friday today. Maybe we can have dinner first."

I smiled. "That would be great. I haven't eaten out in more than a month."

Travis raised his brow. "You broke up with Jacobs less than two weeks ago."

I sighed as I gathered my stuff and walked out with him.

"Well, we hadn't gone out for dinner in a while. He was busy with basketball practice. Turned out, he had tons of extra-curricular activities on the side."

"You're telling me hadn't taken you on a date in a while?"

"He picked me up, we grabbed a bite or two. We had ice cream sometimes. He picked me up at the mall. We were in a relationship. Did we have to go on dates all the time?"

"I'm not a fan of relationships. But I believe he should have taken you out on real dates at least twice a month. You know? Go to the movies, and have a nice quiet dinner together, go to the fairs, go stargazing."

I laughed. "Wow! Travis Cross! No wonder you're the ultimate heartbreaker on this campus."

He grunted.

"Now, since your ex-boyfriend was not such a great fan of romance, let me take you out on a date you deserve."

I laughed. "Date? I didn't think—after our educational date—I would go out with you again."

He raised his brow. "I am, after all, your safety guy. Part of my job is to pick up your shattered pieces and put them all back together."

I laughed. "Well, good luck with that."

\*\*\*

I tried to look okay, but I wasn't. I was scared about a lot of things. I was scared that I wouldn't find the right guy by the time I was thirty-one, and I was scared that Trip wouldn't be the last guy who would cheat on me.

Damn, I was even afraid that I would die a virgin. Or if not, I was afraid that the person I would lose my innocence to would treat me like I was unimportant the next day, would think low of me, or worse, would cheat on me with a filthy slut like Trip did.

"Did you hear the news?" Cindy called me that night.

"What news?"

"A girl was dumped in the fields a mile from school."

The hairs in my neck rose. "Really?"

"Yes. They don't know who it is yet. They're trying to identify her. They're still finding out whether or not she was from town."

"Geez! I thought this was one of the safest towns there is."

"I know. It's nerve-wracking, right?"

Just then, I heard a stumbling noise outside my door.

"What the heck..." My heart pounded in my ribcage.

The door opened and Travis barged into my room. He was breathless, like he had been running, but his face brightened as soon as he saw me sitting on my bed.

"There you are!" he said, his voice full of relief. "You weren't answering your phone!"

I looked at my mobile and realized that I had twenty missed calls, all from him. I left it on silent mode, which is why I didn't hear him calling.

"I'm sorry. It's on silent. Why? What's wrong?"

"They found a girl somewhere. She hasn't been identified yet. I just thought I'd check up on you. And when you didn't answer, I rushed here."

I smiled at him. "I'm here. I'm not that girl."

Travis took off his jacket and sat on my couch. "You really had me worried."

"I'm okay, Trav."

"You shouldn't be alone here."

"As if I have a choice," I murmured.

"I'm still here, you know!" Cindy said on the other line.

"Sorry, Cindy. Travis dropped by. I'll catch up with you later."

"Sure. He sounded really worried! That's very sweet!" Cindy said before she hung up.

I stared at Travis. "What were you saying?"

"You shouldn't be alone here," he said.

"I'm not alone," I said. "I've got two maids living downstairs."

"That's not enough to keep you safe."

"I'm safe. And besides, I always believe in fate. You have to go, you have to go."

He raised his brow. "Well, I promised your brother I would take care of you. That means I will fight fate to keep you alive."

I smiled. "That is really sweet."

"No. It's just me keeping my promise. I told you, I don't make promises I don't keep."

"Relax, Travis," I said. "I'll be fine. I'm not so fragile, you know."

"Nevertheless, I'll stay here until they find out who that girl is. And if they find that she's a local, that means we have a psychopath within a few miles' proximity, and I'll make arrangements for you to stay somewhere safer than here."

"Thomas wouldn't be that paranoid, you know."

"Thomas always believed in the goodness of people. I'm the cynical one, remember? And unfortunately for you, I was the one who lived." There was pain in his voice.

I sat on my bed quietly for a while, just looking at Travis. He was handsome beyond belief, but his eyes were sad, his soul broken.

"You still miss him, don't you?" I asked, standing up from my bed and sitting next to him.

"Don't you?" he asked back.

I sighed. "Every day."

I realized that I was…sad, too. Very sad. And I felt alone. Thomas was not the only one who left me. My mother and my father did, too. And all I had left was…Travis. This wonderful, beautiful boy who pledged to take care of me forever.

I couldn't help it. Something came over me. I stared at Travis. He was staring at me intensely, too. And somehow, I saw him in a different light. Something about him was so deeply enticing and exciting that I was not able to stop myself. I lunged forward and gave him a kiss on the lips.

I closed my eyes. My lips still on his, I wound my arms around his neck. It seemed like time and space froze in that one magical moment…that one magical kiss.

And then when it moved again, it moved in fast forward. Everything went so fast. I felt his arms around my waist as he pulled me to him. I felt his lips gently bruising mine in heart-stopping kisses.

I didn't think, I only felt. And the intense emotion I felt was nothing like I had ever felt before…with Trip, or with any other guy. And now, I realized that I wanted something. And I wanted it with Travis.

"Take me, Travis," I whispered. "Please…"

And just like that, I felt him stop. He pulled away from me. His face was flushed and his breathing rugged. His eyes closed and he raised his face, as if he was steadying himself, trying to get ahold of his emotions.

"I mean it," I said quietly. "Better you than some random guy…than some boyfriend who will cheat on me."

He opened his eyes and stared at me disbelievingly. "What…what are you…asking from me?"

I took a deep breath and boldly said, "I want you…to…be my first. I want to know what it is like. I want you to be the one to show me."

He closed his eyes again. When he opened them, I couldn't read them anymore. They were deep, all emotions hidden. He almost looked mad.

"I'm sorry. I shouldn't have kissed you," he said. "I guess I forgot who you were."

"Who am I, Travis? Some silly little girl who doesn't know better? Thomas's little sister? I'm not young anymore, Travis! I'm the same age as you! And I'm a woman already! I'm not a girl anymore! Stop treating me like one!"

"What do you want me to do?"

I opened my mouth, but no sound came out. Suddenly, I couldn't say it. I couldn't ask him again.

Travis's eyes narrowed. "See? You can't even say it out loud! You don't know what you want, Brittany Anne!" he said in a frustrated tone, calling me by my full name. He stood up from the couch and headed for the door. Then he stopped and looked at me again. "Why me?"

I took a deep breath and struggled to say something… anything… coherent. "Because…you're safe. Somehow, I see you as my angel. You've always been there for me, to take care of me. And I didn't

78

want to throw away my...virginity to someone I didn't know and would never know in my future."

He stared at me icily. "You read too many romance novels," he whispered hoarsely. "I'm no angel, Brianne...especially not in bed." He turned toward the door again. "I promised to keep you safe until they found out whether the girl was a local or not. I'll sleep on the couch downstairs. I don't think it's wise for me to be in the same room as you right now."

And he closed the door behind him.

I threw myself on my bed. I felt embarrassed beyond belief. Moreover, I was afraid that I might have destroyed my friendship with Travis.

How could I have done that? I'd already asked him to be my safety guy, and now I'd asked him to be my...*deflowerer*! And even Travis didn't want me. His kisses sent me spinning like no other kiss had ever done before. And mindlessly, I'd decided I wanted it to be him. The safe guy to give myself to for the first time. Because I knew he would treat me with respect, would not kiss and tell.

I knew him. He wouldn't be gone from my future. He could never cheat on me because he wasn't my boyfriend. And whenever I thought of my first time, I would think of him dearly. I wouldn't loathe myself or the guy. I wouldn't want to turn back time and take it all back.

But he didn't want me. Because I was a virgin? I was inexperienced? I knew nothing about pleasing a guy! I was boring! No man would want me. Not even Travis, who was supposed to be a player...who craved a woman's company more than anything else. I wasn't good enough...not even for him.

# Chapter Eight

Everybody forgot about the girl whose body was dumped a few miles from our town. She wasn't a local. She was tattooed, and there was evidence of use of drugs. Her body was probably dumped after an accidental overdose, as there were no signs of violence on her, not even bruises.

I was glad, because if there was a murderer in town, Travis would have to hang around to make sure I was safe. And I didn't want to see him again after that night. I was too embarrassed, too ashamed.

I believed he felt exactly the same. He was gone when I woke up the next morning. Therese, my maid, told me that Travis sat on the couch all night that night. He waited until the house was up at sunrise, and then he left.

"I was startled to find him sitting like a statue in the couch. He was not moving, lost in his thoughts," she had said. "He didn't look like he slept at all." Well, he wasn't the only one who wasn't able to sleep that night.

The last thing he had said to me was that he didn't want to be in the same room as me. He was a gentleman. He didn't say the words to my face. He didn't want me, and it was best he walked away.

Now it was one week to prom, and I didn't have a date.

"A lot of guys are thinking of asking you out. Find out who is decent enough, at least," Cindy advised.

"I wanted someone as hot as Trip so I wouldn't look like a loser to him."

Sure enough, three days before the prom, a guy named Alexander Jackson pinned a rose to my locker, with a note that said:

*Roses are red, violets are blue, I may be football captain,*
*but I guess I lack the courage to ask you...*
*But I'll only get my answer if I ask, really...*
*So here goes: Will you go to prom with me?*

I had to smile at his attempt at poetry. It was sweet, actually. I pulled up a picture of Alexander Jackson in my mind. Football captain. Broad shoulders, muscular build, blond hair, dark eyes. He wasn't as handsome as Trip, but he was more charming. Plus, his eyes were always laughing. I guessed he'd do well to replace Trip as my prom date.

I placed the rose inside my locker. Then I stuck a post-it outside my locker and wrote: *Yes.*

I was nervous to go to art class. For the three classes that I'd had, Mr. Atkins had asked us to paint in our own chosen locations. It was great for me because I didn't want to see Travis. But now there was no escaping him. We'd have to hand in our masterpieces.

We were asked by Mr. Atkins to express, in whatever form, the meaning of life…our lives. My art piece was a little bit dark and sad. It was a combination of colors and hues in an abstract form. Greens, violets, and oranges mixed beautifully on the canvas. Somewhere there was a tree, somewhere there was a boy standing at the end of a road. I liked to think it was Thomas. Waiting there for me. The only reason why I was able to move on. He was gone, but I lived. And I would keep on living for both of us.

"Mr. Cross submitted his work earlier this week. He won't be able to make it to class today," Mr. Atkins announced.

Honestly, I was relieved.

Relieved because I didn't have to see him. But I was also a little upset. Because it meant that he was employing all means possible to avoid me. I didn't want him to. I had lost Thomas; I didn't want to lose Travis, too.

Mr. Atkins looked at my drawing for a while, and then he smiled.

"You don't always have to be sad, Miss Montgomery," he said quietly. "But I admire your talent. You should consider art school when you graduate."

Before Mr. Atkins dismissed us, he handed me a piece of parchment rolled into a scroll.

"This is Mr. Cross's work," he said. "Kindly give it to him. I've already graded it."

"Can't you give it to him next time?"

He shook his head. "Mr. Cross will not be in for the next three classes. He's taken a special assignment for me outside of class."

He handed me the rolled parchment, tied with a black ribbon.

"No rush. I've already told him what his grade is."

When I went home that night, I decided to clean up my paint cabinets and organize my paintings.

I found a familiar painting of candles and a romantic bed in a hotel room. I scowled at it and then threw it in the bin.

I figured that wasn't going to happen. I needed to let go of that dream. I needed to accept that high school boys were just not that romantic—or even considerate.

I was disappointed to have painted such a romantic picture of how my first time was going to be. The image was so vivid, so accurate. And it was never going to happen. It was just a dream. Maybe someday, when I found the right guy, it could come true. Now, I just didn't care anymore.

With Alex...I would just let things flow. I won't sell myself out but I would stop thinking that fairy tales exist and boys are all prince charmings. If things get deeper with Alex, then maybe he's the one. Although if I had a choice I know who I really wanted to be my first. If I would shoot for special moments and unforgettable firsts... there was only one perfect guy who deserved it. But sadly, he didn't want me.

The next afternoon, Cindy and I planned to go to the mall to buy clothes.

"Aren't you going to buy some nice lingerie?" she asked.

"What for?"

"Well, who knows? Maybe that will be *the* day. Don't you want to wear something that will haunt Alex's nights and make him ask for more?"

"Is that necessary? I mean...I am curious about sex. But I don't have high expectations about my first time anymore, you know. I'm not even sure if I am going to like it. And besides, I'm just letting things flow. Not sure if the moment or the guy would be right. I'm letting fate decide."

"Okay." Cindy rolled her eyes. "But just in case Alex does some grand gestures in the next couple of days and he turns to out to be your romantic whirlwind romance, don't you want to at least look nice under your prom dress?"

"I have nice Victoria's Secret lingerie."

"Yeah, like Lycra gym bikinis!" She rolled her eyes.

"What else could be better than that?"

"Silk. Strings."

"I don't want to look like a slut!" I rolled my eyes.

"All right. Whatever suits you. You would have made more effort with Trip, you know."

"Because I thought I was in love with Trip and he was in love with me. And I was sure I wanted to keep doing that with Trip...exclusively!"

"And with Alex?"

"I haven't known him long enough to feel anything deep. I am curious. He is sweet and good-looking. I think he's a good guy. But maybe I'm overthinking this. I was dreaming too much that I'd give my V-card to some guy who would treasure it like it was some God-given gift or something. But look what Trip had in mind for us, and he was my boyfriend for a year."

"You know what, you *are* overthinking this. Just rip off the bandage! At least Alex won't cheat on you...because...you aren't officially dating exclusively yet. He might ask you to go steady after that, though. Would you agree?"

I shrugged. "We'll see. I'm not in a hurry to get heartbroken again."

The prospect of dating Alex is... okay, I guess. If the world wasn't mad, then I would have a better prospect than Alex. It's not that he's bad. He's... okay. But he didn't charm me as much as Trip did on our first date. And his kisses didn't make me insane like... Travis's nerve-wracking kisses.

*Travis.* Yeah, I didn't know he could send my emotions spiraling through the roof in less than a minute of making a move on me. How could he instantly make me want to go to bed with him with just a couple of kisses? Was that the side of him that he was hiding from me? The charming side that even Tom didn't want me to see?

*Now there's something worth trading my V-card for,* I thought glumly. Then I groaned. I have got to stop thinking like this about Travis Cross! He's like my designated guardian for Christ's sake!

My thoughts were interrupted when I heard a commotion behind us. Some kids were rushing toward the gym.

"I wonder what that's all about!" Cindy said.

"Maybe Trip was caught on top of a cheerleader again. That would be a lovely second!" I said wryly.

84

"Hey, Matt!" Cindy called one of the guys rushing past us. "What's going on?"

"Fight! In the boys' locker room!" Matt replied and he rushed toward the gym.

"Interesting!" Cindy said excitedly. "I wonder who."

"High school boys!" I said, rolling my eyes. "Come on, Cindy, let's go."

She pouted. "Can we at least hang around for ten minutes? I want to know what that was about."

"I never figured you to be a gossip," I muttered under my breath. But I didn't have a choice. I was catching a ride with her and I knew she wouldn't rest until she found out what the fight was all about.

"Let's go closer!" she said, pulling me with her.

I let her drag me to the direction of the gym. However, I froze in my tracks when I saw Travis going out of it, looking like he was on a warpath.

Since that night I kissed him… I haven't stopped thinking about him. And now that I'm seeing him in the flesh again made my heart pound in my chest, and I think I forgot how to breathe. If I were to be really honest, I would say that my curiosity for sex was only encompassed by my keenness to feel Travis's mind-blowing kisses again.

"What's the matter with you?" Cindy asked me, noticing my stiff reaction. Then she followed my gaze and saw Travis coming closer toward us.

"I think we should go!" I said to her.

But Cindy looked star-struck, staring at Travis heading toward us. His hair was wet and disheveled. He had an angry look on his face. It took me a moment to realize that he was staring at me as he came closer to us.

"I think he's headed this way," Cindy whispered.

I should have run, or made an effort to hide. Travis was excellent at getting ahold of his emotions and keeping his feelings to himself. But right then, he was not making it secret that he was furious…raging mad, even.

He stopped in front of me and searched my face. My heart probably stopped beating altogether, and I wasn't sure how I was able to breathe.

"You're not going to prom with Alexander Jackson!" he muttered under his breath.

"What?"

"Tell Alexander Jackson you're not going to prom with him! Not in this lifetime!"

How could he ask me to drop my prom date at the last minute? He wasn't my boyfriend, nor my brother!

I shook my head. "I'm not going to prom without a date!" I said angrily.

He raised a brow. "You're not!" he said. "*I'm* taking you!" And he started to walk away.

I stared at his back. How could he make this choice for me after he rejected me... after he made me feel wanted for one minute before shooting me down the next?

And then suddenly, I realized... did he change his mind about what I asked of him too?

With all the courage I could muster, I said, "This isn't just about prom, you know!"

He stopped on his tracks and stood motionless for a second. Then he turned around to look at me in the eyes. He took a deep breath and said, "*I know.*"

My heart suddenly dropped to my toes. I don't know how I knew, but I was sure that we were referring to the same thing. In his eyes, I saw concern, pain, and the overwhelming desire to...protect me.

He nodded slightly, and then he turned around and headed toward his car and sped off. I was left standing there like a statue, staring after him.

"Oh my God!" Cindy breathed behind me. "What just happened?"

"I'm...not sure actually."

"He's...taking you to prom! This is a game changer! I know you weren't sure about Alex. But come on, no matter how hard you deny it, you and Travis Cross have the hots for each other." Cindy said, almost jumping up and down.

"I wonder what happened to him in the boys' locker room," I said.

Matt walked past us.

"Hey, what happened?" Cindy asked him.

Matt gave me a weird look first and then he said, "Well, Trip Jacobs and Alexander Jackson were bantering about some sort of bet."

He looked at me again. "Cross was there. He didn't like what he heard, I guess. He went for both of them."

"What?!" Cindy was shocked. "Where's Trip and Alex?"

"Still there. Trip lost a tooth. Alex had a bad shiner, I think," Matt replied, and then he started to walk away.

"Wait!" Cindy called. "What was the bet about?"

Matt shrugged. "I'm not sure. But I was told it has something to do with you, Brianne."

"Wow!" Cindy breathed. She turned to face me as soon as Matt walked away. "Well, there goes your knight in shining armor."

I pulled her toward the parking lot. "Let's go."

When we got into the car, Cindy smiled at me mischievously. "So? Have you changed your mind about buying lingerie?"

# Chapter Nine

I looked at my reflection nervously. I was wearing a bright lavender gown that hugged my body to perfection, with a skirt that flowed flirtatiously a few inches above my knees.

I hadn't spoken to Travis since that day he told me he was taking me to prom. I found out later that Trip had been making bets with his friends about who would be able to pop my cherry at prom. I said yes to Alex, who was more than willing to do the job that Trip was supposed to have done had I not caught him on top of that cheerleader. It was all a bet for him. Alex was cunning enough to use flattery and poetry to lure me into his lair. They had been bantering about it in the locker room, cheering that prom was *the* day. Trip had apparently been cajoling Alex into taping the whole thing to make sure he wouldn't cheat on their bet.

The whole campus must have known their evil plans. I'm pretty sure that, had Alex caught our fornicating on tape, there would have been a scheduled film showing.

I was on the Campus Bulletin Gossip Board again, of course!

*Whose virtue was up for grabs? Looks like football team captain's plans blew up in smoke when a rebellious heartthrob chose to defend our girl's unwanted honor. What interest could our heartthrob have in our girl, I wonder?*

Travis must have just finished gym class and overheard Trip and Alex. He got furious and was not able to stop himself from demonstrating his martial arts skills to them. Alex wanted to complain about the whole thing, but Trip was still on probation and he didn't want further trouble. So Travis got off the hook. Not that he wouldn't be able to do anything about it. I'm pretty sure one phone call from his father to the school board would prevent the whole drama from ever being on his record.

I stared at my reflection again. I didn't put on much makeup. I didn't want to overdo myself. This was Travis, after all. He'd seen me at my worst. I wasn't trying to impress him. If he hadn't changed his mind about tonight, I didn't want him to think I was trying to look pretty for him. He had more than half the girls on campus already doing that for him. He was just there to do a job. For me. For my sake. Because I was tired of being the clueless, innocent, little virgin.

But that didn't stop me from buying a fresh pair of Victoria's Secret undergarments. I was wearing a light lavender slip and string bikini underneath my cute prom dress. I didn't know what to buy, but Cindy suggested it looked classy and just a little bit sexy. If Travis (or any guy for that matter) saw beneath my clothes, I would at least want to look elegant and classy.

I showered in chamomile and jasmine bath oils for like an hour. I applied the same scent of lotion and the same scent of perfume. I was sure I smelled sweet, innocent, and fresh, not that it was the first time I'd ever bathed in floral oils. I did it at least three times a week anyway. I liked to smell nice…even for myself.

I was positive I looked nice. I curled my hair and tied it in a bun at the top of my head. Some tendrils escaped to frame my face. I looked simple but nice. I wasn't planning to catch any attention. Two days wasn't enough to make people forget about the locker room fight that Alexander and Trip had with Travis Cross. In fact, two days wasn't enough to make anybody forget the show of emotion from Travis Cross. If he hadn't been such a hottie, he would almost have been the campus outcast, as he seemed so uninterested in any high-school drama.

I wasn't sure if he really meant he would take me to prom. If he didn't show up, I wouldn't go at all. Not after slapping Alex in the face and telling him that he needed to find a new prom date quickly!

The doorbell rang. I jumped up from the bed. I took my purse and staggered downstairs to the door. When I opened it, I found Travis looking down to me, wearing a white tuxedo. His hair was sleekly brushed up, with a lock falling over his forehead, giving him a sleek and mischievous look. He was as dashing as ever.

My heart pounded in my chest.

*This is Travis!* I reminded myself.

"You look…" he started but trailed off.

"Nice?" I asked, uncertain. That was what I was aiming for.

He shrugged. "Yes, if that's the word you prefer."

I smiled. "Yes. You're not too bad yourself."

He offered his arm to me, and I took it. He led me to his Bentley and opened the passenger door for me.

We drove toward the hotel in silence. I felt my hands, they were cold and shaking. I was nervous as hell. Travis looked...devilishly handsome! And if I were any other girl, I would think that there was no better man to go to bed with for the first time! But I wasn't any other girl! I was Brianne...his best friend's little sister. He wasn't any other guy. He was my...safety guy.

"What was the word you were aiming for?" I asked as we neared the hotel where prom was held. I wasn't sure if he understood what I meant. When I said I preferred the word *nice*, he had been about to say something else. I wanted to know what that was.

He looked at me for a second, but he didn't answer. He parked his car at the front of the hotel and rounded it to open my door.

He stared at me for a long moment. I raised my chin to him, determined to let him know that he needed to answer. I had to know what he really thought about the way I looked tonight.

He dropped his eyes to his shoes, as if in defeat. When he raised them to me again, they were full of mixed emotions.

"I was aiming for the word...*ravishing*." And as if he were ashamed of his own thoughts, he turned away from me. He held his arm to me but refused to meet my eyes. I guess I wasn't the only one who was uncomfortable about the whole thing. More than being uncomfortable, I think Travis felt...guilty...embarrassed...ashamed.

*Is he ashamed of being with me tonight?*

My thoughts were interrupted by Cindy, who met us at the entrance. She was with Allan. Allan nodded at me and extended his hand to shake Travis's.

I knew people were looking, people were talking. It was not like Travis to show up at school dances. He didn't have any friends. People barely knew that we knew each other.

We hung out with Cindy and Allan. Travis and I were barely talking, barely touching. It was getting awkward.

"Nervous?" Cindy whispered to me.

I shrugged. "Yes. And scared half to death!"

Cindy laughed. "You won't be if you didn't want him in the first place, you know."

I asked myself if that was true. Did I really want him?

Yes! But God, this is Travis I'm talking about. Our relationship might change forever after this.

And then I realized who Travis really was to me. Yes, I cannot deny that he is devilishly handsome and that I long to feel his kisses once again. But, on the other hand, he was supposed to be the most comfortable guy on earth for me. That's why he was my safety guy. Maybe...I shouldn't have asked him to...be something else. To do something that he wasn't supposed to do. This task was not meant for him. Maybe I shouldn't force it. Maybe now, it's best if we just enjoy prom the way it should be enjoyed.

I felt him tug at my hand. "Let's dance," he said.

I nodded and let him pull me toward the dance floor.

Slow music played. Travis stared down at me, and my heart pounded in my chest.

He pulled me to him and massaged one of my hands. It was cold and sweaty. He narrowed his eyes. "You're nervous."

I took a deep breath. "Travis... maybe this wasn't such a great idea."

He raised a brow. "Don't hurt my feelings. I always thought I was a graceful dancer."

I glared at him. "You know very well that wasn't what I was talking about!"

"What were you talking about?" he asked innocently.

"Travis!" I could not believe he was making me say it out loud.

He chuckled. "But didn't you say...better me than some random guy or some boyfriend who would cheat on you?"

"I know...but...you're my safety guy! You're not supposed to make me feel as nervous as I am now!"

He smiled as if he had triumphantly gained something. "Good. Then we're off to a good start!"

"I'm not...sure I am doing the right thing now."

"You are," he said. "I'm the one going to hell for this."

"Why?" I asked.

He shook his head and didn't answer. Instead, he pulled me toward him. He wound his arm around my waist tightly, his other hand kept massaging my hand.

"You need to relax," he said. "You're too tense."

I had no idea how I could get rid of that weird feeling. There was electricity, there was thrill...but I was too scared, too nervous to feel anything else. I was sure I didn't want to feel ashamed of myself the first time I was going to do it. And not only that, I remembered the look of shame in Travis's eyes.

"You don't want to do this, either," I whispered to him. "Don't lie to me, Travis. I could see it in your eyes. And I don't think I want my first time to be with a guy who…didn't want me. Even for just tonight. Maybe it isn't right. Maybe we shouldn't do this."

"I think you're reading me all wrong," he said. "And it's too late to back out now."

"No, it's not," I protested. "We haven't done it yet. I'm still a virgin!"

He stared at me for a moment and then he leaned forward so he could whisper in my ear. "You won't be by the end of tonight,"

My heart pounded in my chest. I felt his hand slowly massage my back until it rested at the top of my bodice, the part that was bare. The touch of his skin was electrifying. I almost forgot to breathe. "Travis…"

"Sshhh…"

His other hand crept on my neck, and I felt his breath on my ear. He massaged my neck very gently, and then I felt him nip at my earlobe. An unfamiliar emotion crept through me. I let out a moan.

"Travis…" I whispered again.

"Don't say my name…" he said.

"Why?"

He took a deep breath. "Because I promised to protect you and take care of you for as long as I live." He pulled away from me and stared down at me. I saw confusion and shame in his eyes. "I'm not supposed to do this."

Guilt crept through me again. "But you are doing it because I asked you to. Because you protected me from Alex…and Trip…because, you knew I was better off spending this night with you."

"Those…and some other reasons," he said. He held me by the neck and gently pulled me to him. "I think you're ready now, Brianne."

It took me a moment to realize that I wasn't trembling in fear anymore. I could feel thrill more than fear. How could he know that?

He pulled away from me and led me toward the exit.

93

I wondered where we were going. I certainly hoped he didn't plan to do this at the back of his car, although the backseat of the car he brought was pretty spacey.

Was that why he didn't bring his sports car? If he'd planned for the backseat, I would strongly protest and tell him to just take me home. My room was a lot better, and if he didn't agree, I was better off not spending the night with him at all.

We entered the elevator. Instead of pressing the ground floor, Travis pressed P.

*He rented a Penthouse room?*

It seemed like it took forever to get there. When the elevator opened, he took my hand in his.

"You rented a room for us?" I asked.

He raised a brow. "Since your brother is going to kick my ass in hell for this anyway, I thought I should at least do this with class."

I rolled my eyes. Of course! He was Travis Cross, anyway.

He swiped his access card at the last door on the floor. It opened into a spacious room. The living room was lit just right, setting a mood in the room. He led me toward the couch. There was an ice bucket with a bottle of wine in the center of the table. Travis picked it up and poured each of us a glass.

Chardonnay. The one wine I actually liked. Did he remember?

"We shouldn't be drinking, but I know you only like Chardonnay," he said.

I smiled. *He remembered!*

"You know me too well, I guess."

He gave me a rueful smile and said, "Not yet." And somehow, I knew what he meant by that.

I was still uncomfortable. Still nervous.

I looked up at him. "Thank you...for doing me all these...weird favors."

He narrowed his eyes at me. "Don't thank me just yet," he said. "This may destroy us, you know."

"Destroy us?"

"You're...my friend...a dear one. And you know I don't love that easily," he said quietly. "Now, you see what you're making me do?"

"We won't let it destroy us then," I said. Maybe this was a mistake and maybe I wasn't entirely sure why I asked him to do this.

But I'm sure of one thing. I won't let this destroy what we have…
what we are.

He shook his head. "Don't speak too soon," he said. "You may
choose to stay away from me after the night is through."

"I won't," I said. "I'm not going to lose you, too, Travis." And I
knew I meant that.

He reached out for my hand. "I pray…that you can still say the
same thing later." He pulled me toward him. He stared at my face for a
long moment. Then he said, "What a silly little girl…"

"I'm not a girl anymore."

He shook his head. "After tonight, you won't be."

My heart pounded in my chest. Travis led me toward the
bedroom. When he opened it, my heart dropped to my chest. The room
was lit by candles everywhere. The floor was covered in rose petals.
There was a California king bed in the middle. The room looked
familiar…somehow. It was…like the room I painted…the painting I
threw out.

"How did you…" I started to ask.

"I found your painting," he said. "Doesn't take a genius to know
what's going on in your mind when you were painting
that…considering you threw it away after…" He didn't continue.
"Anyway, I thought you deserved this. More than anyone."

I stared back at the room again and almost gasped. "I thought you
said you were no angel in bed."

"I'm breaking all the rules for you, can't you see?"

It was absolutely perfect. The candles were situated almost in the
same places as in my painting. It was like that portrait came to life.

I felt Travis's hand on my shoulder as he eased me into the room.
Then I heard him whisper in my ear, "Do you like it?"

I nodded slowly because I couldn't speak. I felt more nervous than
I was when I went into the room with him.

"You're trembling," Travis said.

"I have every right to be."

He chuckled. "Now you realize what you asked of me?"

I shook my head. "I still mean it. Better you than anybody else.
And I will not lose you after this, Travis."

He fell quiet for a while. Then he pulled me gently so I could face
him. He searched my face. Then he said, "Close your eyes, Brianne."

Reluctantly, I closed my eyes. I felt his breath on my face. "Don't look... just *feel*," he said.

Then I felt his lips on mine as he kissed me. Gently at first, his mouth guiding mine until I started kissing him back. My arms went around his neck and I let him kiss me. It was nerve-wracking. My world started spinning, I felt my knees weaken, and I clung to Travis as if I were clinging to life itself.

He stopped kissing me and leaned his forehead against mine. "This isn't right..." I heard him whisper, more to himself.

My eyes flew open and I looked back at him. His face was torn, full of emotions I couldn't read. His look was dark and he was flushed, out of breath.

"What did I do?" I asked nervously. "What's...wrong?"

He stared back at me but didn't reply.

I felt like crying. I didn't know what was going on. I felt silly. I felt stupid. And even Travis, who was supposed to be the most honest person in the world to me, felt something was wrong.

"Tell me what's wrong?" I asked, unaware that a tear had escaped my eye.

He smiled ruefully, as if in defeat. He reached forward and wiped my cheek with his thumb.

"What's wrong, Travis?"

He took a deep breath. He held my face between his palms and pulled me to him again. And just as his lips were an inch away from mine, he said, "The way I feel *right!*"

Then he kissed me again. Hungrily. As if he were letting go of all his shields, all his reservations. I felt wonderful. His kisses were making me feel emotions I hadn't felt in my life at all. Without breaking our kiss, he gently guided me toward the bed until the backs of my knees hit the edge.

He took off his coat and then he leaned toward me again. He kissed me again as he gently unzipped my gown. When it fell to the floor, I let out a moan. It seemed like Travis was sending all my senses of reason and sanity flying out the window.

How could I feel like this about Travis? How could he undo me this way?

When he pulled away from me, the look on this face was dark and unfathomable. It was like he was fighting all the demons inside of him.

"Travis..."

"Sshhh..." he whispered. "Don't say my name," he said.

"Why?"

He shook his head. "I'm not supposed to do this. This is not supposed to be me." He took a deep breath. He took something from the bed, and I saw him it was a piece of black scarf. He placed it on my eyes like a blindfold. "I don't want you to see me like this."

"Like what?"

It took a moment for him to answer, and when he did, he answered very carefully. "Like a predator."

My heart stopped beating in my chest. I almost lost my breath. Then I said, "Then you can't look at me, either. You can't see me... like a prey."

He chuckled softly. "Then we have a deal. Don't look...just feel." He covered my eyes with the scarf. "Let's...you and I...forget who we are...for a moment."

I nodded, and I couldn't agree with him more.

I felt him on top of me. He kissed me again, gently at first...and then as if he had finally unleashed the 'predator' inside him, he kissed me like it was the last time he would ever kiss a woman in his life.

*** 

When I opened my eyes again, it was already dark in the room. The candles had burned out, and I could only hear a quiet snore beside me. I was not resting on soft pillows, but on a hard, firm chest. I could feel strong arms wrapped around me, keeping me safe and warm.

I looked back at the events that had transpired only a couple of hours before. I remembered the gentle tearing pain. He tried as much as he could not to make it hurt. But it was inevitable.

In those few moments of pain, he held me in his arms and allowed me to whimper. And after that...I remembered warmth, I remembered pleasure. When it was over, I remembered being held. Aside from his quiet moans, I never heard him speak again. As if he was trying to conceal his identity from me. He didn't want me to remember who he was. I would be allowed to remember only the moment.

He shifted beside me. I felt him caress my arms gently. Then I felt him tilt my chin gently and he kissed me again...passionately. He lit the fire in me again. He never uttered a word. But he touched me in places I longed to be touched without knowing I'd wanted it. I let out moans of pleasure. And when I reached the gates of heaven, I wanted to scream his name, but I stopped myself. I couldn't know him like that. And he couldn't know me like this. He wanted me to keep my promise...that I wouldn't lose him. Because I couldn't afford to lose him.

He was my safety guy, my protector. But that didn't stop me from feeling right! From wanting to stay like that with him forever...at least, in those few moments of heaven. I didn't see him. It was too dark. He had turned off all the lights in the room. The drapes were shut. He too, didn't want to see me this way...a wanton...woman.

When I opened my eyes again, it was already morning. I was tucked comfortably in bed but unlike an hour ago, I was alone. There was a little light coming from the window. I reached out for the lamp on the bedside table and turned it on. I realized that it was already almost noon.

I found Travis sitting at the edge of the bed, his back to me. He was already dressed. He was quietly waiting for me to wake up.

"Trav..." I started. I still wasn't sure if I was allowed to call him by his name.

He inclined his head gently, acknowledging me.

"Good morning," he whispered. "I need to go. I just didn't want you to wake up and find me gone. You deserve better than that."

I felt warm. Even in a situation like this one, Travis found a way to be a gentleman.

"Where are you going?"

He took a deep breath. "Far away from you."

Instantly, panic gripped me. "What? But you said...you promised I wouldn't lose you."

He shook his head. "And you won't. But I hope you understand that I need to do this. I need to...stay away for a while. I have made arrangements to send you home safely."

He stood up from the bed and picked up his coat from the couch. He still refused to look at me.

"Why are you going away?" I asked quietly. A deep pain was threatening to shred me to pieces, and I didn't understand why.

"I promised to look out for you. I promised to keep you safe at all times. I do not want to break those promises."

"Why?" I asked. "Am I in danger?" I was trying to control the anger inside me.

He took a deep breath and then finally he turned to me. His face was torn, pained...almost broken. But he still looked as handsome as hell.

"Yes, Brianne," he whispered. "I underestimated some things. I'm a few seconds away from breaking those promises. You are in danger...*grave* danger...of me." And he turned toward the door and left quietly.

I wanted to cry. But I knew I couldn't. I had done this. I made Travis do it. I knew I had to do what I could to help him keep his promises. I had to give him his space. I could not remember...

# Chapter Ten

I was excited to start my new life. For once, I would live in a house where I did not have to wonder when my parents were coming home, or if they were coming home at all.

The last time I'd seen them was graduation day. They decided we would be a family once more. It was also the first time I'd seen Travis since...since he started staying away from me. He didn't go to the stage to take his diploma. But he appeared out of nowhere just as I was posing with my parents for a photo.

Emotions overwhelmed me. After that...night...he kept a good distance from me. I wanted to tell him that it was going to be okay, but I had to remember that it wasn't me who had a problem with what happened between us. I knew I had to respect his decision and the space he asked for.

I missed him like crazy and I almost regret what I asked him to do for me. I realized that though it was the most amazing night of my life, worth every second of giving up my 'first time' for... nothing is worth losing Travis for. If I lost him, it would be like losing my last good memory of Tom. And I can't give up my one remaining connection with my brother.

I hugged him tightly when he approached us. Even though he was brilliant at disappearing from my life, somehow I knew that he was still there. Still watching me. Still keeping his promises to Tom to keep me safe.

"I missed you," I couldn't help whispering to him. He gave me a gentle smile.

"I missed you, too," he said softly, as his arm wrapped around my waist.

I pulled him toward my parents so we could all take a picture...as a family.

"So, am I safe again?" I asked him. When he disappeared, he told me it was because I was in grave danger...of him. I wanted to know things were going to be back to the way they used to be...the way they should be.

He smiled at me gently. "I guess it's safe to say so." I trusted that he was telling the truth. Because if there was anybody who could take hold of his strong emotions, it was Travis.

I smiled at him brightly again. "It's nice to have you back in my life. It was difficult not having you around."

He fell silent for a while. Then he reached down and intertwined our fingers. He pulled my hand to his lips and placed a gentle kiss on the back of my hand. "It was hell trying to stay away from you," he whispered so quietly, I almost didn't hear his words.

My heart pounded inside my chest, and I knew I was blushing a bright shade of red. I was thankful when we reached our parents. It gave me a chance to let go of his hand, so he could hug both of them. Then we took a picture...as a family.

Travis chose to go to a university in the same city as me. I was happy about that. At least I would find comfort in the fact that he was close by. That I could run to him when I needed him...and he could run to me so he wouldn't feel alone.

That...wonderful, amazing night that happened between us was best left forgotten...or at least the memory of it tucked away in a safe, special place...until there was absolute need to call on it.

I aced Mr. Atkins's art class, and he gave me very high recommendations. At first, I was hesitant. But in the end, I took his advice and chose the fine arts program at Southern Connecticut State University.

I was geared to take over my mother's gallery someday. I would probably try to exhibit something of my own. I lived in a dorm near the campus. I also joined a dance club. My roommate, Sarah, was a dance major, and I developed a passion for contemporary dance.

I went out on dates once in a while, but nothing really stuck.

I didn't see Travis regularly. I did receive emails from him, asking me how I was. We would text each other, chat for hours on weekends, as if we hadn't spoken to each other in years, talking like we were just there side-by-side with each other. It felt nice to know that he was always nearby. Travis and I didn't need to be together every day to remember how much we meant to each other.

One Saturday, I was hanging out with Sarah at the public pool.

I welcomed the heat of the sun on my skin. It was almost spring break, and we were sitting at one of the poolside tables. I was wearing a yellow two-piece suit.

"Do you ever think about what you will do? I mean...I'm pretty sure I'll still be unmarried by thirty. I might be dating someone seriously, but I don't think marriage would already have been an option by then. That age is too young. What if you'll be in the same situation? What if...by thirty, you're not yet married, or worse...not even close to finding Mr. Right? Isn't there a way out of your family's...crazy tradition?"

I laughed. "I wish it was just a tradition that I could break. But with all the unfortunate coincidences happening to my relatives who broke the rule...I'm scared that it's actually a curse. But don't worry— I have a plan," I replied.

"What? Like...die? Or disown your own family?"

"Relax. I've got that sorted out," I said. "I will be married by the time I'm thirty-one. I won't be 'cursed' or 'disgraced.'"

"You're so positive!" She rolled her eyes. "You're gorgeous, I know. But we both know that these days, finding the right guy requires luck, too. What makes you so sure you will be married by then? You know guys can't be forced into marriage nowadays."

I smiled at her. "I've got...a backup plan."

Sarah raised a brow.

"You know, one of those boy-friends who promises to marry you at a certain age if you're still single by then?"

"A safety guy?"

I nodded. "Yeah. I've got one of those."

"Wow! Good thinking!" She giggled. "And you plan to stay with this guy for the rest of your life?"

I shook my head. "Until I find the one."

"What if he finds the one ahead of you?"

"I doubt that. You see...you've got to find one of those guys who is happy staying a bachelor for life. You tell him he stays married to you on paper only and for purposes of appearance. But he can continue being...a player for all you care. And when the guy for you finally arrives, you can file a divorce, taking nothing from each other and then remaining friends," I said to her. "Brilliant plan, isn't it?"

"Yeah." She smiled at me. "I think...I'm going to get myself one of those...safety guys. But I won't be as...unrealistic or crazy as you. I'll set the bar at...thirty-eight. Before menopause."

I looked away from her and turned to the bar instead. And I went still for a second. It was like I was seeing a ghost all of a sudden. I had to blink a couple of times to make sure that I wasn't dreaming.

But that familiar blond-streaked black hair was unmistakable. He was looking at me, too. He nodded in acknowledgement, and then I watched him stand up from the bar and make his move toward me.

My knees were shaking. I stood up from my seat. It'd been so long since I'd last seen him. Sure, we got in touch all the time, but seeing him then made me realize just how much I'd missed him.

I smiled at him as he made his way toward me. He gave me a crooked smile that would make any other girl's heart stop beating. But my own heart was pounding in my chest. I ran toward him, and it was like I was running toward home.

I didn't hesitate. I threw myself into his arms. He caught me and gave me a tight hug. I closed my eyes and his fresh, masculine scent filled my senses. I closed my eyes and drowned myself in his embrace. I let myself be locked into safety. And I knew there, no one could touch me.

"I missed you," I whispered to him.

"I can tell," he whispered against my ear. I wanted him to say he missed me too, but for Travis to say things that gave away a hint of emotion at all was within the range of rare and non-existent.

I gently pulled away from him so I could look into his eyes. "What are you doing here?"

"It's a public pool, and just in case you've forgotten, I go to Yale. We're in the same vicinity."

"It didn't feel like that for the past couple of months," I protested. "I haven't seen you in like..." I trailed off, trying to recall the last time I saw Travis.

"I know. Months!" he supplied for me.

I knew Travis wasn't Thomas, but it was certainly sad not having a sibling around. Thomas was also protective of me. And Travis was doing the job he was supposed to be doing...sometimes even overdoing it. Except for the past few months, when he'd just let me be.

I leaned forward and hugged him again.

"Sorry if you came here to find some girls!" I said, giggling. "I missed you—and all this hugging will lessen your chances of hooking up with another girl."

He laughed. And instead of pulling away, he hugged me tighter. This surprised me. I expected him to push me away.

"I did find a girl," he said. "She's gorgeous as hell. I feel sorry for the guys who were thinking of introducing themselves to her. Because now, she's like putty in my arms."

I pulled away from him and gave him a playful punch in the shoulder.

He laughed. "You didn't come here with a date, so I guess it's safe to buy you a drink."

I nodded. "But wait, I'm with..." I turned around toward Sarah. I found her chatting with a cute guy, but somehow her attention was divided between me and him. I turned back to Travis. "Never mind. Sure!"

Travis wound an arm around my shoulder again and I put an arm around his waist. He didn't pull away from me. Instead, he leaned forward and gave me a kiss on the forehead.

We sat at the bar and Travis ordered some drinks for us. "How is school?"

"Wonderful! It's almost break. Are you going home?"

He shrugged. "Depends on where my father will be."

"Travis..." I narrowed my eyes at him.

He sighed. "You know he's a difficult man."

"You're not too easy, either," I argued.

"Wow! That coming from the person who could practically extort anything from me. How difficult could I be?" He rolled his eyes.

"You know you are!" I said, and then I smiled. "And thank you. Because you make it too easy for me to change your mind all the time."

"I don't always like it. But you know I find it so hard to say no to you." He rolled his eyes again and drank his beer. I had to smile at that.

"Let's go home," I said—an idea had come to me. "You and Thomas talked about taking a camping trip down at your lake house on your first spring break, right?"

He narrowed his eyes at me. "You know very well that's not going to happen anymore."

"Well, you were doing what Thomas was supposed to be doing...protecting me. Let me do what he's supposed to be doing with you. I'll go with you instead."

"One whole week with you? Wow! I'd rather be under the same roof as my father!"

"Lie!" I snorted. I knew that Travis hated nothing more than being in the same room as his father.

"Nevertheless, it's supposed to be a guy thing, princess," he said. "We were planning to take a hike in the woods and go camping. You're...too delicate for that!"

"Of course not! I'm not so fragile, you know."

"But that's how I see you. And if you camp with me, I'll be paranoid about your safety—it will be far too distracting," he said.

I sighed. "All right. I get your point. I was just...offering."

"Thanks, but no thanks," he said. "And I plan to stay as far away from my father as possible."

"Really, Travis, I do not understand why you hate him so much."

"We didn't not see each other for months only to talk about my dad the first time we see each other again, right?"

I laughed. "You gotta talk about him some day, you know."

He sighed. "I know. But don't hold your breath. It's not going to happen this year."

I smiled at him. "So, what about you? Any girlfriends? Serious relationships?"

He looked at me for a while and then he said, "How can I hope to have a serious relationship? My fate is tied to yours, remember?"

I raised a brow at him.

He took a gulp of his beer. "I'm good at keeping my promises, *cherie*. Sure you know that by now. I won't break my promise to be your safety guy. So, only after you tie the knot with another guy could I even hope to start finding someone I will have heirs with."

Now I felt guilty. I was keeping Travis from finding his own happiness.

"Travis..." I started.

"Save it," he cut me off. "I don't mind. In fact, until you asked me to be your safety guy, I didn't think I would get married at all."

"Thanks! That makes me feel loads better," I said. I took a deep breath and gave him a serious look. "Even if it was just a favor, Travis...I hope you smile a lot at our wedding, okay?"

He was taken aback by what I said. And then, as if something inside him softened, he reached forward and touched his palm to my cheek. "I'm pretty sure it won't end like that, Brianne. I'm almost sure you will be married to a man who is head-over-heels in love with you…before you're thirty-one. A lot of guys would be lucky to have you."

I turned away from him and thought for a while. I sure hoped he was right. I was glad I was safe from my family's curse, but a bigger part of me wanted the real thing, too. I stared back at Travis's handsome face, then I raised my glass to him and said, "Toast to that!"

He smiled and touched the bottle of his beer to my glass.

Sarah sent me a text message.

*I'll go ahead. Looks like you're taken care of! Details! I want every little bit of it!*

I smiled. I could just as well have been the luckiest girl within a mile radius. Travis looked a lot hotter than the last time I saw him. He'd grown taller, and his muscles and abs were well-toned. His face matured, but only just a little bit. At first glance, he'd grown colder. But when he looked at me, I could still see the boy who used to pull my hair and make me cry a lot when we were eleven years old.

Looking at his abs, a memory threatened to come to my consciousness, but I immediately shut it out. I was not allowed to do that. I couldn't allow that memory to taint the way I saw Travis. He was dear to me. He always would be. And I couldn't allow myself to think of him as something else…even if that night was probably the most romantic night of my life.

"So, do you have plans tonight?" he asked.

I shook my head.

"Let's have dinner. We have a lot to catch up on."

"You honestly mean to say you don't check up on me without my knowledge, Travis Cross?" I teased.

He gave me one hard, guilty look. Then he turned away. "Still, hearing from you is a lot better."

My eyes widened. I was just joking. I couldn't actually believe that I was right. "I don't believe this!" I glared at him. "Travis James Cross!"

He raised a brow. "I told you I'm good at keeping promises. I had to make sure you're safe…all the time."

He stood up and paid our bill. He waved at the waiter and then he took my hand in his. I refused to budge.

"So, just exactly how do you do that? Do you station bodyguards around me? Undercover agents?"

He narrowed his eyes. "Don't be silly."

"Then how? How do you check up on me without asking me…without me knowing you are?"

He sighed. "Let's just say that the head of security at your university and your dorm are good friends of mine now. I just told them to keep a special eye on you, make sure you're safe, and to call me if something seems just a little bit off." He held his hand out and motioned for me to walk ahead of him.

I walked toward the locker rooms and then turned to him. "I'm going into the locker room. Do you have security cameras all over the place as well?"

He raised his face toward the sky. "Oh, God! You're still the same difficult…complicated girl!"

"And you're still the same paranoid guy! Why?"

"Because…" he trailed off.

"Because you're good at keeping your promises?"

He took a deep breath. "That. And some other things."

"Like what?" I continued glaring at him.

He sighed in defeat. "Because I don't want to lose what's left of what I love."

I was taken aback. I stared back at him. He reached out and touched my cheek with his palm. "You know you and Tom were the only ones I had for a very long time. I was alone for more than half of my life. That makes it easy to grow up ruthless…cold. You and Tom were my family. But Tom's gone, too. And now…it's just you." He shook his head and smiled ruefully. "Can you imagine what kind of person I'd be if I were to lose you, too?"

I bit my lip to keep myself from crying. I couldn't say anything. So instead, I reached forward and gave Travis a hug. He hugged me back.

"So don't go and die on me, too, okay?" he whispered.

I shook my head. I pulled away from him gently. "Couldn't you just pick up the phone and ask me if I was doing okay?"

"I can easily do that," he replied. "After all, if you pick up the phone, I can automatically say you're safe, right? It's the times I can't be there that I worry about."

"I'll be fine, Travis," I said. I smiled at him. "I'll fight to help you keep your promise to my brother."

"Good! So now that you know my one weakness, how much do I have to pay to keep you silent about it? For a moment there, I felt like such a weakling!"

I laughed. "No, Travis! You just became *human* to me!"

When I came out of the locker room wearing a pair of shorts and a shirt over my swimsuit, I found Travis waiting for me just outside.

"Where do you want to go?" he asked.

"Home," I replied. "At least to take a shower and to change into decent clothing."

"Why? What's wrong with what you're wearing?" he teased. "You're making a good first impression on the guys right now."

I raised a brow at him. "No, I prefer to repel boys by giving an impression that I'm a smart, boring, and prudent virgin," I said dryly.

He looked at me pointedly. "I beg to disagree with at least two of the words you just said there."

"The smart and prudent ones?"

"Actually the boring and...virgin ones." He stared at me with a serious expression on his face. "I have it on good authority that you are *not* either of those things."

My face turned beet red. I stood there open-mouthed. When he turned to me again, he wasn't smiling, but his eyes were somewhat dancing. I could tell he was teasing me.

"So, do you want to drive?" he finally asked.

I snatched the keys from him and walked toward the exit as fast as I could. Damn! That guy knew how to stir up unfamiliar and unwanted emotions from me. Was it not enough that he could already read me like a book?

When we came out to the parking lot, I discovered that Travis was driving a new, sleek red Ferrari. I gulped, and then I handed him his keys back.

"Why?"

"I'm not sure I could afford to pay you back if I dented your car."

"It's fully insured," he countered. "And please! Have I ever taken money from you?"

I shook my head. "You drive. Just drive especially slow."

He gave me an amused expression and then took the keys from me.

I didn't have to tell Travis where I lived; he knew exactly where it was. He parked in front of my building. I was about to open the door, but he was quick to come out and open the door for me.

"For a cold, ruthless guy, you're such a gentleman," I teased him. "I pity the girls who fancy seeing themselves marching down the aisle with you."

"I'm pretty sure they will be disappointed. I've already promised somebody I'll wait at the altar for her."

"If only to save her from humiliation," I said.

He nodded. "So do a better job at finding your Prince Charming. You deserve better than having a cold, heartless man as your groom."

"You're not heartless, Trav."

"Ahh...many would actually disagree with you."

"They don't know you better than I do," I said, gathering my bag. I headed toward the building. Then I turned to him. "Fifteen minutes."

He leaned on his car and nodded.

I took the stairs to my room. When I opened the door, Sarah was already there. Her face brightened when she saw me.

"Oh my God, oh my God!" she screamed. "Who *is* that hottie you were with? What happened?"

I put my bags on my bed and took off my shirt.

"That's Travis Cross."

"Who is he? Did he drive you back?" Sarah asked.

"Yes. I need to take a quick shower and change into something decent. He's waiting for me."

Sarah immediately ran to the window to peek. "Holy Crap! He drives a Ferrari?" She turned to me accusingly. "Who is this guy and how long have you been seeing each other?"

"We're not seeing each other," I replied, wrapping myself in a towel. "He's...I mean, *was*, my brother's best friend."

I took a shower as quickly as I could. When I came out, Sarah was waiting by the door to ambush me.

"Does he go to our school?"

I shook my head. "He goes to Yale."

"So, are you, like, hooking up?"

"Hell no!" I answered quickly. "We're...the dearest of friends. Like family. And you know what they say about not hooking up with your buddy's sister, mother, or exes?" I reminded myself briefly that Travis had done that *once* already, but I knew it almost didn't count,

110

since I asked him to do it as if he didn't have a choice. And we agreed to forget that night ever happened at all.

"He is...*very* handsome, Bry," Sarah said. "I'm so jealous!"

"Don't be," I said. "We're not dating, nor will we ever date!"

"So does that mean he's...free?"

"For you?" I asked. When she didn't answer, I said, "No. Don't even think about it. He may look like the epitome of grace...but Travis Cross is...a devil in angel's skin. He'll break your heart."

"Really? He looked like he'd go to hell and back for you," she protested.

"He will," I said. "But only because he promised my brother he would look after me for as long as he lives."

Her eyes widened. "Wow!" she breathed. "How lucky can you be?"

I raised my brow at her. "Not very lucky, apparently. Because I had to lose my brother in exchange for having a hot guy like that protecting me and looking out for me."

Sarah bit her lip. "I'm sorry, Bry. I was insensitive," she said.

I smiled. "It's okay. But that's the reality, really. Travis's fate and mine...we're involuntarily intertwined at the demise of my beloved big brother. We were the only family he knew. I lost my family the day I lost my brother. So, it seems like...it's just the two of us now."

Sarah sighed. "But still...wow!"

I laughed at her. "I can't believe you! But then again, that's not an uncommon reaction toward Travis Cross."

I took my bag and then headed toward the door.

"Will you be home tonight?"

"Of course, albeit quite late," I replied.

"Have fun!"

Before I left, I turned toward Sarah again. "And, Sarah, you know that safety guy I was telling you I have?"

She nodded.

"Well, that's Travis Cross," I said. Then I turned away, leaving Sarah dumbfounded with her mouth hanging open.

# Chapter Eleven

Travis took me a private house party that night. It was hosted in a six-bedroom house owned by one of the guys he knew from one of his classes. They served alcohol. We shouldn't be drinking, but I figured that Travis was with me, a few glasses of margarita wouldn't hurt. But I didn't realize I have very low alcohol tolerance, I think I almost passed out after my fourth glass. Travis decided it wouldn't be good for me to come back to my dorm looking witless, and he thought it was better for me to spend the night in his apartment. I think he was right.

When I woke up again, it was already afternoon. I slipped out of bed and went to Travis's luxurious bathroom to take a shower. I put on the same jeans I had worn the day before and the extra halter-top I could fit into my bag before I left home.

I was trying to zip the back of my blouse, but somehow the zipper was giving me trouble.

"Damn it!" I cursed. The thing about living with a girl roommate is that you always have somebody to zip you up when your clothes prove to be difficult.

Just then, from the mirror, I saw Travis approach behind me. He saw me struggling with my blouse. Without a word, he took the end of the zipper and gently but firmly pulled it up to zip it.

I smiled at him. "Thank you."

He looked into my eyes from the mirror. "Hungry?" he asked.

"Yep. And still a little dizzy," I replied.

He stared at me as if he was measuring me up, deciding if I was sober enough to handle myself inside the bathroom. When he was convinced I was going to be okay, he said, "I'll just take a quick shower and let's go to lunch."

Half an hour later, I was feeling a little better after I'd had a soda and some hot Chinese noodles.

"Heaven," I breathed.

"Do you remember half the things you did last night?" he asked.

My eyes widened and I felt nervous. I prepared myself for what he was about to say.

113

"You made out with one of the frat boys."

"Shit!" I gasped. "You're kidding!" Did I really do that? I couldn't remember anything.

He laughed. "Of course I am," he said. "Did you really think a guy can come less than a foot away from you when you're with me?"

"Thanks!" I muttered. "You're my potential-boyfriend repellant!"

"That I am," he said, taking a sip of his soda.

"Continue doing that, Travis, and I really will end up marrying you! I still have to be married by the time I'm thirty-one, remember?"

He laughed. "You're right! I should actually be pimping you. Fancy guys who go to Yale—what do you want? Blue eyes? Green eyes? Blond hair? Black hair?" he teased.

"Stop that, Travis!" I said. "Let me find my own boyfriend at my own time. Besides, I've learned a lot from Trip. I would only be worrying about my relationships four years before my deadline. College is just about having fun."

He nodded. "Good. Just warn me if anybody sticks around long enough."

"Why?"

"Because I don't want you to mess up your chance to marry the guy of your dreams."

"Why would you do that?"

"I won't. But...Brianne...do you even notice the kind of relationship we have?" he raised a brow at me, asking me a serious question.

"We're...friends. And we're really close. I don't hide anything from you. I can tell you everything. You're the only family I have. I love you, like I loved Tom."

"And you sure hug me a lot," he pointed out.

I shrugged. "I hugged Tom a lot, too."

"Except that I'm not Tom. I'm not your brother."

I stared up at him, wondering what his point really was. Was he telling me I should stop being affectionate toward him? *Oh God, this is embarrassing!*

I looked away from him. But he was quick to tilt my chin up so I could look into his eyes. "Don't get me wrong, princess. I like it when you hug me. And just in case you didn't notice, I hug you a lot, too. When Tom was alive, I saw how affectionate you were with each other and I always wished I had a brother or a sister that I could share that

114

bond with. I always envied him...because he had you." Pain and guilt crossed his face. "Now...I have you...I have what you had with him. I'm happy. But it...came with a great price."

I bit my lip, and pain stabbed through me again as I remembered Tom.

"I'm just saying we both like what we have. We know the tie that binds us together. Tom was more a brother to me than a friend. And the worst pain I went through when I lost him...there is only one other person in the world who felt that exact same pain. Only one person went through what I went through. That's you, Brianne. But this relationship...your future boyfriends might not always understand this...because they know I'm not your brother. We're not related by blood at all. So...if you fall in love and get serious with a guy, let me know."

"And what? You'll stay away?"

He smiled ruefully. "I think I've proven that no matter how bad the circumstances are, I still can't stay away from you. After all, how can I keep you safe if I am not around? But I won't make it difficult for you, Brianne. I know where I should stand. I'll draw my boundaries once the right guy for you comes along."

I smiled at him and leaned forward to kiss his cheek. "Thank you, Travis."

I don't know why...I wasn't entirely happy about what he said. A part of me felt surprisingly...sad.

After lunch, I told Travis that I needed to go shopping. Travis patiently walked around the mall with me while I bought some clothes. He sat on couches and when I came out after trying on some clothes, he told me whether they looked okay or not, or he shrugged or grunted, which, according to my interpretation, meant either 'okay' or 'no way.'

When I walked into a lingerie shop, he rolled his eyes. "You're not serious, are you?"

I laughed. "Then don't come inside. Stay here. I'll do this alone."

It'd been months since I'd last bought undergarments, and I took that moment to buy different colors and styles. Most of them were my usual, lacy-elegance and cottony-innocence types of undies and pajamas.

115

I realized I didn't have a sexy pair of underwear. The last time I bought one was when I was with Cindy. When I bought a nice pair of underwear…in lieu of my night with…

I shut the memory out and instead concentrated on the two styles of night garments. One was a green, lacy, long-sleeved nightgown with a deep neckline and ruffles down to the ankle, but with a slit all the way up to the thigh. The other one was a lavender spaghetti-strap nightdress with lace over the silk breast line that ended inches above the knees.

They both looked nice. I held them both in front of me, and I couldn't decide which one to buy. I was not even sure when I would wear them. But they just might come in handy, I thought. And besides, how often did I get a chance to shop for underwear?

Just then, Travis came from behind me and took the green nightgown from me and placed it back on the rack. I stared up at him. He stared at me for a moment. He gave me a wink and then he sat on the couch and scanned through a magazine. I knew I was blushing. I turned away from Travis and took the lavender nightie along with the rest of the items I want to buy to the counter.

*No! No! No!* I tried to calm myself. I don't think I gave the cashier the right amount of cash and I was sure the look she gave me was meant to say, *Stop smoking your socks, okay?*

I took a few short breaths to calm myself before I faced Travis again. He stood up from the couch and headed out of the shop without looking at me.

When Travis drove me back home, it was almost eight in the evening.

He parked in my driveway and rounded the car so he could open the door for me.

"So, this was a nice catch-up," I said.

He nodded.

I looked up at him. I could see the contours of his handsome face illuminated by the moonlight. I could tell why hundreds of girls went crazy for him. Even I, in some small weird moments, found myself dazzled by him.

"We should really do this more often, Trav," I said. "It's a shame that we don't see each other often when we're in the same city!"

He smiled. "I guess you're right. We should hang out more."

I nodded. Then I held out my pinky to him. He and Thomas hooked pinkies and bumped fists when Thomas was alive.

The look on his face when he saw my pinky was hard and pained. But he managed to raise his eyes to me and smiled. He hooked his pinky to mine and gently bumped his fist with mine, careful not to hurt me even just a little bit.

"Stay safe, until we see each other again," he said.

"Stay sane…until we see each other again." I smiled.

I turned toward my dorm again. Just then, my phone rang. An unregistered number appeared on the screen. I answered it.

"My new number," Travis said.

I turned around to face him. "When did you change your number?"

"The other night."

"There are only two possible reasons why you would do that."

He grinned. "The first one you thought of." *His father.*

"And the second reason?" *Girls.*

He chuckled. "Not even close. I don't loosely give my number around, sweetheart."

I laughed. "All right, I'll put it on my speed dial," I promised him. "I mean it, Travis. I hope we can see each other more. College life can be…scary. It's nice to know I have an ally close by."

He nodded. "Anyway, you have my number. Call me anytime you need me."

"Thanks, Travis." I smiled at him. "Drive safely…if not for your sake, then for mine."

"For you, I will." He gave me one last wink and then he drove off.

When I got to my room, I stared at Travis's number for a while. I saved it on my speed dial, and then I smiled to myself.

"You said you weren't sleeping with that guy!" Sarah interrupted my thoughts.

I sighed and put my paper bags on the bed.

"I'm not."

"Where did you sleep last night?" she asked accusingly.

"Just because I slept in his apartment does not mean I was actually sleeping with him."

"I don't understand how you could spend one whole weekend with a guy as hot as that and not feel anything!"

I smiled at her. "I love him," I said. "As I would my lost brother. He's a replacement brother. I probably am a replacement best friend. He's got a complicated life. He's alone most of the time. He feels that the people he loves usually leave him, and so he finds it difficult to love."

"And you're honestly telling me that…you never felt anything for him?"

I hesitated for a while. I saw Travis as a brother. Okay, there were times when he actually stole my breath and made me blush from head to toe. I guess Travis was right. Although in my heart I wanted to treat him like Tom, a huge part of my brain knew that he wasn't really my blood. But I couldn't entertain any of those thoughts. That was precisely the reason why he tried his best to make me forget that night…

I looked up at Sarah, hoping she couldn't see the hesitation or doubt in my face. "It's especially hard when you grew up with the guy. I was used to always having him there."

I guessed I would always have him around from then on. Remembering Travis and how at ease and emotionless he was when he zipped my blouse, and chose that lavender nightdress, what happened between us at prom seemed eons away. It was like he didn't remember it at all.

Well, of course! He was, after all, Travis Cross! That night was probably just another night for him. And I was just another girl. And if that were the case, I refused to be part of a statistic. The memory of that night was best left forgotten.

# Chapter Twelve

I went home for spring break. The house was the same as it was when I left it; my parents still weren't around. Cindy decided not to go back that break, so I was alone at home and totally bored.

It was only my first day back. I laid down on my bed and played with my phone. On impulse, I pressed the button to dial Travis's number.

"Everything well?" he asked after two rings.

"I'm so bored!" I complained.

"What do you want to do?"

"No idea! Are you busy?"

"Nope. Just playing pool," he replied. He didn't say anything for a while, and then he said, "Okay, I'll give you something to do tonight."

"What?"

"Pack your bags. I'm taking you to the lake house tomorrow."

Sheer excitement went through me. "You're not joking, are you?"

"Do I look like I have a sense of humor?"

I laughed. "No, you don't. But I know you do," I said. "That would be awesome! What do I have to bring?"

"Your clothes?" His tone almost added *"Duh!"* to his question.

"What about sleeping bags?"

"Forget it," he said. "I'll take you to the lake house, but we're not camping there. It's not safe enough for you."

"Okay. What time you will pick me up?"

"Six-thirty in the morning," he replied.

"Yay! I can't wait!"

I hastily packed my clothes and anything else I thought I would need for the next couple of days. I went to sleep early that night. When I woke up around three in the morning, I found Travis sleeping on my couch. I smiled to myself and went to the cabinet to get an extra blanket, and then placed it over him. Then I went back to sleep.

We both woke up early and were ready to go by six-thirty in the morning.

"How did you get in last night?" I asked.

119

"I still have your keys," he replied.

I laughed. I'd forgotten that I gave him an extra set of keys just in case he needed to crash for the night.

"Your parents are home?"

He shook his head. "I don't know. I don't care. I don't go to my parents' house anymore. I don't want to risk running into him."

"Then where do you stay?"

"I have my own properties here and there."

"Your own?"

"My grandparents from my mother's side left me with the means to live comfortably...even without my parents," he replied. "Do you wonder why my father hasn't been able to ground me or force me to bend to his will since I was fifteen?"

I shook my head. I did always wonder about that.

"Because I've been living like an adult since I was fifteen, Brianne," he said. "My grandparents' lawyers...they found a way around it. I got money that my father couldn't touch, and I gained access to it earlier than he thought I would. I could actually sue my father for everything that he did to me. But I let it pass...for the sake of my mother, and the family name."

Before we drove off, I asked him, "Can we make a stop?"

"Where?"

"Thomas," I replied.

He looked at me for a while and then he nodded. We drove to the town's cemetery. I brought flowers and lit a candle. I realized that the wax on the candleholder looked fresh. As if somebody had just lit one before me.

"Someone was here," I said.

Travis took a deep breath. "Me."

I looked at him. "When?"

"Last night," he replied curtly.

I smiled and reached out to squeeze his hand. "You still miss him."

He looked at me and then he looked back at Thomas's tombstone.

I imagined Travis standing at my brother's grave for hours, just talking to himself, as if Thomas was right there beside him. I felt pain shoot through my chest and there was a lump in my throat that kept me from speaking.

Travis put an arm around me. "I told him I was going to the lake house with you. I promised him I'd keep you safe."

I hugged Travis. I couldn't help thinking how different things would have been if Thomas had lived. The three of us would have had a blast at the lake house. And even if they didn't like it, I still would have found a way to convince them to take me camping with them.

"Thank you, Travis," I whispered. "We're not so different, you and I, you know."

"Why?"

I stared up at him. "When Thomas died, you were all I had, too."

He gave me a tight squeeze and kissed my forehead. "So don't make it difficult for me to keep you, okay?"

I nodded. "Promise I won't lose you, too?"

He nodded. "I promise." Then he leaned his cheek against my forehead.

***

Travis's family had a huge house overlooking the lake. Although they barely stayed there, they still kept at least three maids and one help boy. When we arrived, the whole house was lit. Everything has been prepared; the whole house was cleaned. It was like they'd spent hours preparing for the "master's" return.

"Welcome back, Master Travis." A familiar old lady greeted us by the door. I recognized Mrs. Beets, the Cross's oldest family maid. She smiled at me. "Welcome, Miss Brittany." She still called me by my full name.

I reached forward and gave her a hug, which startled her for a moment. I guess in the world of the rich, the maids don't often receive hugs. "It must have been years since I last saw you, Mrs. Beets!"

She smiled. "Yes, it had been a long time, Miss Brittany." Then she looked at Travis. "I prepared an extra room when you said you'd be bringing a friend with you. I didn't realize it was Miss Brittany. Would you rather she stayed in the same room as you?"

I laughed. "I can take the room, Mrs. Beets. Travis always takes the couch when I sleep in the same room as him. And I think he's here to unwind. I don't want him to feel uncomfortable."

Mrs. Beets nodded. "Certainly. Come, I'll show you to your room. Leave your bags. Jonathan will take them up."

The guest room I would be staying in was huge, and the bed was luxurious. It had a huge balcony that connected to Travis's room. It overlooked the lake, and I was pretty sure the view would be splendid at night.

"You find your accommodation suitable to your liking?" Travis asked behind me, appearing from the glass doors of his bedroom.

I nodded. "Yes, thank you," I replied. "When was the last time you came here?"

He sighed. "Too long ago. Thomas was still alive then. I promised to take him here after freshman year."

"And instead, you took me."

"Close enough."

"That's the reason why you changed your mind about coming here?"

He nodded. "I planned to come. And I wasn't gonna do it alone."

"So I'm doing you a favor instead."

He smiled. "Thank you for telling me you were bored."

That night, we drank at the gazebo by the lake. We told each other stories about our college life. Travis was taking up business administration at Yale. His father wanted him to go to Brown, where he went, but I think I was one of the reasons why Travis chose Yale. He had to be close to where I was to look after me. I was touched by his dedication.

The moon was shining brightly over us. I'd had a couple of shots of flavored vodka, and I was pretty sure the world was spinning gently.

"Want to go for a swim?" I asked him, suddenly feeling brazen.

He raised a brow. "Are you out of your mind?"

I shook my head. I stood up from my seat and took off my shirt and shorts. I was wearing a two-piece suit underneath. I gave out a squeal and jumped into the water. It only took a second for Travis to jump in after me.

I laughed.

"You're really out of your mind, you know!" he grunted.

"You said we were here to have fun!"

"Yes. But I also promised you'd be safe," he argued.

"It is safe!" I countered.

"Just the same, stay close!" he ordered.

The water was cold. The lake was illuminated by only the moonlight and the little light coming from the gazebo over us. It was

122

so different from the college life I'd just left. Here, it felt peaceful. And then when I saw Travis's careful, protective eyes watching me, I smiled. It felt very safe, too.

"You met any friends in college?" I asked him.

He shrugged. "Just acquaintances."

I raised a brow. "You keep to yourself, as usual?"

"I want to stay focused. People come and go in your life. I don't see the need to be emotionally involved with them."

"Oh, come on! I can't be the only person you love in your life," I said.

He raised a brow. "You're lucky you were Tom's little sister!"

"Yeah. Otherwise, I don't think you'd even care at all," I said.

He gave me a serious look, but he didn't say anything.

"Right?"

He sighed. "It doesn't matter what could have been. You're important to me now," he said in a cold, irritated voice.

I smiled at him. "Thank you."

We swam for another half an hour. Travis never kept his distance. He followed me wherever I swam as if he were afraid I would not emerge from the water every time I went under it.

When I realized it was getting colder, I swam toward the gazebo and started to climb the stairs. But the rails were slippery, and I just landed right back in the water. Travis was behind me and caught me before I landed in the water with a big splash.

He had a firm arm around my waist as he held me against him. I stared up at his handsome face illuminated by the moonlight. I struggled to breathe properly at that moment. Travis was heartbreakingly handsome. Too cute…even for me. But I couldn't see him that way. So I shook myself back to reality and laughed.

"Sorry," I said. I held on to the rails again. Travis didn't let me go until I pulled myself up the ladder again. This time, I held on to the rails more firmly. When I climbed each step, Travis climbed after me. I felt his body against my back, making sure I didn't fall off again. I climbed the ladder slowly, and he took each step after me until I reached the last one and walked toward to our table. The cold breeze blew, and I immediately shivered.

It was an unplanned swim, and we hadn't brought any towels.

Travis took his buttoned shirt from the chair and put it around me, keeping me a little warm.

"Come. Let's get you back to the house," he said calmly.

"Don't you feel cold?" I asked.

"I'm impervious!" he muttered under his breath, and I wasn't sure if he was talking to me or to himself.

He started to walk toward the house. It was too cold, and I was shivering, hugging Travis's shirt around me. I couldn't walk fast enough.

Travis raised a brow as he watched me walk toward him. Then he muttered something under his breath and without warning, he took a step toward me and scooped me up into his arms.

"Hey! I can walk perfectly fine!" I protested.

"Yes. But at that rate, we'll reach the house next weekend!" he argued.

Travis strode toward the house. I was thankful he carried me. It was still a good fifty yards' walk, and Travis's body heat kept me from shivering even more.

Once inside, he still didn't let me go. He climbed the stairs and only set me on my feet in front of my bedroom door.

"Thanks!" I said.

He looked at me for a while and then he said, "Goodnight. We'll go biking in the woods tomorrow."

I smiled. "I thought you didn't want me near those woods."

"I said I wouldn't allow you to camp. But biking should be fine."

"Thanks, Travis." I went inside my room. Only after I closed the door behind me did my breathing became even. I didn't know the effect that Travis sometimes had on me. I felt as affectionate to him as I did with Tom, but it was different, too. Travis could steal my breath, make my heart pound wildly inside my chest, and make me blush from the roots of my hair. But right then, that was not something I wanted to entertain.

I woke up early the next morning. I went to the kitchen where Mrs. Beets was preparing some ingredients to cook our breakfast.

"Good morning, Miss Brittany. I see you're an early riser."

"Not all the time," I said. "What are you cooking?"

"Ham and cheese omelets."

"Can I cook?"

She looked at me for a moment as if she was appalled by the idea.

"It's okay. I want to prepare something for Travis," I said and I went to the counter to look at the ingredients.

I walked to the fridge and gathered butter, onions, ham, mushrooms, and cheese.

Mrs. Beets helped me by slicing the ham and vegetables. Then I heated the pan and started cooking. In a few minutes, my omelet was perfect. Mrs. Beets cooked the bacon and toasted the bread.

"We'll have breakfast on the patio," I said to her.

"Certainly. I will ask Maria to set the table." She smiled at me. "It is very good that you are taking care of the young Master."

I laughed. "I think it is the other way around. He's taking care of me."

"But still, I have not seen anyone else actually reach out and make him feel...loved. Except for your brother, of course. That is why Master Travis was devastated when..." She trailed off, and then she looked at me carefully.

"I was, too," I said sadly. "Travis and I are not so different. I guess that is why we're looking out for each other."

Mrs. Beets nodded. "I think you're the only family he has left now. His parents barely really cared about their son. They kept him very well provided-for. But they forgot that he needed love more than he needed the money."

"My parents haven't been too mindful of me, either. Since my brother passed, it has been difficult for me to get their attention. Travis seems like the only family I have now, too."

"Then it is good that you still have each other," Mrs. Beets said. "Go wake him up. Breakfast is ready."

I knocked on Travis's door, but there was no answer. I opened the door gently and peeked in. I found him sleeping on his tummy, snoring quietly on the bed. He was shirtless and I could see the contours of the well-toned muscles in his back. He was wearing only a pair of black pajama pants.

I tiptoed and tapped his shoulders lightly.

Things happened so fast, and I didn't have time to think. I felt myself whirling, or flying, and then landing on the soft mattress. I closed my eyes and whimpered silently. I lay still on the bed, waiting for any sign of movement. I realized that I was on my back on the mattress. There was a heavy weight on top of me, pinning me down, holding me firmly by the shoulders.

Then I heard a deep intake of breath. I felt Travis lean his forehead against my chin.

"Dammit, Brianne! What were you doing in my bedroom?" he asked in a hoarse voice.

He released my shoulders, but I remained pinned between his body and his mattress. I opened my eyes. I realized that I was shocked and scared. "I…was going to wake you up to tell you that breakfast was ready. I cooked omelets for…you." I stared back at his handsome, guarded face, completely scared that he might strangle me.

He narrowed his eyes as he stared back at me. "*You* cooked for me?" he asked as if he found it so hard to believe.

I nodded. Travis's expression immediately softened.

"Damn! I'm sorry!" he said. And he leaned forward to put his arms around me. He rolled from the bed, taking me with him so that I was lying on top of him instead. He hugged me to him. "I'm sorry. I thought…" He fell silent for a moment. "I guess…I've lived alone too long. I wasn't expecting anybody to be at my bedside when I woke up. I'm sorry. I'm usually not a violent person."

I didn't say anything. We lay there for a while. I tried to recover from my shock while Travis held me in his arms, comforted me and caressed my head.

"I'm sorry," he repeated quietly. "I hope you can forgive me."

I knew Travis would never hurt me. It was his thing to be defensive all the time. He wasn't expecting anyone else to be in his room.

"I forgive you," I whispered. Then I looked up at him. "Do you have death threats that make you so defensive, even in your sleep?"

He took a deep breath. "Force of habit, I guess," he replied. "My father had his bodyguards kidnap me in the middle of my sleep many times in the past. I…learned to be alert even when I had my eyes closed."

"Why…would your father do that?"

"Because I didn't bend to his will. Because I disappeared on him all the time. Because I refused to come home when he was in town. He had to…employ harsh means to get his son to see him. I had to learn how to defend myself against his bodyguards."

"Why do you have such a broken relationship with your father?"

"Didn't I tell you not to hold your breath for that story? I'm not going to talk about it. Not for a very long time."

"But he would know you're here. Won't he come look for you here?"

126

"He won't come here. Unless he wants to be arrested for trespassing," Travis replied.

I propped up on my elbow so I could stare back at him. One of his arms was still secured around my waist.

"But isn't this your family's estate?"

Travis reached forward to push a lock of hair away from my face. "This is *my* estate. My grandparents left it to me when they died. My father is not allowed to come here."

"Why?"

"It's early morning, princess. I don't want to ruin my day by talking about him," he said, raising a brow at me.

I don't know how it was possible, but Travis looked even more endearing in the mornings. The warmth in his face, the sleepy eyes, and the disheveled bed hair looked even sexier on him.

I gave myself a mental shake. I pulled away from him. "Breakfast is ready," I said. I stood up from the bed and held my hand out to him.

He smiled, took my hand, and allowed me to pull him out of bed.

"I guess this will be the last time I will sneak up on you in your sleep," I said.

"Maybe I should learn to look first before I attack," he said apologetically. He reached up to cup my face in his palms. "I'm really sorry, Brianne. You know I would never hurt you."

I smiled up at him. "I know, Travis. I forgive you."

He smiled, and then gently he pulled my face to his and kissed my forehead.

I looked up at him. "Come, breakfast's getting cold and you promised you'd take me biking today."

We went to the woods on mountain bikes. I rode in front of Travis. He didn't like the idea that I was not in his line of sight as we rode. The path led to a meadow overlooking the lake, and we stopped for a while to admire the view.

"It feels so different here," I said. "Like we're far away from the rest of the world."

"I used to come here a lot...when I was younger. Here it didn't make a difference whether my parents came home or not. My father almost never set foot on this property. It wasn't his. It belonged to my grandparents."

"Did you ever come here with Tom?"

He shook his head. "We planned to. But we never got the chance."

I took a deep breath. "Would you rather you were with him today?" I asked absent-mindedly, looking at the beautiful view in front of us.

Travis didn't answer immediately. Then he said, "No. I wouldn't want *you* not to be here, either."

I stared back at him and smiled. "When we were kids, we fought a lot," I said. "I hated you. You teased me a lot. And I couldn't understand how Tom could be best friends with you."

"Who would have thought we'd grow this close, right?"

"Who would have known that Travis Cross would learn to love me like a sister?" I giggled.

"Who would have known I would learn to love at all?" he countered in a sober voice.

I felt for Travis. He could be one of the smartest, one of the cutest guys I had known, and also one of the richest...but somehow, something inside him was torn and broken. It was like if he hadn't been so smart and so in control of his emotions, he would have been all over the place, spreading chaos.

"Maybe you should try to fall in love," I blurted out. "Maybe you'd see the world differently if...you had a woman who made your world spin." I smiled at him teasingly.

He raised a brow at me, as if what I'd told him just plain insulted him.

"And then what? There are only two possible endings to that. Either I make her fall desperately in love with me, and then I shred her soul to pieces and leave her heartbroken, or *I* love her desperately, I would give her everything and give everything up for her and she...leaves me. And my already-damned soul is shred to pieces." He shook his head. "I don't want to bestow such a tragedy on another human being."

I almost got mad at Travis. How could he be this negative? How could he be so bitter about love?

I bit my lip to keep myself from saying what was on my mind. Instead, I stared at the view ahead of me and decided just to tune it out. There were times that I couldn't understand the twisted and sad way Travis saw life...and love. When he said those words, I couldn't help wondering if he was a hopeless case. He was so...cold.

I didn't speak to Travis until we were close to town. I rode the bike as fast as I could, as if I were riding alone. He knew I was pissed off, but he didn't say anything.

Just then, I saw him overtake me, and he stopped in front of me, forcing me to brake and glare at him. He raised a brow.

"Stop, okay?" he said. He took a deep breath. "I'm sorry."

"What are you sorry for? You didn't do anything wrong to me!"

"I know I pissed you off."

"It's my problem for caring, Travis!" I snapped, getting off my bike. He got off his bike, too, and stood in front of me.

"I can't help how I feel right now!" he said.

"I can't help being pissed off, either!"

"What actually made you mad? You know me better than anybody else!" he said, trying his best not to lose his temper.

"*That!* Because I know you're not the vile, ruthless person you were trying to be! Otherwise, I would not have asked you to be my safety guy!" Anger and other unidentified emotions swept through me. Before I knew it, I was losing my temper at him. I wanted desperately for him to see the person I saw whenever I looked at him. I wanted him to realize what a beautiful person he was.

I continued glaring at him. "And you know what? That person who you would shred to pieces could be me, Travis! Did you think about that? In a few years, if fate compels me to call on your promise to marry me, I would have to live with you, and I could be that person you tear apart! It's like you're telling me I was all wrong about you! That you're hopeless! That no matter what, you just don't give a damn! That you didn't care! That…I gave myself to a guy who didn't care! And would never ever care! That…"

Travis pulled me into his arms, preventing me from finishing that sentence. "Stop!" he said firmly, but his voice was pleading. "Don't say that!"

I realized that I was crying. In my anger, I couldn't help but bring up the night we spent together…the night that I was supposed to forget. Travis held me by the nape of my neck, keeping my face pressed against his chest. One arm circled my waist into a tight hug.

"You're not supposed to remember that," he whispered to me gently.

"Maybe my memory is a lot better than yours," I sobbed against his chest. Now I'd really opened a whole can of emotions I didn't even know I had. Travis and I never spoke about that night, nor the reasons why he stayed away from me after that. "That night was not just a part of a statistic to me. Unfortunately, the first guy I gave myself to…I was just one of many girls to him!" I muttered angrily.

Travis fell silent for a while and then he inhaled through my hair and tightened his arms around me. "Just because he is not supposed to care doesn't mean he really doesn't care. Just because he's not supposed to remember, doesn't mean he could forget," he whispered.

"Which one are you?" I asked.

He took another deep breath before answering, "The latter. That night…was the only night that mattered to me," he said. "So, please don't say that I didn't care. Because I did. Even though I was not supposed to."

I pulled away to look into his eyes. He stared at me for a while. I could see all sorts of emotions cross his face as if he was having a hard time fighting his feelings, too. Then slowly, he leaned forward. I thought he was going to kiss me. I closed my eyes. I realized I wanted him to.

But then I heard his deep intake of breath. I opened my eyes. He was able to stop himself from doing what I thought he was going to do. "I cannot lose you, Brianne. Not in any way," he said. "And for that, I must not remember what happened that night."

I bit my lip as I took a deep breath. "Why?"

He heaved a sigh. "Because…because I would go after you if I kept remembering! I would pursue you. I would seduce you. It took me a while to get you out of my system after that night." He shook his head. "I could only be one guy or the other. And I chose the one that has less risk of breaking you…of losing you."

I blinked back at him. "Travis…what are you saying?"

"I'm saying I'm like two people trapped in one body. One is the guy who vowed to protect you from all sorts of pain for as long as he lived. The other…wants you and craves you in ways you do not know of." He took a deep breath and he looked at me with shame in his eyes. "I'm a player, Brianne! I'm one of those guys I need to protect you from! Do you understand my pain?"

I closed my eyes for a moment, and then I nodded. He smiled at me ruefully. "And I know you think better of me. You have faith in me. Let's just hope that someday, I can be worthy of that faith." And he leaned forward and kissed my forehead. He lingered there for a moment.

I didn't know what to feel. Happy? Because somehow, Travis did not seem so immune to me, the way that I sometimes was not immune to him. Scared? Because this meant there would always be this sexual tension between us that threatened to tear us apart forever. Confused? Because I didn't know which of the two feelings I would rather feel.

"I'm sorry, Travis," I said to him. "I complicated us. Because I asked you to...because I was selfish! I didn't even know what it would do to you...to us! I am so sorry!"

Travis hugged me again. "I'm not an angel, Brianne," he said. "You cannot blame yourself for this entirely. Have you forgotten? Nobody could force me to do something I didn't want to do. How sure are you that I didn't want you before you asked me to...be your first? How sure are you that I only saw you as Thomas's silly little sister? As my own sister?" He heaved a sigh again.

I raised my chin to him. "Do you?"

He looked at me with that pained expression again. And in a frustrated voice, he said, "Do you think I would have taken you that night if I did? Nothing about that night felt *wrong*! But it's not going to change anything. I still promised to protect you...from whatever pain, whatever harm. I promised I wouldn't hurt you. I'm not going to risk your feelings...your safety. And I wouldn't betray Tom that way. I know he would never agree. When we were growing up, he already warned me. When I told him once that I thought you were beautiful, he told me that I could have all the girls in the world...except for you. I knew I couldn't have you from the start.

"When you asked me to take you, it was like...giving the devil a chance to step into heaven. I tried so hard to forget who you were that night. And I tried harder to forget what happened afterward. That night haunted me day and night. It wasn't enough. There's a beast inside of me, whose need for you cannot be satiated by just one night." He took a deep breath. "But I'm not going to lose control, Brianne. Not with you. You deserve better. You deserve a guy who can give you his heart and soul...completely. Whose personality is just as positive and sunny as yours. A guy who won't suck the life and sunshine out of you and leave you in the cold."

I felt for Travis when he said that. He was honest enough to tell me that he was not immune to me...but he could not offer me what I deserved. I couldn't lose Travis in any way, either. And even though there was this tension between us, I knew we had to fight it. All we had was each other.

I smiled at him. "Thank you," I whispered. "For being honest," I said. "And for keeping your control. For shielding me from the beast inside you. That must take a lot of work."

He chuckled humorlessly. "Tons!" he said. Then he looked at me seriously. He leaned his head toward mine. He took a deep breath. "Don't make it any harder for me, okay?"

I giggled. "I promise not to seduce you."

"Sometimes that's a problem," he said. "For a gorgeous girl like you, you achieve seduction without trying!" He took a deep breath. "But it's my problem to deal with. Not yours. And it helps when we're together more. Sometimes, becoming numb needs a lot of practice."

"So I guess, this is one of the conversations we had that we must forget…must never speak about ever again."

He nodded. "Put it in your memory vault. Lock it up and throw away the key."

I pulled away from him. "Promise." I held my pinky out for him.

He smiled and then he hooked his pinky with mine. "I mean it, Brianne. I'm still your safety guy…and from me, you will always be safe."

# Chapter Thirteen

Two years later, my parents' divorce was finalized. My mother would take permanent residency in Manhattan; my father would station himself in Boston. No battle for custody—I was already of age. My parents decided to give the house to me instead of selling it and dividing the profits between them.

I was angry. My parents had decided to abandon the house...the happy house where Thomas and I had grown up! Where they last saw Tom! I refused to let the memories go. They could divide all their properties except this house...I could not believe they were walking away from it and all the memories it had.

I was in my room, and as always, I decided to channel my emotions onto the canvas. I didn't know what I was painting. But it was a mixture of dark blues, blacks, violets, swirling around in angry patterns. I was on the brink of crying. That day marked the end, not just of a chapter of my life, but of a whole story.

I swirled the violet paint on the canvass angrily, not knowing what I was really painting, but somehow expressing how I really felt. Tears rolled down my cheeks, but I refused to let a whimper escape from me.

Just then, I felt strong arms encircle me, pulling me away from the canvas.

"Stop it," Travis whispered behind me. He took the paintbrush from my hand.

I stared at his handsome face, and then I completely broke down.

Travis bent and scooped me off my feet and carried me to my bed. I couldn't stop crying. I knew my parents' marriage had crumbled a long time before. But the finality of it brought up so many sad and angry emotions that I almost couldn't face.

I felt Travis's lips on my head. "Sssshhh..." he said in a soothing voice. "I'm still here."

The following years, my life was a series of ups and downs. People came and went for the next five years. My mom trained me to manage her art galleries.

I dated guys and had two relationships. One didn't end well.

Eric.

He was wonderful, smart, and funny. We jived a lot, and it seemed like I was talking to my girl best friend every time I was with him. He was very comfortable. In fact, *too* comfortable. We'd been seeing each other for three years, and I decided to take it to the next level. I thought he would do it, but three years without initiating intimacy was just plain weird.

I planned a night for us in my apartment. I lit candles, set the mood. When he opened the door and I was wearing a silk nightgown in front of him, he broke down to tears.

*Not good,* I said to myself, and I went to him to ask him what was wrong.

"I've not been honest with you," he said. "I was…probably just using you…to deny what I really wanted. What I really am!"

"What are you talking about, Eric?"

"Brianne, I'm gay."

I almost fainted. No wonder we'd been seeing each other for so long and he'd been dodging intimacy as much as I had…maybe even more!

So I wasted three years there when I was actually a ticking time bomb. I had to be married by the time I was thirty-one. Well, I would be, anyway…to Travis Cross, if I didn't find my own guy.

As for Travis, he'd built his own company that was set to compete with his father's. It seemed like a game of chess between the two of them. One man trying to teach the other a lesson, the other trying to show the other that he was much smarter.

Travis stayed mostly in Manhattan, but he also traveled a lot. But no matter how busy he was, he never failed to see me on my birthday. He would show up for a day, give me an extravagant present, like a piece of diamond jewelry, and then we'd spend the whole night talking and catching up, and it always felt the same. Like we were together all year long.

Eric didn't mind Travis. In fact, he liked it when Travis dropped by and joined us for dinner. Now, I think Eric might have been interested in Travis more than he was ever interested in me.

"But I do love you, Brianne!" Eric said. "Just not in an intimate way. And I promise I'll always be here for you. I'll always be your friend."

So instead of making love, Eric and I spent that night in bed. I was locked in his embrace, my head on his shoulder, and he told me the secrets he couldn't tell anybody else.

Now, Eric and I are still very good friends. He dates once in a while, trying to find his own Mr. Right.

I then dated a guy named Christian. He was a tall, dark blond guy with startling green eyes. He was very cute and very ambitious. He was a lawyer with dreams of becoming a partner in his law firm one day.

I wasn't painting much. Chris made me see that money came faster when you managed a business. It takes a while to sell a painting for a good price, but buying and selling other people's paintings brings home the money faster. And I needed the money. I had a wedding I needed to save up for.

With Chris, I didn't have a problem with intimacy. He was the best friend of my old friend Cindy's brother. We met at a party Cindy threw. He asked for my number, and he asked me out the next day.

We'd been dating for two and a half years. The future seemed very bright for me. I was beginning to think I might not need Travis Cross to enter into a ceremony he completely didn't believe in.

When I started dating Chris, I had been successfully managing one of my mother's galleries. I learned the commercial side of the business. Instead of painting my own masterpieces, I learned the logistics and the financial side of managing a gallery. I did miss painting, but I needed time for this. And time seemed to be quite a luxury for me at the moment, especially with a guy like Chris, who seemed to be living in the fast lane.

The relationship was comfortable, cozy, and smooth sailing. Christian was a stand-up guy with a lot of principles in life. He was ambitious, and he guided me in managing one of my mom's galleries. Sure, he was uptight most of the time, but he taught me to be tougher and to go after success. I might not succeed in painting my own masterpieces, but at least I had galleries to manage in the future.

The only time I felt I was being artistic at all was when I joined Sarah's dance group. They had dance shows once in a while, and I always managed to get a part in one of their performances. I begged Chris to watch me, but he always had a case to work on whenever there was a show. I could tell he was not really thrilled by my dancing.

I told him that he just must think that it was a form of exercise for me to keep my muscles toned and my heart healthy.

Travis caught up with me every once in a while. Whenever he was in town, we'd have dinner together. He was also been quite a busy man. Whenever I saw him, I couldn't help throwing myself in his arms. Being with him felt like I was still the old me. Careless and carefree.

We never talked about Chris or Travis's own women. When we were together, it was like there was only the two of us in the world. In two years, I only got to see Travis about one or two days a month. So whenever we saw each other, I felt like I was always running out of time and I had to make the most of it. I told him things I couldn't tell Chris or Sarah. My dreams, my fears…what was left of the old me.

"What are you doing with a guy who changes you so much?" he asked me once. We were on the balcony of his hotel suite. I was sitting beside him, and he had an arm around my waist with my head resting on his shoulder.

I sighed. "I have to make something of myself, too, Travis. I have to survive on my own. I'm not trust-funded like you. The minute I graduated college, I was on my own in this world. I can't afford to paint and dance all the time and expect that money will just come pouring in on a daily basis."

"But are you happy?" he asked.

I stared up at him. He was studying my face, reading all the hidden emotions behind the façade I'd been putting up for years. "If I didn't have a roof over my head and I starved to death, I would certainly be sad, Travis," I said.

He smirked. "You're crazy if you think I would allow you to get that far!" he said under his breath.

I laughed. "I know you won't," I said and rested my head on his shoulder again. "But, Travis, I have to survive on my own, you know."

I felt him shake his head. "No, you don't," he said. "Your fate is tied to mine, remember? So that means you *never* have to be alone for as long as you live."

"For as long as *you* live," I corrected him.

"No," he said. "I'll find a way to take care of you even in the afterlife." He chuckled.

I felt a heavy lump in my throat. Suddenly, hearing him say that broke my heart. I couldn't…and I mean *couldn't*…imagine living my life without Travis in it. No. Just thinking about Travis dying was just too painful for me.

I didn't know it, but I was crying silently. Suddenly, Travis pulled away from me and tilted my chin up so he could look at my face.

"Why are you crying?" he asked.

I shook my head. I wiped the tears from my cheeks. I pulled away from him and looked at the view of the city in front of us.

"Brianne," he insisted. "What did I say wrong?"

I stared at him. How could Travis say it like that, as if he didn't think he meant a lot to me?

"That I would lose you one day," I murmured.

His expression softened. He reached out and pulled me into his arms again. I felt him kiss the top of my head. "I'm sorry," he said. I wrapped my arms around his waist and hugged him to me while I continued crying on his chest. "But there are things beyond our control, *cherie*. I'm just saying that even if I'm gone, I'll make sure you live a comfortable life."

"I don't need a comfortable life, Travis," I said. "I need you to be in it...*always*. And promise me you will be!"

"Ssshhh..." He took a deep breath. "I promise, princess. You won't lose me."

"I love you, Travis," I whispered and I felt him kiss the top of my head.

He took a deep breath. "I love you, too, Brianne. Promise me I won't lose you, too."

I smiled. "I promise."

Chris hadn't met Travis yet. Chris knew that my parents and I weren't close. He knew that I had an old friend whom I constantly kept in touch with, the only other person who reminded me of the happy family I used to have. And somehow, Chris never seemed interested with my "oldest friend." I tried to tell him about Travis, but he seemed so uninterested and he usually changed the topic. So I just stopped trying over the years. Whenever I disappeared for a day, I would tell him that I was catching up with an old friend, and he'd tell me to go ahead and knock myself out, just don't do anything silly.

It's good that he trusted me, not that I intended to do anything silly with Travis. Travis and I were no longer teenagers with raging hormones who couldn't get their emotions under control.

"Why don't you ask your old friends to come with you?" Chris said whenever I asked him to come to my family reunions with me.

Well, Travis was always invited to our reunions anyway. But I wanted Chris to meet him and my family. But somehow, he was always busy impressing his bosses and his clients. I got how ambitious he was. I just wished that he would pause for a moment to come to my dances or my family reunions.

He couldn't really blame me for being disappointed. The most important male figure in my life had set the bar really high for my future boyfriends. Travis probably earned about a hundred times more than Chris, and he still had time to come to my family reunions.

My first Christmas with Chris was a disappointment. I was so looking forward to it, but, unfortunately, he told me that he had to go to work. The CEO of one of the companies they were working on to hire their legal services held a major Christmas Eve party and his boss nominated him to attend for their firm. He was eager to impress and ditched our holiday plans of renting a cabin in the woods.

Since Chris waited until the day before Christmas to tell me that he's bailing on me, it was too late to fly out to where either of my parents were to spend Christmas Eve with them. So when Sarah told me she was having a 'singles Christmas Eve' party at her place, I decided to go. I could tell she truly felt sorry for me. But I tried to smile as much as I could, and pretended I was having the time of my life.

"Give me a real smile." Sarah teased as she handed me a cocktail.

"I'm okay," I said to her, taking a sip of my drink.

"No, you're not," she said. "You're disappointed. I know you'd rather be spending this evening cuddling up with a guy who would envelop you in warmth… and comfort and love."

I rolled my eyes. "Shut up, Sarah." But I know she was right. Christmas Eve is a pretty good time of the year to spend with someone you love.

My phone rang.

"*Cherie*," Travis greeted me cheerfully on the other line and for the first time since Chris told me he was cancelling our holiday plans, I smiled for real.

"Hey you!" I greeted back. "So, how does a business mogul like Travis Cross spend Christmas Eve? Are you at some VIP Christmas party in Manhattan or some VIP club that only allows entry to the rich and the famous?"

It took a while for him to answer. Then he said, "Actually, I'm standing in a snowy street in front of a line of apartments that has a coffee shop on the corner and an old bookshop that only sells travel books."

For a moment, I couldn't understand what he was saying. And then it occurred to me that Sarah's apartment has a coffee shop in the corner street and a travel bookshop.

"In Connecticut?" I asked.

"George Street, to be exact," he replied.

I couldn't believe what he said. I didn't know what to say, but I felt like tons of frustration and sadness were lifted off my chest. I actually ended up laughing. Sarah looked at me like I was out of mind.

"Okay. I don't know why you find that amusing, but I would appreciate it if could come out of your friend's apartment."

When I finally stopped giggling, I hung up the phone and stared at Sarah.

"What is going on with you?"

I gave her a big smile and then I hugged her. "Merry Christmas, Sarah. Thanks for inviting me and trying to cheer me up."

"Where are you going? Is Chris outside? Did he cancel his plans?"

I shook my head. "Not Chris. Travis."

She gave me a teasing look.

"Stop that. Travis is family. Anyway, catch you later."

When I came out of Sarah's apartment, I found Travis standing across the street. I didn't hesitate. I ran to his arms and he caught me. When I pulled away, he looked at me and smiled.

"How did you know where I was?"

"I was in town. I got an invite to this party. I got bored after thirty minutes and excused myself. I went to your place, but nobody seemed to be home so I tried Sarah's."

"I could be at Chris's."

"You could be. Except that I think I saw him at this lame party without you. I did the math."

"You haven't met Chris. How could you know how he looked like?" I asked.

He just raised a brow at me but didn't answer.

139

I rolled my eyes. Immediately, I knew he had him checked out when he found out I was dating him seriously.

He smiled at me apologetically. "Sorry, *cherie*. I can't help it."

"I'm sure," I said dryly.

"You asked me how a busy businessman like me spends Christmas Eve. Well, there you go. Attending a prestigious VIP event, talking and laughing with a lot of people I don't really know or care about. Talking about politics or Wallstreet. Listening to a bunch of phony people talk about their latest shiny cars or luxurious yachts. You could say I should be a hero for lasting thirty minutes." He grinned. Then he pulled away from me and intertwined our fingers. "Now, let me show you how I really want to spend my Christmas Eve."

We walked for a couple of blocks until we reached the park. The trees were covered in Christmas lights and we can hear faint sounds of music from afar. There was a skating rink in the center.

"Ice skating?" I asked him, laughing.

"It's been a while." He grinned at me boyishly. "You up for it?"

I smiled at him widely. "You bet."

We spent an hour skating. It had been months since I last saw him and it was a good time to catch up with each other. We teased each other, chased each other around the park in skates. For a while, it felt like we were kids again and we didn't have a worry in the world. And when the snow started falling, I laughed like I did that one time when I was eleven, when Tom, Travis, and I had a snow fight in our front yard.

I stayed in Travis's suite that night. He gave me a pair of earrings with diamonds and colored precious stones. We stayed up almost all night talking. And just when I thought my day would suck, in the end, I got to spend Christmas Eve cuddled up with a guy who enveloped me with comfort and love.

The following Christmas, Chris came through. We did rent a cabin in the woods. By twelve midnight, I sent Travis a text message that says, *"Merry Christmas, Travis. I hope you're having a great time wherever you are. Miss yah. Lots of love."*

After a minute he replied, *"Merry Christmas, cherie. I'm having a nice time, but nothing beats last year's Christmas. Miss you too. I'll see you soon."*

After our little trip to the cabin, Chris finally agreed to come with me in our family reunions. He wasn't available the last time we had one and this year, he said he will definitely make an appearance. My Aunt Victoria would be having an anniversary celebration. Chris filed his leave in advance and made sure he was all mine that day.

The day before we were set out to take a road trip to my aunt's place, I found Chris in my apartment after I came home from the studio.

"Hey," I greeted him, giving him a peck on the lips. "Not busy with a case today?"

He shook his head. "Finished all my work yesterday. Remember, we have your family reunion tomorrow?"

"What did your boss say about you being on leave for a day?"

He shrugged. "He's fine with it. I work overtime all the time. I was hoping to make partner in three years."

I smiled at him. "And I'm sure you will. You're great!" And I knew that with all the hard work he put in, it wouldn't be long before he achieved his goal. Chris was two years older than me. Being a partner at his age would be a great achievement. I knew it would make him really happy.

I noticed a package sitting on top of my table. "What is this?"

"Oh, delivery came for you," Chris replied.

I looked at the box.

"Who is Travis Cross?" Chris asked.

My face brightened at the mention of his name. I excitedly opened the box. Inside it, there were two smaller boxes. There were cards on top of them.

I read one.

*Please send Aunt Victoria and Uncle Boons my apologies. I won't be able to make it to their wedding anniversary. But please send them my love with this present.*

I opened the box for Aunt Victoria. I was surprised to see a matching pair of *his and hers* gold and diamond bracelets. One for her and another for Uncle Boons. "Wow!" I breathed. The gift looked expensive.

"Cousin?" Chris asked as he read Travis's note for my aunt and uncle. He looked at the box with the bracelets. "Rich cousin?"

I shook my head. "No," I said. "A dear friend. Family friend."

I picked up the note on top of the other box.

*Brianne, I saw this and thought of you. I may not be with you all the time, but know that you're always in my thoughts.*

141

*Love, Travis*

I opened the box and found a gleaming diamond tennis bracelet inside it. My breath caught in my throat. The bracelet was absolutely beautiful.

"Please tell me this family friend of yours is as old as your Aunt Victoria!" Christian muttered under his breath after reading Travis's note and seeing the bracelet he gave me.

I giggled. "Don't be silly!" I said to him.

I took the bracelet from the box and put it on. The fit was perfect—no need to be resized, and it looked amazing on my wrist.

When I looked up at Christian, he was reading the guarantee card that came with the bracelet, certifying the clarity and carats of my diamond bracelet.

"How old is this guy?" Christian asked again.

I didn't figure Christian to be a jealous guy, but I answered him wearily. "Does he have to be old?"

"To afford to give jewelry as expensive as this?"

I sighed and put the jewelry back in the box. "He's twenty-nine."

"Twenty-nine!?" Christian looked back at me disbelievingly. "How...do you know this guy?"

"We grew up together, Chris. Remember the 'old friend' that I always catch up with?"

"Your old friend is a *guy*?"

*Oh, shit!*

"He was my brother's best friend," I replied. "He's family to me. In fact, when my parents decided they didn't want to be a family anymore after my brother died, Travis was the only family I had left."

"But his message in the card is too mushy, too cheesy to be just friends!" Chris muttered.

I laughed. "You can't seriously be jealous, can you?"

He sighed and then he pulled me into his arms. "I guess I am," he said. "I love you. And I want to stick around for a very long time. I want to be the only guy in your thoughts!"

I smiled at him. "And you are," I said. "Travis is a dear, dear friend. He sort of took my brother's place in my life when Tom died."

Chris smiled. "Okay. But next time you go out with this guy, I want to go with you."

I smiled widely. "Sure. I've been wanting to introduce you to him for years," I said. "He's like a brother to me, Chris. It would mean a lot to me if you would be on good terms."

Chris leaned forward and gave me a passionate kiss on the lips.

I was in Chris's arms that night. His touch comforted me, made me feel warm. *I know this man,* I thought. I longed for the comfort of his arms…to know that he would be there in my future. He might not always hit the spot, but it was the cuddling after that I looked forward to most of the time. After all, that's what intimacy is all about.

The next day, I introduced Chris to all my relatives. I sincerely hoped this would not be the last time Chris would come with me.

"Tell Travis Cross I won't be able to forgive him!" my aunt Victoria said. "His presence is much more wanted than his present."

I laughed. "But that is a lovely present, Aunt Vicki!" I argued.

She beamed. "Oh, it is! Look at the cut of these diamonds! Leave it to Travis Cross to gift in style!"

"Comes with the money!" I giggled. "Travis has tons!"

"I cannot believe this is your aunt's twenty-fifth anniversary. She seems…so young," Chris said after my aunt left us alone.

I laughed. "We have a tradition in the family," I told Chris. "All women should marry before they turn thirty-one, or earlier. But definitely not after."

"And what happens if you don't get married by that time?"

"We turn into frogs," I replied.

"What?" He looked at me seriously.

I forgot that Chris almost didn't have a sense of humor. He was a person who was serious about life, and nothing about that was a laughing matter.

"Just kidding. I think we're…'cursed' and are a disgrace to the family. I don't know if it's true. But somehow, some of my cousins and aunts have gotten bad luck in love and relationships after they disregarded the tradition."

Chris fell silent for a moment.

"Something wrong?" I asked.

He shook his head. Then he looked at me and gave me a smack on the lips.

My mother made a late appearance.

"I'm sorry I'm late, sweetheart." She kissed me on the cheek. "Where's Travis? Did you come together?"

143

I shook my head. And then I took Chris's arm. "I came with Chris, Mom," I said. "Remember, I told you about him."

"Oh, yes. I'm sorry." She shook Christian's hand. "I forgot you had a boyfriend now. I guess it was just force of habit for me. I was so used to you and Travis being together all the time, and you always come to these gatherings with each other. Where is he?"

I shook my head. "If I had to guess, I'd say he was somewhere in Europe, buying out one of his dad's companies. Or in a bedroom with a woman. You know him. Business and women are all he cares about."

My mother narrowed her eyes. "I beg to disagree," she said. "I think there's nothing he cares about in this world more than you. He almost raised you when your father and I weren't there for you, remember?"

"I'm a big girl now, Mom," I said to her. "But yeah, Travis did great doing *your* job!" I knew there were pain and anger in my voice. But I couldn't help it.

My mother bit her lip, but instead of saying something back, she just nodded and then stepped back and joined my other aunts.

"That was...rude," Chris said behind me.

I sighed. "I know. Disrespectful. But I couldn't help it. I'm harboring all these bad feelings toward my parents. When I lost Tom, I lost them, too. They chose to mourn in their own worlds and left me behind."

"And this Travis character didn't leave you behind?"

I shook my head. "He promised my brother he would look out for me. For a while, he was the only family I had left."

"Sounds like a real hero," he muttered.

I looked back at him. "Chris, please. Don't! I can't let you antagonize Travis. He's too dear to me...he's like the brother I found when I lost Tom."

"We've been dating for two years and that name never came up," he said. "And now, he's all over the place."

"I always told you about him," I said.

"Yeah. Formerly known as 'old friend.'" Chris rolled his eyes.

"Chris...Travis is like my brother."

"But he isn't," Chris pointed out. "It feels uncomfortable to know that there's another guy who isn't a blood relative checking up on your girlfriend, you know."

144

I sighed. Travis had mentioned this to me years ago. He had said that not all my boyfriends would understand the kind of relationship that we had.

"Travis may not be a relative by blood, but he has been more like family to me than any of my blood relatives ever were," I argued. "Please? Let's just drop this? I don't want to argue about Travis. I never had a problem with him being in my life with any of my previous boyfriends."

"That's because your previous boyfriend was a fag," he muttered.

"And I'm not going to let you talk about Eric that way, either," I said to him. "He's a decent guy."

Although Chris tried to hide it, I knew that things weren't perfectly fine. He was quiet on the way home.

I invited him to spend the night with me, but he shook his head. "I have an early meeting tomorrow. It's best I stay in my apartment. It's closer to the office. I'll see you Wednesday."

I nodded and kissed him goodnight. When I closed the door, I couldn't help feeling that something was off between us. I wished I would understand exactly what and why.

# Chapter Fourteen

Wednesday, I surprised Chris by showing up in his office. He was having a chat with one of his lady colleagues. He was surprised when he saw me at the door of his office.

"Brianne!" he beamed. He came to me and gave me a kiss. "I thought we weren't meeting until seven."

"I thought I should pick you up for a change," I said. "I hope it's not a bad time."

He shook his head. "It's perfect!" He turned to the blonde sitting in his office. "Alana, this is my girlfriend, Brianne."

Alana was a beautiful blonde with startling blue eyes. She was wearing a pencil-cut suit that hugged her body to perfection. She smiled at me brightly. "It's nice to finally put a face to the name. I've heard so much about you."

She extended her hand to me and I shook it. Standing beside Alana made me feel out of place. I was wearing a pair of skin-tight jeans and an off-the-shoulder floral blouse, a Juicy Couture cross-body bag, and no make-up at all. My hair was tied in a careless ponytail with some tendrils loose around my face. She was wearing an Armani suit and perfect makeup, not a single hair out of place.

Seeing her made me feel that I should have dressed up more, so Chris and I would look…more suited for each other. But I guessed it was too late for that now. I told myself I should tab that thought for next time.

Chris left early and we had dinner together. Even then, I felt like he was lost in his thoughts, like something was really bothering him.

"Is this still about my aunt's anniversary?" I asked him when he took me back to my apartment.

He shook his head. "I'm just tired. I have a lot of pressure at work."

"Do you want to stay the night?" I asked him. "I can help take your mind off the pressure."

He narrowed his eyes. "I didn't bring a…condom," he said.

I was taken aback. It was the last thing I expected him to say.

147

"Well, we did that once before. I'm pretty sure it isn't that time of the month for me."

Chris shook his head. "It's best we take extra care," he said. "It's...too early for that kind of pressure."

"What pressure?" I asked him.

"Family," he sighed.

"When I asked you to stay the night, I didn't say 'Come, impregnate me!'" I said in an irritated voice.

He took a deep breath. "Either way, I'll see you tomorrow. I have tons of things I need to sort out."

He left without another argument. When I went to bed alone that night, I tried to remember when Chris started acting differently.

It started the morning that Travis's package arrived. But then again, we didn't talk or argue about Travis anymore. I thought it had to be something else. And when did he ever find the idea of sleeping together abhorrent? Or pressuring? He never did before. But now...it seemed like he was avoiding it. Why?

***

I didn't see Chris for another two days. I made no effort to call or text him. He had issues to sort out. I wanted to give him space to think and realize that he was being ridiculous.

My phone rang, and my heart jumped. *Finally!* He was calling me! But it wasn't Chris.

"I'll be in town tonight, *cherie*. But my flight to New York leaves at three in the morning. Just thought I'd catch up with you," Travis said on the other line.

My heart immediately gave a leap. I felt like crying. I realized I'd just missed him so much.

"Pick me up?"

"Fifteen minutes."

I was on my front steps in ten minutes, waiting for Travis. I was dressed in a long floral skirt and a white sleeveless top. I wasn't wearing any makeup. Whenever I was with Travis, I didn't have to worry about what I wore at all. There was no pressure to look suited for each other. And that felt comforting. With Travis, I didn't have to hide who I was, or pretend to be something I wasn't.

After two minutes, a red Ferrari parked in front of me. He got out of the car wearing a pair of jeans and a black jacket, which made his hair look darker.

"*Cherie*..." he greeted me in a low voice.

I gave him a tight hug. "I missed you," I said to him. "You should come visit me more often."

He raised a brow. "Why, I thought you had a boyfriend."

"I do," I said. "But you're irreplaceable."

"Don't scare me," he said. "I hope you're not prepping me for a big favor I can't say no to."

I laughed and pulled away from him. "Of course not!"

He opened the passenger door for me.

"Where are we going?" I asked him.

"Have you eaten?" he asked.

I shook my head.

"Let's go to dinner and then we can have coffee. Unfortunately, I can't drink. Flight schedule's a bummer."

Travis told me how successful he was becoming in his business. He'd been having some battles with his father, but he was winning most of them. He sounded focused and determined to prove his father wrong. I could sense the antagonism in him every time he mentioned him.

"Why do you have to fight with your father all the time?" I asked him. "Why is it your mission to see him on the ground?"

He had a hard expression on his face. "It's not like he doesn't deserve it, you know." I could see anger and resentment on his face again.

"Travis...when will you stop this?"

I reached forward and touched his cheek with my palm. I thought he was going to pull away. But instead, he held his hand up to hold my hand between his cheek and his palm. He closed his eyes for a moment. Then he took a deep breath. To my surprise, he turned sideways and kissed my palm. Then he released my hand and gave me a sober, pleading look.

He shook his head. "Don't ask me that, Brianne," he said to me. "My mother has been begging me to reconcile with my dad. She hasn't succeeded. But I beg *you* not to ask me the same thing."

I bit my lip. It was touching to know that somehow, he still felt he couldn't deny me anything. And I knew I would not ask him to do it unless I understood the real reasons behind it.

"Not now," I said to him.

He took a sip of his coffee. "So, how's the boyfriend?"

I shrugged. "Something's off. Lately, he's been acting weird," I said. "I think he suddenly realized your existence in my life and he's...jealous."

"I told you, you should have stuck it out with Eric!" he said, but I knew he was joking.

"Eric must have been more interested in you, you know," I giggled.

"But he's a nice guy," Travis said. "I want to meet this Christian."

"Why? You're going to have him background-checked?" I asked him.

"What makes you so sure I didn't do that two years ago when you started dating him seriously?" he challenged me.

"Travis!" I glared at him, daring him to deny it.

He took another sip of his coffee and didn't say anything.

"Unbelievable!" I muttered. "When will you stop?"

"Never," he said under his breath. The serious look on his face made me feel that he meant that.

"And what did you find out about Chris?"

"Did I make an effort to warn you or tell you to stay away?" he asked. "I'm only after your safety, Brianne. Your relationships are still your own business. And speaking of relationships, shouldn't you be concerned about how fast this Christian will propose to you?"

I stared back at him. "Why would I worry about that?"

"Because, you're twenty-eight now, *cherie,*" he said. "Tic-tock, tic-tock."

I remembered I'd told Christian about the fact that women in my family had to marry before they turn thirty-one. And apart from being jealous about Travis, Christian had also acted *off* when I asked him to sleep over. He'd immediately told me that he didn't have a condom with him and that he didn't want to take that much of a risk.

Now, I guessed I knew what he was cranky about. He thought there was pressure to settle down, and he wasn't sure if he was ready.

"Do you want to live with this guy for the rest of your life?" Travis asked me solemnly.

I bit my lip. *Do I? Am I ready to get married and stay married, have kids, raise a family? And more importantly, with Christian? Am I going to be happy for the rest of my life...with him?*

Travis sat back in his seat, reading my expression like a book. "Hmmm...interesting."

"What am I doing, Travis?" I asked him.

He reached out for my hand. "Living your life. Not letting the burden of your family tradition affect you. It's not easy to say the person you're with is the one you want to be with for the rest of your life. For some, it's easy. For most, it's too damn hard. I think you need more time, Brianne."

"But I don't have time," I said to him.

The expression on his face was hard to read. He squeezed my hand. "You do," he said. "But I can't tell you what to do. You have to figure out this one yourself."

I hugged Travis tightly when he dropped me off at my doorstep.

"I'll miss you," I said to him. "Please come more often."

"Your boyfriend will not like that."

"It doesn't matter. I'll handle that."

He kissed my forehead. "Stay safe, and call me anytime you need me."

"I love you, Travis."

He smiled at me. "I love you too, Brianne."

When he left, I wanted to cry. What was I doing? I was dating a guy who had changed me more in two years than anyone had in all my twenty-eight years. I couldn't even see myself being happily married to him yet. He wasn't even close to proposing to me. And I hadn't even begun wondering how much my relationship with Travis would change if Christian proposed and I said yes.

Travis was right. I needed more time to figure out my life. I wasn't ready to spend the rest of it with one guy. I wasn't sure that Chris was the one for me. And I was positive he wasn't sure he wanted me forever, either. But I had to decide soon...or I would be cursed for life.

\*\*\*

Chris knocked on my door the next day.

"Finally, you showed up," I said. My voice was cold, and I was determined to let him know that I wasn't happy he'd made no effort to contact me.

He marched inside my apartment. When he turned to me, his face was flushed and he looked furious.

"Is this your Travis Cross?" he asked and showed me a picture on a magazine.

I snatched the magazine from him and stared at the picture of Travis with a headline that read, *The New Generation of Cross Magnates: Younger. Richer. Smarter.*

I skimmed through the article. It was a write-up of the major changes that had been made to Cross Magnates since Travis had bought out the majority of their shareholders in his brilliant move to kick his father out.

I looked at the portrait of the cold, manipulative man next to the article. He was handsome as hell. But his eyes lacked the warmth they usually had whenever he looked at me.

I looked back at Chris and handed him the magazine.

"Yes," I said.

"You were with him last night, weren't you?" he asked.

"How did you..."

"I was about to surprise you," he said. "I was thinking, this guy could look geeky anyway—maybe I was being silly. I was just about to park in front of the building when I saw a Ferrari stop in front of you and its young, handsome driver give you a hug as if he wouldn't ever let you go! And that's when the plate that said TJCROSS caught my eye! I realized you'd been lying about him the whole time!"

"What? Lying? What did I lie about?"

"You told me nothing was going on between the two of you!" he spat back at me.

"There's nothing!" I insisted.

"I followed you! I watched you! You two sure like touching each other!"

I laughed humorlessly. "We're affectionate with each other! But then again, don't you get affectionate with your relatives? Closest friends? I hug Eric when I see him, too, and that doesn't seem to be a problem with you."

"Eric is gay!" He showed me the picture of Travis in the magazine again. "This guy is straight! He looked like he'd just stepped off the

152

cover of a magazine, he drives a Ferrari, and he's a billionaire! He's what every guy aims to be before they're forty! And he's only *twenty-nine!*"

"I cannot help your insecurity, Chris! But I don't think we should argue about this anymore! Travis is a part of me! He's a part of my family, the people I hold dear. If we're going to be together, you must accept him. And you have to trust that we're platonic—nothing else!"

I motioned for him to go. He didn't argue. He closed the door behind him with a bang.

***

I had dinner with Eric the next day. I talked to him about my fight with Chris. He smiled at me apologetically. "Chris is very ambitious. He loves you. And he's very proud. I guess he needs to resolve this within himself. He feels insecure. Travis is that one guy a boyfriend doesn't want his girlfriend to ever know in her life. He's...too much competition! The only way the guy will feel safe about Travis Cross is if his girlfriend is Travis's sister or cousin. Other than that, there's just no way. I mean...he's as handsome as Lucifer himself! He's brilliant. Some business critics call him a genius. And he's a billionaire!

"And that's driving Christian crazy. If I were straight, I would have felt the same way when you introduced Travis to me. I wouldn't have felt right. I would never believe that two gorgeous people wouldn't have the hots for each other at some point, at least once in their lives!"

My phone rang, and it interrupted my thoughts. I had taken a deep breath before I answered Chris's call.

"Hello."

"How was he in bed?" his voice sounded rough, as if he was drunk.

"What?"

"How was Travis Cross in bed?" he repeated and then he laughed bitterly.

"I don't know what you're talking about, Chris!"

"Don't lie!" he said. "Cindy told me."

"Cindy told you what? I haven't seen Cindy in months!"

"She's visited for a day," Chris said. "And just enough for me to find out about your past, Brianne!"

153

"What past?"

"I said don't lie!" he shouted. "You slept with Travis Cross! The lucky bastard! He's smart, he's rich, he's successful, he's handsome...and he was your first, wasn't he?"

My heart pounded in my chest, and I felt like all the blood in my body had drained completely.

"It's not true what you said to me! All this brotherly, platonic shit!" he said angrily. "You're attracted to him, and I'm pretty sure he wants you, too! Cindy told me you were pretty tight in high school! And you were the reason why Travis Cross went to Yale when he was set to go to Brown! Because he wanted to be close to you! What guarantee do we have that you only slept with each other at prom? Nothing! For all I know, you could be...fuck buddies!"

"Stop that, Chris!" I raised my voice this time. "That was a long time ago! Nothing's happening now! I swear to God! Travis and I will never happen!"

"Well, if that is true, you're just gonna have to choose! Him or me? Decide now! If you choose me, you are forbidden to see him or talk to him, email him or text him. I cannot allow that!"

I stared at Eric helplessly. I couldn't believe what I was hearing. "You can't ask me to do this, Chris."

"But I am! It's the only way we can be together! I cannot allow anything that has to do with Travis Cross!" He took a deep breath. "I can't look at him and not think about how he turned you from a girl to a woman! That he's been inside you. That the first man you ever trusted your body with was him! That's too...much! *Too much!* So, choose!"

I took a quick moment to imagine my life with Travis. It was the way it used to be. Safe. Comforting. I had a family. I had somebody who could read me like a book, protect me with his life and make me laugh out of my wits. Who would inspire me to turn even my darkest paintings into colorful pictures of sunshine and happiness.

Then I imagined my life without Travis, and I felt like my heart had just shattered into a million pieces. It was like losing my childhood, my family...it hurt the same way it did when I lost Tom. My stomach twisted into knots and I almost forgot how to breathe. My heart felt so heavy and there was a lump in my throat. And suddenly, I knew the answer to Chris's question.

"I love you, Chris," I said to him. I took a deep breath. "But I cannot live in a world where Travis Cross does not exist. You can't ask me to give up a huge part of me and expect me to live a normal life."

Chris took a deep breath as if he hadn't expected me to say what I'd said. "He's more important to you than anything else. Brianne...two weeks ago, he was just an *'old friend'* that you caught up with once a month! How did I not see this coming? How did I not know that there was this other guy who meant the world to you?"

"You would, if you paid more attention to me," I murmured. I realized it was true. Chris didn't care about what was going on in my life. It took him two and half years to show his face to my family. He never asked me about the friends I saw, hung out with, or caught up with. He was always content with the fact that I was changing myself and my ways for him.

"Damn it, Brianne!" he cursed. "How could this guy ruin us? He was stealing you from under my nose!"

Travis was right. Our relationship was difficult for some guys to understand or accept. That's why he kept a safe distance from me. Without telling me, I realized then that he'd drawn boundaries between us. He hadn't turned up on my dates with Chris. He only showed up once or twice a month, and he didn't demand that I spend too much time with him. Because he wanted to give me a chance to make this work. But still...my relationship with Chris was pretty messed up. Because Chris was one insecure, self-centered man. I wasn't sure I wanted to spend the rest of my life with someone like that.

"I meant it when I said that I wasn't cheating on you. I've never cheated on anybody. Travis and I are friends...the best of friends. He didn't want to touch me! But I asked him to, because I was young and stupid and under the pressure of high school immaturity. Maybe Cindy should have told you that part. Maybe you should have asked her for the full story." I was sobbing but fought to keep a steady voice. "I love you, Chris. But I choose Travis." And I hung up on him.

I stared at Eric brokenly. He inched closer and put an arm around me. I rested my head on his shoulder. I closed my eyes and tried to calm my raging emotions. I didn't know how to feel. Devastated? Confused? Angry? Relieved?

155

"Things will be okay," Eric said. "Either Chris comes to his senses...or Travis comes to his—although I'm hoping it will be the latter."

I pulled away from Eric. "Shut up, Eric! You know very well that Travis and I are just friends."

"I know you are," he said. He sighed. "But nobody could take care of you better than Travis could, you know?"

"I don't need just that, Eric. I need somebody who could also love me...exclusively. Somebody I can fall in love with, and somebody who can fall in love with me."

"What did you and Christian break up over?"

I took a deep breath. I could feel something twist inside my chest. If I hadn't been resting my head on Eric's shoulder, I would have been afraid of fainting. "He found out about prom."

"What about it?"

"Travis...and I...we slept together at prom."

There was silence and Eric stood still. I pulled away from him and stared at his shocked expression.

"That's bad!" I groaned. "But I was young. I was...immature! I caught my boyfriend cheating on me. I'd been hoping to sleep with him. I was probably the only girl in school who was a virgin! And then the guys were making bets on who could take my V-card. I was stupid!" I sighed. "I asked Travis to help me out. He didn't want to. But when he found out that the guy taking me to prom was in on the bet, he beat him up and told me to dump the guy! He took me to prom instead."

"And so...he took you to bed, too?"

I sighed and then I nodded. "But it was just one night. It was against his will! He almost couldn't do it!" I laughed humorlessly. "I have no memories of Travis's face in bed. He wanted both of us not to remember that night. He blindfolded me. He kept his eyes closed during the act. He didn't want us to mention each other's names. He turned off all the lights afterward, and it was impossible to see the face of the guy sleeping beside me.

"Then he didn't show up for weeks. When we saw each other again...all memories were forgotten. I'm not even sure it was Travis at all! All I know is that...I was with a guy on prom night. He made love to me. He taught me what to expect when a man and a woman come together in bed. He made my first time romantic because he said I deserved it." I shook my head. "But I'm not supposed to remember. I've never spoken about it with him. Travis and I don't see each other that way."

Eric stared at me wearily. "Did you forget?"

I laughed humorlessly again. "I didn't have a choice! I…was blindfolded! I never saw his body touching mine! I didn't see him over me, kissing me, or entering me. I have no memories of making love to Travis. I have memories of making love for the first time…being with a guy for the first time…but I can't place Travis's face with the memory. I'm sure he didn't even take a peek at my face that night. Otherwise, he would never have been able to touch me. He'd be too guilty. Travis valued his friendship with Tom more than anything. He felt he was betraying Tom by touching me."

"Why did you choose Travis?"

I sighed. "Because I cannot be with a guy who could ask me to give up whatever is left of my ties with my family…whatever is left of my ties with Tom," I replied. "Travis took care of me when my parents couldn't…wouldn't. When I lost Tom, Travis eased so much of the pain! We may not be related by blood, but we have this bond now. I cannot be with a guy who would be selfish enough to ask me to sever those bonds!"

Eric nodded. "I understand. Chris is insecure, but that's not reason enough to ask so much from you. Give him time. He might come back to his senses."

When I went home that night, my heart still felt heavy. I wanted to strangle Cindy for betraying me…for not leaving it up to me to tell Christian about that night with Travis. But then again, I wasn't even sure I planned to tell Christian…or anyone for that matter…about prom night. I was not supposed to remember…I was supposed to forget.

And although that night was probably the most amazing night I'd spent with a man…I couldn't remember Travis in it. That guy had unnerved me, brought my emotions back to life, made me scream, made me whimper, made me want to stay in his arms forever. It was romantic, sensual, terrifying…it was exciting, addicting…it was everything I'd ever dreamt of and more…so much more.

I was pretty sure no other night with any other guy could measure up with that night. But I didn't know that guy's name. I couldn't place Travis in that memory. He was so much different from that guy I went to bed with. The Travis I knew now would never touch me like that. Even if I begged him to!

I thought about Chris and all his promises, all the nights that we spent together. I realized that I was counting on the relationship to last. Long enough to get me through my family tradition. I realized that I was hoping that after one more year with Chris, he'd be ready to propose to me. But even that would have been a mistake. Travis was right. I did change so much because of him.

Another pain stabbed through my heart. I remembered decorating the apartment with him. He helped me choose the furniture. The whole apartment was a shade of earth tones. Formal. Calm. Professional. So much like Chris! He had such mature taste. I gave up the neon lights because I wanted to fit into Chris's world...to fit his taste. So he would love me enough to want to marry me and save me from my family's curse.

I was deeply saddened, and I felt alone. I wanted to cry, but the tears still wouldn't come. Maybe I was mad at Chris! Maybe it hadn't sunk in yet. Maybe I was in shock!

I had a hot bath, and then I slipped into a comfortable cotton spaghetti-strap cami and matching shorts. I sat on the couch and closed my eyes. I didn't think I could sleep in the bed now. The memory of Chris would haunt me, and I knew I would never be able to sleep.

The doorbell rang and I jumped in surprise. I looked at the clock on my wall; it was one in the morning. My heart pounded in my chest.

*Chris!*

Had he changed his mind? Had he come to tell me he was sorry?

I was shaking when I went to the door. I took one deep breath before I turned the knob and opened it.

My breath caught in my throat. All of a sudden, I realized just how lost I'd really felt all those years. And how sad I really was. It felt like my world was crumbling! I felt like I'd lived in Chris's world for two years, and now I was on my own in the world he molded for me, and I didn't know how to live there alone. And I needed someone to hold me and tell me that it was going to be all right.

I closed my eyes and allowed myself to be caught by Travis. He enclosed me in his arms, kept me warm as if he were telling me that I didn't have to worry. Even if my deadline was looming over me, I didn't have to worry about another failed relationship. He was there. And no matter what happened, I would be safe.

He lifted me off my feet and carried me. He settled me on the couch, took off his jacket, and gathered me in his arms again. I closed my eyes, inhaled his scent, lost myself, and finally...I was able to cry my heart out.

# Chapter Fifteen

We had a dance show the next day. Before going to the theater, I dropped by Chris's apartment to pick up some of my stuff. I'd left some of my dance clothes at his place.

He wasn't there, but the girl named Alana was. I was tempted to ask her what she was doing in Chris's apartment, but I guess I didn't have to be a genius to guess that.

I was even more heartbroken than I was before. We'd been broken up less than twenty-four hours, and there was already another woman in his house.

Sarah was close to berating me for showing up a few minutes late.

"I dropped by Chris's apartment to get my stuff," I said, motioning at the box on the floor.

"Wow! That does not look good!"

I laughed humorlessly. "It doesn't. But I can't think of that now! I need to dress up!"

I focused on my dance pieces. I had one with Sarah and some guys. It was a contemporary piece that told a story of a girl who was in love with a guy all her life, but he didn't have eyes for her. He wanted another girl who was coveted by many others. I was the coveted girl. Sarah played the lead part. It was a difficult piece with many twists and turns and some lifting. It was acting, not just dancing.

We got an encore at the end of our performance. Sarah performed brilliantly, and I was pretty sure I provided a good supporting performance.

We rushed backstage. I had another piece coming. It was a lyrical hip-hop dance. Until a month before, I hadn't even known I could dance hip-hop.

"What happened?" Sarah asked me as we changed into new costumes.

"We broke up!" I said.

"Why?"

"He didn't want to be pressured about marriage at this stage. You know I have a deadline. And then he was so insecure about Travis! He asked me to choose between the two of them."

"And of course you chose Travis," she concluded.

"You know how important Travis is to me. He may be a difficult man who seems like he doesn't have a care in the world, but for years, he's taken care of me. He's kept me safe, made sure I was provided for."

"I know," she said. "Even though you say you cannot love each other romantically, I know he's just as important as the air that you breathe. But I can't blame Chris, either. Travis Cross is one guy you hate to compete with!"

"But he isn't competing with Chris!"

"I know. But Chris would never feel that way. He'd always think that no matter what he did, there was another guy in your life who would always do better! Always smarter, always richer...has that amount of history with you. He could never measure up."

"Does it even matter that he's the one I was in love with?"

"It should. But maybe some things are more important to Chris than...the fact that you're in love with him," Sarah said.

I finished fixing my hair and stared at myself in the mirror. I had on a lot of makeup. It was necessary, if I didn't want to look like a corpse on stage.

Just then, one of the production assistants approached me with a bouquet of roses in her arms.

"This came for you, Brianne," she said.

I stared at the roses and then at Sarah.

"Maybe Chris wanted to apologize," she said.

I shook my head. "There was a woman in his apartment when I went by. Two words: revenge sex. How could I forgive him for that?"

"But didn't you say Travis stayed with you last night?"

"But I didn't sleep with Travis!" I argued. "I fell asleep on the couch beside him. When I woke up we were still on the couch, and we were both fully dressed!"

Sarah giggled. "All right, all right! Case stated. Read the card!"

When I read the message, I was surprised to find that it hadn't come from Chris.

162

*You were lovely onstage. I'll wait for you after the show.*
*Love,*
*Travis*

I was smiling widely, and tears welled up in my eyes. I was deeply touched by his thoughtfulness. I never told him about the dance shows I was participating in. How could he have known?

Sarah rolled her eyes. "Oh, my God! Will you please just snap out of it and marry the guy?"

I laughed. "I'm sorry. I just didn't expect it."

"He's always watched you! What do you mean you didn't expect it?"

"No! I don't even tell him about the shows."

Sarah was taken aback. "But...he..." She trailed off.

"What?"

"He asked to be on our mailing list a couple of years ago," she said. "He purchases tickets in advance. I get contacted by his secretary for every show. I'm pretty sure he's seen all our performances. I thought you knew!"

I was shocked. I shook my head. "No. I never did."

Our conversation was interrupted by a production assistant calling us to go backstage to wait for our cue. And as we danced into our finale, I had a big smile on my face. I knew, for the first time, I had somebody in the audience watching and cheering for me.

***

I couldn't help crying while in bed that night. I remembered being there with Chris...all those nights he kept me warm. All those nights we shared our thoughts and dreams with each other. And now, I couldn't help thinking that he was sharing the night with Alana!

*They could be having mindless sex right now!* I thought. Alana seemed experienced enough. She might be a tigress in bed. I'd be out of Christian's mind in no time.

Suddenly, my bedside lamp was turned on and I felt Travis sit on the bed beside me. I was really glad that he'd stayed with me. I was pretty sure I couldn't do this alone.

He gathered me in his arms and allowed me to cry on his chest. The expression on his face was dark, cold...fathomless, and I knew he was trying to control his emotions.

"When I went to his apartment to get my stuff, I found one of his lady colleagues there. It looks like...he's sleeping with her now," I said. "She's blond. She looks tough, and smart. She's sophisticated. Professional. She's a lawyer as well. Her personality is quite strong. She's very pretty!" I whimpered. "I guess he was telling me he could replace me with someone prettier...someone who has more...success, much more going on in her life. I really felt small...and I couldn't believe it only took him a couple of hours to throw it all away. Two years!"

Travis didn't say anything.

"Chris is a very ambitious guy! He's got so much control. He wanted me to be...a lot of things. I tried to change that. For two years, I built my life around him. I just didn't expect it to end this way."

Still, Travis kept quiet. But he continued holding me against his chest. I stared up at him. Usually, he would offer a sarcastic remark or tell me what a moron Chris was. But now he wasn't saying anything. "Are you okay?" I asked him.

He took a deep breath. "I was trying my best to tune it out," he said in a harsh tone. "Because I'm a few seconds away from hunting that moron down and punching all his teeth down his throat!"

I smiled at him. "Thank you," I said to him. "I don't think I can be alone for this. Not here," I said. I looked around my apartment. "We painted these walls, you know. He chose the colors. He chose the bed...he chose almost every piece of furniture that I have here."

"Thank God!" he said sarcastically. "I was afraid your taste had gotten boring! It's a relief to know you weren't the one who decorated your apartment."

"Is it boring?" I asked him.

"It's not you," he said. "I noticed it the first time I came here. I know you would never settle for colors this...*safe*. You'd be more creative."

"He didn't come to a single show I had," I said. "I didn't play a major part in any of the shows, but it would have been nice to have someone in the audience cheering for me."

"You had someone," Travis said quietly.

"I didn't know that," I said. I stared up at him again. His expression was sober. "Thank you for watching me, Travis. Even if I didn't know it, you were always there. Did you really come to my shows?"

He nodded. "Every single one of them," he replied. "You were brilliant! I wonder why you haven't had a starring role in the dances."

"I am a part-time member," I said. "I did it for fun. Sarah and the others work there full-time. They do it for a living. I was doing it to keep myself sane. Now I realize I was dancing to get in touch with whatever's left of the real me. The me that Chris never really appreciated."

"Do you even like managing a gallery?"

"I don't hate it. But I always feel it could be my paintings I'm selling," I said.

"Why don't you pursue that path?"

"I need the money," I replied. "I'm not as rich as you, Travis Cross."

"You don't have to be to pursue your dreams," he said.

"I need to do it for Mom, too," I said. "She needed help managing her galleries."

"You can do that and paint, you know."

I sighed. "Chris would never approve."

"You're not with him now," he pointed out, his voice showing signs of irritation.

"I know. Another relationship gone to waste," I said. "I'm not getting any younger. I need more time."

"You have time," he whispered.

I took a deep breath. "I need to find a guy who can fall in love with me and rush me to the altar. I cannot do that before I'm thirty. There's just no way! I'm just starting to get over a breakup. Relationships take hard work. And I can't just magically find a guy who can propose to me and save me from my family curse!"

He fell silent for a while. Then, he said quietly, "I'm sure you can figure this out, Brianne." He pulled away from me and stood up from the bed. "Get dressed."

"What? Why?"

"You're not staying in this apartment an hour longer," he said. "You can't get over that guy if everything around you reminds you of him."

"Where am I going?"

"I have a hotel suite that I have prepaid for a week, and I'm not using it," he said. "Maybe it's best you stay there for a while."

"Are you serious?"

He raised a brow. "Do I joke about these things?"

I smiled. "No, you don't."

"Grab some clothes. You're staying with me for a while." And he exited my room, not giving me a chance to argue.

As I packed up my clothes and some essentials I knew I would need, I thought about what Travis told me. That I had time. He'd told me that before, but he said he'd leave it to me to figure it out.

I had to be married before I turn thirty-one. How could I find a guy who would propose to me in such a short span of time? And even if I worked on a relationship really, really hard... like what I did with Chris... it still would not guarantee a wedding.

I needed at least another three years...to find someone. To fall in love again.

How could Travis think that I had time?

Unless...

An idea kept playing in my head...I would have time...if I called on Travis's promise. If we got married, I would have years ahead of me to get my life back on track, and if I did stumble upon somebody and fall in love with him, it will be easy to divorce Travis and we go back to the way we used to be. If the guy I found really loved me enough, he would understand that the marriage between Travis and me was just an arrangement.

A month before, I had been hoping Chris would pop the question on my birthday! Now I was thinking of asking Travis to marry me instead.

I loved Travis so much. Could I really ask him to make that huge sacrifice?

Thirty minutes later, we were standing in Travis's luxurious hotel suite.

"Wow!" I breathed. "This is expensive," I said. "Do you have business in Connecticut that allows you to rent a suite like this?"

"I do," he said. He stared at me for a moment. "You."

I smiled. "Just me?"

"I meet with some investors here once in a while. But mostly, I come here to check up on you."

166

"Must be a pain keeping tabs on me," I murmured.

He raised a brow at me. "I've been doing that for more than a decade. Suffice it to say, you're a part of my routine." Then he took a deep breath and said, "And I would have done the same thing you did if another person asked me to give you up."

I stared at him blankly. I hadn't told Travis why I broke up with Chris. I'd just told him that Chris had been unreasonable and that he was jealous. But I never told him that Chris had specifically asked me to choose between the two of them. And that I'd chosen him.

"How did you know?" I asked him.

"Eric," he replied. "He called me as soon as he dropped you off. He told me everything. I intended to pay Chris a visit first so I could give him a good beating before I came to your place, but I figured you would be alone and you needed me more than Chris needed a shiner."

I smiled at Travis ruefully.

"I was waiting for you to tell me," he said.

I shook my head. "You don't need to know. I am such a burden already. You don't need to feel guilty about this. You don't deserve that."

He touched my cheek with his palm. "You're never a burden, Brianne." He pulled me toward him and gave me a kiss on the forehead.

I inhaled the sweet, masculine scent of Travis. And now, more than ever, I realized that I'd chosen right. I would be ten times more miserable had I chosen Chris over him. Because I knew I could never lose him. I knew how painful it had been to lose Tom. It would be just as painful to lose Travis. No matter how cold, unattached, and unemotional Travis appeared to be, I knew he really cared about me. He was that one person I could always depend on...that one person who would never betray me.

"Nevertheless, do you want me to talk some sense into this guy?" he asked.

Even if Travis explained himself to Chris, we could never go back to the way we used to be. He'd been with Alana. He left her at his apartment at the exact time he knew I was going to drop by. He was rubbing it in my face that they were together now. That I was replaceable.

And Travis was right. This wasn't me. I used to be fun! I used to be all colors and hues. I was reduced to the timid, insecure, boring little girl trying to fit into Christian's world. I needed to find myself again.

"Do you want to? Do you think it's the right thing to do?"

Travis stared back at me and he shook his head. "No. To both your questions."

I nodded. "I thought so."

"Although, I hope there is something I can do to ease your pain. To make things right."

I looked up at Travis. I knew the time had come to call in the favor I'd asked him when we were sixteen years old. I needed time. He needed to buy me some! But it would be too much to ask. I felt like I was asking him for his life so I could extend mine.

I bit my lip and took a deep breath. "You're right, Travis. I do have time..." I stared into his eyes and took a deep breath. "And I think I'm going to need it now." I was not sure if he'd gotten what I meant, yet I didn't want to say it directly.

What could I say? The choices that popped up in my head said, *Travis, I'm desperate, will you marry me?* and *Travis, do you want to commit suicide now?*

I didn't think either was suitable at the moment. The first one was the best, but I'd be damned if I proposed to a man!

He searched my face. Then he closed his eyes and raised his face toward the ceiling for a while. When he looked at me again, his eyes were unreadable.

He took a deep breath. "This is not going to be easy for you, either, you know."

I nodded. "I know. But I have you beside me, so nothing is too hard."

"Brianne, I have needs..." he started.

"And you're welcome to have them fulfilled as per usual," I cut him off mid-sentence. "Just...don't let my parents or my close relatives find out. Don't have it printed in gossip columns...at least not for a year or two."

He took a deep breath. He narrowed his eyes and said, "I need an heir, Brianne."

That made me take a step back. "That...that wasn't part of the conditions."

"*Your* conditions. You haven't heard mine yet," he said.

"When? You're too young to be a father," I said.

168

"My parents had me when they were thirty-one." His voice was hard, as if he was trying to make me understand one serious complication in our arrangement.

I took a deep breath. "In two years, we can have IVF if you really want. If...if by then, we're still together."

He narrowed his eyes. He shook his head then pulled me to him and gave me a kiss on the forehead. "You can be so naïve sometimes, Brianne," he whispered in a frustrated voice. "It may be one of the reasons why you have me wrapped around your finger."

"I do?" I was surprised. It wasn't easy for Travis Cross to admit any sign of weakness. "I thought it was because Thomas asked you to give me everything I needed."

"That too," he replied. He sucked in a deep breath. "Just promise me we'll discuss my condition after two years."

I nodded. In two years, I might have found Mr. Right, or we could always discuss the possibility of having in-vitro fertilization.

Travis smiled at me. I didn't know whether he'd said yes or no. I stared up at him.

"Sleep in the bed—I'll take the couch," he said. "I have a meeting first thing tomorrow morning. I'll give you a call in the afternoon."

Though I tried so hard, I just couldn't force myself to sleep that night. It's difficult when you don't know whether you're engaged or not. What would I tell my family? How would I introduce Travis? Had he said yes already? Was he my fiancé? Damn it! All these questions were killing me!

A while before, I had been crying my heart out because of my breakup with Christian. Now my heart was pounding wildly in my ribcage, and I didn't know whether I wanted to jump for joy or reel with excitement.

*Damn!* Only Travis Cross could do this to me. After all these years, I still couldn't figure out how he could evoke such feelings within me when he shouldn't have had any effect on me at all.

\*\*\*

I woke up at noon the next day. Travis was already gone. I contemplated going back to my apartment, but I knew that would depress me even more. For hours, I hadn't thought about Chris. All I thought about was Travis's answer and the status of our relationship.

169

Was I supposed to introduce him as my fiancé? Should I call my parents?

Because I was getting restless, I decided to go to the dance studio. I danced my worries away, and for a couple of hours, it seemed to work.

When I got back to the hotel suite, I took a nice, hot bath. The phone in the bathroom rang.

"It's six p.m.," Travis said on the other line.

"And?"

"And you're invited to join me for dinner at Le Divalle."

I giggled. "Wow! That's...expensive! And formal! Am I allowed to ask why?"

"No reason. I've arranged for the hotel car to drive you there," he said. "See you at seven."

When I got out of the bathroom, I was surprised to find a big box sitting on top of the bed. I must have been in such a hurry to take a hot bath that I hadn't noticed it sitting there when I came in. I opened it. There's a card on top of the tissue cover that read, *Wear me.*

I pulled out the cream silk cocktail dress from the box. There was a matching pair of sandals that came with it.

I tried it on. It hugged my body to perfection. It was backless, and the hem ended above my knees. I tied my hair into a bun and curled some tendrils to flow around it, and then put on very light makeup. When I put on the glass sandals that came with the gown, I was satisfied by my reflection. The girl staring back at me was far from Alana. Alana looked tough, like she meant business. The girl in front of me looked elegant and lovely. Her facial features were soft and angelic. She looked like the girl who could make even devilish guys like Travis Cross bend to her will.

I took my purse and then went down to the lobby.

"We have a limo waiting outside," the concierge said, and he had a member of the hotel staff assist me to the entrance.

Before I got inside the limo, I heard someone call, "Brianne?"

When I turned around, I found Christian staring back at me. He had just valet parked his car. Alana's arm was around his.

I raised a brow at him.

"You look... different," he said under his breath. Alana gave me one antagonizing look.

"Why? Did I grow an extra head?" I asked him, raising my brow.

He stared back at me, quite dumbfounded.

"That was a joke. But I forgot you don't have a sense of humor." I took a deep breath. "Anyway, thank you, if you meant that as a compliment," I said haughtily. "If you don't have anything else to say, I need to go. Travis is waiting for me." I turned my back on him and got inside the limo. From inside, I could still see him looking at me until Alana made a pout and pulled him away.

I had fresh pain inside my chest, but I knew I had to fight it. At least now, I'd managed to stun Chris for a change!

I was taken to *Le Divalle*. It was an elegant, strictly reservations-only restaurant and the most expensive in the city.

"Travis Cross," I said at the reception.

Immediately, the receptionist smiled and led me inside the restaurant. I was hoping to see Travis at one of the tables, but I was led to another door.

"Where are we going?" I asked.

"Mr. Cross made special arrangements. You'll be dining by the poolside."

When she opened the door again, I was stunned to find the poolside decorated with candles and flowers. Even the pool itself was adorned with floating candles and a lighted balloon in the middle. There was a table at the center, with two waiters standing at the sides.

"Do you like it?" I heard Travis ask behind me. I spun around and found him staring at me. I couldn't read the expression on his face.

He took my hand in his and led me to the table. He pulled a chair out for me.

"What's all this?" I asked him. "And you had to make me dress up?"

"You look lovely, by the way," he said.

I laughed. "Travis? I'm getting scared. What's all this about?"

He shrugged. "I just want to have dinner with you. Take your mind off things."

I raised a brow. "Promise? There's no catch to this?"

He nodded. He motioned for the waiter to bring us wine. We had Greek salad as an appetizer and then finally, pasta and salmon were served as the main course.

It did take my mind off things. It made me feel loads better remembering Chris's confused expression when he'd seen me earlier. And being with Travis here made me feel much more secure. The way

171

he prepared everything was…as romantic as a fairy tale, and yet as comfortable as home.

"Where did you go today? You weren't in the hotel when I dropped off the dress."

"I was at the studio," I replied.

"Figured as much." He looked at me for a moment and asked, "Do you want to stay here, Brianne? Or do you have plans of living somewhere else?"

"Right now? I think a change would be good. I am…close to asking my mother to transfer me to another city. Maybe I could do well managing another branch. Or maybe even better, I'll try painting something this time."

"Good" He nodded. He reached somewhere under the table and handed me a box of Godiva chocolates.

I laughed. "You're not planning to make me fat, are you? Or do you believe that chocolates are the best breakup buddies?"

He shrugged but instead of replying, he smiled at me crookedly.

I opened the box. It was a collection of heart truffles in milk, white, and dark chocolates. There was a huge heart chocolate in the middle with an engraving at its center.

*Voudrais tu m'épouser?*

My heart caught in my throat. I didn't speak French, but I knew that phrase sounded so familiar!

I stared at Travis. He was smiling boyishly at me. But he looked nervous! For the first time, I saw a different Travis Cross. One that didn't look confident of his calculated movements.

He stood up from his seat. He held a box in front of me and then he bent down on one knee.

I covered my mouth with my hands. I wanted to scream. I wanted to cry. *He didn't have to do this!*

He took a deep breath. "Brittany Anne Montgomery, I promised to take care of you for the rest of my life. For years, you've been the only thing that I've cared about in this world, the only thing that I loved. You've been the only family I have. And now, I hope to make that official. Would you do me the honor of becoming Mrs. Brittany Anne Cross? Will you marry me?"

Tears rolled down my cheeks. I couldn't say anything. I felt like I was going to die any minute.

I nodded. "Yes, Travis. I will marry you. You know I will!"

He chuckled boyishly and then he took my hand and slipped a huge diamond ring on my finger. He brought my fingers to his lips and kissed them.

He stared at me for a long moment, and then he took a deep breath before pulling me into his arms. The waiters cheered around us. And as if it wasn't perfect enough, the skies suddenly lit in a display of spectacular colors.

"Did you do this, too?" I asked.

He nodded. "I wanted it to be perfect for you."

I rested my head on Travis's shoulder as we both watched the wonderful fireworks display. It felt... surreal. This was more than what I'd dreamt of. I'd hoped for a dreamy proposal from Chris, but not like this! What Travis did for me was not just a dream. It was a fairy tale!

I didn't know this side of Travis. He was usually sarcastic, distant...unattached. He did show me that he had a loving and caring side. But this was different. This was nothing like the Travis Cross I'd known at all!

The Travis I knew, the Travis that everybody knew could be cold and ruthless. No one knew of his pains, his weaknesses, maybe except for me. He almost seemed invincible. I would never have expected him to propose to any woman like this. His proposal was so wonderful...so romantic...so perfect!

Travis was looking at me when I looked up at him. He wiped my tears with his fingers. "Why are you crying?"

I took a deep breath. "Why do you always have to make everything perfect for me? Why do you always go through all this trouble just to make sure my dreams will come true?"

I didn't expect him to answer. But he held my face between his palms. "Because you deserve it," he whispered.

"You didn't have to propose to me!" I argued. "I asked you to do this. Why did you have to propose like this?"

He chuckled. "Because I *will* marry you. It's not a fake wedding. The engagement is real. And every bride needs to be proposed to first before she gets married. You, more than anybody, deserved a proposal like this," he replied. "In fact, if your ex-boyfriend hadn't screwed up and had decided to marry you instead, I think I would've been disappointed if he hadn't proposed to you this way...or at least some way close." He looked me in the eye and added, "The engagement is official. You have a ring on your finger. So now, you can officially call me your fiancé."

"Even if it was just a favor? Even if I just asked you to sacrifice a huge part of your life?"

He shrugged. "You are a huge part of my life, too. For a long while now, you've been the only family I have had. I told you I didn't intend to marry at all. But if I do this with you, it won't be that bad, will it?"

I laughed and hugged him. "No, Travis. I don't think it will be bad at all!" I took a deep breath. "I love you. Thank you for doing this for me."

He held the back of my head and took a deep breath. "I am doing this because you are probably the only person I love in my life."

I stared up at him. "I didn't know you could love at all," I teased, trying to make the mood lighter.

He grinned. "Me neither."

Travis may sound like a formidable force—manipulative, shrewd, and ruthless in many ways—but I knew how torn and broken he was inside. And sometimes, he wasn't afraid to show me that side. After all, it is tiring to be so strong all the time.

He stared at me seriously. Then he said, "Close your eyes, Brianne."

I did as he said. I felt his breath against my face. My heart pounded wildly inside my ribcage. Gently, I felt him brush his lips against mine. I tensed against his lips, and he sucked in a deep breath. "Do you realize that this is something you should get used to?"

I blinked back at him. "But didn't we agree…"

"That we would not go to bed, yes. But do you want your parents and your relatives to suspect that?"

I shook my head.

"Then you should know that they expect us to make a show of affection toward each other." He gave me a reassuring smile. "Don't worry. I promised to protect you from the beast inside me, remember? I'm still good at keeping my promises."

I understood that. I didn't want my relatives to think I'd just commissioned Travis to marry me to escape the so-called family curse, whether or not there was truth to it. We did have to show them that this was a love match. Though nothing would happen in the bedroom, they didn't need to know or suspect that.

I nodded at him. "Would you care to try again?" I asked him boldly.

He sucked in a deep breath, as if this was difficult for him, too. Then he leaned forward, and I closed my eyes. I felt his lips on mine, and he gave me one gentle kiss. And then he kissed...*really*...kissed me. Passionately.

It was a mixture of a whole lot of emotions for me. It was a combination of thrill, fear, excitement, weariness...it was nerve-wracking, it was mind-blowing, and sanity-disturbing!

*How could I feel like this every time Travis kisses me?*

When the kiss was over, Travis leaned his forehead against mine and sucked in a deep breath.

"That's enough...for now," he whispered.

I knew I was blushing violently. Travis smiled when he saw my flushed face.

"I can make you blush," he whispered. And I wasn't sure if he was teasing me.

"Didn't you know that a long time ago?" I raised a brow.

He touched my warm face with his fingers. "It's good to remember."

Travis had been with a lot of women. I was just one of the many that he'd kissed like that. I doubted that he felt anything when he kissed me. I doubted that I could stir any emotion in him, the way he stirred so many emotions in me. And for that reason, I felt embarrassed. But I refused to let him see that.

"I'm not always soft-hearted or sensitive," he warned me.

"You almost never were," I said to him. "But I know you are. I know you have a good heart, Travis."

"You have so much faith in me," he said and hugged me to him. "This is not going to be easy for either of us."

"I'm ready for that. Just promise I will still have you when all this comes to an end."

He took a deep breath and tightened our embrace. "I promise, *cherie*."

I smiled against his chest. I knew he meant that. After all, Travis was so good at keeping his promises.

# Chapter Sixteen

When we got back to the hotel, Travis and I sat on the bed and talked. We were…well, basically planning our future. Although we were not lovers, we were betrothed and whether we liked it or not, we had lives that we would live together, for the next two years, minimum.

"You said you were thinking of moving cities," he said.

"Yes."

"Then come to Manhattan with me," he said. "You can manage your gallery there instead. You can paint all you want. I'm pretty sure there are dance studios that would be happy to accommodate you."

"That sounds like a plan." I smiled. I found that proposal interesting.

"I have an apartment there. You can move in with me."

"Why? Can't I rent my own?"

"Useless," Travis replied. His tone told me that he thought my idea was ridiculous. "When do you intend to get married anyway? You're approaching your deadline, *cherie*. Didn't you want to get married before that?"

I nodded. "Are we getting married in New York?"

"It's up to you, really. We could get married at home. Or in New York, whichever you prefer."

"New York is expensive," I said. "I don't think the money I have saved up is enough. But in any case, I intend to have a small ceremony."

Travis raised a brow. "Did you really think I would let you pay for our wedding?"

"But, Travis, this is a favor!" I protested. "You already gave me this lovely ring! Which…I will return when we divorce, by the way. So you don't have to buy a new one for your real fiancée."

He smirked. "You are my real fiancée," he reminded me.

"I mean…you know what I mean!" I said in a frustrated tone. Our relationship seemed to be getting harder and harder to define with each passing day.

"Well, in any case, you won't be spending a dime on our wedding. I've been saving up for it since I was sixteen years old," he said.

"You have been?"

He nodded. "I promised to be your safety guy. I had to make provisions for this event, you know."

I sighed. "You really have the answer to everything, don't you?"

"Not everything." He took a deep breath. "So, are you fine with moving in with me...to my apartment in Manhattan? I personally do not like my fiancée staying in an apartment decorated by her ex-boyfriend!"

I laughed at that. Travis sounded like he was irritated and insulted at the same time.

"And besides, maybe you'd like to get married in two or three months," he said. "It's not forbidden for engaged couples to live together prior to the wedding."

I nodded. "You state your case well, Mr. Cross," I said. "Do you have a guest bedroom?"

He raised a brow. "My guest bedroom is a third the size of my room and has no walk-in closet. No way I would let you stay there. And besides, why would we stay in separate bedrooms?"

"Because nothing will happen between us, remember?"

"Yes, but that doesn't mean we can't share a bedroom." He raised a brow.

"We certainly can't share a bed!" I protested, blushing violently.

He laughed. "Yes. But my bedroom is big enough to accommodate you. And I can always add a couch big enough to be a bed and I'll spend my nights there. Same bedroom, separate sleeping arrangements."

I looked terrified. Would I really be living with Travis? Staying in the same bedroom as him for the next two years?

He narrowed his eyes. "You haven't thought this through, have you?"

I shook my head. "At least not this far."

He slightly shook his head. "Oh God, Brianne!" he said under his breath. Then as if he were talking to a ten-year-old, he said, "We're going to get married. We will live in the same house and we will stay in the same room. We don't want to risk your parents or any of your relatives dropping by our apartment and finding us living separately. If they found out that this marriage is an arrangement or a favor I'm doing for you...you'd be 'cursed' no matter what."

I sighed. He had a point. "I guess you're right."

"Furthermore, we will show affection as if we really are a happily married couple. We can kiss, we can hug, and cuddle with each other, but..." He paused, giving me a hard expression. Then he continued, "We will not have sex. And in two years, you promised to discuss the possibility of having at least one son with me."

"Wow. You got that one mapped out." I knew only that I had asked Travis to do this for me, but it seemed that he'd given it more thought than I had.

"I have to. I don't want to confuse the do's with the don'ts!" he muttered under his breath. "Are you going to be okay with all the rules?"

I nodded slowly. Then I said to him, "Women."

"What?"

"We need to discuss the issue of your women," I said. "I know you're a player, Travis Cross. How would your marriage to me impact your...sex life?"

He narrowed his eyes at me and then he said, "Let that be my problem."

"I said it was okay for you to continue your usual activities," I said. "But I can't let my parents know or think that you're cheating on me. They love you like a son, Travis. If they thought you were hurting me, that would change. And I couldn't let that happen. You don't deserve that."

"I told you...let *that* be *my* problem," he said in a more serious voice, as if telling me to shut up, as if he didn't want to discuss the subject matter anymore.

"Do you have a mistress? Girlfriend? That I should know about? I mean...not that I care, really. I just want to know if I need to watch my back."

He raised a brow. "What do you take me for?"

I sighed. "Travis...I...don't know your relationship profile. I know there's been a string of women. I just want to know if anybody from that string actually stuck."

He sighed and said, "No one has the right to hold a gun to your face or stick a knife to your back. You should be safe. There were women...but no one stuck for more than a couple of weeks."

I was surprised. "Why?"

"Because I'm a difficult man, Brianne!" he said in an irritated tone. "No woman will want to have a relationship with me! No woman *can!*"

His voice was so forceful, it made me turn away from him. I swallowed hard and then I turned around to get up from the bed and walk out of the room.

I heard his sharp intake of breath as I exited the bedroom, and before I knew it, I felt him pull my arm, and then I was enclosed in his tight embrace. I closed my eyes. I didn't hug him back. He didn't say anything, but he kept hugging me tightly, and I was almost afraid I would be crushed.

"I don't want to fight with you, Brianne," he whispered softly. "Especially not on the first day of our engagement." It seemed that he was struggling for words. "But it is true...as you will soon find out when you live in my world. I'm a difficult man. I'm ruthless! Heartless even! I do not care about other people's emotions. Maybe that is why I was getting better at my game. Because I see things logically all the time. I make decisions based on what I think would be most profitable. Regardless of what's at stake. I'm a stone, you know!"

I shook my head. "If you were a stone, Travis, you wouldn't be standing here, holding me!"

Instead of letting go, he hugged me tighter. "You're probably the only one allowed to see me...weak. Maybe it's because you're the only thing left to remind me what it's like to feel love...and pain." He took another long breath. "Maybe it's a good thing that you're the one I'm marrying. If it were somebody else, I'd probably just break her heart, shred her to pieces."

"And you can't afford to hurt me...because you promised Tom you wouldn't."

He sighed but chose not to answer that. Then he pulled away to look at me in the eyes. "I'm sorry I raised my voice at you. I will try my best not to let that happen again."

I smiled at him. I took a deep breath and I stood on my tiptoes so I could give him a kiss on the lips. I knew I wouldn't normally do that. But it was something that I would have to get used to. Something that I should be comfortable doing from now on to make it easier to pretend in front of everybody else. He was my fiancé now. Everything was real.

He took a deep breath and leaned his forehead against mine. "You're a good man, Travis. I know you are. You can pretend to be ruthless all you want. But nothing can change the way I see you. I know you have a heart. And I know that even though you're just doing this as a favor, I still am a lucky girl to have you for my husband."

He smiled ruefully. "You have so much faith in me, Brianne. Sometimes I don't think I deserve it."

"You do," I said and gave him a hug again. "And I won't stop believing in you, Travis."

***

The next day we were in Manhattan. Travis took my hand in his as we entered his building.

I couldn't help but notice that everybody on our way upstairs seemed to have frozen in place when Travis walked past them. Everybody greeted him formally, *Good afternoon, Mr. Cross.* And then the path seemed to just open up for him, like everybody in the building knew better than block his way.

Travis walked past every single one of them without a word, not even a nod. It was as if he didn't hear them…they didn't exist, except for the bellhop who brought my bags up.

A man in an Armani suit opened Travis's penthouse suite.

"Mr. Cross," he greeted Travis. He didn't smile, either. But I didn't miss the quick look he gave me.

"Call the landlord, Karl," Travis said in a cold, commanding voice.

"Right away, Mr. Cross," Karl said. He turned to the bellhop, gave him a tip, and immediately asked him to go.

Travis turned to me. When he saw me standing beside a couch eyeing him curiously, he said, "You can sit, you know. This is your home now."

"Oh. I was waiting for you to tell me what to do," I said wryly.

Travis didn't miss the sarcasm in my voice, but instead of answering back, he turned away from me and went to the bar and poured himself a whiskey.

Karl came back with a man in his fifties. They stood behind Travis.

"Mr. Cross. Welcome back," the man greeted him.

Travis got straight to the point. "This is Brianne Montgomery," he introduced me to both Karl and the landlord. "She's my fiancée. She's going to live with me in this apartment. Tell all your staff that I want them to treat her with the same courtesy you give me. I don't want any of your guys giving her problems. Am I understood?"

The man nodded. "Yes, Mr. Cross."

Travis turned his back on them. That must have meant they were dismissed now. They turned around, and the man nodded at me. I stood up from my seat and ran after them just as they were about to reach the door.

"I'm sorry, I didn't get your name," I said to the older man.

He stared back at me blankly. "Excuse me?"

I smiled at him brightly. I extended my hand to his. "You can call me Brianne."

He shook my hand and smiled. "I'm sorry, Miss Brianne. My name is Andres Ferguson."

"Nice to meet you Mr. Ferguson," I said.

Then I turned to Karl. He was staring back at me in wild amazement. "I'm...Karl Dereks. I'm Mr. Cross's P.A.," he said in a voice that was too feminine to belong to a straight man.

"It's nice to meet you," I smiled.

Mr. Ferguson nodded at me and then he exited through the door.

"Are you hungry, Brianne?" Travis asked, walking toward me and Karl.

I nodded. "Kind of."

"What do you want to eat? We can have food delivered."

I shrugged. "Asian cuisine should be fine."

Travis nodded and turned to Karl. "Go to Pearl de Oriente. When you get there, read me the menu. You can bring the food over."

Karl nodded.

I glared at Travis. He raised a brow at me.

I turned to Karl. "I'm new in the city! Perhaps if I go with you, I can start learning the streets of New York."

"You will not walk the streets of New York, there's no need for you to know them."

"How do you expect me to get around?"

"I'm arranging for a limo and a driver to be at your disposal wherever you go."

"Great! Lovely!" I rolled my eyes. "No, thank you. I'm not crippled. And I need to make new friends in the city. Perhaps Karl is a good start." I turned to Karl. "I'll come with you."

He was open-mouthed as if he was appalled that I was daring him to defy Travis's command. But I pulled him by the arm and started for the door. Then, just before we stepped out of the apartment, I turned to Travis and said, "*I'll* read you the menu!"

I pulled Karl with me, closing the door behind us. He was still staring at me widely.

"What?" I asked.

He shook his head. "You're going to get me fired!"

I laughed. "If he fires you for this, let me know," I said. "I'm pretty sure I can make him hire you back."

He gave me a weird look and asked, "*Who are you?*"

I laughed at that. "I'm Travis's angel counterpart," I joked.

When I called Travis to read him exactly what was on the restaurant menu, he didn't even make me start. "Order whatever you want, and bring the same thing for me. Karl has my credit card. He'll pay for the bill."

"Are you sure you don't have a personal preference?" I asked, provoking him.

"You know I'm not going to let you read that menu!" he said in a frustrated voice.

"I don't mind, Trav."

"Brianne…are you testing my patience?"

"Hmmm…nope. But maybe I want to find out just how short your temper really is," I said evenly.

"Very short," he answered curtly. "So please hurry home." Then he hung up the phone.

Karl stood in front of me open-mouthed. "Okay, so I'm personally your fan now!" he said.

"What are you talking about?"

"That is just amazing! I think this is the first time I ever saw someone stand up to Travis Cross!" he said.

I laughed and then turned to the waiter and ordered three of their beef set specialty.

"Why three? Their servings here are massive," Karl said.

"Yes. The other one is for you."

Karl shook his head. "No, no. I can't."

"Consider it my treat," I said to him, smiling. Then I turned to the waiter. "Please don't put sesame seeds on one of the sets."

"Are you allergic to sesame seeds?"

I shook my head. "But Travis is."

"How did you know that? I've worked with him for three years and that never came up. Who are you and where did you come from?"

I laughed again. "I've known Travis since we were ten," I said. "He was my brother's best friend."

"How did you...end up engaged?"

"Ahhh..." I hesitated. I didn't know how to say this. "Spur of the moment, I guess. Things just sort of happened. But before that, Travis and I were...like the best of friends."

"How could you be best friends *and* engaged to an intimidating man like that?" he asked. "And how can you spite him...and make him bend?"

"I don't really have an answer to that," I said. "Since my brother died, Travis sort of...took it upon himself to take care of me. We've known each other for years."

"And that makes it easier for you to stand up to him," Karl said. "Do you mind if I look at your ring?" he asked.

I nodded and extended my hand to him. "Didn't he ask you to pick this one out?"

He shook his head. "I know rings. This is gorgeous! The design is nothing like you'll see in the shops today. It's absolutely out of this world!" He looked at me. "Perhaps this is an heirloom?"

I pulled back my hand and stared at the design of the ring. The center stone was probably four carats or more, and the diamond was very clear. There were stones and carvings on the side that made it look elegant and classic. It was a beautiful ring. And I knew it was more expensive than any of the rings I'd dreamt of wearing whenever I thought about being proposed to.

"Where do you live?" I asked him.

"Same building as you," Karl replied. "Travis was generous enough to rent an apartment for me. Part of my package." And he seemed really happy.

We walked back to the building. "Are you sure you're okay? You walked a couple of blocks!"

I laughed. "I'm a part-time dancer. I have much more stamina than you think."

"You dance?" he asked. "Ballet?"

I shook my head. "Contemporary. And sometimes jazz, hip-hop. I'll probably try breakdancing soon!"

He grinned. "Wow! You're cool! No wonder he's smitten with you."

When we reached the lobby of the building, I told him that he could have lunch in his apartment.

"But Mr. Cross might need something."

"And I'm here to take care of that. I'm sure he will not need a rundown of what happened to his businesses while he was gone. Just go to your apartment and enjoy your lunch. I'll bring our lunch up. And besides, he might be pissed off with me when I get back. You don't need to be there when we have our verbal judo!"

I took the paper bags from Karl when we entered the elevator. He pressed his floor.

"Are you sure this is okay? I'm worried."

I smiled at him. "I promise you won't get 'disciplinary action' for this."

He grinned. "You're a breath of fresh air, Brianne Montgomery. I think you really are what a guy like Travis Cross needs in his life."

When I opened the door of Travis's apartment, he was leaning on one of the walls, watching me come in.

"Where is Karl?"

"I sent him to his apartment to have lunch."

He narrowed his eyes at me.

"It's lunchtime, Travis," I said. "The guy's been waiting on you for hours. He needs nourishment if you want to keep your assistant for a very long time. And whatever you need for the next hour, I think I can handle it."

I placed the paper bags on the table and prepared our food. When all was ready, I came to find Travis. He was sitting on the balcony, staring at his wonderful view. He seemed lost in his thoughts.

I knew that he was raging mad at me right then. Travis was used to having things in order. I was slowly disturbing that balance, and I knew he wasn't happy about it.

But he was too tense all the time. I knew he didn't have to apply military tactic to everything he did. The Travis I knew still knew how to have fun, how to let things go. He used to be so mischievous and naughty when we were growing up. He even managed to joke and laugh whenever we saw each other in Connecticut. Now, here in his own world, he seemed engulfed with an invisible cold, tough case.

"Lunch is ready," I said to him.

He slowly stood up from the chair and faced me. I smiled at him. He didn't smile back.

I sighed. And because I didn't know how to please him better, I stepped closer to him and gave him a hug. He didn't hug me back, but I kept my patience.

"You said it wasn't going to be easy for me to live with you," I said. "Well, it isn't going to be easy for you, either. Because while you're cold and ruthless, I'm warm and sunny, remember?" I stared up at him. "Do you want me to stop smiling all the time?"

He stared down at me for a long moment. And as if realization had seeped through to him, he took a deep breath. He wound his arms around me and gave me a kiss on the forehead. "No," he whispered. "I wouldn't want you to stop smiling at all."

I smiled. "I love you, Travis," I said to him. I meant that. I might not love him as a lover, but I knew I loved Travis with all my heart.

"You're the only thing I have left to love," he whispered.

I pulled away from him. "Come. Lunch is waiting."

***

Over the next week, I settled into Travis's apartment. He was busy most of the time, but he checked up on me almost every hour. He left at eight in the morning and came home between eight and eleven at night.

I usually waited up for him. When he came home, I took off his coat, put his shoes back on the rack, and asked him if he'd had dinner. Usually, we had midnight snacks together on his balcony, and he told me bits and pieces of what had happened during the day.

"I'll go to the gallery tomorrow," I told him one night. "I haven't called Mom yet. Perhaps I will surprise her. I sent her my resignation from our branch in Connecticut. She told me she would talk to me when she gets back from Paris. That's tomorrow."

Travis nodded. "I'll send a car to drive you."

I shook my head. "I can take the train, Travis. You don't have to worry about that."

186

He raised a brow at me. "You're my fiancée, Brianne. You won't take the train."

"You don't have to spoil me, Travis. I'm just an ordinary girl," I said to him.

"Brianne, could you please…at least for the first few weeks while you're still settling in…just allow me to do this," he pleaded.

I sighed in defeat. Then I nodded. "Okay. But once I'm settled, the car and driver need to go."

"What time are you coming home?" he asked.

I shrugged. "I'll go around noon. I'll probably be back around five. Why? Do you need anything?"

He shook his head. "Just give me a call if you do."

I slept on the bed, Travis slept on the couch in the bedroom. It was big enough to be a bed. Once or twice, when I couldn't wait up for him, he slept in the guest bedroom, just so he wouldn't disturb me when he came in.

Living with Travis was not as hard as I thought it would be. There were a couple of times that I still stared in space and thought about Chris…the last man I was in love with. But anger immediately crept in when I remembered Alana and how she was in his apartment a couple of hours after Chris and I broke up.

I had yet to give up my apartment. I'd sell my stuff…as soon as the idea that I'd be living with Travis for a very long time sunk in.

My mother was surprised when she saw me at her doorstep the next day.

"I saw the limo, and you're the last person I was expecting to step out of it!" she said, hugging me.

"It's nice to see you, Mom." I hugged her back.

We sat at the coffee table by her glass window.

"What happened? You are resigning? And now I see you in Manhattan, being driven around in a limo."

I took a deep breath. "Well, I might be living in Manhattan for a while."

"Why are you leaving your life in Connecticut behind? Everything okay?"

I nodded. "Everything's fine." Although I still thought about Chris once in a while.

187

"I would like to have you here. I need help managing this branch when I travel most of the time," she said. "And I think you'll be safer here."

I raised a brow and giggled. "This city is not crime-free, Mom."

"True. But Travis is here," she said. "I know you'll be well looked-after here." She looked at the limo outside. "I take it you have seen each other already."

I smiled. "How else could I afford that?"

"He spoils you," she smiled. "By the way…are you still with that guy you brought to Aunt Vicki's party? Is he…getting close to popping the question? You're gonna be thirty soon, you know."

I sighed. I shook my head. "No, Mom. Unfortunately, that didn't work out."

She was taken aback. "Oh my God, sweetheart," she sighed. "You've broken up? Why? I thought you'd been dating for a while now."

I nodded. "But apparently, he has so much insecurity in life. He doesn't sit well with…our marrying-early tradition."

My mother looked at me apologetically. "Oh, sweetheart. It doesn't matter," she said. "I married your father young and look where we are now. Don't mind the stupid family tradition. I don't think it's true. It's better to wait for the right man to come."

I laughed. "Thanks, Mom. But I'm not going to be the subject of table talks and family gossip, or risk being 'cursed' in love for life. I do intend to get married this year."

"Well, this Chris character should come to his senses! He should know what a beautiful, amazing woman you are!"

"I'm not marrying Chris," I said to her.

She looked confused and then her eyes drifted off to my finger. She immediately pulled my hand to examine my ring.

"What the…" she started. "This is expensive! And it looks like an heirloom! Are you marrying royalty?"

I laughed. "No. But I know he's rich. Although that isn't the reason why I'm marrying him."

"You just broke up with Chris. How come you're marrying another man? Chris didn't propose to you and you dated him for two years. How long have you been seeing your fiancé?"

I shrugged. "Forever, I guess." Because Travis and I never really started dating, I couldn't figure out the right answer to that.

"Who is this guy?"

"Take a wild guess, Mom. I think I've only known *one* filthy rich guy in my life," I replied.

She was thoughtful for a while, and then her eyes widened. "You're kidding!"

I shook my head and smiled. I think I was blushing, too.

"I didn't even know you two were dating!" she said. Then she narrowed her eyes at me. "Don't tell me you two just got drunk one night and then you got pregnant and you decided to get married. Because I will kill Travis if that is the reason!"

I laughed. "Relax, Mom. That's not it," I said. "I guess…Travis and I had always thought we'd get married one day. We treat each other like family anyway. I guess marriage is the way to make it official."

My mother stared at me as if she was reading me. I felt nervous for a while, afraid that she might see through me, but what did I have to hide?

I loved Travis; he loved me. That was true. We didn't love each other like lovers, but still we loved each other nonetheless. That counted for a lot. We promised to look after each other for the rest of our lives. That was a lifetime vow in itself. He did propose to me; I said yes. I had an engagement ring. The wedding would take place in a couple of months. So in truth, there was nothing to be guilty about. This engagement was as real as the real thing.

"Are you happy?" she asked.

I would not be 'cursed' by my family. I would not join their Hall of Shame. I would marry a guy who loved me and would take care of me better than any other guy could…and would do a better job than my father ever did. I was recovering from my breakup with Chris in record time. I had a new life to look forward to. I didn't have to worry about losing Travis, at least for the next couple of years. What could be happier than that?

I nodded. "Yes, Mom. You know I am."

She smiled at me and tears rolled down her cheeks. "I have been…a bad mother, Brianne. I abandoned you so many times, and in so many ways. But I'm glad you turned out okay. And I'll always be indebted to Travis for looking out for you during those times that we couldn't. Travis…is one of the many things we will always thank Thomas for."

Tears rolled down my cheeks, too. Because now, more than ever, I felt that I was not only doing the safe thing by marrying Travis. I was doing the right thing.

When I got back to Travis's apartment, I was surprised that he was home. The table was set for two. He emerged from the balcony with a beer in his hand.

"There you are!" he said. "I have a surprise for you."

I smiled excitedly. "Really?"

He took my hand in his and pulled me toward the balcony. There, I saw an easel and a cabinet full of art supplies.

"Oh my God!" I breathed.

I realized just how much I'd missed painting. I felt nostalgic and excited at the same time. Travis just reminded me what I'd been missing about myself all this time.

"I figured you'd want to start making that masterpiece of yours. Paint the world, the way you see it."

I lunged forward and gave him a hug. "Thank you, Travis!" For years, with Chris, I'd barely bought a brush. He wasn't fond of seeing me being idle and just painting. He never told me to stop painting, but he also didn't encourage it. And now, I realized just how much I'd really missed it, how much I missed that part of myself.

Travis hugged me back. "You're welcome, *cherie*." Then he pulled away from me. "How did your chat with your mother go?"

I smiled at him. "Great! She cried, of course. She said she felt indebted to you forever since you've been taking care of me since I was…fifteen."

He looked at me with a sober expression on his face. "And now I will take care of you for the years to come."

"Until I find the right one," I said, examining the canvass on the easel.

He didn't answer. When I stared back at him, his expression was fathomless.

"Do you mind at all, Travis? That you'll look after me for a couple years more?"

He pulled me to him again. "I'm not worried about that," he said. "With me, I'm sure you're taken care of. It's after the divorce that I'm worried about."

I stared up at him. "Why?"

"I will only give you a divorce if you are sure that you've found the right one. That the guy you find will give you the life you deserve."

"And you're willing to stay married to me until I find him? What if...I find him after five years, or ten years? Will you stand by me for that long?"

"Yes," he replied without hesitation.

"What about your own life, Travis?"

He took a deep breath. He pulled me against his chest and inhaled through my hair. "You're going to be my life now. Before you, I wouldn't think about marriage at all."

"You're saying that because you haven't found her yet. But someday, Trav, you will find the girl you want to spend the rest of your nights with."

He chuckled humorlessly, as if he thought that was an offensive joke.

"I'm not kidding! When you do, you'll want to marry her...and stay married to her for the rest of your life," I said.

"Is that what you were looking for?" he asked. "A guy you wanted to stay married to for the rest of your life?"

I giggled. And then I nodded. "Yes. And a guy who wanted to stay married to me forever. Because he loved me...because I ignited his senses, and he couldn't live a day without me. Not just because I forced him into this fate a long time ago."

He fell silent for a while. Then he said, "Until you find him, I'll stand beside you."

Tears rolled down my cheeks. I hugged Travis tighter. "Thank you, Travis."

"For what?"

I took a deep breath. "For you."

# Chapter Seventeen

In the mornings, I made sure I was up to make coffee for Travis before he left for work. I did his tie and helped him put on his suit.

He smiled at me. "You'll do a good job at being Mrs. Cross," he teased. "I'm beginning to get used to this."

I laughed. "And who said you were difficult to live with?"

Travis rarely came home at eleven in the evenings anymore. Most of the time, it was earlier than that, and we had dinner together.

One night, he came home late and I had fallen asleep on the living room couch waiting for him. When I woke up again, I was already back in the bed with Travis snoring quietly on the couch.

I had a chat on the phone with Karl one Friday night. He warned me that Travis was in a foul mood. He'd had a meeting with his father, and it didn't go well.

"Like how bad?"

"Really bad. Travis was pushing his father to the wall, making him realize that he didn't have any other choice but to sell. When the older Mr. Cross realized he was losing more and more to his son each day, he tried different tactics."

"What tactics?"

"Since he couldn't win with Travis arguing about business, he decided to throw a few insults on the table," Karl replied. "He called him insulting names. This way, he knew Travis would never fight back. The guy still has some respect for his old man. I salute him. Anyway, just to give you fair warning if he comes home cranky! He has a dinner meeting with one of our shareholders so he'll be home late. You may want to be asleep already when he comes home. We stay out of his way when he's on the warpath. I wonder what you do."

"Thanks, Karl. I'm sure I can handle that."

I waited for Travis that night. I was in the bedroom when he arrived at ten. He gave me a smile that didn't reach his eyes and didn't say anything. He went to take a shower.

I was sitting on the bed when he came out of the bathroom wearing only a pair of boxers. He sat on the couch without a word. He looked lost in his thoughts.

I climbed out of bed and approached him. He gave me one hard look, when I looked down at him. Somehow, I could see his soul through his eyes. He was filled with anger and pain—feelings he was struggling to hide. He took a deep breath and then he wound one arm around my waist, pulling me to him. He rested his cheek against my belly, his arms tight around me. I hugged his head to me. I realized that he was in tears. But he was quiet. He didn't let out a whimper or utter a word. I continued caressing the back of his neck gently, letting him know that somehow, I heard the words he couldn't say.

We stayed like that for about fifteen minutes. Then I gently pushed him back to the couch and he pulled me with him. I sat on his lap and rested my head against his shoulder as he continued holding me.

"Do you want to talk about it?" I asked quietly.

"No," he whispered. "But I would like you to stay with me for a while."

I nodded. I circled an arm around his waist and hugged him, too. We stayed on the couch quietly. After a while, I must have fallen asleep. When I woke up, I was locked in Travis's arms. We'd both fallen asleep.

I felt Travis's arms on me tighten. He gently caressed my arm. I looked up at him. He was awake, too.

I leaned up and kissed his jaw. He caressed the top of my head and continued holding me.

"I know it's your father," I whispered and he sucked in a deep breath. "You don't have to be affected by him so much."

"For someone who's family, you'd actually expect the man to behave better."

"Why do you hate each other so much? I've been asking you that question for years. You never told me. Maybe I can understand your pain better if you tell me." I propped up on one elbow so I could look into his eyes.

He sucked in a deep breath and then he said, "My father is a soulless man. He beat up my mother. There were times he even…" He took a deep breath. "He even raped her." I watched Travis struggle to remember the painful memories. I rested back on the couch, against

194

his shoulder, to make it easier for him to tell the story. I caressed his arm to provide whatever form of comfort I could. "He beat me, too. When he got drunk, he'd lock me up in closets, hit me in the head. He almost drowned me in the tub when I was nine." I was appalled, but I refused to let a whimper escape me. Travis didn't need that.

"He and my mother didn't really want a child. They didn't want the responsibility. When my mother decided she'd had enough, she just moved out of the house...she didn't consider me in the equation. When I was in high school, I started excelling in sports and academics. That's when my father realized that I was smart. He started taking interest in me. I was going to be a trophy that he could be proud of. But I had a rough childhood. My father had at least three mistresses." He took a deep breath.

"He saw women as toys that he could play with. At an early age, I was exposed to loose, gold-digging women." He paused for a while. Then he continued, "My father's birthday gift to me when I was twelve was a woman twice my age. I was young, Brianne!" he said in a rough voice. "I was innocent. I felt..." He trailed off. "Molested! I lost my virginity to one of the women my father picked up somewhere. How twisted is that?!" He took a deep breath and for a while, I thought he was struggling to continue. I reached out for his hand and squeezed it to make him understand that it was okay. He could tell me his secrets. He was not alone.

He kissed the top of my head, and then he took a deep breath before he continued his story. "From then on, I felt ashamed of my family. I think I disowned them a long time ago. That's why I ran away from him whenever he'd come home. I'd sleep at your house. There were times when his bodyguards found me. They would force me to go home. They'd tie me up and carry me to my dad. And I would receive a good beating afterward."

I propped up on my elbow again. I stared into Travis's eyes. He was crying. I realized then just how torn and broken he really was. And I felt for the boy he used to be. The mischievous kid I used to hate when I was younger. Underneath the strong, naughty façade was a scared little boy...abandoned and abused.

"I was alone from the time I was ten. Then I had your family," he said. "Before Thomas died, you were all I had. He knew everything. He didn't tell you. I asked him not to. I was afraid my father would abuse me and my mother more if anybody knew. And I was afraid of what my father would do to your family, too.

"When I was a teenager, I was a mischievous daredevil. But can you blame me? I got the concept of right and wrong from a few maids, butlers, nannies, and mostly the television. I started taking care of myself. I started choosing what I wanted to learn in life. I was racing even before I got my driver's license." He sucked in a deep breath and fell silent for a while.

I stared up at him. He gave me one hard look. I saw guilt, remorse, and hatred cross his face all at the same time. Then he said in a broken voice, "You're going to hate me for this, Brianne." I didn't understand what he meant, but I dared not interrupt him. "That day…I got into a challenge with a bunch of kids. The bet was high. My Porsche. Tom warned me not to mind the kids from the other town. They were a bunch of lawless imbeciles. But I was too full of my own ego. I agreed to the bet—to race.

"The night before, I had an argument with my father. It was those times that I was already rebelling against him. I told him I had an important thing to go to. He didn't listen. He had his bodyguards kidnap me, tie me up, and lock me in my room. I wasn't able to make it to the race. But Tom was driving my car then. He waited for me to come. But I never showed up. I would forfeit my car…or my life if I didn't show up. Between Tom and me, I was the racer, the better driver. But Tom stood in for me…so I wouldn't lose my Porsche or risk being beaten to death by those guys. But damn! I would have given them all my cars…if I had known what was going to happen." Tears rolled down from his eyes.

My heart pounded inside my chest and I was confronted by a mixture of emotions. "Tom…took your place. He raced for you."

Travis closed his eyes. More tears rolled down his cheeks. "He died…I lived."

I couldn't understand the pain I felt. I cried once again for the brother I had lost. The sweet, happy-go-lucky, standup, responsible kid who was trying to look out for both Travis and me.

Travis crushed me into his arms. "I'm so sorry, Brianne," he whispered. This time, I couldn't control the tears that rolled down my cheeks. "Tom asked me not to tell you what really happened that night. But I can't lie to you anymore. I can't let Tom shield the truth from you just so you would think better of me. You see, Brianne, I'm not a

196

good person! I'm the reason why you lost your brother. I caused you all this pain, this misery. You lost your family because of me. You're alone because of me!

"Tom always sacrificed himself for the things he held dear. He would do anything for the people he loved," Travis said remorsefully. "I wish I hadn't been one of them! Because if I hadn't…then he would still be alive!"

Travis looked at me, shame and regret evident on his face. His expression was pleading, as if he were asking for my forgiveness. "I'm sorry, Brianne! I was the reason Tom was taken from you. And I will never forgive myself for that! I will never forgive my father for that night! If he…had been a good father…if he had learned how to listen to me…if he had just given me another punishment, like…grounding me or taking away my luxuries…I would still have found a way to make it that night. I would have saved Tom."

I could see Travis's guilt, his pain. He had carried this secret all these years. Every time he looked at me…he felt tormented for causing my brother's death.

My heart broke for him. It wasn't his fault. It was an accident. It must have killed him to carry this burden for almost half of his life.

I leaned forward and hugged him. To assure him that I didn't blame him…that I wasn't mad at him. "But, Travis…it could have been you, too!"

"That would have been better. I was meaningless compared to your brother! He had so much going for him. I didn't mean anything to anybody. The pain wouldn't have been much if I died and he lived!"

I pulled away from him. Now I was mad. "Don't say that! You meant something to us!" I said to him angrily. "And you mean the world to me now!"

I wanted to slap him in the face for thinking so lowly of himself. For thinking that nobody would care or cry if he died.

He hugged me to him again. "Sshhh…"

I couldn't stop crying now. I didn't…and wouldn't…hold my brother's death against Travis. It wasn't his fault. But I couldn't help getting mad at him for thinking nobody in this world would mourn for his death…that he didn't make a difference in anybody's life…especially in mine. Because I could never imagine my life without Travis, in the past, and now in the future.

"You always underestimate us, Travis! You underestimate the care and the love that the people around you have for you. Even now. You still think you are alone. You still think nobody cares for you. Nobody loves you." I whimpered against his chest. "Tom would have been devastated if you died in that race! I wouldn't be where I am now if you weren't with me all these years," I whimpered. He didn't say anything.

"You're so focused on the love that was not given to you by your parents...you fail to notice the love and respect that *are* being given to you by the other people around you. Tom would have felt the same way you did! He would have wanted you to live! I won't blame you for his death. It was his time. And maybe he chose to go. To give you a chance to find the love you deserve. So you could build a family of your own and make it so much different from what your parents built for you." I took a deep breath.

"You've become cold and ruthless! But I know you're not like that inside. You hide so much of your emotions. There's nothing wrong with risking it, Travis. You showed Tom love, and you never regretted it when he was gone. Because you've done your part. Because 'til the end, you were brothers! But now, you refuse to open up yourself and love another. You're becoming the same person that you hate the most—your father!" I propped up on my elbow and stared at him again. "You're better than that, Travis. I know you are. I believe you are."

I took a deep breath. "You're a smart man. People respect you for that. You don't have to be an asshole all the time. You make people's lives difficult, and I know you're doing that on purpose! Because you refuse to show any sign of weakness. Being thoughtful, considerate, and sweet doesn't make you less of a man, Travis.

"You have to risk your heart. Because someday, these people will not be around you anymore. But at least, you won't regret making them a part of your world. You don't have to live alone all the time. Because if you just open your eyes...you'll know that you're not. There are a lot of people in your world who care about you."

He stared at me for a moment and then touched my cheek with his palm. "Will you stay with me for a long time?"

I smiled gently. "You know I will." And I meant that. I realized I hadn't really understood Travis that much...until now. He had been deeply hurt when he was a boy. He was a victim of pain and neglect.

The first person who really cared about him was taken away from him. From then, it was easy to distant himself...so he wouldn't feel any more pain. So he wouldn't feel abandoned again. And I couldn't blame him for feeling that much anger with his father. Anybody would feel the same. I would break if that ever happened to me.

Travis took a deep breath. "I was...afraid to need you, Brianne," he said. "But God knows I do!" He crushed me into his arms once again.

I smiled. It was probably the first time that I could do something for Travis. For years, it had always been the other way around. He had always been there for me. I rarely ever did anything for him.

"I'm here for you, Travis." I reached up and leaned my forehead against his. "Don't ever push me away."

He chuckled humorlessly. "I'm going to marry you, Brianne. You got me tied down, how could I push you away?"

I glared at him. "You know very well that's not what I meant."

He stared at me deeply. "Do you really think you can save me?" he asked softly.

I smiled slowly. "I can. I will." I leaned forward and gave him another kiss on the jaw. Then I rested my head on his shoulder again.

He held me against him tightly. We lay there for a while, lost in our own thoughts, and yet savoring each other's warmth, knowing that the bond we shared had just become stronger than ever. I understood him better. And now he knew he could trust me to stand beside him, the way that he had always stood beside me.

I heard him suck in a deep breath. "I could get used to this, you know."

"What?"

"This...easy, comforting conversation," he whispered. "This...marriage."

"It couldn't be that bad," I said.

He shook his head. Then he kissed the top of my head. "No. It's not bad at all." He reached for my hand and brought it to his lips. He kissed my fingers. "Goodnight, Brianne."

I took a deep breath. "Goodnight, Travis."

And we fell asleep in each other's arms on the couch.

# Chapter Eighteen

The next Friday night, I was having coffee with Eric. He was on a business trip in Manhattan. He figured he'd see me first before he went back to Connecticut.

We were interrupted when my phone rang. My heart pounded when I saw Chris's number on the screen.

"Chris. What's he calling me for?"

"Realizing what a big fool he's been?" Eric suggested.

I answered the call. "What?"

I heard Chris's intake of breath on the other line. "Brianne..." His voice was sober. "I've been waiting for you in your apartment."

"What? Who told you to go there? I should have changed the locks! I cannot believe you had the nerve to actually use your keys!"

He didn't say anything for a while. He took another deep breath. "Are you coming home anytime soon? It's been nearly two weeks now. And I see no signs of you. I dropped by the dance studio, hoping you'd be there. Sarah told me you'd gone to Manhattan."

"I'm selling everything in that apartment!" I muttered.

"Are you...moving to Manhattan for good?"

"Yes. Why not? Everything I love is in Manhattan!"

"Including Travis Cross?" he asked.

"*Especially* Travis Cross!" I snapped. "Did you call me for a good reason, Chris?"

He took a deep breath. "I guess...I just want to apologize for everything. I was...I don't know what came over me. I talked to Cindy again. She told me everything. She also told me that you didn't see Cross again until graduation. That he avoided you after the huge favor you asked of him."

"I still don't see this as a good reason."

"You were a stupid girl in high school, weren't you?" he asked, and he chuckled humorlessly. "I was even more stupid for letting jealousy cloud my thinking! I'm so sorry, honey." He was crying now.

I bit my lip, trying to get a grip of all the emotions enveloping me. But out of all those feelings, I recognized the most potent one—anger.

201

"If there's a way…if there's ever a way that I can make that up to you, I would do anything! I love you, Brianne! I promise I'll never forget that again. And if…if you say that you and Cross are like brother and sister more than anything…I will believe you. I will…get to know the guy! I'll do anything just to be given another chance!"

"How many hours after we broke up did you sleep with Alana?" I asked him.

Silence.

Then a sharp intake of breath. "That's…not fair, Brianne! I was drunk! I was a mess!"

I took a deep breath. "How stupid do you think I am?"

"I know you're not stupid! I was just shooting for another chance. I realized how…different you were! I guess I had to be with Alana to realize what an amazing woman I was already in love with! And I may never forgive myself for hurting you. But I want just one chance. And I will use that to make it up to you. Even if I have to make it up to you for the rest of our lives!" He kept on crying. And I felt like crying, too.

"Brianne…I realized that it's you. I miss the warm smile you have when I wake up in the morning. I want to have kids with your hair, your eyes, your smile…and you can teach them how to paint, how to dance. I was so wrong…" He paused. He sucked in a deep breath and then he said, "There are more important things that matter in life. And I want my life to be filled with your laughter, your smile. If…if you'll have me…we can plan our wedding! Cindy told me about your family tradition and how pressured you were to get married by the time you're thirty-one. I would rather rush you to the altar…than not have you at all in my life! I guess it takes something like this to realize a lot of things. I love you! I am not asking for much. Just a chance!"

I didn't say anything. I couldn't. Tears were rolling down my cheeks now, but I didn't want him to realize that.

Why would Chris call me and ask me this now? Now that I had started settling in my new life? That I had gotten comfortable with my life with Travis? That I was beginning to find a routine with Travis?

"I can't," I said. I tried my best to keep my voice steady. "I can't trust you anymore, Chris. I didn't do anything wrong. I was happy…all in love with you, introducing you to my family…and you went all cold, accusing me of sleeping with the person who's probably the only close family I have left…the only tie that binds me to my brother. And if that wasn't enough, you slept with Alana. You wouldn't have touched her if you didn't have the hots for her long before we had a fight. You weren't just devastated! You were waiting to find an excuse to justify…having a *taste*! And I can't be with a guy whose love and loyalty for me was…so weak!" I took a deep breath. "And it's too late now, Chris! I can't go back!" And I hung up on him.

Eric didn't say anything. He put an arm around me to provide the only thing I needed at that moment—comfort.

"If I didn't know your sexual preference, Eric, you would be flying to the street corner by now," I heard a cold voice say behind us.

I didn't turn around. Instead, I quickly wiped my eyes and my cheeks.

Travis sat in the empty seat in front of us. My efforts to hide my tears were futile. He was, after all, the one person who could read me like a book.

"Who died?" he asked icily.

I glared at him.

"I guess Christian came to his senses and wanted our girl back," Eric replied for me.

Travis narrowed his eyes. "I hope you didn't say yes."

"Of course not," I said. "He…said he'd marry me right away. He'd make it up to me for the rest of my life."

"Did he also say he'd give you the moon and the stars?" Travis asked sarcastically.

"Well, at least he's realized this now," Eric said. "You could have gotten back together with him…had he not slept with somebody else. And you were right. He wouldn't have touched that slut if he hadn't been interested in her beforehand!" Eric smiled at me encouragingly. "You did the right thing, sweetie."

When I looked at Travis, I saw that he was staring at me with a cold, measuring expression. He was reading my wordless reactions toward Christian. I blushed. It was one of those times when Travis stared at me like that and I felt unnerved all of a sudden.

I turned away from him for a minute. When I looked at him again, he gave me a crooked smile.

Eric told us that he was meeting another friend in half an hour, and he'd leave us alone. He promised to visit again the next month.

I was left with Travis. He stood up and placed some bills on the table for the coffee that Eric and I drank.

"Where are we going?" I asked.

"Let's take your mind off your stupid ex. I don't like seeing you this way," he said, pulling my hand.

"What way?" I asked.

He turned to me. Then he took a deep breath and said, "Having second thoughts about marrying me."

I stopped in my tracks. That wasn't my intention. I never had any second thoughts about marrying Travis. Of course, it only felt natural to feel pain again after Chris called, but the thought of breaking off my engagement with Travis never really crossed my mind.

Especially now...when Travis and I had formed a bond different from the one we used to have. When we now both seemed to feel comfortable about the prospect of marrying each other. When our relationship had changed from being the best of friends to being betrothed. When recently, I found myself constantly finding comfort in his arms, and he seemed comfortable in taking down his cold, ruthless mask in front of me.

Travis raised a brow at me, as if challenging me to deny that. I glared at him. He wasn't trying to hide the fact that he was pissed. He continued staring at me with a cold expression on his face.

Because I didn't know what else to do or how to prove to him that I never had second thoughts about our engagement, I reached up and gave him a quick kiss on the lips.

Then I walked away as fast as I could. I was pretty sure I was blushing like hell. Travis caught up with me after a few seconds. We walked in silence.

Finally, I looked up at him. He had a grin on his face, one that I had never seen before. It was mischievous, boyish, and teasing. I glared at him again. Finally, he laughed. Without saying anything, he took my hand in his and intertwined our fingers.

***

We went to dinner. Then we went to check out the bars. I had too much to drink, and I was tipsy and laughing all the way home.

I don't remember much, but I know I was still able to shower and dress into a matching pink silk cami and shorts.

When I woke up again, I found myself in bed, locked in Travis's arms.

I stared up at him. He smiled at me. "Good morning, angel," he whispered.

I smiled. "Good morning, Travis."

I glanced at the clock on our bedside table. It was already nine in the morning.

"What are you up to today?" I asked him.

He shook his head. "I thought I'd spend the whole day with my fiancée," he said. "After all, another guy is vying for her hand. Perhaps I should show her that she's still better off marrying me."

I laughed. "Will you let it go? You know I'm not going back to Chris," I said. "I haven't changed my mind. I'm still going to be Mrs. Travis Cross. And besides, shouldn't you be relieved that you have a chance to be off the hook? Off the vow I forced you to take fourteen years ago?"

"Fourteen years ago, I probably wouldn't have stopped you from going back to him," he said. "But things have changed now, haven't they?"

I stared up at his handsome face. He was right. Things had changed between us. It was like neither of us thought of marrying the other as a last resort anymore.

I rested my head on his shoulder. "Yes," I whispered softly.

He gave me a tight squeeze and I felt him kiss the top of my head. "When are you going to start preparing for our wedding?"

"When do you want to get married?" I asked.

"Three months?" he asked. "Is that enough time for you to prepare?"

I propped up on one elbow and stared back at him. "That soon?"

"I figured you'd want to be married before your thirtieth birthday," he said.

"Yes. But don't you need more time?"

"For what?"

I shrugged. "Get your women accustomed to the fact that you have to be discreet because you have a wife now?"

He fell silent. Then he took a deep breath. "If that is the case, then you need not worry about that at all."

"I can be toxic to you. I'm sorry," I whispered.

He reached for my hand and then brought it to his lips. "You don't need to say sorry. You are my fiancée. That is real. I will marry you. That's real too. So don't feel as if everything you ask of me is a favor.

205

Remember, I am Travis Cross. Nobody could force me to do something I don't want to do."

I felt touched by what he said. I closed my eyes for a moment. Somehow, I could not imagine myself being in Chris's arms anymore. Because, there in Travis's arms…I felt much safer.

Travis and I decided to spend the day at a resort. I had been indoors too long, and I missed swimming and basking in the sun.

We ran into Karl in the corridor on our way out. He looked lost in his thoughts, as if he was trying to compose some sentences.

"Karl!" I called him.

He froze when he saw us. "Good morning, Miss Montgomery. Mr. Cross."

"Are you okay?" I asked him.

He nodded.

Travis raised a brow at him. He didn't need to say anything, and I could tell Karl swallowed hard before opening his mouth to speak.

"Sir…" he started. "I was…going to ask if…if…if I could take Monday off…I mean…I don't think it's going to be a busy day…"

"Don't you think it's up to me to say if Monday is a busy day or not? If you're not busy, Karl, maybe I should start reviewing your job description…or your salary package," Travis said in a cold, unemotional voice.

"Yes, sir," Karl said immediately. "I'll be in the office on Monday!"

And with a slumped shoulder, he turned on his heel and walked toward the stairs, obviously not wanting to share the elevator with us.

I glared at Travis.

"What?" he asked.

"You didn't even wait to hear what he was about to ask you! For all you know, he needs to take the day off because one of his loved ones is sick! Just because you don't have family doesn't mean everybody else around you doesn't have one, either."

"Of course I have family. You. Not my fault if you rarely get sick I don't have to take a day off work."

"How could you be so…insensitive to the people around you?"

Travis took a deep breath. "Let's not fight about this, Brianne," he said. "Don't ruin our day because of one of my employees."

"You only look at Karl as an employee," I said. "But if you really look closely, you will see that the guy cares about you. He knows what

206

you want and do not want! He's sensitive about your preferences and your needs."

"You make me sound so gay, Brianne! Cut that out."

"You know what I mean, Travis!" I said, this time raising my voice. "Karl takes his job to a different level! He's a high-caliber employee. You should be lucky you have him as your assistant."

"And I thank him enough every time he gets his paycheck. More than enough, actually, if you know how much he's earning."

"And because of that he's lost his right to be...treated with consideration?"

Travis sighed. The elevator door opened into our parking lot. "What do you really want me to do, Brianne? Just say it and I'll do it, and let's get it over with."

"I want you to find out what Karl wants to do on Monday and give him the day off if it's reasonable to do so."

He handed me his phone. "You thought of it—you do it."

"That's beside the point. I'm not Karl's boss," I said. "You are!"

"But since we got engaged, you've become the boss of me. Override my orders to my employees if you see fit!" he muttered, and then he turned toward his car.

I dialed Karl's number.

One ring.

"Yes, sir?" Karl asked in an alert voice.

"Travis runs a military rule in the office, doesn't he?" I asked, my tone light and teasing.

It took a moment for Karl to respond. "Am I...am I on speakerphone?" He really sounded scared.

"Of course not. You're on friendly grounds, don't worry."

"Thank you, Miss Montgomery. How can I assist you?"

"Why were you going to ask for a day off?"

It took a moment for him to respond. "Well, my grandmother is sick. I wanted to drive to Jersey to visit her for the day." His voice actually sounded teary.

"Oh, I'm sorry to hear that," I said sincerely. "Okay. You can take a day off."

"But...but Mr. Cross will not..."

"Will not contest that. I'll send you a text confirmation. Go visit your grandma. And buy her a box of cookies from me. Charge it to Travis's card—I'll just pay him back."

Karl didn't say anything for the next ten seconds.

"Karl?"

"Thank you, Miss Montgomery," he said. "My grandmother and I are very close. I really appreciate this. You're...a wonderful woman. You are the woman that Travis Cross needs."

I handed Travis his phone back.

"Happy?" Travis asked.

I raised a brow at him. "Yes. Because Karl's grandma is sick. I felt good about giving him the day off on your behalf."

I turned away from him. I heard him sigh, and then he gave my arm a tug and pulled me to him into a hug.

"Okay, it's done," he said. "Can we please stop fighting now?"

"I just want you to learn, Travis. Learn to be sensitive to the people around you. You'll know that more than half of them care about you sincerely."

He sighed. "I'll try...next time."

Travis checked us in to a suite. We had breakfast on the balcony and watched the people sunbathing by the poolside.

"Do you do this much?" I asked him.

He shook his head. "Rarely. The apartment has an indoor pool. I'm on the priority list."

I raised a brow.

He sighed. "It means they can kick anybody off of the poolside if I choose to go for a swim."

I narrowed my eyes at him. "People are at your disposal, and sometimes you like using the privilege."

He looked away from me and took a sip of his coffee. "What is the use of having privilege if you aren't going to use it?"

Logical. But then again, it wasn't right. Travis's disposition was improving. But I knew a total makeover was impossible overnight.

*Baby steps,* I thought to myself.

I stood up from the table, still angry but refusing to have another argument with Travis.

"I'll go change," I excused myself.

I took a quick shower, applied lotion on myself, and then finally changed into a two-piece suit.

I heard a knock on the bathroom door, and then Travis peeked in when I was trying to tie my halter-top bikini. I looked at him in the mirror.

"I was wondering what was taking you so long," he said. He opened the door. He was already in his board shorts.

Seeing that I was struggling to tie my top properly, he walked over to me and took the strings of my top in his hands. Carefully, he tied the strings. I felt self-conscious. I was only wearing matching boyshorts, and my back was bare in front of Travis as he tied my suit into a nice, secure knot. I was pretty sure I was blushing.

When he was done, he stared at me in the mirror. He took a deep breath. "Will you forgive me if I promise I will schedule my swims to make sure Mr. Ferguson need not kick anybody out of the pool from now on?"

I stared back at him. I realized then that he was trying to change his ways...for me...because he was slowly trying not to be such a difficult, ruthless man...the man he was all those years...the man his father made him to be.

I nodded. I turned around to face him and held my pinky up for him. He stared at it for a moment, and then he hooked his pinky to mine and smiled at me.

# Chapter Nineteen

I went to Travis's office on Monday. Since Karl wouldn't be in, I volunteered to help him out in case he needed assistance. But when I got there, I was the one surprised. There was an easel at one corner of his office, and the coffee table had a box of Godiva chocolates and a bouquet of roses on top of it.

"Is it always like this?" I asked him, looking at the lovely roses.

He stood behind me and wrapped his arms around my waist. "I have a special visitor today. I thought she'd like to indulge in a box of sweets."

I laughed and turned around so I could face him. "And the easel is for?"

He smiled and wrapped his arms around my waist again. "So you can paint or draw and leave me alone to my work."

"I can paint at home—why did you agree that I come here if you weren't going to need me anyway?"

He shrugged. "I just want you to be here." He hugged me to him. "I hope it isn't too much to ask."

I smiled. "No, compared to the favors I ask of you, this is nothing!"

Travis made some phone calls and did some work on his computer. He looked at me once in a while and he smiled or winked at me when he caught my eye.

I drew a picture of Travis in black and white. I painted his serious face: boyish, dangerous, handsome as hell. I stared at the painting when I finished it. His eyes were mesmerizing, and I felt warm knowing that familiar face. My knight. My angel.

"I look nothing like that!" he said, coming up behind me. He wound his arms around my waist and pulled me to him.

"Or course you do!" I protested.

"My hair is all wrong," he said.

I laughed. "I had to change that a little bit. I like your hair better when it's disheveled."

211

"My employees will not take me seriously if I come to work looking like I can't afford to buy a comb," he said laughing.

I turned around to face him. And playfully, I ruffled his hair.

"Don't!" he protested, but it was too late.

I was laughing. He closed his eyes in defeat. Then he leaned forward and gave me a quick smack on the lips.

"You're going to pay for that," he whispered.

"I'm holding my breath!" I laughed.

He pulled me to him and gave me a hug. I hugged him back. I didn't know the wonderful feeling seeping through me right now. It was familiar and yet it was strange. It was comforting, and yet it was terrifying. It was exciting, and at the same time, it was disturbing.

I closed my eyes. We'd gotten more affectionate with each other. And it was just right. He was, after all, my fiancé. The only thing that set us apart from normal betrothed couples was that the reason we became engaged was a condition preset and agreed upon fourteen years prior. But other than that, nothing was fake, everything was real, everything was official. And that gave Travis all the right to kiss and hug me. He didn't need to ask.

A knock on the door interrupted us.

Travis rolled his eyes. "Come in!" he called.

A woman in her fifties came in. "Mr. Cross, your father is on line one."

Travis's face hardened. "Tell him I am currently busy." I raised a brow at him and gave him one hard look. He sighed and turned to the woman. "Thank you, Mrs. Denver. I'll take the call."

"You're...you're welcome, sir," she said. She had smiled at me before she left. I smiled back graciously and then I turned toward my painting, leaving Travis be to speak to his father.

He was silent, and I could only guess that he was tuning out their conversation.

Then finally, he said, "Are you done?" He took a deep breath again and then he said, "Goodbye." He hung up.

He leaned back in his seat and squeezed the skin between his eyes, and I could see that he was trying his best to control his emotions. Travis's father was the one person who could instantly throw him on a warpath.

Then I realized that I probably was the one person in this world who could calm him down just as fast as his father could anger him.

I put down my pencil and took off my gloves. I went to stand beside him, touching his shoulder gently. He looked up and then he pulled me to him and made me sit on his lap. He gave me one tight hug and I hugged him back.

When I pulled away from him, he looked like he had his emotions under control. He took a deep breath. He smiled at me and then he said, "Let's get married, love."

***

I told Travis we could just go to Vegas and marry quickly. He raised a brow at me as if I had somehow offended him. He didn't say anything, but the look he gave me was enough to make me run to his computer and start searching for the best wedding coordinators in town.

I scheduled a meeting with three of the people I thought were the best in the business.

"When's your meeting?" Travis had asked before we went to bed that night.

"I've got one at eleven. Then another at one in the afternoon. The last one will be at three."

"The limo will take you around," he said.

"Is that really necessary, Travis?" I asked.

"For my peace of mind, it is."

The next day, I was waiting for a lady named Leona at Art Café. I ordered a cappuccino. She was fifteen minutes late already. I opened my notebook and made a note of this.

*Running fifteen minutes late. No text. No calls.*

When she finally arrived, she was with another girl, who I could only guess was her assistant. Leona had dark hair and gray eyes. She was wearing a tight Chanel suit.

When she sat on the chair in front of me, she extended her hand to me.

"Leona Watson," she said in an elegant voice.

I didn't miss the curious stares she was giving me. It was like she was measuring me up. I knew that she was one of the best in the industry, and she was also one of the most expensive. I was very curious to know why.

"Brianne Montgomery."

"Are you related to the Montgomerys who lived on Sixth?" she asked.

I shook my head. "I'm...new in town, actually."

"Hmmm..." she nodded. "Where do you want to get married?"

"I am from South Carolina. My relatives are mostly there. My fiancé also grew up there. Maybe, if he agrees, that's going to be the venue."

"We charge double for out-of-town arrangements," she said frankly. "Do you mind if I ask you what your budget is?"

"I'm...not sure, actually. My fiancé will be...will be taking care of the expenses." I hadn't checked with Travis to find out how much he was willing to pay for the wedding. I really didn't want it to be grand. A simple one with our relatives there would be just fine.

"Well, I think it's important that you know the budget first. Then we can decide what type of wedding you can afford," she said, her expression haughty now. Even her assistant was looking at me with a bored expression on her face.

"Actually, I have no idea. I was hoping to hire a wedding coordinator who could give me an estimate," I said honestly.

"Okay, in that case, I'll give you my standard rates," she said. She held out her hand, and her assistant immediately handed her a paper. She gave it to me.

I scanned through the figures. She charged per hour, and if my math was correct, her whole fee was enough to pay for a small wedding itself.

"What do you do for a living, if I may ask?" she said with a smile, which I was sure was fake anyway.

"I...paint," I replied.

"That's nice! Do I know any of your work?"

I giggled humorlessly. "Not unless you were one of my art professors."

"O-kay." She seemed eager to end the meeting.

I was distracted when I saw my limo pull out of the parking slot and then slowly drive away.

"Hey!" I whispered to myself.

Leona was looking at the limo, too. Then she turned back to me. Clearly, she didn't think it was mine.

*Damn! I should have dressed in an outfit that screamed Chanel, too!*

I was dressed in a pair of skintight denim capri pants and a lavender off-the-shoulder blouse. My hair was just tied in a pony. I hadn't worn any jewelry, except for my engagement ring, the stone of which was turned inward towards my palm. I wasn't really the type to show myself off through jewelry and expensive clothes. But lately, it had seemed quite important.

Well, I was not really rich. I made average income at my mother's gallery. I didn't have a luxurious lifestyle. And ever since I'd gotten engaged to Travis, he provided for all my basic needs. I didn't have to pay for the roof over my head or the food I ate. Over the years, he'd lavished me with expensive jewelry. I actually had tons of gold and diamond bangles, earrings, and necklaces in my safety deposit box in Connecticut. They had all come from Travis. By the time I had graduated from college, I no longer felt the need to buy jewelry for myself anymore. I felt I already had so much *bling* compared to any other woman my age.

I turned back to Leona. She smiled at me. "So, would you like to give this a bit of time? I can give you an exact quote later, although I doubt it will be much lower than that."

I was distracted again when I saw a beautiful red Bentley pull into the parking space vacated by the limo.

"I handle mostly A-list clients," Leona continued. "I'm sorry, but I can't give you a rate lower than that."

I stared back at her. She had really gotten on my nerves this time. She wasn't only belittling me with the way she looked at me: she was doing it with her words now. "I wasn't asking for a lower rate, was I?" I asked in a cold, irritated tone.

She smiled. "Of course not. I just want to be honest from the beginning. We don't want us to waste each other's time. And I usually charge ninety percent in advance. I'm quite strict, and I'm also picky with my clients. What does your fiancé do?"

"Why don't you ask him yourself?" I asked as I watched Travis get out of his car.

Leona followed my gaze. I heard her gasp. She probably recognized Travis. If she didn't, the license plate that said TJCROSS probably told her who my fiancé was.

"But that's..." She blinked back at me. "You're marrying Travis Cross?"

I smiled. Finally, I'd gotten her open-mouthed. "Yes," I replied haughtily. "So, perhaps, Miss Watson, you will try to make a better presentation of your services? Or perhaps try making a bit of effort to treat me the same way you treat your other clients? I'm interviewing two other wedding coordinators in a couple of hours. Perhaps you would care to make a better impression?"

Leona looked embarrassed. Travis was just in time to catch at least the last three sentences I'd said and immediately figured out the situation.

He smiled at me and then he leaned down to give me a kiss on the lips. "I'm sorry I'm late, love. What did I miss?"

I stared back at him. "You didn't say you were coming!" I said to him. "Did you send the limo away?"

He nodded. "I'll be your driver for the rest of the day, Mademoiselle." He looked back at the two ladies sitting in front of us. Immediately, his expression turned from boyish to cold. He raised a brow. "I take it you are one of the coordinators my future wife is looking to hire?"

Leona nodded nervously.

Travis leaned back in his seat and took my hand in his. He intertwined our fingers. He stared at Leona haughtily. "The budget for this wedding, as you may have guessed by now, is unlimited. I want my fiancée to have the best wedding money can buy." He looked at Leona's calling card in front of me. Then he stared back at her. "Impress me!" he said in a cold, commanding voice, which made Leona buckle in her seat.

She fiddled with her hands nervously. And then she said, "I'm...Leona...this is Jennifer..." She referred to her assistant.

"I'm not interested in your names. I'm interested in what you can do for us," Travis said in cold and bored voice.

"Sure, Mr. Cross," Leona said.

If it were any other person, I would have given Travis a glare. But in this instance, I thought Leona deserved this treatment.

She must have spoken for a whole fifteen minutes, giving us a rundown of their previous work, references, and contacts. Travis just sat in this seat, but I knew he wasn't listening. He'd decided not to hire Leona. He just wanted her to make an effort to treat me like any other client.

216

When Leona was finished with her monologue, Travis didn't say anything. He just sat there, looking at my notebook. He took my hand in his and brought it to his lips. Then he noticed that the stone of my engagement ring was turned inward. He pushed it with his finger so it was facing the proper way.

I didn't miss the silent gasp from Leona when she saw my ring. It was impressive, I knew. But I had been afraid it was attracting street muggers.

"Do you...do you have any other questions, Mr. Cross?" Leona asked uncertainly.

Travis looked at her for a moment. Then he turned to me. "Are you interested in anything else? You, my love, will have to make the decision on this. I'll go with whatever you decide. But personally, I prefer you chose somebody with a better work attitude."

I shook my head. "No." I turned back to Leona. "Thank you for your time."

Leona looked terribly embarrassed.

Travis put a stack of cash on the table for our bill. "No change," he told the waiter, who nodded gratefully. Travis must have given a tip twice the amount of the actual bill. Then he took Leona's card. "I'll keep this. I'll have my assistant give feedback to your boss. I'm sure he or she will be happy to hear about your excellent interpersonal skills," he said sarcastically.

Leona stood up from her seat. "Mr. Cross, please," she pleaded. "I'm truly sorry. I should have treated Miss Montgomery better. I am at fault. But I have a kid in school. And I need this job—"

"You should always put that in your mind before you meet people," Travis cut her off.

"I know. But I beg you..." Leona was close to tears now. After all, making people cry was probably one of Travis's easiest skills. "My boss would fire me if somebody like you complained to him."

Travis raised a brow. "Don't worry, I will remember to compliment your hair." And he turned his back on her.

Leona looked at me pleadingly. I reached out for Travis's hand and gave it a squeeze.

"Travis..." I whispered. "No blood, no foul," I said to him. "Let's leave Miss Watson alone. I'm sure she just had an off day. She won't get our account...let that be punishment enough for her."

217

Travis stared at me for a moment. Then his expression softened. He leaned forward and gave me a gentle kiss on the lips. "Because *you* asked," he said. He tossed Leona's calling card back on the table. "I won't be needing your contact details ever."

Then he pulled me toward him and we headed for his car. Travis opened the passenger door for me and I got in. I glanced back at Leona again. She was staring at me. Then she gave me an apologetic smile and gathered her things.

"Were you really going to complain about her?" I asked Travis when he got in the driver's seat.

"Yes," he replied. "And that was the least grave thing I had on my mind."

I sighed. I reached out and squeezed his hand. "I guess I don't make an impressive fiancée."

He raised a brow. "On the contrary—you are. A woman who can draw men's attention without makeup and can provoke another woman's jealousy without wearing expensive jewelry or clothes...don't you think you're impressive enough? Why do you think I want to get married so soon?" he teased.

I giggled, and then I asked, "Speaking of that, why *do* you wanna get married so soon?"

"Didn't you want to get married before you turned thirty? Wasn't that part of what you asked me?"

"Yes. But the so-called 'curse' won't hit me before I turn thirty-one. I still have time. Why did you want it earlier?"

He sighed and reached for my hand. "Because my father is making a beast out of me. I want us to get married before that happens. You deserve a better groom than that," he said in a frustrated tone. He stared at me for a while. "And the sooner I start a new family...the less remorse or hatred I will feel toward my old one."

"But, Travis..." I started to remind him that we would only stay married until either of us found the love that would last us a lifetime.

"I know," he cut me off, knowing what I was going to say. "But you're going to be my wife for at least two years, remember?" he asked. "Until then, you are my family. You've always been, anyway. Maybe we're just making that official."

I smiled at him. "Yes," I said. "I think so, too."

218

# Chapter Twenty

I had my bachelorette party back home. Friends from college and from the dance club and a couple of my relatives were there. We had it at a little resort. Somebody actually rented a stripper.

I was extremely embarrassed when the stripper danced for me. I was pushing Sarah to take my seat at the center of the room.

"Come on, Brianne! You're not getting any from your fiancé— why not just have no-strings-attached fun with that cutie?" Sarah asked.

"Because I don't want my other cousins to think that I'm not faithful to Travis!" I argued. But honestly, had I only slept with two men in my life. One was my boyfriend of two years. And I was marrying the other one in a couple of days.

"For someone who's not really in a relationship with your fiancé, you're pretty damn loyal!"

"If you do this, I'll do anything you want!" I begged her.

"Okay, fine! He's cute anyway," she said, making her way to the stripper.

We had too much to drink that night. We were laughing and goofing around. I'm pretty sure I passed out.

When I woke up, I was in a room that was quieter than the one I passed out in. I was lying comfortably in bed.

I saw Travis lying on the couch in one corner. He was sound asleep. I don't know how it happened, but I found it endearing that he found me. The male stripper had been trying to flirt with me all night, and I had tried all means to get away from him.

"How did you find me?" I asked Travis during breakfast that morning. He had rented a room for us in the same hotel where I had my bachelorette party.

"Don't you know me well by now?" he asked.

"Travis knows everything!" I teased.

He reached out for my hand. "I was just making sure nothing bad would happen to you."

"With a bunch of silly girls?"

"Well, there was a man, wasn't there?"

"Yeah. But I'm sure he's harmless."

There was a hard look on Travis's face. Then he said, "When I knocked on the room around three in the morning, one of your cousins was appalled to see me. There were...some people having sex in the bedroom. She thought it was you...with the stripper," Travis said uneasily. "I thought so, too, to be honest."

I raised a brow. "Why did you think it was me?"

"Because you're the bride," he replied. "And easily the most attractive girl in the room. That guy must have been trying to hit on you all night."

I giggled. "He was. But I begged Sarah to take my place."

He narrowed his eyes. "Really? Did he look like an ogre?"

"Completely the opposite."

"Then why didn't you..." He shrugged and chose not to continue his sentence.

"Maybe I don't do that just for the fun of it...or just because there's an occasion that calls for it, no matter how once-in-a-lifetime it seems," I said in an irritated tone.

What a weird thing for your fiancé to ask you. That actually made me remember that this marriage between Travis and me was really just an arrangement...to save me from shame. Nothing more.

For months, I was floating on air, finding comfort and happiness in the change in our relationship. I thought even though he didn't say it, he somehow felt that we...belonged together. That he was as comfortable as I was with our new setup...the new course our relationship was taking.

But I was wrong. No matter how affectionate we had gotten, it didn't change the way we really were. He didn't think I belonged to him. I should feel the same.

I felt a sharp pain in my heart, which made me angrier at myself. *I can't...won't...feel this way about Travis.* I trusted him with my life. But I didn't think I could trust him with my heart. He was saving me until I found the man of my dreams. It would be too much for me to start asking him to *be* that man.

I took a sip of my coffee and stood up from the table. "I better take a shower," I said. "Thanks for breakfast."

I took my time inside the bath. I was in the tub, staring at the pristine white tiles in front of me. I couldn't understand why, but I felt really disappointed and…sad.

I didn't speak much with Travis afterward. He knew he'd offended me. He read me like a book. But he didn't say sorry, didn't try to console me. He was looking at me wearily, but he didn't attempt to apologize. When he dropped me off at the hotel where our wedding was going to be held, he didn't even kiss my cheek or squeeze my hand.

"See you," I whispered.

He stared at me for a while, and then he nodded and left.

*Now he's just being weird!* It was not fair that he could read me like a book, but I couldn't even decipher his thoughts. This mind-reading thing should work both ways!

The next night, it was his turn to have a stag party. A part of me was worried, but I tried my best to shake off that feeling.

Travis had every right to have fun tonight. This night was no different from any other night. If he was allowed to sleep with any woman while married to me, he was definitely allowed to sleep with the stripper at his stag party.

There was a knock at my door. I opened it, and Sarah walked in. We rented rooms in the hotel. My bridesmaids and some friends occupied my floor, and all the groomsmen and some of Travis's acquaintances occupied a whole floor in the other wing of the hotel. We decided to arrive three days before the wedding to ensure that everything went according to plan.

"You busy?" Sarah asked.

"Yes," I muttered. "I'm actually going to Mars. My spaceship leaves in ten minutes."

Sarah raised a brow. "Ha-ha! You're very funny," she said sarcastically. "Seriously? You have plans?"

"Yeah. I plan to pop a sleeping pill and doze off to Neverland as early as eight." The minute that was out of my mouth, I realized it wasn't such a bad idea. I didn't like feeling the way I did.

For months, I'd slept in the same room as Travis, and I was getting perplexed now that I didn't even know where he was.

"You're agitated!" Sarah said accusingly. "You're worried he'll sleep with the stripper, aren't you?"

"Of course not! He can do that if he wants to!"

221

Sarah laughed. "Wow! The contrast between your words and your tone is very convincing!"

From the beginning, Travis had made it clear that he'd be nothing more than a groom who would meet me at the altar. Other than that, we were free to see other people. I was free to find my Mr. Right, and he was free to sleep with whomever he wanted.

But I couldn't seem to shake off that feeling. Yesterday, Travis and I had this silent argument about the stripper at my bridal shower. He really thought I would sleep with the guy. Well, I was not like him! I didn't sleep with just anybody!

*I shouldn't feel like this,* I thought. *I cannot drive myself crazy with the thought of him having sex with another woman. Nothing can happen between us. I gave him full permission to have his needs fulfilled elsewhere.*

Although, I couldn't help but wonder why I had hoped that the changes in our relationship somehow meant something to him. That the new bond we had formed as an engaged couple would matter more to him than a few seconds of ecstasy with another woman.

"Come on! Get dressed and let's go down to the bar," Sarah said. Because I didn't want to drive myself crazy anymore, I decided having drinks with Sarah was a better idea.

Three hours later, I couldn't remember why I wanted to drink myself to oblivion at all. In fact, I think my subconscious fully took over. I was drinking too much alcohol and laughing so much with Sarah. I don't know how long we stayed at the bar. I remember Sarah flirting with the bartender. I was just laughing my heart out as if everything around me was a joke.

I must have passed out at one point. I dreamt, I felt. I laughed and didn't care about anything else. Then, I dreamt about Travis. I remembered his arms around me…touching me, kissing me.

"Travis…" I whispered as I hugged him to me. He didn't speak. He kept kissing me. I remembered being afraid and excited at the same time.

*"Don't look…just feel…"*

It was fifteen years ago. But I went back to that night…in my dreams. I exploded in a million different colors and a mix of emotions. I remembered him the way he touched me. How could one touch undo me like that? How could a few moments with him make me want to explode? It'd been years…but still, nobody had touched me the way Travis touched me that night. Nobody even came close!

"Travis!" I screamed his name as I reached my peak. I clung to his body, and he held me against him, catching me.

When it was over, I remembered him walking away, tearing my heart into a million pieces. I needed to be safe from him, he said. But I could never be safe with anybody else…only with him!

The door closed behind him and I was left alone in the cold bed, with only the pillows to hug to myself.

Suddenly, I woke up. It was still dark in the room, and I had a very bad headache. I was panting and my heart was pounding wildly. The memories of my dream came back to me.

*Travis.* I dreamt that he shared the bed with me. He unnerved me…made me feel every bit wanted, every bit loved…every bit a woman. I turned to the other side of the bed. It was cold and empty.

I'd had the most vivid dream. It was like I could still feel Travis inside me, even though I knew it had been more than a decade earlier. That dream…was one dream I didn't want to wake up from.

How could I remember that night as if it was only yesterday?

I was marrying Travis in less than twenty-four hours. It was wrong to expect more from him…he'd already given me so much.

I'd had too much to drink. I didn't even remember parting with Sarah or going back to my room. I must have stripped all the way from the door to the bed and just dozed off.

I put on a robe and gathered my clothes from the floor, and then I took a shower. I met Sarah for breakfast. I was still a little dizzy.

"What happened last night?" we asked at the same time.

We laughed. "Wow! I'm never gonna drink that much again!" I said.

"Well, you were trying your best not to think about Travis's stag party."

There was that pinch in my heart again.

Where was Travis? Since the day before when he thought I would sleep with the stripper, I hadn't really spoken to him. I'd been mad at him for thinking I would sleep with just anybody. But I guessed that's what he wanted to do. So I didn't have to ask where he was. He was supposed to have a separate bedroom in the hotel. I wouldn't barge in there! I was almost sure he was there with one, maybe even more than one, woman.

Sarah ordered coffee for us.

"How much did we drink last night?" I asked, laughing.

"I'm not sure!" Sarah replied. She squeezed her temples with her fingers. "But I'm guessing it was a lot! I don't remember how I got back to my room!"

"Me, neither! I remember laughing a lot, though!"

"I remember flirting with the bartender!"

"Maybe he took you back?" I teased.

"I wouldn't have minded that!" she laughed.

"Didn't you...spend my bachelorette night with the stripper? What happened to that?"

She laughed. "Nothing," she said. "It was one night of fun!"

I narrowed my eyes. "It...didn't mean anything to you?"

She shook her head. "Men can't be the only one enjoying these...one-night-stand things!" She stared back at me. "Don't tell me you haven't had a one night stand?"

"Well, when I was younger, I did spend the night with a friend. But we both decided it was just...sex, nothing more, and we won't do it or speak of it again. Does that count?"

"Yeah, that will do."

But Sarah didn't know that that night did mean something to me. It was the best night of my life. Nothing had come close. And until I found the guy I would really spend the rest of my life with, I doubted another night would.

***

The night before my wedding, I had dinner with my family and friends. Travis wasn't there. We weren't allowed to see each other twenty-four hours before the wedding. My family was quite the superstitious type. They still follow this old tradition.

*Well, I'm sure there are plenty of things he can do with his time!* I thought angrily. He was probably still locked up in his room with that stripper they gave him for his stag party!

I sighed. *What is happening to me? How can I start believing in this marriage? When did I start thinking that Travis was really mine?*

Travis's mother came up to me after dinner. She smiled at me and gave me a hug.

"Take care of him," she whispered to me. "Travis has always had a soft spot for you. If there's anybody who can control him, it's you." She had tears in her eyes as she gazed at me. "I hope Travis will be happier with you than he ever was with us. I hope that now, he finally finds the family that he truly belongs to. He'll be a good husband and a great father. Thank you for giving him a chance at that life."

I felt guilty. Nobody, except for Sarah, knew that I was marrying Travis because I didn't have a choice at the moment. Everybody else thought we were really in love.

"Hello, gorgeous," Eric greeted me from behind.

I beamed at him and gave him a hug. "I'm so glad you made it!"

"I wouldn't miss this for the world!"

"When did you arrive?"

"Last night. In time for Travis's bachelor's party," he replied.

"*You* were there?"

"Travis didn't have many friends," he laughed. "But it wasn't much of a party anyway."

"Why?"

"Well, it was just drinking, playing pool, and then when the girls came out, even Travis's college friends couldn't push them to him. He seemed to be in a foul mood and acted as if he couldn't wait for it to be over. He played pool and told his college buddies to f off whenever they tried to introduce a girl to him."

"Wasn't there a stripper in a cake?"

"Well, there was. But actually, she danced for almost all of us...except for the groom, who gave her a scowl as she approached him. Travis can be very scary when he wants to. I thought the poor girl was going to cry." Eric laughed. "And he left earlier than any of us."

"He left?"

Eric nodded. "Don't worry. I know he left alone."

A part of me was glad because all my worries about Travis sleeping with the stripper were nothing. Then, a part of me was again bothered because I hadn't seen him in two days. Though he wasn't with the stripper, it could still mean he was with someone else. Maybe a past fling, a former mistress.

But what right did I have to complain, really? It wasn't right that I'd asked Travis to give me at least two years of his life and demand that he give up other women.

That night, just before I went to sleep, I heard somebody knocking on my door.

"Who is it?" I asked.

"It's me," Travis said on the other side of the door.

My heart pounded in my ribcage. What could he be doing here? He was gone for two days, and he appeared just when we weren't allowed to see each other anymore!

Did he come to call off the wedding? What would I do if he refused to marry me now?

My hands were shaking when I opened the door slightly. I stood behind it, refusing to show myself to him.

"You know we're forbidden to see each other," I said nervously.

"I know," he said. "But I can't resist."

"Travis, we both know that's not true!" I said.

But sometimes, I had this unfamiliar feeling that wished that was true…that Travis was a normal groom, excited to see his bride at the altar…that he felt a tiny inch of excitement over this wedding…because sometimes, I did. I felt ecstatic about the wedding and nervous that Travis didn't feel the same.

And now that Travis was coming to me on the eve of our wedding, when he wasn't supposed, to scared me.

*Oh my God, he's really going to call it off!*

"Travis…what do you want?" I asked.

He heard him sigh. "I need to see you."

"Why?"

He didn't reply.

"Travis…we're not allowed to see each other. Unless…you came here to…call it off?" My voice was weak and weary.

"What?" he asked sharply.

"I…was thinking you wanted to call the whole thing off at the last minute. I can't think of any other reason why you would want to see me now."

I heard his sharp intake of breath, and then suddenly I saw him reach out for the key card inserted in the room's main switch. I had already turned off the lamps in preparation for sleep but had left the main light on when Travis knocked on my door. But now Travis had switched off all lights, and suddenly, the room was enveloped in darkness, illuminated only by the moonlight coming from the balcony.

I felt a push on the door, and then suddenly, a figure was standing in front of me. I stared up at his silhouette. Even in the dark, I could make out the contours of Travis's handsome face. I could tell there was a glitter in his eye as he stared down at me.

"I didn't come here to call off the wedding," he said. "Didn't even cross my mind."

Relief washed over me.

"Then what are you doing here?" I asked.

"I..." He trailed off. Then he took a deep breath. "I wanted to...make sure you're prepared for tomorrow's...kiss."

"What?" It was the last thing I expected him to say. I think he was lost for words, too. Like he wanted to tell me something but had decided not to.

"I will kiss you...thoroughly, as that is expected of me. After the ceremony and during the reception," he said. "I don't want you to think I'm taking advantage. I just want to make sure you know."

I giggled. "I know that. The wedding is real. You didn't have to ask, Travis."

He was silent. When I stared up at him, I realized that he was staring intently at me in the dark. My heart suddenly stopped beating. I felt his breath on my lips. Then he whispered, "Then I'm not going to ask now." And I felt his lips on mine.

The kiss was gentle at first. And then his arms came around my waist and he kissed me...thoroughly, desperately, as if he was trying to tell me something that he could not put into words. I wound my arms around his neck and kissed him back. I savored that moment. It was like in my dream that night...it felt wonderful...it felt real.

When the kiss was over, he took a deep breath. "Like that," he whispered. "Tomorrow, expect that I'm going to kiss you exactly like that."

I giggled nervously. "I won't be surprised, then."

He pulled away from me. "Goodnight, Brianne. I can't wait to meet you at the altar tomorrow."

I wanted to cry when I heard that. Suddenly, I realized I wanted it to be true!

# Chapter Twenty-One

For once, my parents decided to behave in front of each other as they walked me down the aisle.

I was nervous as hell, my palms were sweating, and my heart was pounding wildly inside my chest. Did every bride feel like this? I felt scared...terrified. I felt self-conscious that every eye was on me.

But when I raised my face toward the altar, I saw Travis standing there, looking magnificent in a tux. He was looking at me intensely...as if he couldn't take his eyes off me...as if I were the only woman in the room. He was looking at me the way I wanted my real groom to look at me. Tears welled up in my eyes.

He looked down to me as he took my hand from my father. He gave me a crooked smile that made my heart stop beating altogether.

"Hello, beautiful," he whispered.

"Hey," I managed to say.

He raised my hand to his lips and gave it a kiss. Then he guided me toward the altar.

Travis held my hand all throughout the ceremony. I was nervous, but I felt lightheaded...and happy. I knew there was no place on earth I would rather be...and I couldn't think of a better man to share this moment with.

*"You may kiss the bride."*

I watched nervously as Travis lifted my veil, stared at me deeply for a moment, and then leaned forward to give me a deep kiss on the lips.

The touch of his lips on mine was the same every time he kissed me—electrifying, mind-blowing, heart-stopping. He wrapped his arms around my waist and pulled me to him as he deepened the kiss.

After what seemed like eternity, he pulled away from me and watched my face carefully. I was pretty sure my blush was making me turn violet. And as if that pleased him, he gave me a crooked smile again. Then he pulled me to him in a tight hug.

"Mrs. Travis Cross," he whispered.

I didn't know why, but I liked the sound of that.

It was a grand celebration at the resort. My wedding was probably the biggest wedding my family had had since they started their stupid family curse. I hadn't spent a single cent. Travis refused to make me or my father pay for anything. He made special arrangements with my coordinator that I didn't know about. Like the grand fireworks at the reception. They were big and lasted for at least twenty minutes.

Travis surprised me by smiling and laughing a lot. Just when I thought he'd be bored, or would give me endless do-it-and-get-it-over-with attitude, he actually looked like he was having fun.

He was always beside me, entertaining our guests. He would reach out and give me a hug once in a while. Even after our kiss in the church, he gave me a couple of smacks on the lips.

When I gazed at him under the fireworks, I saw a man different from the Travis I had known all my life. This was a boyish Travis I was looking at.

Then he stared down at me. I saw something in his eyes, something I couldn't decipher. It was as if his eyes were asking me something. That look on his face was somewhat guilty, somewhat pleading. And yet, I couldn't even guess what exactly he was thinking about.

He tilted my chin up and then slowly, he leaned forward and brought his lips to mine. Right there, in the middle of the fireworks, I wound my arms around his neck and lost myself in that kiss.

I didn't want that kiss to end. It was…like the kiss we shared fourteen years ago…when he took me…the kiss that haunted me again the other night when I had my dream about Travis and the night we had spent together.

When the kiss was over, Travis stared back at me, his eyes like liquid sapphires…as if he was desperately asking for something…like he was trying to read something in my expression, and he was getting frustrated that he couldn't get his answers.

"Is something wrong, Travis?" I asked him. The look on his face wasn't just making me nervous. It was terrifying me. I felt like something was definitely wrong. Travis was so good at keeping in his emotions. But now, the sad and confused look on his face told me that he was somehow going through some emotional turmoil.

He shook his head. Then he pulled me to him again and hugged me tightly.

"Everything's going to be okay Brianne, right?" It took me a moment to realize that it wasn't a statement. He was asking me a question. I pulled away and blinked back at him.

"Of course, Travis. We're going to be fine," I assured him. I meant that. No matter what happened, I wouldn't let anything destroy what I had with him. We wouldn't lose each other...even after this marriage ended.

He leaned forward again and gave me another thorough kiss on the lips. When I pulled away from him, his expression had already changed. The boyishness was back. He had an easy smile on his face, and then he leaned his forehead against mine.

"Tom must be itching to kick my ass in heaven," he whispered.

"Why do you say that?"

He shook his head. "I've kissed you too many times today."

I laughed. "You married me today. It's the least I can do for you. Tom would understand that you are doing me a favor. And some things are...necessary."

He laughed. "Do you really think you just pushed me to accept this fate? Do you really believe I'm doing you a favor?"

I took a deep breath. "I don't just think that. I know that. And you don't have to pretend otherwise. I'm still thankful for you, Travis. Not just because you married me today. I thank you for everything you've done for me since I've had you in my life."

He leaned his forehead against mine. "You're more than I deserve, Brianne," he said. "And I thank you. For being my only family for years."

He kissed me on the nose. When he looked back at me again, there was a certain glitter in his eyes. He smiled dashingly, and he never looked more handsome to me. His smile was genuine, and it reached his eyes. Clearly, whatever emotional turmoil he had been going through a while ago, he had gotten hold of it now. I wondered how he did that. I wished I had that ability sometimes.

I realized I was happy to make Travis look like that. And I wanted to see him more like this...unmasked...carefree...*human*! He used to be dark and cold...I wanted to see him warm and happy. Even for just a little while.

There were cheers from our guests when the fireworks finished. They encouraged us to kiss again. With a sly smile on his face, Travis leaned down and gave me a thorough kiss on the lips once again.

231

When he pulled away, I saw that confused and broken expression on his face again, but he was quick to mask it with a grin. He gave me a gentler kiss on the lips, and then he hugged me. "We're going to be late for our honeymoon," he said.

I pulled away from him and blinked back. "But... Travis... we... promised not to..."

He laughed. "Yes," he leaned forward to whisper in my ear. "But sex isn't the only thing married people do on a honeymoon. We can do all the rest."

I giggled. In a way, I was embarrassed. I was becoming too defensive. I constantly reminded him about our deal, when he might not even have been interested in that! He might have gotten used to just kissing me and hugging me. But making love was an entirely different story. We both knew that our relationship was...special. Unique. It was beautiful the way it was. To cross the line...would put so much at stake. And I didn't think either of us was prepared for the consequences.

"Okay." I smiled at him. "I'll go on a honeymoon with you...and do everything but have sex. But I have one condition."

He raised a brow. "Okay. So remind me again who's asking whom a favor here?"

I laughed. "I know. But still, I have something to ask you."

He sighed in defeat. "All right, Mrs. Cross. What is it?"

"I want to see *you*, Travis." I placed my hand on his chest. "The man trapped inside. No masks. No reservations. No defenses."

He narrowed his eyes as he stared at me. "Brianne... you're... extorting so much from me."

I smiled. "I deserve it. I want to know my husband."

"Don't you know me better than anyone already?"

"I want to know the man you haven't shown anyone else. The man maybe even you do not know," I said. "Let go of your mask, Travis. For me. Even for just a short while. Let that be my wedding gift."

He stared at me for a while. Then he closed his eyes. He pulled me to him and gave me a hug.

"You're scaring me, Brianne," he whispered.

"You don't have to be afraid. I love you just as you are, Travis," I said. "It doesn't matter who you are. I know you have a softer side. And I want to get to know that man."

He leaned his forehead against mine. "I may not know how to let go of my mask, Brianne. I've been so guarded since I was a kid."

I pulled away from him and looked into his eyes. "Follow your heart. Go with what you feel. Take the thinking, analyzing, calculating cap off your head. I think you'll be just fine."

He sighed. "You're asking me to be a trusting, gullible, romance-believing loser."

I laughed. "Maybe. But promise you won't fall in love with me?"

He raised a brow. "Ha-ha. Very funny."

"Just giving you a fair warning. I can be very charming," I teased.

He rolled his eyes. "Trust me, I know. How else did we get here?" I couldn't help laughing at that. Then he stared at me for a while. "How sure are you that it will make a difference? Maybe this is really me. Masked or unmasked. There's nothing much underneath."

"You don't have to put a mask on if you don't have anything to hide underneath, Travis. You know that. You won't be so guarded if you have nothing to guard," I said. "Just learn to let go. And I'll go on this honeymoon with you."

"Again, I'd like to remind you that you asked me to do this fourteen years ago. I didn't even have to plan a honeymoon getaway."

"Then why did you?"

He took a deep breath. "This marriage is real. I just want it to come as close to the actual thing as possible. Even if we just spend time talking to each other all week. You need to be able to stand me long enough, you know."

"We live together, Travis. We've lived together long enough for me to say that I can stand you."

"Nevertheless, everybody expects it. I want you to have a story to tell when you're asked."

I stared up at him. He really was sweet. No matter how much he tried to hide it. And more and more, I wanted to see him the way he really was.

"Thank you," I said. "I mean it, Travis. No masks for you."

He sighed and then he nodded. "And no holding back for you?"

"Wh-what do you mean?" I blinked back at him.

He gave me a mischievous, crooked smile. Then he pulled me to him and leaned forward. Just as his lips were an inch away from mine, he said, "Exactly what I said. Don't hold back, my lovely wife." And he devoured my lips.

The world started spinning. I held on to Travis for dear support. His previous kisses were…comforting, enthralling, exciting…and with a hint of desperation, as if he was begging for something. Now, this kiss…was invading, as if he meant to conquer, to seduce…it was mind-blowing…a kiss that you lose all your memories to. The kiss that made me forget who I was and who he was that night I gave myself to him.

When he pulled away, I could barely open my eyes to look at him. I was embarrassed. I gave in. It seemed like I gave my everything in that kiss.

When I was brave enough to look at him again, he was looking at me carefully. There was a look of triumph on his face, and yet, that didn't make me feel ashamed. It made me feel happy that somehow, I made him feel good.

"Do we have a deal?" he asked.

I smiled. "I would give up everything to get to know the real you."

He raised a brow. "I hope by the end of the week you'll still think that it was all worth it."

"Don't worry. I have a feeling I'll still feel that way. We have a deal." I held out my pinky to him. He stared at it for a moment. His expression softened. Then he hooked his pinky with mine, but instead of pulling it away like he was supposed to, he twisted our hands and brought my fingers to his lips. He kissed them gently. Then he stared at me. "Deal."

***

We barely had time to say goodbye to our guests. I had to get out of my wedding gown quickly and fix my hair.

"Did you bring all the lingerie we brought you?" Sarah whispered to me.

"Shut up, Sarah. You know what the deal is."

"Well, I was hoping that had changed now, with all the kissing and hugging! You guys couldn't take your eyes and hands off each other all day, did you know that!?"

"Then we put on a good show," I laughed. "Well, kissing is part of the deal. We decided not to pretend in that area, to make it look natural. The only thing we decided not to do is…" I trailed off, heaving a sigh.

"It's a pity!" Sarah said. "It looks like *that* would go effortlessly well for you, too."

I rolled my eyes. "Come on, Sarah! I don't want to think about that."

"Why? Because you don't find him attractive?"

I sighed. I didn't want to lie. I did find Travis attractive. Very! There were plenty of times that I lost my breath when I stared at him...or when he stared at me. I felt proud when we were together because I knew that devilishly handsome man belonged to me...at least officially or publicly. I loved kissing him. His arms felt so safe...like home. I knew I was in so much danger of falling in love with him, too. But I had to remind myself who he was...what he was to me and what our relationship was.

I loved Travis. With all my heart. If I lost him, I would be devastated! As much as I was with Tom...maybe even more so, since I'd been with him longer. I knew he loved me. We might have been husband and wife, but that didn't change what we were...what we would always be: the best of friends.

"No, it's not that. Travis is the one guy I can't risk to lose. And he promised my brother he wouldn't touch me," I said. I didn't know what it was, but when I heard myself say that, it sounded like I had a trace of regret in my voice.

"But you want him to?"

I sighed. Deep inside, I knew the answer to that. "It doesn't matter. Because from the beginning, I've known that if there's one person who can keep a promise, make that promise his bible, the creed of his life, it's Travis. I'm afraid to entertain any other possibilities. There's just...*so much* at stake here. Whatever happens after this marriage...I *still* want Travis in my life."

"And all the hugging and kissing all over the place is...?"

"Part of the deal," I replied. "Part of the change in our relationship. He's my husband. We're two friends, married to each other, making a life together, but not sleeping with each other. Kissing is necessary. He can kiss me if he wants. When I asked him this favor fourteen years ago, I only told him that he couldn't sleep with me. I never told him he couldn't kiss me or hug me. And besides, it makes it look real if we're naturally affectionate."

"Hmmm...I don't know what you're smoking, but I have to warn you...it's not farfetched that one of these days, you'll wake up and find yourselves head-over-heels in love with each other! Maybe you already are," she said. "You already love each other to begin with. And it looks like you love making out anyway."

I hated to admit it, but I thought Sarah was right about one thing. I did love making out with Travis!

I barely had time to wash off my makeup and take the clips and little flowers out of my hair when Travis stepped into my room saying we should be off. He already had two bags ready.

"What about my clothes?" I asked.

"All in there," he said. "I ordered a whole set of clothes for you. One of the qualities I like about Karl is that he's very meticulous and very thorough. You can grab a couple more things you want to bring. But I doubt you'll need anything more." Then he said goodbye to Sarah and told me he'd wait for me in the lobby.

Sarah gave me a box. She said that was her wedding surprise for me. "Honeymoon-handy stuff." She winked, and I actually glared at her. But I decided to bring it along with me. I had no time to open it and screen the contents.

In less than an hour, we were onboard the plane to Bora Bora. I reclined my seat and made myself comfortable.

Travis reached forward to touch the circles under my eyes. "You're very tired."

I smiled. "I am. It's been a long day. But everything was perfect." I reached out for his hand. "Thank you, Travis. You're wonderful. And you laughed and smiled a lot."

He grinned at me. "I promised you I would."

I reached forward and touched his cheek with my hand. "Thank you." I pulled him toward me gently. He leaned forward and gave me a gentle kiss on the lips.

Then he gathered me in his arms and I rested my head on his shoulder.

"Sleep now, love. I'll wake you up when we get there."

We checked in to a luxurious hotel. We were staying in an over-water bungalow, luxury suite with a private plunge pool.

Before we entered our bungalow, just at the doorstep, Travis grinned at me and then without warning, he swept me off my feet and carried me in his arms.

I laughed. "Wow! This honeymoon couldn't be more real."

Our suite had a huge deck and a deep tub that gave a spectacular view of the ocean while you bathed. It offered a restful atmosphere, and at the same time, it was quite private.

There was one king-sized bed. Although there were chairs and sofas, I noticed that there was no couch big enough for Travis to sleep on. An unfamiliar emotion crept through me. I felt nervous; however, there was another hint of emotion there that I didn't want to entertain.

"Do you like it?" Travis asked as I checked out our plunge pool.

I beamed at him. "I love it!"

I took a shower as soon as we got settled in. It was a long flight. Travis and I had an early dinner on the deck. We talked about what had happened at the wedding and the funny characters that made up the guest list.

"Was your mother surprised you suddenly...got married?" I asked.

Travis shook his head. "No," he replied. "And I don't think she really cared all that much."

I frowned. "Travis..."

He sighed. "Love...you asked me to take my mask down. This...is me being honest about what I feel about my parents. I...have no emotion for either of them."

"Your mother came to me," I said. "She asked me to take care of you. I think she cares about you more than you know...more than you allow. She...thanked me for giving you a chance to have a better family than the one they gave you."

"You've been my only family for a very long time, Brianne. What family was she talking about?"

"Travis..." I whispered.

"Brianne," he cut me off and reached out for my hand across the table. "Please..." He took a deep breath. "I don't want to think about them. For now, I don't want to think about anything else but you. You have my full, undivided attention for a whole week. Please...let's talk about this some other time?"

I realized that he was right. I could not force Travis to have a better relationship with his parents overnight. So much had happened. It would take time to heal all the wounds.

I nodded. He raised my hand and kissed my fingers.

I felt warm. Somehow, this new Travis in front of me...was far sweeter than I ever imagined he could be. He was open about the way he felt, and he gave me fair warning about not liking the topic we were discussing.

We rested for a while, and then we decided to take a dip in the pool. When I came out on the deck, Travis was already in. There were candles around the pool, and there was a bottle of Chardonnay beside him.

"Wow," I breathed. There was a full moon, and it illuminated the lagoon and the pool perfectly.

I took off my robe to reveal a two-piece string bathing suit that Karl had included in my bag.

I felt a little self-conscious. The suit was tinier than what I usually wore, and I could feel Travis's eyes on me as I got into the water.

When I reached the center, I raised my eyes to him. He was staring at me intently. He gave me a crooked smile and motioned at me to come closer to him.

I moved toward him shyly. When I was in front of him, I raised my eyes to him again.

"You're gorgeous," he whispered.

"Thank you. But remember, I told you not to fall in love with me," I teased.

He snorted and said, "Yeah. I remember you saying something like that." He stared at me deeply. He pulled me gently and then he leaned forward and gave me a gentle kiss on the tip of my nose.

I thought he was going to kiss me on the lips. I was expecting it. Travis and I had agreed on many things. But we hadn't really agreed that making out in private was part of the deal…although, I didn't think I would mind if that was the case.

I stared up at him. He raised a brow. "Disappointed?" he asked, reading my expression.

"Of course not!" I lied. I was embarrassed. Was I really that transparent?

He laughed. "My lovely wife! Have you forgotten who you are talking to? Or *lying* to?" His eyes were dancing and he had a teasing grin on his face.

I took a step back from him. "You're so full of yourself, Travis Cross!" I glared.

He was quick to put his arms around my waist, pulling me to him. I continued glaring. He smiled at me devilishly and said, "That's a pity you aren't disappointed. Because I am!" And without warning, he kissed me on the lips.

I didn't know what to feel. It was like sparks of fireworks erupted around us and illuminated the skies with a million different colors. The air was cold, but I felt fire under my skin, and I slowly felt myself losing control. I kissed Travis with as much enthusiasm as he kissed me. I pulled him to me and kissed him with so much intensity, so much passion.

Just then, he stopped and gently pulled away from me. I stared back at him in panic. I was afraid I had done something wrong.

Seeing the look of alarm in my eyes, he quickly hugged me back and chuckled softly. "Easy, love," he said. "I'm only human. Don't make me ask you for something I know you cannot give."

Understanding dawned on me. I laughed. "I'm sorry," I said. "Was that too much?"

He leaned down and kissed me gently on the lips. "A little. But still tolerable."

I leaned my head on his shoulder. "What's going on between us, Trav?"

He chuckled softly. "You're my wife, Brianne. I think I'm entitled to a few kisses once in a while. I would love to have more, but that part is totally up to you."

I stared up at him. "Travis...we can't..." I started. "You know...I can't give myself to you and not ask for a lot of things in return. We have a *beautiful* relationship. Something that is more important to me than anything else. Are we willing to risk *that* for this desire that we both feel? It would complicate things for us even more. Don't make *me* ask you for something I know *you* cannot give."

He stared at me for a long while, then he heaved a sigh. "Fair enough. I think you stated your case well. And because I'm such a masochist, I'm going to kiss you as much as I want. Let Tom kick my ass in hell later!" And he kissed me again...as thoroughly as he did before, so that I almost forgot my whole monologue from a minute before.

We stayed in the pool for another hour. Talking and drinking Chardonnay. It was a perfect setting, and I had a picture in my head of what a blissful picture we made. I couldn't wait to get to my easel and paint it on canvas.

It was already past midnight when we emerged from the pool. Travis wrapped a towel around me. I felt a tingle in the nape of my neck as he brushed his lips against the base of my neck.

"Travis..." I moaned. "Stop!"

He took a deep breath. He gave me a gentle kiss on the neck one last time and said, "Get dressed before I cannot control myself."

I turned around and smiled at him. I got on my tiptoes and gave him a kiss on the lips, and then I went into the room. When I was alone in the bathroom, I stared at myself in the mirror. My lips were probably bruised from kissing, my face was flushed, and I had a big smile on my face that I couldn't wipe off.

"What is wrong with me?" I scowled at myself. I felt like a silly little girl. And for Travis Cross no less! Well, this was a honeymoon after all, and I'd promised him I wouldn't hold back.

I emerged from the bathroom wearing a silk nightgown that decently ended above my knees. Travis took one hard look at me and groaned, "So help me God!"

I laughed. "This is the most decent one your assistant packed in the bag."

Travis shook his head in frustration. He gave me a smack on the lips, and then he went into the bathroom. I lay on the bed and switched off the lights. The room was illuminated by the moonlight coming from outside. I could hear the faint gushing of the waves below us.

I still had a big smile on my face. I don't know what was going on between Travis and me, but I was almost certain I was enjoying it. I promised not to hold back what I felt. I promised to go with the flow... so Travis could let go of his control.

Once again, he'd admitted that he wanted me. But that wasn't what I wanted. My relationship with him was too beautiful to risk for just a 'want,' a desire. If I allowed him to touch me, I would want him to 'love' me...as in *fall* in love with me. And I would want to be the only woman in his life from that point forward.

I knew Travis would want to stay with me forever after that. But that wasn't enough. If he stayed with me, I wanted him to do it because he felt I was the only one for him. Not because he was honor-bound to do so, because he didn't want to hurt me. I would want him to stay with me simply because he wouldn't be able to live without me. And I knew...that was too much to ask.

# Chapter Twenty-Two

When I woke up the next day, my head was resting comfortably on Travis's shoulder. We had our arms around each other, as if it was a natural thing for us to sleep in the same bed.

"Good morning," I greeted him.

He smiled lazily. "Good morning." He leaned down and kissed my forehead gently.

I stretched in bed lazily, and then I stood up and disappeared into the bathroom.

We had our breakfast in one of the restaurants of the hotel. We chose a spot overlooking the ocean. It was a beautiful view, and I was almost sorry I hadn't brought a sketchbook with me.

After breakfast, Travis and I decided to swim on the beach. We went kayaking, and then we sunbathed on the shore. There were some couples there, but it wasn't crowded and was easy enough to mind our own business.

We walked on the shoreline just before sunset, our fingers intertwined.

"It's beautiful here," I said.

"Yes. I'm glad you like it," he said. "I wanted to give you the honeymoon you deserve, Brianne. This is your first marriage, after all."

"Whatever happened to that guy who told me he'd just be a mere groom who would meet me at the altar?" I teased.

He sighed. "You also told me to put my mask down." He stopped walking and pulled me gently so I would face him. "I guess this is me. Do you like what you see?"

I stared back at him, and I saw a picture of a boy with a broken soul, a man who had let go of the control he had held on to for decades of his life. He was torn, he was broken...but he was sensitive, he was sweet...he was every bit as loveable as I thought he would be.

I took a deep breath and struggled to find my voice. "I don't like it. I *love* it," I whispered, and I threw myself in his arms and gave him a big hug. "If you could only stay like this with me forever, Travis…"

He took a deep breath and hugged me back. "That would mean weakness, vulnerability…I can't always allow that, Brianne."

"Not even with me?"

"Don't you already love me the way I am?"

"Yes…but now, I know you have two different sides," I replied. "And *this* is the guy I want to be with."

He sighed. "You're lucky I love you," he said. "The favors you ask of me are far too weird…too difficult."

"At least I didn't require you to give up half of your fortune!" I laughed.

He raised a brow. "You did, actually."

I blinked back. "When?"

"When you married me," he replied. "You own half of what I own now."

"But this is not…"

"What? This marriage is real, Brianne," he said. "You're my wife now. That's not a fake, make-believe thing. We didn't even have a prenup."

"But you know why we got married, right?"

He narrowed his eyes at me for a moment and then he said, "Why *did* we get married, Brianne?"

I stared back at Travis. Looking at his handsome face and his intense, piercing eyes, I forgot the real reason why I'd called in the favor I'd asked fourteen years earlier. It was like…nothing else was important now. At that moment, there was nowhere else I would rather have been…no one else I would rather have been with…not even Christian.

"Because…" I started. Because I really couldn't think of the reason why I'd married him, I thought about the reason why he'd married me. "Because I asked you this favor fourteen years ago. And you were one guy who could keep your promises."

He took a deep breath. "Yeah. I guess you could say that." He pulled away from me and we started walking again.

I stared up at him. "You sound like you're tired of doing me all these weird favors!" I teased.

"It can be exhausting," he grinned back at me.

I glared at him and pretended I found that offensive. "Okay, fine! Don't do me any favors ever again!" And I walked out on him.

I felt him pull me, but I struggled to get away from him and I started running away.

He made one wrong pull. But he was also quick to realize it. Quickly he was beside me, pulling me to him and hugging me.

I realized then what had happened. I was wearing a bikini top, and in my efforts to get away from Travis, he had accidentally pulled the strings that tied my top to my body. He enclosed me in his arms before anybody around us could notice what happened.

I was aware that I was half-naked and touching skin-to-skin with him. I buried my face in his shoulder in embarrassment.

When I stared up at him, his eyes were dancing.

"Dammit, Travis!"

"I'm sorry," he whispered. "It was a slight miscalculation on my part."

I pinched him on the side as hard as I could.

"Ouuuch!!!" he moaned. "Do you want me to let go of you now?"

I panicked. I shook my head. "No. Please don't," I begged.

Travis chuckled. He fixed my top in place and then he tied the strings on my back in a secure knot.

"Next time, tie your tops more securely," he said, staring down at me, his eyes laughing.

"Next time, pull somewhere or something else," I said evenly.

He laughed. "Yes. Next time." And he leaned down to give me a kiss at the base of my neck that sent shivers down my spine and almost turned my knees to jelly. *How is Travis doing this to me?* I thought, getting more and more frustrated with myself.

I breathed in the scent of him and hugged him to me.

I wondered what would happen when we got back to Manhattan, when we truly started making our life together. When Travis started becoming the reserved, unemotional, cold, ruthless man he wanted to be again. When I started holding back all my feelings for him to prevent myself from falling in love with the one guy I couldn't afford to lose in my life. When I started forgetting how wonderful and blissful this honeymoon had been. And how it was everything I had ever dreamt of and more.

We played like little kids on the beach. We built sandcastles, we chased each other on the shore. Every time he caught me, he would sweep me off my feet, carry me in his arms, and take me to the water. Travis laughed more that day than I had ever heard him in my entire life. His eyes had a certain glitter in them. He looked more boyish, and more than that, I thought he looked happy. And it warmed me to know that *I* made him happy! After all the things that Travis had done for me, I wanted to do something for him this time.

We watched the sunset together. I was cradled in his arms while we sat on our deck. The scene before me was far more beautiful than I could ever have imagined. And it was more special because I was in the arms of a man whom I trusted with my life, a man I knew would go to hell and back to protect me, save me, and keep me happy.

"Are you happy, Travis?"

He took a deep breath. Then I felt him kiss my temple and inhale through my hair. "For many reasons, Brianne…I think I am."

That made me smile. He gave me a squeeze and I stared up at him. His beautiful eyes were unreadable. They were staring down at me, speaking to my soul, as if there were something he wanted to say to me that he couldn't, as if he were pleading for something, asking for forgiveness, or looking for answers.

Panic swept through me. A while ago, I had been happy to hear him say he was happy. Now I felt really sad because I knew that something was up. It was as if Travis was really in pain, but he was trying his best to look happy…to make me happy.

"Is…something wrong, Travis?" I asked.

He took a deep breath and then he shook his head. Instead of answering, he bent down and kissed me on the lips. He kissed me thoroughly, passionately. There were a thousand words hidden in that kiss, and I wanted to cry because I wanted to understand them…I wanted to know what he wanted to say. I wanted to know everything about him…every hidden layer of his soul. But I knew it was too much to ask of him to tell me everything. At least for now.

The sun went down and Travis and I were still kissing. When I pulled away, I almost felt embarrassed. I was feeling more than one emotion, more than one spark. I was ready to ignite, and I was so close to breaking all the rules just to be with him.

I went inside the bungalow to take a bath as I was still dressed in my two-piece suit, with sand particles covering my body. Travis followed me inside.

I didn't speak. I was trying to calm down because I was ready to invite Travis to join me in the bath or in bed. Damn! He wasn't the only one struggling to control his desire.

At the door of the bathroom, I made the mistake of looking back at him. I didn't shield my eyes. All my emotions...hunger and yearning...were readable on my face as I looked at the one man who could read me like a book! When I looked at him, it seemed we had the same thing on our minds.

Things happened quickly. Before I knew it, his lips were on me again. He pulled me to him, a little rougher than usual. His tongue invaded my mouth in kisses that were meant to devour and conquer.

My own hands weren't helping me. I was pulling him, kissing him back with as much hunger and eagerness.

When he freed my lips, he nuzzled my neck. I let out a loud moan as I pulled his neck as if I could get him closer than he already was. I realized we were in the shower already. I was leaning against the bathroom wall helplessly. I allowed him to kiss me the way he did in my vivid dreams of him.

I remembered what it felt like...his skin against mine, his lips devouring me...taking me on an intense ride of passion.

But I knew I wasn't dreaming this time...the feel of his skin against mine was as real as it would ever be.

"Damn it, Brianne!" he cursed softly against my skin. "Stop me!"

"Travis..." I whispered his name. He nuzzled my neck and somehow, I couldn't think about stopping him. It was like my mind was a complete blank.

"Tell me to stop, love," he begged. But he himself didn't make any move to end the madness that was taking over both of us at the moment. His arms around my waist were getting tighter each second, in sync with the urgency of his hot kisses against my lips and my skin.

I took a deep breath. In all honesty, I wanted this—just as badly as Travis did. I wanted this to happen. I wanted Travis to take me...right then and there. I was losing all sense of control, all sense of reason. I realized that I wanted Travis more than I had ever wanted any man in my life! I wanted the very first man I had been with...I want to feel him again. Moreover, I wanted to freely touch him and look at him as he made love to me.

"Travis..."

His lips found mine again. He kissed me, softly bruising my lips, sending me closer and closer to my breaking point.

"Brianne...you have to stop me!" he said in a hoarse voice wrapped with lust.

"Why?" I murmured the only syllable that could escape my mouth at the moment.

"Because...I'm a few seconds away from taking you again!" he said, his voice filled with warning. "And *that*...will change everything between us!"

Something about what he said made me blink back to reality. When I opened my eyes, I found that Travis had stopped kissing me. His eyes were teary, his expression dark and intense. He was staring at me deeply, begging me to comprehend what he was trying to say.

He took a deep breath. "The next time I take you, Brianne...I will not allow you to forget anymore. And I will not disappear like I did before. The next time I take you...I will ask you to put all your bets on the table, and risk *everything*." He took a deep breath, controlling his emotions. "I'm a few seconds from unleashing the *beast* inside me. The beast I was protecting you from for so many years. And once it's out, Brianne...I won't have the strength to lock it up anymore." He stared at me for a long while, allowing me to absorb every word he said. "So if you want me to remain the same safe guy you've always had...please...stop me *now*."

I felt like Travis had taken me to a crossroads. He was making me choose between two paths. One path led to the same comfortable refuge that I have always had...with the same Travis who would protect me from every beast, including himself, who had asked me to forget what had happened between us many years ago...because he felt so guilty about taking me. And another path led to something uncertain...something more exciting, something more terrifying. Something that would allow both of us to explore the passion we felt for each other...but could come at the expense of the bonds of friendship we had cultivated for years.

And somehow...I realized that I was not ready to risk Travis for *anything*. Not yet. Even though I knew I wanted him with so much passion and intensity, I also knew that I loved him with every bit of my soul and that I would die if I ever lost him in any way. And there was a huge chance that I might...because I would expect him to commit to me. I would not allow him to touch any other woman, even if that made him happiest. And I knew that would be too much to ask. And Travis had already given me so much in the past. He'd already given me his life. It would be too much to ask him for his heart.

No, Travis Cross was not something I could afford to gamble with.

"I'm not going to lose you, Travis," I whispered. Then I took a deep breath and said, "So...please *stop*." My voice was broken. I know I didn't sound convincing. I wasn't even able to convince myself.

Travis smiled at me ruefully. I couldn't read his expression. I wasn't sure if he was disappointed or relieved. He reached for the knob behind me and turned on the shower. I shivered at the cold water running against my skin.

Travis took a deep breath and stared at me for a while. Then he said, "I guess we both need a cold shower."

I don't know how long we stood there. He was standing at arms' length away from me. Both his hands were on either side of my face, caging me in as he leaned against the wall to support his weight. His face was turned toward the floor and his eyes were closed as he let the water run down his body. He didn't touch me or look at me. I leaned against the bathroom wall, feeling the cold water run over my skin, trying to calm my pounding heart and my raging nerves.

I remembered Travis's face in my dream many nights ago. He gently and passionately took me. It was everything I wanted it to be...it was every bit as wonderful as I thought lovemaking should be. In my dreams, I came to my peak twice...he never abandoned me, he gave me pleasure, and he caressed me in ways I wanted to be caressed. He screamed my name over and over when he reached his peak, and then he held me as tightly as he could when it was over. It was everything I could ever dream of, maybe even more. And in my dreams, he didn't ask me to close my eyes. He didn't ask me not to say his name. He said my name as if it was the sweetest word that could come off his lips.

I realized I wanted it to be real. That dream I had a few nights ago made me reach the edges of my passion even in my sleep. I wanted to feel it. To see if it was every bit the same in reality.

But it would take a lot for me to know. My relationship with Travis was far more important than any dream and fantasy that I might have. Travis was real. And I was not going to give him up just to know whether or not he could make my dreams come true.

When he raised his face to me again, he seemed to have calmed down. He looked apologetic and frustrated at the same time, but he managed a rueful smile.

247

"I'm sorry," he whispered. His voice was so gentle it made me want to cry. "I shouldn't have put you through that."

"I'm sorry I didn't stop you earlier."

He leaned forward and gave me a gentle kiss on the nose. "This marriage is going to be harder than I thought it would be."

"Because it isn't real?"

"The marriage is real, Brianne. It's just waiting to be consummated," he replied. "And the moment I touch you, there will be no going back for either of us."

I sighed and leaned forward to hug him. I could feel him still hard against my abdomen. He hesitated to touch me. He managed a few deep breaths and then I felt an arm encircle my naked waist.

"Why does it have to be this complicated?" I asked him. "I thought it was going to be easy."

He sighed. "It would have been very easy…if I didn't want you so damn much!"

I smiled. In a way, I felt flattered by his confession. The usual, guarded Travis wouldn't say that too easily. I felt happy to know that he wanted me that way. Because I knew I wanted him as much. But then again, I had to remember that Travis was a player to begin with. It was natural for him to want me this way. He told me once that he was a predator. If I gave in, I didn't think I would allow him to play with other prey, too. I would want him to stop with me…I would want to be the only one. And that complicated our situation even more.

I pulled away from Travis, but he stared down at me. He smiled and then he kissed me gently on the lips again.

"I'll go to the other bathroom…before we start this rollercoaster ride again," he said. I smiled at him apologetically and he grinned at me. "It's not your fault you're too damn beautiful!" He kissed me one last time, and then shut off the water and grabbed the towel on the towel bar.

I waited for him to exit the bathroom before I turned on the shower again. I sat on the floor and allowed the water to run over my skin until I calmed the blood in my system down.

# Chapter Twenty-Three

The next several days were bliss. It was like there was nothing else in the world but Travis and me. We still kissed, but we both knew where our limits were. We tried not to come close to the edge. We knew we both might not have the strength to stop a second time around.

We watched the sunset together every day. Sometimes on the deck, sometimes in the pool.

One time, we were lying on a hammock by the beach. I was in his arms, comfortably resting my head on his shoulders with one of his arms wrapped around my waist.

"It's almost over," I whispered as I watched the sun go down behind the horizon. But I didn't mean the sunset. The next day we would set back for New York. And somehow, I felt my heart breaking.

Travis heaved a deep breath. "I know," he whispered. "Tomorrow, I put my mask back on. And you're free to push me back when I come any closer to you."

I stared up at him. "It doesn't have to be like that, Travis."

"Yes, it does," he said softly.

"Why? Can't we stay like this forever?" I asked. "Can't you take your mask off for me for good?"

He shook his head. "This guy is weak, Brianne. He won't be able to protect you...from himself."

I rested my head back on his shoulder. I guessed he was right. Without his mask, Travis couldn't resist getting his hands on me...couldn't resist kissing me whenever he had the chance. I wanted it. If he didn't resist, I wouldn't have the power to push him back, either. If he didn't control himself, we were both in danger of breaking each other...tearing each other apart...losing each other. Why did it have to be complicated? Why did he have to be Travis...the guy who was as important to me as the brother I had lost?

Travis tilted my chin up so I could look into his eyes. He stared at me deeply. With a broken expression on his face, he said, "Whatever happens...please don't forget...I would never intentionally hurt you, Brianne. And I would do anything for you. Just say the word."

I sighed, trying my best to control the emotions overwhelming me all at once. "I love you, Travis. I think I would die if I ever lose you."

And I knew I meant that.

That night, we stayed on the deck and had some drinks. Travis had his usual beer, and I had a mild cocktail. There was a lover's moon in the sky, and it illuminated the pool and the beach in front of us beautifully. Travis's face against the moonlight was perfect...he looked like a dark angel. I felt a flood of pride sweep through me. I didn't know why but somehow, it felt good to know that it was me he was kissing now. But who knew what would happen to us when we went back to the real world?

I opened Sarah's box of honeymoon tricks. Travis and I had a laugh when I pulled out some naughty stuff from the box, like edible underwear, lubricants, and flavored oils.

There was a game there called "Sssshhhh!!!"

"'Ssshhhh!!! The newlyweds' honesty game,'" I read from the caption.

Travis raised a brow. "That's interesting."

I read the caption further. "'This is the game to play to get to know your new wife's or husband's deepest, darkest secrets prior to your honeymoon. Know the answers to questions such as *'Are you really hitting the spot?' 'Are you the best he or she ever had?' 'Where exactly is her g-spot?' 'What's his or her secret fantasy?'* Play the game to improve your connection to your partner. But a word of warning! Some questions may be better off answering with a lie!'" I had to laugh at that. I stared up at Travis. "Shall we play it?"

He raised a brow. "We're not a normal couple. What good could it to do for us?"

I giggled. "Nothing, maybe. But it sounds like a hell of a laugh!"

Travis held his hands up. "All right, whatever gives you a kick." He grinned.

I read the instructions. The game actually required the players to lose a piece of clothing or do something kinky depending on the question. The more interesting to a player the answer was, the higher the bet, the kinkier the action would be.

"Hmmm... now, this is interesting," Travis said, grinning.

"Forget it! We're not going to do that," I glared at him. "Let's just read the questions and take turns answering them."

He raised a brow. "Now, where's the fun in that?"

"Come on, Travis! I'm just curious about the game. It's not like you have an important board meeting to catch, you know." I took a card from the deck and read one question out loud. "When did you lose your virginity?"

I looked at him. He raised a brow at me. Suddenly, I realized I knew the answer to that. I smiled at him and handed him the deck of cards. "Your turn."

"Shouldn't we answer each question both ways?" he challenged me. "It's not fair to know a secret only one way."

I rolled my eyes. "Fine. But I didn't have to answer that question, either. You know exactly when I lost my virginity."

He narrowed his eyes at me and then he shook his head. "Hmmm...actually, I don't think I recall that."

I didn't anticipate that I was going to feel bad when I heard what he said. I raised a brow at Travis and gave him a haughty look. Of course! How could he remember? I was only one of the girls he'd been to bed with...one of the statistics. How could I have possibly made that night special to him?

"I don't have to answer that!" I insisted, refusing to look at him, not letting him know that he'd actually pissed me off.

Travis stood up from his chair, came close to me, and quickly placed my face between his palms, forcing me to look at him.

I raised a brow at him. "Hey..." he said. He smiled at me sheepishly. "Senior year. May eleventh. Twelve-thirty a.m., Paladine Matrimonial Suite 1403. You were eighteen years old. I was the guy who took your innocence away from you. I touched you twice that night." He stared at me and then he heaved a sigh. "Just because I asked you to forget doesn't mean I could will myself to do the same thing."

I bit my lip. *He remembered!* "Maybe you just have a very good memory."

He chuckled as he released me. "Believe me! It's one of those things I wish I didn't have." He sat back in his seat. "Next question?"

I picked another card from the deck. "Have you had a partner of the same sex?"

"Hell no!" Travis answered immediately.

I laughed. "Too defensive there, chief!"

"Next question?"

"Are you not interested to know *my* answer?" I asked.

251

"No," he said.

"Why not?"

"Because I already know the answer," he replied. "And I can say I'm thankful my wife is as straight as I am."

I laughed and picked another card. "Where's your weakest spot?"

He shrugged. He thought for a moment and then he said, "I guess it's my ear."

I tried to think what was mine. Chris was the only man I had been with after my first time with Travis. And I couldn't remember a spot that made me weak, or made me shiver.

Travis raised a brow at me. "Honestly, you don't know?" he asked.

I shook my head. I didn't remember Chris ever kissing me on some part of my body that made me instantly mindless.

"I really can't think of any. Maybe I don't have a weak spot."

Travis raised a brow at me again. "Come on. Think again."

"Well, I can't remember Chris dwelling on a particular spot that...made me *weak*."

"Maybe this Chris character is a moron," Travis whispered under his breath.

"I heard that," I said to him. "Could be true, actually." Honestly, I thought I'd felt more sensual with Travis in the previous week than I'd ever felt in the years I was with Chris. With Chris, it felt like a task, an obligation that we had to fulfill because couples were supposed to do that to strengthen their relationship. But if it hadn't been a requirement, we might not have done it at all.

With Travis...it was like, we didn't have to do it...we knew we couldn't do it...and yet we were like two opposite poles of magnets pulling toward each other, and we had to find the strength to stop.

"Next question?" I asked Travis. In a way, I felt embarrassed that I couldn't tell him where my weak spot was.

Travis picked up a card. But before he read the question, he stared at me from under his lashes. "The base of your neck," he said in a low voice.

I blinked back at him. "What? There's no way you could know that!"

He raised a brow. "Really, Mrs. Cross, would you like me to prove my point?"

I bit my lip. I knew I was red all over. I shook my head. "No," I replied in a weak voice. "I'll take your word for it. Next question."

He gave a look that was meant to unnerve me...make me blush. And when he was sure I'd blushed enough, he gave me a smirk and said, "Your ex is officially a moron. I've known that since we were fifteen, *cherie*."

I glared at him. But I knew he was right. One night when we were young, he'd trapped me in his bedroom when I came home past my curfew. He sort of nuzzled my neck for the first time. I trembled and almost fell to the floor. Amazing how Travis had realized that in three seconds and Chris never did in the two and a half years we were together.

Travis gave me a crooked smile before reading the question on the next card. "Fantasy place you want to do it?"

I laughed. "Gosh! Hmmm...I'm not an exhibitionist. I would like it to be in a bed of rose petals." I looked at Travis shyly. "I'm boring."

He shook his head. "You're romantic. Me? Funny, I fancy a pool."

"A pool?" I echoed.

He nodded and pointed at the plunge pool beside us. "As long as it's private."

I laughed. "Wow! And I actually thought Travis Cross would think about...fitting rooms or something."

He frowned. "I'm actually discreet in my sexual affairs. And any woman who would allow me to do it with her in a public place...actually turns me off."

"Hmmm... interesting fact about Travis Cross." I smiled. I picked out another card from the deck. This one had a long question, followed by series of question marks and a red heading that read, "*Answer with Caution!*"

"Interesting card," I said. I read the first question. "Did you have sex seventy-two hours prior to the wedding?"

I knew the answer to this on my side. But suddenly I realized I wanted to know what Travis's answer was, too.

"No," I answered. I read the follow-up questions. "I guess the rest are all N.A.'s for me." I looked at Travis. "Your turn."

He narrowed his eyes. "Are you really interested in my answer?"

"Well, it's not like I will file a divorce if I don't like what I hear," I laughed.

He sighed. "Ask away."

"Did you have sex seventy-two hours prior to the wedding?"

He stared at me soberly. "No," he whispered.

"Come on, Trav! You can lie better than that," I teased. But deep inside, my heart was pounding inside my chest. *Why the hell am I nervous?*

"I didn't have sex before my wedding," he said. "I...made love." His voice had a hint of pain, and suddenly the air seemed to be full of the same intense emotion that he felt.

"To whom?" I asked quietly, reading the next question. *The stripper in the cake?* I wanted to add.

He sighed. "To an amazing...wonderful woman."

I guessed he didn't want to say the name of the girl...if he actually still remembered.

I read the next question. "What were your thoughts during that time? Did you realize anything vital about yourself?"

Travis stared at me seriously, as if deciding whether to answer the question or not. Then finally he said, "My life. The reason why I live. The core of my existence."

I stared back at him. Suddenly, I wanted to cry. When he said those words, he sounded so vulnerable...so torn...so broken.

"I realized I had a heart, and it's been beating and breaking...I realized there was one person I could live and die for...and I wanted to freeze that moment for eternity...because in that moment...when she screamed my name...she truly belonged to me."

"Travis..." I couldn't breathe. I realized something. This was what he'd been trying to tell me since the wedding...every time he fell quiet and looked lost. He wasn't just a broken soul...he was also heartbroken when he married me. He wanted to tell me how much of a sacrifice he was making for me. There was...a woman...and Travis couldn't be with her...because he'd kept his promise to marry me. "Travis...you're...in love?"

He bit his lip. Tears threatened to escape from his eyes. "It doesn't matter now, does it?" He smiled ruefully. "Sometimes, it's too late when you realize your world revolves around one person...I thought...it was my body craving hers...but that last time I was with her...I realized it was my heart screaming out for her...I realized too late...she was the air that I breathed...and I would give everything just to see that look on her face again...the look of love shining upon her

254

when she screamed my name and we..." He took a deep breath. "Came together. She told me she loved me...but I didn't tell her how I really felt...how I really feel..."

I looked back at Travis. His eyes were wet with tears. He was broken. Because I'd asked him a big favor...because he pledged his life to me a long time ago...it had prevented him from pursuing his happiness...his own love, when he didn't even know that he was capable of feeling that.

And now...his life was mine...and the heart of the woman he realized he loved was lost to him. He was left with me...the selfish little sister of his best friend...who had become so used to him saving her for half of her life!

"Travis...I'm sorry," I whispered. "I didn't know..."

He took a deep breath. "Don't feel sorry, love," he said softly. "I didn't know, either. I knew...too late. Otherwise, I would have told her...before the wedding...so at least...she wouldn't feel that I cheated."

Tears rolled down my cheeks. Even though I knew there was a part of me that broke hearing that there was another woman in his heart...a bigger part of me ached for the broken man inside Travis...who may have lost the chance to be with the love of his life because he helped me buy time to find the love of *my* life. How truly selfish of me!

I couldn't stop crying now. I stood up from my seat and went to Travis. He caught me in his arms, making me sit on his lap. He put his arms around me, cradled me in his arms, and I cried against his chest.

"I'm sorry, Travis," I said. "I didn't know. Otherwise...I would not have held you to your promise! I would have let you go. I would have set you free. I didn't know you were sacrificing that much for me!"

"Ssshhh!" he whispered. "I guess I also wouldn't have allowed you to cancel the wedding."

"But you can't sacrifice that much for me, Travis," I said. "Now, it's too late! You're married to me now...and you may have blown your chances of being with her."

I realized that even though a part of me hurt, too, I would rather do something for Travis...if there were anything more that I could do to help soothe the pain.

"Tell me, Travis. Tell me how I can make it up to you? To help soothe your pain...tell me what to do."

He looked down to me. His expression was still torn and broken. He smiled at me wistfully. "For now, this is enough, love. What you're doing is enough to soothe a little of my pain."

"Don't you want to pursue her? Do you want me to talk to her and tell her why you married me in the first place?"

He laughed humorlessly. "I doubt that would be of any help at the moment." He pushed a lock of stray hair away from my face.

"You're just giving up?" I asked him angrily. "Don't you want to fight for what you feel for her?"

He smiled at me. "How about you, Brianne? Aren't you going to fight for me? I'm your husband now."

"But I want you to be happy, Travis!" I said.

He smiled. "And I will be," he said. "With you. Like this. Time heal all wounds. For now...I am happy this way with you. I won't ask for anything else just yet."

"I've been unfair! I...always thought you were mine forever...I didn't even think that you also had a life of your own... a heart of your own! I feel like...I stole the one chance you had to be happy!"

He chuckled humorlessly. "I guess I had two chances to be happy. I chose this one."

"But why? Why didn't you tell me?"

"Because you needed me, Brianne," he replied softly. "This marriage was pre-ordained fourteen years ago. Last-minute realizations don't always get factored in."

"Of course they do! Had you told me...that you had a chance at a different life...that would make you happier, I would have...set you free."

"And you would rather your family curse you?"

I nodded. "If that meant you'd be happier for the rest of your life, then yes!"

He smiled at me wistfully. "Then I don't deserve you, Brianne! I guess I should be the one making amends, not you. And I am happy...like this...with you."

"But there's something missing," I said to him. "I can see it in your eyes."

256

He gave me a smile that was full of pain. "One of the downsides of asking me to put my mask down, love. You weren't supposed to see a lot of things."

"But I want to!" I insisted. "I want to know everything. I want you to know that even if you've lost hope in trusting anything else…you can trust me."

He cupped my face between his palms. "I know. It's me…you shouldn't trust. I know deep inside my heart I would never hurt you. But I was afraid that there were some things beyond my control," he said in a broken voice.

"But I do trust you, Travis. And I always will," I said. "I will always believe in you. I want you to be happy…even if…it means you will be happier without me." I knew I meant that. But it hurt to say it. Because I really could not imagine my life without Travis in it.

He shook his head. "Can't you see, Brianne? I cannot be happy without you. My fate was tied to yours the day I promised Tom I would take care of you."

"You don't have to sacrifice so much for me!" I argued.

He smiled ruefully. "I was actually hoping something good will come out of this. When I chose this path…I was hoping…for a miracle. I know we'll be okay, love."

"Miracle?" I echoed.

He shrugged. "That someday, things would fall into place. That we'd both be happy in the end."

I hugged him. "You don't always have to be selfless with me!"

He gave me a humorless laugh. Then he shook his head. "You have so much faith in me, love. I don't deserve it. You must remember the man that I was before I married you. Don't forget who I really am." He shook his head again. "I don't think it's in my nature to be selfless."

"Why do you always try to change my opinion of you?"

"Because I want you to see who I really am," he said. "And see that I cannot change…not permanently, at least."

"You would have changed…for her," I said in a sad voice. "Love changes people, Travis. You would have been a better, happier man if you'd chosen not to marry me…if you followed your heart…if just once, you allowed yourself to break a promise."

257

"My parents never knew how to keep their promises, or their word," he said coldly. "I'm not going to be like them. I have never been."

"Even if you sacrifice your heart?"

He hugged me tighter to him. "Even if sometimes I don't do what's right."

"Yes," I sobbed in his arms. "You shouldn't have married me, Travis. You should have followed your heart. That's what's right."

"But everything about this honeymoon feels right, too, Brianne."

I sighed. I knew what he was saying. Everything felt right…even the part where I was in his arms. I felt like everything was as it should be. I hadn't thought about Christian in a long time. And now that I remembered him, I didn't think I would trade my time with Travis for anything. I guessed it was safe to say that I was totally over Christian.

"Are you saying you don't regret choosing me over the woman you might be in love with?"

He took a deep breath. Then he said, "I've had you this way longer. It may be harder to let go of what we have. I've never regretted my decisions in the past, Brianne. So please don't make me feel like I should start regretting some of them now."

I stared at him. "Travis, sooner or later, I will find the man I have been looking for. We'll divorce and I will remarry. That was the plan, remember?"

He gave me a devilish smile and said, "Who told you I had plans of ever giving you up?"

I giggled. "I told you, you can't fall in love with me," I teased.

He shook his head. "I don't have to be in love with you to want to keep you forever," he teased back. "I told you, I'm naturally a selfish man…greedy, even."

I laughed. "You intend to keep me as your wife forever?"

He shrugged. "Ever wondered why I didn't suggest a prenup?"

I laughed. "Stop that, Travis! You don't need a prenup because you know I will not take a single penny from you! We trust each other enough to know what the real deal is. For all it's worth, I should be paying *you* for your services…but that would make me feel like a dirty old woman." I took a deep breath. I still felt guilty about the whole thing. I stared at Travis. "Who is she?"

He raised a brow.

"The woman…who basically is your life," I added.

I was not sure I wanted him to answer. There might have be a small part of me that ached to know whether when Travis was kissing me, his heart actually longed for the company of another woman.

"Why do you want to know?" he asked.

I shrugged. "No reason. I'm just curious. In all the years I've known you, I've never imagined a woman could actually make you...miserable."

"I'm not miserable, Brianne."

"I knew you were torn and heartbroken when you married me. Now I know why," I said. "I was just curious what she's like...this woman you'd rather be kissing when you are kissing me."

"Don't be absurd, Brianne," Travis said, his tone showing signs of irritation. "When I'm kissing you, I would rather be kissing you. Remember, nobody can force me to do what I don't want to do. So when I'm kissing you, there's no other woman in my mind but you."

"Still...I want to know what she's like. You said she's your life."

He sighed and cupped my face between his palms again. "I think we've played too much of this game now. You're asking too many questions that aren't on the cards!" he said. "But to answer your question...this woman, who is my life...is amazing and wonderful. She has reddish blond hair...beautiful gray eyes. She's a vixen in a beautiful human form," he said solemnly. He took my hand and raised it to look at my fingers. "Her delicate fingers can paint beautiful pictures, colors, and hues. When she dances on stage, she takes my breath away." He stared at me deeply. "She has a good heart, a wonderful soul. She's exquisite, far more beautiful than any woman I have ever known."

I narrowed my eyes at him. "Travis! I asked a serious question!"

He chuckled. "And I answered it truthfully!" he said. "Because it's true. I married you. *You* are my life now."

"You're not going to tell me who she is, are you?"

He sighed. "It doesn't matter, Brianne," he replied. "I would rather try to stay married to you now."

"But we both know where this marriage is headed! I don't want you to let go of your chance at love, too!"

"This marriage will last as long as you want...need it to," he reminded me. "How long will that take?" he asked me matter-of-factly. "And during those years, I don't intend to be miserable, Brianne."

"Then why did you choose to marry me?"

He took a deep breath. "Because I can't afford to lose you…in any way. That would make me more miserable than anything else. And for that, I wanted to kick Tom's ass! He threw us in this situation."

I didn't know what to feel anymore. Travis had just confessed that he gave up the first woman he ever loved for me. He was torn, broken, and miserable, but he chose this path because he would rather have a broken heart than not have me in his life at all. Because his love for me was far greater than any other love he would ever feel for any other woman.

I hugged him again. "How can I help you ease the pain?"

He tightened his arms around me. He took a deep breath. "This. For now, this is enough."

I realized then what I needed to do. Travis had lost his love when he married me. I would try to make up for that. I would fill that empty gap in his heart. I would try to ease the pain by doing what the girl of his dreams would have done had he not married me instead. I would try to take her place…until Travis could be whole again. And I would be patient with him. I knew it was going to be difficult. Because when we got back to New York, Travis wouldn't be as open and as vulnerable as he was now. In New York, he would try to repel my efforts to make him forget. But I would be persistent. This was the least I could do for him. Damned if I got my heart broken in the end!

# Chapter Twenty-Four

We got back to our apartment. As soon as we entered, Travis turned to me and said, "It has been a lovely week, Mrs. Cross."

I smiled at him. "It has been."

"Now, we are at a crossroads again," he said. "I told you I can't do without my mask. The guy you've been with...is far too vulnerable to be able to protect you...keep you safe."

I shook my head. "I don't believe you!" I said to him. "That guy is more capable of protecting my feelings than anybody else."

He narrowed his eyes. "You have to remember, Brianne. I not only want to protect you," he said. "There's a big part of me that also craves you."

I stepped closer to him. "I know what you're capable of, Travis. I know that guy can protect me, too. You don't have to put your mask back on. When you told me...you chose to marry me over pursuing the woman you loved...I promised I would make this choice count. I promised to make you happy, Travis. It's the least that I can do! Before I set out to find the guy I was meant to be with for the rest of my life, I will make this a happy home for you first...until you get over your heartache. Until you're ready to find love again."

He closed his eyes for a moment. When he opened them, I could see tears shining through them. "Do you know there's more than a fifty percent chance that I don't let you go after all this?"

I giggled. "I told you—you cannot fall in love with me."

"But I also told you I was selfish and greedy by nature."

"You will let me go when you know I'll be happy," I said to him. "I know you, Travis. I know you want me to be happy. And now, I want a chance to make *you* happy."

Travis closed his eyes for a moment. Then he pulled me to him and gave me a hug. "God give me strength to let you go when you ask to be set free!" he whispered, more to himself.

When he pulled away from me, he stared at my face. He wiped the tears from my eyes. Then he pulled my face to his and gave me a kiss on the lips. He leaned his forehead against mine and said, "I am a big

261

mess inside, Brianne. I hope you can really fix me...and forgive me when all this...doesn't end the way we wanted it to."

"I won't need to forgive you, Travis. I know you won't hurt me."

He gave me a solemn look. "Always remember that," he said. "I would never hurt you."

I knew he meant that. He chose to hurt himself and the woman he loved just to keep his promise to me. Yes, I would make amends. As long as Travis needed me, I would be the wife he deserved... the family he could come home to.

After dinner, while we were still sitting at the dining room table, Travis reached out and gave me an envelope.

"What is this?" I asked.

"Something you need to accept from me since you've accepted my proposal to be my wife," he grinned.

I opened the envelope and found two cards on it. One was a black Visa card with the word "Infinite" written on it. The other was a black debit card. Both cards had *"Brittany Anne Cross"* engraved on them in gold letters.

I stared back at Travis. "What's this?"

"A credit card and an ATM card," he replied with a teasing grin.

"I know. But why?"

He shrugged. "Because I'm going to provide for you from now on. Everything you ever need for the house, just charge on the card. I love it when you cook for me. The least I can do is pay for the groceries. Although, you could have Karl arrange it for you. But I thought you wanted to be hands-on."

I smiled. "Yes, I do. No way would I ask your assistant to do our grocery shopping. It's a small household anyway. Just because I married Travis Cross doesn't mean I'll live like a spoiled little rich girl now." I stared up at him. "But, Travis, you didn't have to. I want to pay for my share. At least cook for you, pay for the groceries. I mean, you're already not asking me to pay rent."

He frowned. "You're my wife, Brianne. You won't have to worry about spending for anything anymore. You don't even have to work in your mother's gallery. If you want to, I won't stop you. But everything you'll ever earn is yours alone. Please, let me provide for everything else. And every single thing you fancy...clothes, handbags...charge them on the card. Consider them my treat."

"And the ATM card is for?"

"For you," he replied simply. "The pin is our wedding date. Every month, I will put money in the account. It's yours. Do whatever you want to do with it."

I raised a brow. "Like an allowance?"

He sighed. "I don't know how to make you understand, Brianne. This marriage is real. Do you realize that legally, you own everything I own? That bank account should be a joint one. You should have access to what's mine. But I know you'll never agree."

"Of course I won't. I don't even agree with the ATM now!" I argued.

He reached out for my hands and squeezed them. "Please don't argue, Brianne. Just take it. I can argue with this on legal grounds too, and you know I would win. For instance, if something happened to me, my accounts would be frozen for a couple of months before they would all go to you. But during those months before everything is fixed, I want you to have all the means to go on." He took a deep breath. "I promised you once that no matter what happened to me, I would still take care of you. I'm making steps to ensure that promise is kept."

What he said actually brought me tears. I didn't even want to think about what he had just said. Nothing could happen to Travis. Because I would die if something did. He was more important to me than all of the material things he could provide. Didn't he know that?

Travis stood up from his seat and pulled me into his arms. "*Cherie*, I will fight fate for you. You know that. But the coin has two sides. Everything in life is fifty-fifty. I plan my life ahead. I like things to be in order. I don't take chances in life. And I won't take chances with you. I want to make sure you'll always have a good life. Whether I'm around or not."

"I want you to always be around. I don't even want to think of the other possibility."

"You don't have to. It's me who has to deal with that." I had heard the sadness in his voice before he leaned forward to kiss me.

*** 

Travis was standing in our balcony, having a beer. I told him I'd join him shortly, but he didn't know that I was busy doing something else.

263

I was anxiously looking at the clock. Today...was Travis's thirtieth birthday.

When the clock finally struck twelve, I went to the balcony. I was carrying a cake in my hands.

"Happy birthday to you...happy birthday to you..." I sang.

He stared back at me, his eyes wide, as if he couldn't believe I was singing him happy birthday with a cake in my hands.

"Make a wish," I told him.

He smiled at me wistfully and then he blew the candle on his cake.

"What did you wish for?" I asked.

"I'm not supposed to tell, remember?"

I laughed. "Just asking." I placed the cake on the table.

I brought out a paper bag, and inside it was a neatly rolled parchment, tied with a red ribbon.

"What is this?"

"Your birthday gift," I replied.

He chuckled. "That's a first. I don't usually allow people to remember my birthday."

"But people doing something nice for you on your birthday means they care about you. It takes quite a lot to come up with surprises. And usually what the person wants is to see the glimmer in your eyes when you open their surprise. It hurts them when you turn them away and shut them out."

He stared at me and smiled ruefully. Then he opened the parchment roll. It was a painting I'd made for him...a painting of the perfect sunset on the beach, with a silhouette of a man and a woman lying on the hammock, watching the sunset while in each other's arms.

Travis bit his lip. When he stared at me, his eyes were welling up with tears. He smiled. It was as if he didn't know what to say. Then he pulled me to him, and he gave me one hard kiss on the lips.

He leaned his forehead against mine. "Now, how can you question my decision to choose to marry you?" he whispered.

I pulled away from him so I could stare into his eyes. "Because I know you'd be happier if you'd pursued the other option you had."

He shook his head. "On the contrary, I might have been more miserable," he said. "And I wouldn't be in this portrait you painted, which is..." He paused for a while and then he continued, "A picture of bliss."

"It is actually…" I stared at my painting. I felt a surge of emotion sweep through me. My voice was full of emotions when I said, "A picture of bliss."

We got ready for bed. Since we had returned from the honeymoon, Travis and I had been sleeping in the same bed. Sometimes we cuddled; sometimes we stayed on our own sides. It didn't feel weird at all. Instead, everything felt right when I was in his arms. I felt safe…like I didn't have to worry about anything at all. Sometimes, a part of me wished that he thought about only me when I was in his arms…and not wished he had chosen to stay with her instead. I knew I wanted to make up for the loss he felt. But sometimes, I thought there was a part of me that wished I could do more than that…that I could be more than just a patch…a substitute for Travis.

When I came out of the bathroom, dressed in a pair of silk pajamas, Travis startled me by sweeping me off my feet and carrying me to bed.

"Stop it!" I squealed. "Put me down, will you!"

He shook his head and stared at me mischievously. I landed on the bed with a bounce and laughed. I watched helplessly as Travis descended on top of me with a devilish look on his face.

"What are you going to do?"

"Something that will make Tom regret he ever asked me to be your guardian!" he whispered. I saw the Travis I knew when I was a kid…naughty…mischievous. His eyes were dancing as if he was up to no good and proud of it.

I struggled to push him away, but he was quick to get a grip of my wrists and pinned both my hands on top of my head. I couldn't stop laughing. "Travis, please…"

He shook his head. "It's my birthday. Nobody can stop me from doing what I want."

I watched helplessly as he leaned forward and kissed me on the lips. Thoroughly and passionately. He breathed in the scent of me; he devoured my lips as if he'd been holding back from doing so for weeks. Since we'd gotten back from the honeymoon, Travis and I had shared a lot of hugs and occasional kisses. But he'd never attempted to kiss me like that again.

He let go of my wrists, but he didn't stop kissing me. I wound my arms around his neck and kissed him back with just as much passion. I realized I'd missed this...I yearned for him to kiss me like this without reservations...without thinking he needed to protect me more than anything else.

But as always, he stopped and gently pulled away from me. He stared at me with eyes drunk with passion. But I knew he had his emotions in check. He smiled at me.

"You're beautiful," he whispered.

"So are you," I said to him.

He leaned forward to kiss me gently on the lips again. Then he inhaled the scent of me.

Deep inside, I felt my heart twist in knots. I felt a pinch of pain. I wondered if, at that moment, Travis was thinking about her...the woman he loved...the woman he made love to last before he married me...the woman he lost because he chose to marry me.

I realized I wanted him to forget her...and see me instead. I couldn't understand why, but somehow, I wanted not just to ease his pain...I wanted him to draw his happiness from me, too.

I held his face between my palms. Then I leaned forward and kissed him gently.

He stared at me for a moment and then he smiled. "Thank you, Brianne," he said. "For being here. I think I've been celebrating my birthdays alone for most of my life."

I smiled. "I'm here now. And I'll be here for as long as you want me to be."

He laughed humorlessly. "Don't make promises you can't keep, love," he said. "Because if it were up to me...it would be a very long time. In fact, I don't think I'll ever be ready to let you go at all."

I giggled. "And what? We'll stay married forever?"

He stared at me. I expected him to laugh. But when I looked at his face, his expression looked serious. My heart pounded inside my chest. "Aren't you happy with me, Brianne?" he asked in a sober voice.

Tears welled up in my eyes. I knew the answer to that without even thinking, not even blinking.

"I am," I whispered. I was happy with Travis. With him, I felt safe...comforted...loved...taken care of. And I knew he would not break my heart. "Are *you* happy with *me*, Travis?"

I was afraid of his answer. I knew between the two of us, I was the one who didn't have a choice. He, on the other hand, had the choice between the woman who was possibly the love of his life and me. I wanted to know he didn't regret that.

He smiled, and somehow, I saw glitter in his eyes. He leaned forward and just as his lips were an inch away from mine, he whispered, *"It's bliss!"*

# Chapter Twenty-Five

I woke up cuddled in Travis's arms. I opened my eyes lazily.

"Good morning," I said to him.

He leaned forward and gave me a soft kiss on the lips. "Come to the office with me today?" he asked.

I smiled. "Why? I can't sit around while you're working. It will distract you."

He chuckled. "It will distract me all right. But I don't really mind," he said. "You can paint while I read some contracts. I'll work only until noon. Then maybe we can go to a hotel. It's almost the weekend anyway."

My face brightened. "Really?"

He nodded. "Really. I want to celebrate my birthday with you alone, Mrs. Cross."

I beamed at him. "Wait for me. I'll go dress and pack some clothes."

I had a big smile on my face as I packed our stuff for the weekend. I realized that somehow, I hadn't thought much about Christian since I'd gotten engaged to Travis. Damn! I hadn't even thought about how I would hunt for Mr. Right since I'd married Travis. I realized that...now, my world revolved around him and our marriage.

I didn't realize that a smile had crept to my face. I was happy! I didn't think I'd been happier than this. And I thought we gotten married only to buy me time to find Mr. Right. But at that moment...*Travis* felt so right!

If only...if only he hadn't been in love with somebody else when he married me. I still wondered who she was. Maybe a former fling or a mistress, and maybe he realized at the last moment, before he married me, that she'd meant more to him.

We were a couple that didn't sleep with each other. But since we'd gotten married, it seems we did everything else that married couples did. We kissed, but we made sure we didn't step close to the line. I was not sure how he was having his needs satiated, and frankly,

I didn't want to think about it. I wondered if he still saw her, if he'd been with her since he married me. He didn't attempt to make love to me. He always stopped before we got so close that we'd have to make a choice again. I wondered if during the times he wasn't with me, he actually made some effort to see her.

I couldn't really be jealous, could I? I was the one who'd taken his life and his love away from him. I might have been the legal wife, but it was when he was with me that he was cheating. Because we both knew that his heart belonged to someone else. He was only mine on paper. But everything else that was Travis...belonged to her.

And suddenly, this realization made me feel sad. So sad that I felt almost heartbroken. Maybe I really believed that he was happy with me. Everything he showed me was genuine, sincere. And every time he kissed me and held me, he made me feel that I was all that was on his mind. I had no suspicion that he was ever thinking about somebody else. Damn! I didn't even feel that he was having his needs satiated somewhere else. He made me feel that I was enough for him. What we had was enough to keep him happy.

When Travis opened his office, his staff was there, and they all cheered, "Happy Birthday!"

Travis was surprised. It seemed that many of his employees were uncomfortable...scared, even. I remembered Karl telling me that the last time they surprised Travis, he didn't like it and told them never to do it again.

I stared at Travis. I was afraid that he would shout at everybody and tell them to get the hell out of his office.

But instead, he raised his brow and asked, "No confetti?" His tone was light and teasing.

Finally, they were all able to breathe...in relief.

"We were afraid you wouldn't like the mess, boss," Karl said, and then he motioned for somebody to bring the cake.

Suddenly, the whole room started singing Happy Birthday. I joined them. A big cake was brought in front of us and at the end of the song, and Karl said to Travis, "Make a wish."

Travis took a deep breath. He closed his eyes for three seconds, and then he blew the candle. We all cheered after.

"Speech! Speech! Speech!"

"You guys are pushing your luck, huh!" Travis said, but he was chuckling. Even I was amazed by this transformation. I was ready to put my hand on his mouth just in case he said something rude or insensitive to his employees, like he would normally do.

He took a deep breath. Then he said, "Thank you all for remembering. I guess I never really allowed you to in the past...and I do apologize for that. But I really appreciate your efforts...and the cake." He turned to me. "I want to thank my lovely wife. It's an amazing feeling not to wake up alone on your birthday as I always did in the past. I wish to celebrate the rest of my birthdays with you by my side." And he turned to his employees. "And you, too, of course. Thank you all. Lunch is on me. Karl, please take care of that. I'll be leaving after lunch, so anything you guys need me to sign or review, my office is open until noon. And if you have finished your tasks for the day, you're free to start your weekend early. But please, join us for lunch."

There should have been an encore after that. But instead, his employees were open-mouthed. They were silent...and I was afraid they were in shock.

He stared back at their blank faces. "I must have been such an ogre in the past, huh," he said to them.

Karl was first to recover. "Thank you, boss! And happy birthday again!"

I clapped my hands first, and everybody started cheering after that.

When everybody left his office and we were alone, I went to him with a big smile on my face. My eyes were pretty teary.

"Why?" he asked.

I shook my head. I gave him a hug. "I'm so proud of you, Travis. Did you really mean what you said?"

He hugged me back. "You must know that all these years, I lived in ruthlessness, insensitivity, brutal truth, and sarcasm. Do you think I would lie about what I feel now just to make other people feel good?"

"No. I don't think you can," I giggled. "You're starting to see things on the bright side now."

"That's because I have my sunshine with me," he whispered. He pulled away slightly to look me in the eyes. "That's you, love."

I smiled at him. "It's good to know I'm not the only one benefitting from this marriage."

"Who told you you were benefitting from this marriage at all?" he asked me with a mischievous grin on his face.

271

I laughed and raised my finger to him to show him my engagement ring. "Diamonds are a girl's best friend!" I teased.

He narrowed his eyes. "If diamonds are all it will take to make you stay, then I won't have a problem at all. But we both know you don't need or even want diamonds at all, Brianne."

I pouted. "Sure I do. I especially love my engagement ring."

He smiled. "That was my grandmother's," he said. "She left it for me a month before she died." There was pain in Travis's voice. "You know, my grandparents were the only ones in my family who ever loved me at all. When they died, I was left with nannies and butlers. Then I met Tom and your family. Then…there was only just you."

"What about…" I took a deep breath. "Her?"

He narrowed his eyes. "Who?"

"The woman you said you love…the woman you…made love to before you married me."

A mix of emotion instantly returned to Travis's face. Pain, guilt, remorse, anger. I think I read it all in a span of five seconds, and then he took hold of his emotions and his expression became steady again. He took a deep breath and held my face between his palms.

"There's only just you," he repeated.

"But Travis…" I insisted. "How can you ignore what you feel? How can you…"

He stopped me by giving me one hard kiss on the lips. "There's only you, Brianne," he whispered again. "My wife." And he kissed me thoroughly.

A surge of happiness seeped through me. Travis was trying to make this work. He was trying to make *us* work. He was trying to belong in this marriage…because that would mean he belonged to a family again now. And that was more important to him than anything he felt before…or felt now…for any other woman.

I painted while Travis read through contracts. I caught him staring at me several times. He would wink at me when he caught my eye, and I would smile and blush.

Noon came, and we had lunch in one of the office's conference rooms with the rest of the staff of Cross Industries. The atmosphere was fun and light.

Karl came up to me when Travis was on a phone call. "You're a miracle worker, Mrs. Cross," he said. "And I thought that man was hopeless."

I laughed. "He's making an effort to change. And I think I like him better."

"His old man is starting to use different tactics now. He learned that Travis got married," Karl said. "The older Cross said he would only give up his shares of Cross Magnates to Travis if Travis could give him a grandson."

I stared back at Karl. "And what did Travis say?"

Karl shrugged. "He told his father that if he had kids, his father would never be able to stand within a mile of them." Karl chuckled. "But when do you plan to have a baby? That would be the fastest way to change the old man's mind. I think he's getting old and tired of the game. He just doesn't want to admit to Travis that he's losing. He doesn't want to be the first to make a move to reconcile with his son."

"Why does he want a grandson?"

Karl shrugged. "He knows he may not be able to fix his relationship with his own son. He might soon retire. He needs somebody to give the fruits of his labor to. And he knows Travis would never accept them. So he thought he'd name Travis's son his heir instead. Your kid is going to be a prince, sweetheart. He's going to be richer than his father," Karl chuckled. "When do you intend to have kids, anyway?"

Karl didn't know that nothing was happening between Travis and me, and the chances of having a kid were between nil and zero. So I just shrugged and gave him a smile.

"He loves you very much, you know," Karl said.

I didn't say anything. I knew that was true. Travis did love me a lot. But he was not *in* love with me. Not the way I thought I was starting to be.

That realization crept up on me like a thief behind my back. I turned red, and suddenly I felt dizzy...nauseated even. I looked at Travis, who was speaking on the phone in one corner, and I realized that...I was falling in love with him...if I wasn't already!

I no longer had the will or the intention to find my Mr. Right while I was married to Travis. It had seemed since our honeymoon that there was only him in my world...and my life had taken a different route.

Suddenly, I felt like everything I had eaten was starting to work its way back up my throat.

"Excuse me," I said to Karl.

Immediately, I went to the ladies' room. I got there in time to reach the sink and throw up everything I ate that day.

I gargled with water then I washed my face. I stared at myself in the mirror.

*Could it be true? Could I really be in love with Travis?*

Whenever I thought of the other woman in Travis's past, I felt a stabbing pain of jealousy. I didn't even want to entertain thoughts of him sharing a bed with her, or with any other woman for that matter...even though we were not sleeping with each other...even though I hadn't satisfied his needs in that department since prom night.

Whenever he stared at me, I could feel my blood heat up and my heart pound wildly in my chest. I had this aching pain to hold him and kiss him constantly.

For a while now, my objective had been to make him happy with me so he would forget about her. I realized why I was doing it. It wasn't out of guilt. I was doing it for my own personal reasons. I wanted him to get over her...so he could finally fall in love with me, too!

I married Travis because he was my safety guy. Because I needed time to find that one guy who would make me happy. But I'd lost that will now because...I was happy! *Very* happy. With Travis. With this marriage. He was right. This marriage was bliss. The only thing missing between us was a deep physical intimacy, which God knows I wanted so much, too, but I was afraid it would make me lose him forever.

But if Travis felt the same way I felt now...making love would not destroy us...it would strengthen us! But only *if!*

But sadly, I remembered the emotions he wasn't able to hide when I brought her up. There was pain. There was guilt. There was remorse. There was anger. So, even though he told me that there was only just me now, I knew that the woman in his heart was still her.

That made me throw up again. I held on to the sink for a while to steady myself, keep my balance.

An old woman came out from one of the stalls. I smiled at her in the mirror. She was beaming at me. I realized that she was too old to be one of the employees. She must have been a guest in the building.

"Congratulations, dear!" she said as she walked past me.

It took me a moment to realize that she thought I was having morning sickness. But she was gone before I could correct her. I stared at myself in the mirror again, and then I laughed.

It would probably be the end of my world if Christian had left me a souvenir and I'd found out about it too late. If it happened that my ex-boyfriend had impregnated me and I was already married to Travis, my family would not only be ashamed of me, they would disown me altogether!

But that was the least of my worries. I may have asked Travis to marry me out of desperation, but I wouldn't ask him to be a father to my ex-boyfriend's baby! Especially not now, when I realized that I loved him…more than I loved him before. I didn't love him as a brother, or as a best friend anymore.

Luckily, I remembered having my periods in Manhattan. So I knew I was not pregnant after I broke up with Christian. It'd been months since we last slept together. I would have been halfway through the pregnancy by now, and that was impossible since I had still packed a pair of two-piece string bikinis in my bag.

I gargled with water again, and then I fished mouth spray out of my purse. I combed my hair and put on a bit of powder before I went out of the ladies' room.

Travis was leaning on the wall, his arms crossed as he anxiously watched the ladies' room door. His face lit up at the sight of me.

"Are you okay?" he asked.

"Yes," I replied.

He pulled me into his arms and gave me a tight hug. "You had me worried."

I felt good. Especially now that I knew that I was in love with him, his hugs gave me an entirely different feeling. They made me feel whole. They made me feel home. I realized that Travis was the only guy who could complete me. He always had been anyway.

"I just felt a little dizzy," I said.

"Do you want to cancel our plans?" he asked.

I shook my head. "No. Of course not."

He smiled. "Come, let's go," he said. "I can't wait for us to be alone."

I giggled. "Why?"

"It's my birthday," he said. "My three wishes. Peace. Quiet. Brianne."

My heart swelled when I heard that. How could Travis say all those things to me and yet be in love with somebody else? Or was he over her now?

"Are you sure…you don't want to be somewhere else?" I asked quietly. "It's your birthday, Travis. You can ask me anything you want."

He stopped walking. He stared at me for a long moment, and his eyes were unfathomable. I was afraid I'd offended him.

I bit my lip. I knew he was angry.

"Don't make promises you can't keep, Brianne," he said in a cold voice. "I just might take you up on that offer."

I raised my chin to him. *This is it! He will finally admit that he wants one chance…at least one day to be with her!* Damn, it hurt, but I knew I would allow that!

"I mean it," I said brokenly.

He narrowed his eyes at me. He gave me a bitter but devilish smile, as if an evil plan had just hatched in his head. Then he took my hand and walked toward the building exit.

"Travis… wait!" I said. "Where are we going?"

"Where we planned to go," he replied coldly.

"Why? I thought you wanted…"

"You don't know what I want, Brianne!" he snapped.

We reached his car. He opened the passenger door for me. I refused to get in. "What the hell is going on? Where are you taking me?"

"It doesn't matter! I can take you home, or at the hotel, or I can haul you back to my office. Either way, I'm going to make sure you don't break your promise. Now, do you need help getting in the car?"

I glared at him and then I got inside his car. Travis didn't say a word during the entire drive. He'd made arrangements for us to spend the weekend at the Four Seasons. He was driving fast, and I could tell how furious he was.

When we got to the hotel, we were immediately assisted by the hotel staff. Travis took my hand firmly, and we immediately went to our suite through a private-access elevator.

The room he rented was very luxurious. The architecture was very dramatic and posh. But I was too afraid of Travis to actually enjoy looking at the suite.

Once we were alone, Travis finally looked at me. He gave me one hard look. His eyes were dark with fury. He came closer to me.

"What did you say to me, Brianne?" he asked. "You said I could ask you anything I want?"

I took a deep breath. "Travis..." I whispered. "I only said that...because I thought..."

"You thought what?" he asked angrily.

"I thought you wanted to be with her...that woman you said you fell in love with...I thought I was being selfish. That I was taking too much of your time..."

"You have no idea what I really want, Brianne!" he said almost angrily. "But if you meant what you said, I will let you know!"

I had to be strong, and brave. This man in front of me was furious... cold and ruthless again! But I was not afraid of him. I knew that no matter how mad he was, he wouldn't hurt me! I was just afraid of what he would say to me...afraid that he would tell me that what he really wanted was her.

I raised my chin to him in pure defiance. "I mean it."

He smiled at me crookedly. There was a hint of mischief in that smile, and a hint of evil.

His face descended toward mine and he gave me one hard kiss. He devoured my lips as if he had been hungry for a decade. He invaded my mouth as if it were his sole mission to conquer me.

Then he nuzzled my neck, and I let out a moan in a voice I could barely recognize. My knees felt weak instantly and I lost my balance. Travis caught me in his arms. He gave me one hard look and then he picked me up and carried me to bed.

"Travis..." I whispered.

He took off his jacket and his shirt, his perfect abs exposed before my eyes. He got on top of me, and he kissed me again. The world stopped and then it spun ten times faster.

He kissed me savagely, as if he was going to take what he had deprived of himself of for a long time. He was bruising my lips.

"Travis...stop," I whispered.

"This is what I want, Brianne!" he whispered hoarsely. "Are you willing to give it to me?" And suddenly, I realized that his voice was no longer angry, or cold...it was almost...desperate...begging.

"Travis..." I whispered. "I told you before you could have your needs fulfilled as per usual..."

Travis's forehead was resting against my shoulder. His eyes were closed. He had taken a couple of deep breaths before he spoke again.

"I haven't touched a woman since…since we got married, Brianne," he whispered.

This confession surprised me, but more than anything, it made me happy. "Why?"

He sighed again. "Because…because I don't want to cheat on you. And because…" He raised his head so he could look at me. I looked into his eyes. They were like liquid sapphires, almost shining with tears. "Because I don't want anybody else…but you. I know that nobody could soothe this pain I have…could satiate this need I have…just you, Brianne."

"Travis…"

"You said I could ask you for anything," he said. "Now I'm looking at the person I want the most, Brianne. The one thing I want…the one thing I know I cannot have!"

I took a deep breath. God knows I wanted him, too! But the difference between the two of us was… Travis just wanted me. He was not in love with me…the way that I was so in love with him.

"But didn't you promise Tom…"

"I promised Tom I will look out for you for the rest of my life. I promised him I would always make sure you are safe. I think…I am doing a good job keeping those promises. I never promised him I wouldn't touch you…or want you."

"Travis…" I whispered. In truth, my heart was welling up with happiness. But I was also scared. Because I knew I was a few seconds away from giving in to what Travis was asking of me…but I knew that I couldn't share him with anybody else…even if she was the one he loved, I would not allow him to touch her again.

There was too much gamble, too much risk. My heart was at stake already, and now he wanted to put our friendship on the table. And that friendship was my rock…my pillar. It was what kept me alive and kept me going over all those years.

Travis took a deep breath. Then he pulled away from me and stood up from the bed. I immediately felt empty, heartbroken and deeply sad. He refused to look at me again.

"I'm sorry," he said. "I need some air."

"Why are you so mad at me now, Travis?" I asked, trying to keep my voice steady. "What exactly pissed you off?"

He didn't answer. He put his shirt back on and then he headed for the door. Before he left he said, "The way you don't believe it's you I'm thinking about all the time...the way you think I'm thinking about somebody else, when I desperately want only you. The way I bare my soul when I kiss you, hold you in my arms...and yet you still believe I want somebody else." He sighed. "I don't often show this much emotion for another human being, Brianne. You must know because you know me the best. It's frustrating that even *you*...do not believe me."

He exited the room and I lay back in bed feeling confused and upset. But I knew he was right. Throughout this entire marriage, he had been trying to make things work between us. But I had still kept thinking about the other woman. I had kept thinking that he was not yet over her, and every emotion he'd ever shown me, he would have been happier to show someone else. Maybe he really was over her. And there was just me in his life now.

Amidst the tears and the anguish, I fell asleep. In my dreams, I saw Travis...the way I'd dreamt about him many nights before.

He touched me the way I wanted to be touched, the way I needed to be touched. He was reluctant to touch me, because he was honor-bound not to. But I begged him to. I asked him to make love to me. He kissed me in ways that made me forget who he was...who I was. He held me in ways that kept me safe and warm. I screamed his name as I reached my peak. I felt like jumping off a cliff and then feeling Travis catch me in his arms. And then I told him I loved him. He gave me a smile of triumph, and then his body shook as he reached his own heaven with me in his arms.

And I woke up. I was panting alone in bed. I knew that my dreams of lovemaking with Travis were so potent, so vivid because I wanted them to come true with so much desperation. It was him I wanted the most, too!

I realized what I needed to do. It was time to stop fearing what could be...and go after the one thing I wanted the most in my life now. Yes, I might get heartbroken after this. Yes, I might lose my friendship with Travis. But what if he felt the same way for me? Then I had nothing to lose and everything to gain. But I would never know until I took a chance. I believed in Travis. I knew...whatever happened...he wouldn't hurt me.

Maybe now...it was time to put all my bets on the table and raise the stakes very, *very* high!

# Chapter Twenty-Six

It was already nine in the evening, and Travis had not returned yet. Each minute I waited for him, I got worried.

Had he finally given up on me? Had he finally given in to her? Did he think we were hopeless and that he just had to continue with the original terms of our agreement? While I, on the other hand, had decided to keep him for myself, to go after what I wanted, and what I loved, no matter the consequences?

I had food delivered to the room, and I set a candlelight dinner for us. I showered and dressed in an elegant Victoria's Secret nightdress under my silk robe. I wanted to show a bit of effort to Travis...he deserved it after all I'd done to him.

But as each minute passed by, my hopes were going down the drain. It was still his birthday. Maybe he'd decided to have a bit of fun himself. And forget the one person who had caused him pain...me.

Eleven in the evening. The food had gotten cold, and the ice in the bucket had turned to water. In all frustration, I decided to give up. Travis probably wouldn't come back tonight. I called room service to take the food away.

I went onto the balcony. There was a lover's moon again that night. It illuminated the skies perfectly. The city lights proved that people out there still refused to sleep. Proof that Travis could still be out there somewhere...

I sighed. It would have been perfect. But maybe I'd decided to fight just a few hours too late. When I decided to give in...I guess Travis decided to give up.

"What was room service doing here?" I heard a voice ask behind me.

I took a deep breath. "Taking away the dinner I prepared for us," I said in a low voice.

He didn't say anything. I turned around to face him. I didn't disguise the tears in my eyes. He would know immediately that I had been crying anyway.

281

He looked at my face, and then at the silk robe I was wearing. I should have been embarrassed, but I was so angry, I didn't have time to feel anything else.

"I'm going to bed," I said haughtily. "Happy birthday again!"

I walked past him, but he was quick to catch me by the waist, stopping me. He tilted my chin up so I would face him. I stared back at him and raised a brow, making no effort to disguise any emotion I was feeling at that moment. *Let him read me like a book, for all I care!*

He narrowed his eyes. "What were you planning to do?"

"Nothing!" I replied.

"You can lie better, Brianne," he said.

"If you're so smart, why don't you say it out loud yourself?!"

"It's still my birthday, and you promised to give me anything I wanted," he countered.

"Oh, the wishing line expired an hour ago!" I snapped.

Tears seem to fill his eyes and he smiled at me solemnly. "Are you just doing this because it's my birthday?" he asked. "Or is it because you want me as much as I want you?" His voice was a whisper...full of emotion, full of desperation.

I took a deep breath. The anger I felt a while ago was slowly melting away. I just could not stay angry with this man. I realized that he was my one weakness, too. He always had been. I looked into his eyes. "Maybe I realized you're all I want, too, Travis."

His arms immediately came around me into a tight hug. I heard him suck in a deep breath. But he didn't say anything.

"Where have you been, Travis?"

He laughed. "You really had to ask." He caressed the back of my head. "I went back to the office to work...so I could forget we had a fight. The video logs in the building will prove that. And I'm glad you're worried."

Instantly, my heart was filled with joy and relief. Travis bent down to pick me up. Silently, he carried me to the bedroom and settled me down on the bed.

He stared at me seriously...desperately. Then slowly, he kissed me, gently at first, and then passionately. I breathed in the scent of him. He nuzzled my neck, and I clung to him for dear life.

"Travis..." I whispered.

I felt him tug at the strings of my robe. Slowly, he took it off me, and he kissed my bare shoulders. He took off his shirt and then he came down and kissed me again. I wrapped my arms around his neck, and I kissed him back with the same intensity, the same passion.

He stared down at me, with all tenderness in his eyes.

"This will change everything forever, Brianne," he whispered.

I nodded. "I know."

He smiled at me wistfully. "I discovered I'm going to be possessive and jealous. I am going to officially end your quest to find the man of your dreams."

I nodded happily. Tears welling up in my eyes.

"In return, I offer you my protection, my faithfulness...I will try my damn best to fill the shoes of that man you were looking for. I will try to make you happy, Brianne."

Tears filled my eyes. I nodded. I touched his cheeks with my fingers. "As long as you promise you won't touch any other woman...I think that is enough."

He smiled. "I promise," he said in a sober voice. "How could I, anyway? All I want for the rest of my life is you."

He bent down slowly and kissed me again. I felt him reach down to his pants to get out of them until he was only wearing a pair of boxers. There was no disguising how much he wanted me. I could feel him against my abdomen. I let out a moan of pleasure.

Travis slowly took off my nightdress, kissing the skin he revealed. I felt like I was running out of breath. Shards and pieces of my dreams were mixing with what I saw before me. I was unable to believe what was happening between us...that finally, this was happening for real.

"Travis..." I whispered against his skin.

"Brianne..." he whispered.

I clung to him for support. His touch was too electrifying. I was afraid I could not handle the intensity of his kisses and the magnitude of emotion I felt with every caress.

"Travis..." I moaned as he kissed my neck. He was right. It was my weakest point. I instantly turned mindless at the touch of his lips on that spot.

"Open your eyes, Brianne," he whispered softly. I did as he asked. "I want you to look at me, remember me as I make love to you."

I giggled softly. I pulled him to me and gave him a kiss on the lips. "I will never forget this, Travis."

He smiled. There was still something in that smile that was desperate and yearning. I hugged him to me to assure him that

283

everything was going to be okay. That every single thing he promised me a few minutes ago, I promised the same to him.

"This is not a dream, Brianne. This is real," he said. "You're giving yourself to me. I'm pledging my soul to you." And he went inside me.

It was everything I ever expected and more. Fireworks seemed to have exploded everywhere. It was as if all my dreams were coming true at the same time. I ignited with every touch, every kiss. Hearing him moan my name was the sweetest of all sounds I could ever hear.

I could feel him inside me as he had been before…many years ago. It was the same, and yet it was different.

We rode the tide of passion together. My peak wanted to be reached. With Chris, it wouldn't always last long enough for me to get there. But with Travis, I could tell that he was holding back, he was trying to control himself.

"Travis…" I whispered, almost in a plea.

"I know, love," he whispered. "Just trust me," he said.

Slowly, I could feel it build up inside me. I held on to Travis, as I let him ease me into pleasure. Just then, it happened. I couldn't turn back, couldn't hold on. I was left with no choice but to let go…to jump into the cliff.

"Travis!" I screamed his name.

"Brianne…my wife," he whispered.

My release was long and satisfying. It was nothing I had ever experienced before. He waited for me to finish, and then he whispered, "I love you, Brianne." And finally, I felt his body rock as he released himself inside me.

We lay there for a moment, still joined, still locked in each other's arms. I didn't realize it, but tears were rolling down my cheeks. I remembered the words he said to me before his release. I wondered if he was aware he said them.

Damn! It's difficult when for years you've been saying those three words to each other constantly. I desperately wished he meant that a different way this time around.

Travis pulled away slightly and stared down into my eyes.

"Are you okay, love?" he asked.

I nodded. "I am."

He leaned forward and kissed me gently on the lips. Then slowly, he pulled out of me. He lay back on the bed and pulled me toward him.

He tilted my chin toward him so he could stare into my eyes. He searched my face, trying to read my expression, searching for any sign of regret, anger, or even remorse.

I giggled. "I'm perfectly sane, Travis Cross. I know what happened between us. I will never forget it and I'll never be sorry."

He smiled. "Just checking." He hugged me to him again.

I sighed. "I don't have much memory of your face...that first time. I was completely blindfolded. Why didn't you want me to look at you?"

He sighed. "Because I was...ashamed of wanting you too much! Tom asked me to take care of you, not covet you for myself. For years, I was reminding myself that I was forbidden to want you."

"And so you haven't had any memory of ever having me all throughout these years, either," I said.

He sighed again. "Memories of you, your body, how you looked when I took your innocence away from you, even the pain on your face when I first entered you, are so vivid in my mind, I feel like it was only yesterday."

I pulled away from him so I could stare into his eyes. "But, Travis...you were supposed to have closed your eyes."

He chuckled humorlessly. "I couldn't take my eyes off you! I was so...enchanted by how beautiful you were, I couldn't close my eyes. Damn! I couldn't even blink. I was afraid that if I did, you would disappear before my eyes. And I didn't want that."

"You cheated!" I accused him.

"I suffered for it, don't worry," he chuckled. "For years, the memory of your body haunted my existence. And knowing I couldn't have you made it so much worse for me."

"Serves you right then!"

He pulled me to him in a tight hug. "It doesn't matter now, does it? You're mine now."

I smiled to myself. "Yes. And you're mine too, Travis."

"Yes, love. All yours."

I stared up at him. "I can't believe it. We used to be two kids who couldn't stand each other."

He chuckled humorlessly. "*You* couldn't stand *me*. That wasn't the same case the other way around."

I stared up at him. "What do you mean?"

He stared at me for a while and he smiled. "I've always had a crush on you, Brianne." His tone was shy. I was surprised by his confession. "You hated me. I figured the only way to get a little of your attention was to...constantly tease you. But I guess that plan backfired, huh."

I laughed. "It did." I knew I was blushing, and his confession made me happy. "Did Tom know?"

He fell silent for a while. When I looked up at him, he was thoughtful. Then he said, "He did. If there was one person who knew exactly what was going on in my mind, it was him. But he warned me off."

I sighed. "If he were alive, do you think he'd be happy for us now?"

"Yes," Travis replied.

"How can you be so sure?"

He stared down at me thoughtfully. "Because I was also the person who knew exactly how his mind worked and what he was thinking all the time."

I smiled and reached up to kiss his lips. "Hard to believe that from being enemies, we would become the best of friends, and then we'd be lovers..."

He chuckled. He leaned down and kissed me on the lips again. "Lovers? No, love. Tonight, we just became husband and wife."

I playfully slapped my forehead. Yeah! How could I forget that? Travis and I had never dated. We got married first, before everything else. And now, this marriage was consummated. We truly had become husband and wife.

I closed my eyes. I was very happy! I didn't think I had been this happy in all my life. It felt like coming home and being in the only place I knew I would be safe...and being with the only guy I knew could make me complete.

I sighed. "How long do you think this will last?"

"Forever, Brianne," he whispered. "I want you to be my wife, forever."

I smiled. Travis didn't directly say he was in love with me, but for now, it was enough to hear him say he wanted to make this work forever. And I knew no one would care for me as much as he did.

"Have you eaten?" he asked.

I shook my head. "My date sort of stood me up."

He laughed and hugged me to him again. "Your date was crying his heart out in his office because he thought he'd never get to hold you like this at all, no matter how many of his masks he put down for you."

I propped up on one elbow and stared at him. "And how many more masks are you wearing still?"

He shook his head. "No more, love. I just bared my entire soul to you."

I leaned forward and gave him a kiss on the lips. "Good. Because you might break me if you don't."

"It won't be possible for me to break you without shredding myself to pieces first," he whispered.

I smiled contentedly in his arms. He said he loved me. I am not sure if he meant he loved me the same way I loved him...but for now, it was more than enough.

"Travis."

"Hmmm..."

"That beast...that you unleashed...was not terrifying at all. In fact...it was quite gentle."

I felt him shift to prop up on his elbow. He looked down at me. He had a twinkle in his eyes, and he gave me a devilishly naughty grin. My heart pounded inside my chest.

I laughed. "Travis..." I almost regretted what I'd said.

"Challenge accepted," he said in a mischievous voice. My laughter died as he leaned forward and took my mouth in another heart-stopping, mind-blowing kiss.

# Chapter Twenty-Seven

We stayed at the hotel for the whole weekend. We almost didn't go out of our room. We couldn't get our hands off each other. I lost count of how many times we made love. Afterward, we were happy to cuddle in each other's arms.

I had never seen Travis this open or this happy. He was laughing most of the time, and he couldn't resist a chance to pull me into his arms and kiss me.

It was bliss. It was everything I could have ever dreamed of. It was like for the first time in many years, I belonged to a family again. And I couldn't be any happier that I belonged to a family with Travis.

"Are you happy with the apartment, love?" he asked. "Or would you want to move into a house?"

"I've just settled into your apartment," I reminded him.

"Yes. But we need to think long-term now. If you don't want to settle in New York, that's fine with me. I can set up an office wherever you want. Pretty soon, we're going to think about having kids. And I'm not sure you want to raise them in Manhattan."

Kids. I smiled at the thought. Travis really wanted to have kids with me. I really was married now!

"You're thinking about kids now?" I asked, laughing.

"Of course," he replied. "I was a lonely kid when I was growing up. If it's not too much to ask, I would like at least three kids."

"Your birthday's long over," I reminded him.

He laughed. "Fine. I'll ask for a baby for my next three birthdays then."

"Travis, I'm going to grow big if I get pregnant every year!"

"And I'll adore you just the same," he said, giving me a kiss on the lips.

"All right. Why don't we settle here in Manhattan for now? And as soon as I'm pregnant, then we'll think about relocating somewhere else." ‹

"Okay, deal." He smiled. He stared at me for a long while and then he smiled. "You have no idea how happy I am."

Tears welled up in my eyes. "I'm very happy too, Travis."

When we came back to his apartment, Travis looked like he was a changed man. We were greeted at the door by the bellman.

"Good day to you, too, Godfrey." He smiled.

I was surprised because the bellman was not wearing his nametag, and yet Travis surprised us both by greeting him by his name.

It went on when we entered the lobby. He greeted the guys at the concierge by their first names. When he wouldn't have even looked at them before when they had greeted him, he now knew every one of them by first name. And even they seemed to be very surprised.

Karl was at his doorstep when we got to our floor.

"Good afternoon, Mr. Cross," he greeted him. "Mrs. Cross."

"It's Sunday, Karl. What are you doing here?" Travis asked.

It took Karl a moment before he could respond. "Well...I just wanted to ask if you needed anything for today. I wanted to remind you about your meetings for tomorrow."

"I have them on my phone, Karl. No need to come here personally to remind me. Go spend the rest of your free time however you please," Travis said.

Karl smiled. "Right. Thank you, sir. Have a nice day." He nodded at me, and then he left.

When we got inside the apartment, I couldn't help giving Travis a hug. I buried my face in his chest and sighed.

"What's wrong?" he asked.

I giggled. "Nothing, Travis. You're perfect!"

Monday, Travis came home at five in the afternoon. He got me a bouquet of roses.

"What is this for?"

He shook his head. "Passed by a flower shop and thought of you."

I got on tiptoes to give him a kiss on the lips. "I love them. Thank you."

He deepened the kiss. And then his hands crept under my shirt. Electricity shot through me, along with a desire I thought I couldn't handle.

"Travis..." I moaned.

We fell on the couch and Travis stripped off his jacket and his shirt.

"Travis, please..." I begged. I didn't know desire could be this potent, erasing all sense of reason, replacing it with a sense of urgency.

In a minute, we were making love on the couch, whispering each other's name, kissing each other as passionately as humanly possible.

When it was over, we lay there for a while, cuddling each other, while Travis told me what had happened during the day.

"Karl once told me you intended to liquidate your father's company once you acquired it," I said. "Do you still plan to do that now?"

He sighed and hugged me tighter. "Are you going to ask me to stop now, love? I once begged you not to."

"There are other lives at stake, Travis," I said. "Some innocent people whose lives depend on their jobs. One of your father's employees could have a pregnant wife, and losing his job would mean losing their means to raise the baby. You can have your battles with your father…but you have to keep them clean. Make sure…there will be no casualties."

He thought about it for a moment. He took a deep breath, and then he said, "You're too good for me, Brianne. Sometimes, I don't think I deserve you at all."

"But I promised to save you, remember?"

"And you did," he said. "Now, I couldn't imagine life without you…" He took my hand and kissed my fingers. "Or without these fingers touching me, these hands holding me…" He kissed me on the lips. "Or these lips kissing me."

I smiled at him. "I guess it will be like this forever."

He smiled back. "Yes, love. Forever."

Travis never came home late. When he did have a meeting, he let me know beforehand. Sometimes, he asked me to wait for him at a café in the hotel where he was having his meeting. He arranged for the limo to pick me up. After his meeting, we had dinner or coffee together. Travis was not afraid to show affection. He hugged me, kissed me in public. Sometimes, I was afraid we'd get charged with public indecency.

When I told him that, he just laughed. "I think I have enough money to pay that fine over and over again!"

Thursday night, we met Karl in the corridor.

"Coming to see me?" Travis asked.

"Yes," he said. "I was just wondering if Monday would be a very busy day…because…if it is, I can come to the office, but if not, I was wondering…"

"Karl, you can take Monday off," Travis said immediately.

"Really?" Karl's face immediately brightened. "Are you sure? Because if it's going to be busy, I'll be okay. I'll come to work."

"If you want to go to the Bahamas, Karl, you can do so."

Karl was surprised. And then he smiled. "I'll bring a laptop just in case…"

"I'm not going to ask you to do some work on your weekend getaway. Now go, before I change my mind." Travis said.

Karl beamed. "Thank you, Travis," he said. He turned to me. "See you later, Brianne."

We entered our apartment. "You told him he could call you Travis?"

Travis shrugged. "I figured Mr. Cross makes me feel old!"

I laughed and gave him a hug. "You're wonderful, Travis. And no matter how old you are, I think you're still the most attractive man I've ever laid eyes on."

Travis pulled me into a hug and then asked me to sit down on the couch.

"What's going on?" I asked.

He went into our room and then he came back with a folder. He looked at me wearily and then he handed it to me.

I started getting worried. "Travis, what's going on?" I asked.

He sighed. "Everything I own, Brianne…is summarized in these papers here," he replied. "Every bank statement, every piece of property that is under my name is in there. The original copies of the deeds are in my security deposit box, to which you will have access to."

I narrowed my eyes. "Why?"

"Because they are yours, too. I don't want to hide anything from you. When we got married, everything that I was and everything that I owned became yours as well. So you should be aware of them."

"But, Travis…I don't want anything from you. I don't need these."

"You do, Brianne. You're my wife. Before we got married, I had no beneficiaries at all. No one to give the fruits of my labor to," he said. "Well…it has always been you. But that is specified in my will. That's different. But now, you have to be aware of these things."

"Travis, why? I don't need to know."

"Yes, you do," he insisted. "Because if something happens to me...I want to make sure *everything* goes to you. Not anybody else whose only relation to me is a shared DNA."

I raised my brow at him. "Specifically your father."

He took a deep breath and gave me a slight nod. "I want you to be able to fight for your right. And you will be able to do that if you're aware of everything. My father is very, *very* shrewd. And he's getting desperate."

Tears filled my eyes. "Travis..." I sighed. "Please. Don't take this too far. I would rather be penniless any day, as long as I have you with me. I don't need all these." I said, pointing at the folder in front of me. "I only want my husband."

He smiled at me and then sat beside me, taking me in his arms. "And you have me. But you know me, Brianne. I always plan ahead. Always one step ahead of the game. I have to do this."

It was sad to think about a future without Travis, but he was right. The coin had two sides. And the reality was that he had the father he had. I nodded and gave him a tight hug. He hugged me back.

"And I have something else to ask you, Brianne," he said.

I stared back at him.

"What?"

"Whenever you're ready, I want you to learn the ropes at my company."

Now, panic gripped me. "What? Travis...I'm in to arts!"

He laughed. "And you're smart. I'm sure you'll learn fast. And I'll be your teacher."

"And what would you do if I don't learn or if I make a mistake?"

His eyes gleamed. "Well, I'll be happy to teach you a lesson." Then he scooped me up in his arms and carried me to the bedroom. "In fact, I should give you have a glimpse of that now."

I laughed. "Travis!" I landed on the bed with a bounce, and soon, he landed on top of me.

The laughter died in my throat as he leaned forward and kissed me thoroughly.

*** 

Travis had a meeting with his father in LA the next weekend.

"You want to come with?" he asked. "Although, I prefer he doesn't see you."

"Why?"

"My father is the devil incarnate. The less he knows about you, the safer you will be from him."

"And what about you?" I asked nervously.

"I'm his son, Brianne," he replied. "And I can take care of myself."

I nodded. "Okay. I think I'll just go to Connecticut. I need to visit Sarah. Plus, I have an apartment there that I need to vacate. I've got stuff to sell."

He smiled. "Do that. I'll come to Connecticut from LA to pick you up."

"Deal."

He kissed me thoroughly. "Two nights are going to be so long without you."

I smiled. "I know. It's like...I don't know how to go back anymore, Travis."

"Good. Because you're not allowed to go back, love," he said. "I warned you before, remember. When you let me touch you again, we belonged exclusively to each other from then on. It was the plan before. It's the plan now, especially now that you've made me feel all this! I think I'm going to die if I don't get to feel your touch...if I don't know you're mine...only mine."

My heart swelled at his words. "I'm yours, Travis," I sighed. "I guess part of me has always been yours. And now...all of me is," I whispered, and then I kissed him thoroughly.

When I met Sarah Saturday morning, I was pretty sure I was a picture of bliss.

"What have you not been telling me?" she asked. "You look wonderful! And you have a certain glow about you! Are you pregnant?"

I laughed. "Don't be silly! This is not pregnancy glow. Let's just say that I'm totally in love with my husband."

She shrieked. "When did this happen?"

"I guess on our honeymoon, we were...doing a lot of kissing, and it took a lot for us not to sleep with each other. And then...on his birthday, I decided to stop thinking about the consequences and just go for the one man I'd always wanted. The marriage just turned real. And

I'm happy, Sarah! I've never been this happy! I mean…we've only slept with each other for a week, but it has been wonderful. He is talking about kids and settling down in a different city. He's everything I could ever, ever ask for and more."

"I'm so jealous! How lucky can you be? I thought Travis Cross was a devil in angel's skin. But it looks like he changed a lot for you. I guess this is love."

I sighed. "We haven't said 'I love you' to each other since we slept with each other." I thought about it and I realized it was true. "It's funny, because all these years, it was so easy to say 'I love you,' and we said it to each other all the time. Now…we haven't said it in a week."

Sarah smiled at me. "Probably because it means something different now. Before…those three words meant you loved each other as friends or as family. Now…that's no longer the case."

"I just wish he'd say it to me and I would have *no doubt* what he meant, you know," I said wistfully. "Before we got married, he said he was sort of in love with another woman. But he chose to marry me nevertheless…and now, he keeps telling me that there is no one else for him. Only me. I guess that is more than enough. Maybe he didn't love that woman strongly enough. And she's out of the picture now."

"So you did get what you were looking for after all. Your safety guy didn't only save you from the 'curse,' but he also turned out to be the man you were looking for all your life."

I nodded. "And I'm so happy! I've always loved Travis…as a dear friend. But he made me fall in love with him. He is a wonderful husband!"

While having coffee and dessert, Sarah told me about the performance schedules. I wanted to join, but somehow I knew this honeymoon phase with Travis wasn't nearly over yet, and I didn't want to spoil that by putting some distance between us. I wanted him to fall in love with me, too. The way I was so in love with him. And besides, my priorities had changed now. Our family came first.

"It took you that long to go to bed?" Sarah asked.

I laughed. "I was too careful! And Travis is too much of a gentleman! He is a master of keeping his emotions under control. We slipped sometimes, but we stopped just in time."

"Wow! I can't imagine how much self-control that took!" she laughed.

Suddenly, I felt queasy, as if something in the cake I ate had made me sick.

"Excuse me..." I said to her.

I immediately ran to the ladies' room. I threw up everything I'd eaten since the morning. I washed my face with water while Sarah looked at me wearily.

"Sweetheart, are you..."

I laughed. "I can't be, Sarah!" I said to her. "Unless pregnancy manifests itself this early. I mean...I only slept with Travis a week ago. It's too early."

Sarah shrugged. "When was the last time you had your period?"

Damn! I realized I hadn't had my period in a long time. "I don't know. A week or so before my bachelorette party. I might be delayed, but I can't be pregnant."

Then I realized pregnancy was not the only thing that could delay a woman's period. There could be conditions worse than that. I knew because a couple of my aunts had suffered from female cancers over the years.

"Oh my God, Sarah. I think...I need to go see a doctor. What if I'm sick? What if I have a medical condition that actually prevents me from getting pregnant? A cousin of mine had her ovaries removed when she was just in her twenties. It runs in our family. I can't take chances." Tears welled up in my eyes. "I need to give Travis a child, Sarah."

"Hey, calm down!" she said to me. "I know a good doctor. Let's go there now."

Thirty minutes later, I was sitting in the waiting room at the clinic Sarah went to. She was a blonde woman in her forties. She smiled at me.

"Married?" she asked.

I nodded.

"Good." She narrowed her eyes. "Sexually active?"

If I hadn't been under stress, I would have laughed at that question. "Yes," I replied.

"Alrighty. When was your last period?"

I shook my head. "Unfortunately, I cannot remember," I said. "But I don't remember having it last month or this month."

"Feeling anything weird?"

"I threw up this morning."

296

"First time you threw up?"

"Well, last week, too. Once. But that could be just because of something I ate."

"Okay. Lie down on the table, and we'll have a check."

She applied ultrasound gel on my tummy while I prayed so hard that I didn't have cancer or any cysts that would prevent me from conceiving. Travis deserved to have a baby. He deserved to have a family. I didn't want to rob him of the family he had dreamed of just because I was unable to give him children. The only way he could forgive his parents was…if he got a chance to be a better father to his children. That was my plan. And I also didn't want to miss out on becoming a mother.

"I can't see it properly. I'm going under," she said. And she shifted to do a vaginal ultrasound instead.

"Well, congratulations," the doctor said after a few minutes. "It looks like you're pregnant."

It took me a whole minute to process that. "What?" I wanted to be happy. Could they really detect it this early?

"Seven weeks."

"Seven weeks?" I echoed. "Are you sure? It's not just three or four weeks?"

She increased the volume of her ultrasound. I heard a walloping sound, and then it became rhythmic. I realized it was my baby's heartbeat. Tears slipped from my eyes. I felt warmth envelop me, and I couldn't define how happy I suddenly felt.

*I'm going to be a mom!*

"Heartbeat is strong," she said. "You can't hear that if you're only a week pregnant. And the ultrasound says it was conceived around October 25th, plus or minus a week."

Everything else that she said was a blur. She said something about seeing a doctor in Manhattan immediately. I thought there was alarm on her face when she checked me again, but she said the baby was fine, so I didn't care about anything else.

I remember taking a note from her. I remember paying her assistant.

"Hello!" Sarah had to snap her fingers in front of me to bring me back to reality.

I stared back at her.

"Are you okay? What did she say?"

297

"Sarah…she said I'm pregnant."

"Then Travis is going to be ecstatic!"

"Sarah…I'm *seven* weeks pregnant!"

It took Sarah a moment to recover, too. And then she breathed, "Oh my God!"

# Chapter Twenty-Eight

I lay on Sarah's couch. I needed time to figure things out. I would have been jumping for joy now if the doctor had said I was one week pregnant. But no—I was seven weeks pregnant, which meant I was already pregnant when Travis and I had consummated our marriage a week ago. If the time she gave me was right, I had already been pregnant before I even married Travis, and I was pretty sure nothing had happened between us on our honeymoon.

"Christian?" Sarah asked.

"How? I mean, I broke up with him months before I got married."

"What were you doing around October twenty-fifth?"

"I was busy preparing for a wedding!" I replied.

Sarah took out her organizer and scanned through the dates. "Okay, October twenty-second, we all checked in to the hotel in preparation for your wedding. Are you sure you didn't see Chris round about that time?"

I shook my head. "Of course! I haven't seen him in months!"

"Eric?"

"Eric would never even be able to get it up!" I rolled my eyes.

"I was pretty sure I was the one who slept with the stripper." Sarah giggled. "October twenty-fifth, we didn't do anything," she said. "That was the day before your family dinner."

She stared at me blankly. I took a deep breath. She looked at me apologetically and reached out to give me a hug.

"Hey, it's going to be okay."

I shook my head. "No, it's not!" I said. "I'm going to lose Travis because of this. I won't let him answer for a kid that is not his. And, Sarah, do you realize what a shame it is if you do not know how you got pregnant in the first place?"

She handed me a glass of water. "We'll figure it out, sweetie. For now, take a rest. Your baby needs you to."

I must have slept all day. I felt so sad and so scared. When I woke up, Sarah had already prepared dinner for us.

"Come, you must be hungry."

I ate in silence. I still kept picking my brain for what happened during that time. And everything came up blank. I couldn't remember anything significant.

"I was just thinking," Sarah said. "I think I remember where we were round about that time."

I stared at her, scared of what she was about to say.

"We went on a drinking spree," Sarah said. "You wanted to forget the fact that Travis might sleep with the stripper in his stag party. We drank our wits out."

My heart pounded in my ribcage. That was the night I didn't remember how I got back to my hotel room, and my clothes were scattered on my hotel room floor.

"Oh my God, Sarah!" I breathed. "I don't know what happened to me that night. I can't even remember how I got back to my room! And I was...I was naked when I woke up!"

Tears rolled down my cheeks. Sarah hugged me. I wished this were all a dream I would soon wake up from.

After a few hours, everything was still a haze to me. No matter how much I thought about that night, nothing changed. I was left with a dead end. I couldn't remember what had happened after I drank about a bottle of tequila.

"How did you wake up?"

She blushed. "Well, Dante, the cute bartender I was flirting with all night? He got one of his friends to cover him for the remainder of his shift. He accompanied me to my room...one thing led to another. But sorry, sweetie. I don't remember seeing you off to your room. I think I left you at the bar, actually, because I was in such a hurry to go back to my room with Dante."

A memory came to my mind. There was a bartender, there was another guy.

"Which reminds me, I need to pay you back for all the liquor I had that night."

I narrowed my eyes. "I don't think I paid the bill," I said to her.

She blinked back at me. "Well, nothing is free these days!"

"If you don't remember paying, then who paid?"

"Maybe Dante?" Sarah asked.

"Or maybe it's whoever took me back to my room! Whoever did...took advantage of me and left me a souvenir."

Sarah looked at me apologetically. "Do you want to go back to the hotel? We can check."

"We need to go now."

"What? Why now?"

"Because we need to talk to your bartender, and I'm pretty sure he doesn't take day shifts. And tomorrow, I should be ready to face Travis."

Travis called me that night. I hated it, but I had to lie to him.

"I'm sleeping over Sarah's. I feel tired, actually," I said. "I miss you."

He sighed. "I would give everything to have you beside me right now."

I giggled. But he didn't know there was a trace of bitterness to that. "We'll see each other tomorrow."

"That's too long," he sighed. "Next time, you're coming with me on my trips."

"Travis, you can handle a few days without me."

"I discovered I can't. Not anymore," he said. "Take care of yourself while you're there. And be miserable without me."

I giggled. "I am." That was true. I was miserable. Not only because Travis was not with me, but because I knew there was an eighty percent chance our marriage would end abruptly. I couldn't let Travis save me this time.

He didn't say anything for a moment.

"Travis?"

"Love?" he replied.

"I need to go. It's been a long day," I said.

"Okay," he said. "Goodnight."

"Goodnight."

"Brianne..." he said softly.

"Yes?"

I heard him take a deep breath. Then he said, "I love you."

"I know."

"You don't," he said.

"Of course I do. You always said I was the only thing left for you to love, remember?"

"Yes," he replied. "But this '*I love you*' isn't like before."

My heart stopped at that very moment. I even forgot to breathe.

"Wh-what do you mean?"

He sighed. "I mean *I love you*. Do you understand?"

I think my heart broke at that very moment, and immediately tears rolled down my cheeks. "Yes." I took a deep breath. And because I knew I meant it, too, and because I knew tomorrow might change forever, I said, "I love you, too, Travis. The same way you love me."

He sighed. "God, I wish we'd said that to each other before we parted."

I took a deep breath. "Me too." I wished I'd said that to him earlier. I wished I wasn't pregnant and didn't know who the father of my baby was. More than that, I wished I were pregnant with *Travis's* child. That I was only a week or two along, because then I would definitely be sure that Travis was the father. I realized I didn't want to get pregnant with anyone else. Just with Travis. But things were different. And I was a freaking mess because I knew that as much as I loved Travis, I couldn't let him take care of someone else's child. And that moment I heard my baby's heartbeat, love had grown in my heart already. I loved this baby, even though I didn't know who'd fathered him. Because no matter who the father was, I knew that he was mine.

"Well, that will be the very first thing I will say to you when I see you tomorrow," Travis said.

"Can't wait," I whispered.

He chuckled. "Go to sleep now! There are no flights available to Connecticut at this hour. Otherwise, I would be taking them to get to you."

"You have a meeting tomorrow," I reminded him.

"That's a bummer, huh!" he said, his voice full of frustration. "All right, goodnight, love."

"I'll see you tomorrow."

"I'll see you in my dreams."

When we hung up, I couldn't stop crying. The moment would have been perfect. But it was all ruined. Because I knew tomorrow did not bring anything that I should be excited about. Tomorrow, I might lose Travis forever. Actually, he was lost to me the moment I found out I was pregnant with somebody else's child.

Travis had been there for me all my life. He'd saved me over and over in the past. But he couldn't save me from this mess. I would not allow it. It wasn't fair. Even if he insisted, and I have a feeling he would come up with another solution to my problem, I would not let him. He'd done so much already. I could free him of his promises to my brother. He had already fulfilled those promises a long time ago. And I loved him too much to ruin his life.

We checked in to the same hotel where we'd had my wedding. It was ten in the evening when we arrived. After getting our room, we headed to the bar where Sarah and I had gone drinking before my wedding.

A familiar face was there. I guessed he was the guy named Dante. Then another bartender was there, too. He was a blond guy with hazel eyes.

"Two faces I was not expecting to see tonight," Dante said. He gave a dazzling smile for Sarah, and Sarah winked at him.

"Oh, please!" I rolled my eyes. I was starting to have nausea already.

"Sorry," Sarah said. She turned to Dante. "Actually, we're here to ask you for a favor."

"Anything," Dante smiled.

"Remember we were here before?"

"I remember everything, sugar," he said to Sarah, which irritated me even more. But I kept my mouth shut.

"I left with you. And somebody covered for you, right?"

"That would be me," the blonde bartender answered.

I stared at him for a moment. He was familiar. Like I had seen him before, and it could have been that night. I thought, in horror, that this guy could have been the one who took me back to my room.

"What happened after I left with you?" Sarah asked.

Dante was taken aback. He stared at Sarah for a moment and then he said, "Well, you couldn't get your hands off me. Not that I minded. I took you to your room…"

"Not that!" I said in an irritated tone. "She meant, what happened *here,* in this bar, after you left with her."

Dante shrugged. "I wouldn't know, sugar."

I turned to the blond guy. He narrowed his eyes as he stared at me, as if he was trying to place me or remember what happened.

"Don't tell me you took me back to my room?"

"Of course not! I'm married. And faithful."

Relief washed over me. But I realized that the horror wasn't over yet. If he hadn't taken me back to the hotel room, then I must have gone with somebody else. Although, it wasn't really my thing to do one night stands. Maybe on that night, in my agitation about the fact that Travis was having his stag party and could be having fun with his stripper, I had decided to try something wild.

How could this happen now? Now that finally I had found the person I wanted to spend the rest of my life with. Now that I had finally made a family with Travis. Now that I had finally saved him. This would break him as much as it would break me. Maybe even more.

"Did I leave alone?"

"I honestly don't remember. It was more than a month ago."

"I know," I said in a desperate voice. "But could you please try to remember?"

He closed his eyes for a moment. Then he stared at me for a long while.

"I remember Dante didn't come back until five in the morning. You weren't here anymore. You were gone."

"Did you write off our tab?" Sarah asked both the men.

"We don't earn big time, sweetie. And you two had too much to drink. I can't afford to write off that bill," the blond guy said. He turned to me. "I remember now. You were with a guy."

Horror crept through me again. "Who?"

He shrugged. "I mind my own business. And it's not like it's an uncommon thing to have customers flirt with each other here. It happens all the time."

"Where did the guy come from? He just sat beside me, started a conversation, and then I was all over him?" I asked. That didn't sound like me.

He nodded. "Pretty much," the guy replied. "You were laughing a lot. And then I think you started kissing him. You made out here—I had to turn away. And I guess you left with him."

"Who was he?" I asked desperately.

"I don't know, sweetheart," the blond guy said apologetically. "And we don't have security cameras here. We can't help you."

"Why do you want to know, anyway? So you were with a guy for a night. You don't remember who he is. What's the big deal? You're pretty hot. He won't be the last guy on earth for you," Dante said.

I glared at Dante. "How would you feel if a guy you couldn't remember left you a souvenir?"

He backed off. "Ohhh! I'm sorry, sugar," he said. He looked at me for a moment. "Well, I hope it's curable."

304

I looked at him disbelievingly. "It's not a disease!" I turned back to the other guy. "What did he look like?"

He thought for a moment. "Caucasian. Tall. Good-looking fella."

I stared at him, waiting for him to say more.

He shook his head. "I really can't remember any more distinctive features."

"You just described at least thirty percent of the male population of South Carolina. And I'm not even sure what you consider good-looking for a guy!"

"Look, sweetheart. I really can't help you much."

"Who paid my bill?" I asked.

"Ahhh…he did." The guy smiled. "That I remember. You insisted on paying, but you were not fast enough to fish through your wallet. I think you were drunk out of your wits. He paid with an Infinite card. I was impressed. He also gave me a huge tip. Like, one hundred percent of the bill."

"Hey! You didn't tell me that," Dante protested.

"Sorry, pal. I figured you already got the girl." The guy grinned.

"Can…can I see the bill?"

"It's not here, sweetie. And it was over a month ago," he said.

"Is there a way for us to find it?"

"It's in the office," the guy said. "They're not working now."

"Tomorrow?"

"You really want to it that much, huh?"

I nodded.

The guy sighed. "Okay, tell me where to find you. I'll pull some strings and get you a copy of the credit card slip. But there could have been at least ten customers that night."

"Can't you tell which one?"

He shrugged. "Difficult. But that narrows your choices."

"When can you give it to me?"

"Tomorrow, noon?"

"Can it be any sooner?" I asked wearily. Who knew what time Travis would be in Connecticut.

"I'll try. But no promises."

I almost couldn't sleep that night. So I was right—there was a guy. He'd taken me back to my room. What's worse, the bartender told me I had been all over him. So it could mean that I'd slept with

305

him. How could I be so damn loose? How could I flirt like that with a stranger? And how could I not remember?

"No matter how I look at it, that was the only instance that I could have been with a man," I said to Sarah. "Travis slept on the couch the whole time, and I didn't get drunk with him. I would have remembered. That night was the only night I was drunk out of my wits. And it coincides with the week I got pregnant."

"Ultrasound results may change as the week progresses," Sarah reminded me.

"But only plus or minus two weeks. Plus or minus two weeks from that night, I'm still positive I didn't have sex at all! Christian and I were long over by then. Travis and I didn't happen at all until last week."

Sarah squeezed my hand. "Don't stress the baby. Go to sleep now."

When I finally fell asleep, I dreamt of making love to Travis. He touched me in the most sensual way. He was very gentle. I was the wild one. I dreamt about making love and reaching heaven. And then he stood up from the bed and dressed hurriedly.

"Why are you in a hurry?" I asked him.

When he turned around, I recognized in horror that he was not Travis. That face belonged to Christian! I dreamt of making love to Travis, but it was Christian who I was really sleeping with!

"No!" I screamed.

"Brianne! Brianne!" Sarah shook me. I opened my eyes and realized, in relief, that it was all just a dream.

I sat up from the bed and gave Sarah a hug. "Sarah."

"Hey, you were having a bad dream," Sarah said.

I was scared. I might have been in love with Christian before, but I realized I didn't love him as much as I loved Travis now. I didn't think I'd loved anyone as much as I loved Travis. And tonight, I would have to tell him that our marriage was over.

I rushed to the bathroom to throw up. The morning sickness was getting worse now. Even if I planned to wait for a week or so more to tell Travis, he would surely recognize the signs. He would know.

I dressed in a pair of drawstring pants and a comfortable shirt. I came out of the bathroom just in time to see Sarah open the door. She let Dante and the blond bartender in.

"We didn't get your name," I said to the blonde guy.

"Rick," he said.

"So, Rick, did you manage to find something for us?" I asked.

He nodded. He took out a stack of paper and handed it to Sarah. "You didn't get this from me."

I nodded.

"Well, there's about a dozen credit card slips here," Sarah said, rolling her eyes.

"It was a busy night," Rick pointed out.

"Thanks for your help, Rick," I said. I took out some money from my wallet and handed it to him. "For your trouble."

He accepted the money from me. "Anytime. Good luck with whatever you are looking for."

And he left and Dante gave Sarah a wink before he exited the room. I took the papers from Sarah.

"Okay, I hope he only gave us the guys. I mean, no point getting the slips of female customers," Sarah said.

Sarah and I split the papers to search separately. I read the names on my stack, trying to see if any of them rang a bell.

"Tyrone Gomez," I read. "No. Don't recognize the name."

"Jackson Bow," Sarah read.

I shook my head.

"Timothy Reyes."

I shook my head again.

Sarah took another paper. She stared at the bill for a while.

"Oh my God!" she breathed.

I looked at her wearily.

"October twenty-six, one fifteen in the morning," she said.

"Yeah, it could be around that time. What have you got?"

She stared at me with a worried expression on her face. And she handed me the piece of paper.

Her hands were shaking, and that made me extra nervous.

I knew then the name was familiar. Christian? Eric?

I read the copy of the credit card slip. The time and date were as Sarah mentioned. The bill was about four hundred dollars.

I scanned the bill for the name. When I found it, my heart stopped beating altogether.

After reading it a dozen times, I was convinced I was not dreaming. The slip still bore the same name: *Travis James Cross*

# Chapter Twenty-Nine

I was in shock. I almost didn't speak to Sarah for the entire duration of our trip back to Connecticut. We went straight to my old apartment.

It had been months since I last visited it. It was exactly the way it was when I'd left it. Sarah was kind enough to ask a maid to clean it up at least twice a month.

I saw Christian's spare key on the table. He must have left it there when he found out I was getting married. He left a note for me.

*Have a good life, Brianne. I hope he's what you were looking for.*

Tears rolled down my cheeks. I had a good life, all right. And Travis was everything I wanted and more. But I just didn't know what to feel right now.

"The good thing about it is that it's Travis," Sarah said quietly.

"That's not the point, is it?" I asked in a small voice. "Do you realize that I was drunk? I was not myself. I couldn't even remember that night. Travis didn't seem drunk. He signed the credit card slip perfectly well. If it was him...then he...took advantage of me." Tears rolled down my cheeks. "And he promised he would never do that. Travis is the one person I trust. He was the last person I expected to take my clothes off and take me when he knew perfectly well that I was helpless to defend myself. And what's worse...he didn't tell me."

"I'm sure he wanted to. Maybe he was just afraid you'd...react like this. And he was afraid to lose you."

"We consummated the marriage before we even got married!" I muttered. "And he pretended to be a gentleman during our honeymoon." I wiped the tears from my cheeks. "You don't understand, Sarah. If it were any other man, I wouldn't feel this betrayed. But this was Travis. He promised me he wouldn't touch me, wouldn't take advantage of me. And I knew how good he was with keeping his promises. I didn't expect this from him at all."

"Before you work yourself up, why don't you talk to him first?"

I nodded.

The doorbell rang. Sarah looked at me wearily. "Well, I'm here if you need me," she said. "Brianne, you have to remember that this is

Travis. Not any of your past boyfriends. This guy was everything to you, even when you were not in love with him."

Tears rolled down my cheeks. "And that makes it even worse, doesn't it?"

Sarah bit her lip and then gave me a hug. "I'll go. Call me anytime you need me." Then she went to open the door. I heard her say hi to Travis.

"Hey! Thanks for keeping my wife company," Travis said to her.

I didn't listen to the little chitchat. At the sound of his voice, my heart swelled with love, and then, I remembered what he might have done to me before I'd gotten married, and my heart broke. I could help feeling disappointed and betrayed.

I was looking out the window. I knew Travis was behind me. Gently, I felt his arms creep around me. He kissed the base of my neck. I bit my lip to prevent myself from moaning.

"God, I missed you!" he whispered and pulled me to him.

I stared up at his handsome face, and I felt the cold façade I'd built slowly crumbling down. But then I remembered that he had taken advantage of me. And he hadn't told me.

He smiled. "I love you," he whispered. Slowly, he bent down and gave me a kiss on the lips.

I savored the kiss. *It could be our last*, I thought.

Tears rolled down my cheeks. Travis stopped kissing me when he realized that I was crying. He pulled back and studied my expression.

"What's wrong, love?" he asked wearily.

I pushed him away from me. "Travis…I'm pregnant!" I said.

He stared at me for a while, and then he beamed. "Sweetheart, that's wonderful! I'm gonna be a father. Isn't that a good thing? Why are you crying?" He stepped toward me again.

I held my hand up to stop him from coming any closer.

"I'm *seven* weeks pregnant, Travis!" I said to him. "We only started sleeping with each other last week."

I watched his expression carefully. It went from comprehension, to weariness, to a look of pain, and then guilt. He didn't have to admit anything after that. I could read him like a book, too, when you he wasn't so guarded.

"Brianne…" he started.

"Oh my God," I breathed, shaking my head.

He took a step closer to me. He reached out for my hands, but I pulled them away. "Brianne...please. I didn't mean for that to happen. But I wasn't sorry."

"Why, Travis? You said I could trust you."

"And you can!" he said. "I'm only human, Brianne. I'd been controlling what I felt for you for years. Every day, every night for the last fifteen years I told myself that I couldn't want you...because you were forbidden...I could not have you. Then one night, I slipped! I wasn't able to hold back. My desire for you was stronger than I was. I let go of all control!"

"You took advantage of me!"

He shook his head. "I didn't...or at least, I didn't mean to..."

"There's no excuse for what you did, Travis!" I said to him. "And you should have told me!"

"I got scared. For the first time in my life, I felt afraid. I was afraid to lose you...both of you..." He took a deep breath again. "The you that I have loved like family since I was a kid, the one that Tom left under my protection...and the you that I love with all my heart...the only woman I have ever been in love with! You see, Brianne? There was no other woman. It was you all along."

In my mind, I remembered what he'd said to me...*I made love...to an amazing, wonderful woman.*

I sat down on the couch. "You still lied to me, Travis. You were the last person I expected to do this to me. Wanting me too much is not an excuse for what you did."

Travis knelt down in front of me and took my hands in his. He kissed them desperately. When he raised his face to me, I saw the tears in his eyes. "I did not only want you. That night, I realized that I was in love with you. That I might have been in love with you all these years." His voice was full of pain.

"You seduced me. I was drunk! And yet you touched me! I must have been unconscious the moment I hit the covers, Travis. I was helpless! I just lay there...and you took me!"

Travis stared at me, and for the first time that night, I thought I saw a flicker of anger in his eyes. "I..." He started to say something. Then he shook his head, stood up and turned away from me.

"What? Tell me! Lie to me!" I said angrily.

"I didn't lie to you!" he raised his voice. "I would never lie to you."

"Yeah! Be smart with me! You just chose to omit the fact that you *raped* me days before I married you. And how convenient it was for you! You already had the solution on hand, didn't you? You were going to marry me anyway. So you figured you'd test the merchandise first?!"

He narrowed his eyes at me. "I'd already tested the merchandise a long time ago! Why would I need to do it again if that was my intention?"

"Then what was your intention, Travis?"

"I wanted you!" Travis said in low, cold voice. He was angry now, I could tell. But he was trying not to lose his temper. "I tried to stay away from you. I tried to control what I felt. That night...something was different between us! I wasn't able to stop myself. If I knew...how it would all end, I wouldn't have touched a hair in your body! It would be easier for me to take a million cold showers to calm my need for you than to betray your trust! Surely, you must know that."

"Apparently, I don't know you at all! You...were the beast you should have been protecting me from, Travis! You *promised* me!"

He closed his eyes in anguish for a second. When he looked at me again, I could no longer read the expression on his face. "Sometimes, you make me choose between protecting you and giving you everything you ask of me," he said. "That night, I was helpless. I realized for the first time how much our relationship had changed. I realized what you really meant to me."

"And so you just took me? Knowing that I was unconscious of what you were doing?"

He bit his lip to keep from saying what he really wanted to say. And I felt frustrated because I wanted him to explain everything to me. I wanted to understand him. I knew him...he was better than a man who would take advantage of a drunk, unconscious woman just because he had lusted for her for so many years. But he just looked down at the floor, trying to control his anger, trying to bottle it all up again.

"You should have told me before you married me!" I shouted at him.

"I shouldn't have married you at all!" he roared back.

I felt like he had slapped me when he said that. It hurt like a shard of glass piercing through my heart. How could he say that?

Tears rolled down my face. He realized that he'd hurt me even more with what he'd said, but he didn't say anything to take it back or deny it. Maybe he really did feel this marriage had been a mistake from the beginning.

"Did you...do that as part of your plan to win your battle with your father?"

He stared at me disbelievingly. "What are you trying to say?"

"I'm saying your father wanted a grandson, didn't he? Did you take advantage of the time I could not say no to you? You had to make sure you could get me pregnant, even if it meant you had to *rape* me!"

I think that threw him over the edge. He balled his hands into fists and he turned to the wall beside him, then he gave it a hard punch.

"Damn it!" he cursed. "No matter how hard I try, I lose with you, Brianne! I'm tired!"

Now I couldn't understand what he was saying. "You're tired of protecting me? Of the silly little girl your best friend asked you to take care of?"

"I'm tired of making things right for you, only to have it all blow up in my face! I'm tired of not getting a single thing right when it comes to you!" he said in a broken voice, while he leaned his forehead against the wall he had just punched.

"Then don't!" I said angrily. "Just stop, Travis!"

He looked at me coldly. He didn't say anything, but I realized how furious he was. Now, I was looking back at the same Travis I had known many months ago. Cold and ruthless.

"Do you really mean that, Brianne? Do you really want me to stop?"

My heart broke in a million pieces.

*No! I want you to keep trying! Because I know, somehow, we will get it all right!*

I bit my lip. "I...want you to stop fighting fate for me..." I said in between sobs.

He closed his eyes once again. He took a few short breaths, and then he stared at me coldly.

He headed for the door but then turned to me. "It will save us both if you remember everything that happened that night!" And with that, he stormed out the door.

I felt like all my dreams of having a happy family life had gone out the door, too. I was too confused and too hurt. I should have been happy that it was Travis who'd fathered my baby. I should have been happy that there was no other woman all along.

But, on the other hand, the bigger part of me that had complete faith and trust in Travis was also crumbling to pieces. Travis...the man who would never ever betray me...who would not dare touch me without my consent...who would rather hurt himself than take advantage of me. If I didn't have him to believe, what did I have?

No matter how much I tried to justify his actions, I still kept thinking in my mind that he had violated me. And it wasn't like him. Travis would never rape me...or any woman, for that matter. But why did he? If he really meant what he said, that he realized he was in love with me that night, then all the more reason he should have respected me, he should have protected me. And knowing that the only way he would win against his father was by having a son only made it more difficult to understand or forgive him.

I could not imagine how Travis could use me like that. And I don't know how I could trust him after all this! Trust was the main root of our relationship. How could our love survive without that trust?

It had been hours, and Travis still had not returned. I was lying down on the couch. I wasn't whimpering anymore, but it seemed like I had slipped into limbo. I felt like I was floating on air. I didn't make a sound; I lay still. But it was inside that I was in turmoil. My emotions were going haywire. My soul was broken. My heart was shattered to pieces. It was like the pillar of strength that I'd had for years had crashed down to the ground.

Then suddenly, I felt a sharp pain in my abdomen. I tried to steady myself, but the pain was still there. I fiddled with the phone and dialed 911.

Then the throbbing pain became sharp, cutting through my abdomen like a knife. The pain was blinding, and I was afraid it would tear me apart.

Then things suddenly went hazy. I remembered being lifted somewhere. I remembered being sedated. I remembered being carried into an ambulance.

And then...there was nothing.

# Chapter Thirty

*Black.*

I started swirling black paint on my canvas. Allowing it to drip its own pattern down, taking shape, like it had a mind of its own.

This color described my days and what I was now. An empty vessel with a black hole in the center.

For weeks, I felt like I was floating into nothingness. I had nothing to look forward to, nothing to hope for. I was taking one day at a time, taking each breath with the sole purpose of making it to the next. Nothing more. I was alive. But I wasn't really living.

That day I had woken up in the hospital, everything crumbled before me. It was the moment that I felt I'd lost my past, my present, even my future.

The man that I loved walked out of my life with no hopes of ever coming back. The life I wanted to nurture inside me was gone, even before I could fully acknowledge its presence. And then the doctors said I had a small percentage of conceiving life inside me again.

For a while, I blamed myself. I should have been stronger. I should have been calmer. I could take losing everything…but not the innocent life inside of me and the man who had given me that life.

I wasn't a doctor, so I didn't fully understand what they told me at the hospital, and the minute I heard miscarriage and cancer, I completely blacked out. Everything I saw was a blur, and everything I heard was blah, blah, blah.

My friends and my family kept telling me that it wasn't my fault. But the man I'd hurt the most when I lost the baby had completely shut me out of his world. So I knew that he blamed me, as much as I blamed myself. He agreed to the operation. I was told that he had been with me during the time that I was out.

"Your cancer was advancing…it posed a threat to your life. Travis didn't want to wait. He made a decision to save your life," my mother told me. "Regardless of what the consequences might be to your baby. It was a difficult choice."

315

I would have risked it. I wouldn't have agreed to the operation. I would have waited until the baby was strong enough to survive. But I was unconscious, sedated due to the severe pain, and my husband made that decision for me. Surgery was the best option. Removing the affected organ was necessary. I started miscarrying even with the doctors' best efforts. My pregnancy was sensitive. I couldn't fight for him even if I wanted to.

When I woke up in the hospital, I swear I could smell Travis's aftershave on my pillow. My mother told me that he'd stayed with me while I was unconscious. But he was gone the minute I opened my eyes. My already broken heart was shattered to a million pieces. I hugged my pillow to myself and drowned myself on what was left of Travis's presence beside me…his scent, his memory.

*Red.*

I filled my brush with red paint and swirled it on the corner farthest from the black. Now, my strokes were even more defined and less free-form. I brushed the paint upward with as much vigor as one wrist motion would allow.

The red reflected much of what I felt inside, too. I felt broken about losing the life I'd loved inside of me. I felt rage and loathing when the doctor told me that the other ovary left with me was not as healthy as it should be. Treatment was required. But I was told I had about a one-third chance of conceiving again.

The strokes on my canvas became rougher and more urgent as I remembered how angry I was. And worse, I didn't know who to direct that anger at.

At whomever in my family had given me this bad string of genes. At myself, because I should have taken better care. I should have done more. I should have done routine checkups when I was younger so I could have prevented it. I should have paid attention to every missed period or any irregularity in my menstrual cycle. I should have gone to the doctor sooner.

I took more of the red paint and smudged it in downward, circular motion.

I remembered that when the doctor told me that I would have so much difficulty conceiving, I realized I had gotten mad at Travis, too. He'd made that choice for me. I would have risked my life just to have the baby. And even if I'd only had one child in my life, I would have been complete as a woman.

*Blue*

I took a new paintbrush and dipped it in blue acrylic paint. I stroked it lightly on the white space between the red and the black, making stronger strokes in the center and softer where it met the other colors.

It had been months since I'd gotten out of the hospital.

I did call Travis before I was discharged. I could still remember that conversation in my head because it was the last time I'd spoken to him.

"I'm sorry I lost your baby," I said in a broken voice.

He took a deep breath. Then he said, "At least you're alive and safe."

"It doesn't matter now, really," I whispered.

"It does to your family," he countered.

"Why did you do it, Travis? Why didn't you take a chance? I would have waited until it was safer."

I heard his sharp intake of breath. "Maybe...I needed to save you one last time."

That broke me, but I refused to let a whimper escape my lips.

"I won't ever be the same! What's the point of my womanhood if I can't conceive?"

He was silent for a while. Then he said, "The right guy for you will love you enough not to care. At least now, you can't really say I raped you just to get an heir." His voice was so unemotional, it completely made me mad and sad at the same time. I wanted to cry so hard—right after I gave him a good slap in the face.

There was a long silence. Then finally, he asked, "Do you have anything else you want to say to me?"

*I love you.* But I didn't say that out loud. I couldn't. His cold demeanor made me abandon all hope that this phone call would fix anything between us. Travis had caved in. The Travis who'd loved me was now buried underneath the hundred masks he was wearing. I didn't even recognize the man I was speaking to anymore.

"Goodbye," I said weakly.

Again, another long pause. "Goodbye, Brianne."

317

*Purple.*

I took a brush and dipped it in purple. I swirled this around at the point where blue met with red. I continued with my strokes until the blending and continuation of the hues seemed flawless.

I was now back in my apartment in Connecticut. It had been months since I'd gotten out of the hospital. I had my mother move my stuff out from Travis's apartment.

Even after I had completely moved out, I still hadn't heard from him. He didn't call me or attempt to see me. And it broke my heart as much as it made me angry.

I asked my mother for a break. I told her I needed a sabbatical from work. I had a little money saved up. I could take care of myself without working for about a year. And I needed to figure out what I was going to do with Travis and our marriage.

News of our separation reached the ears of some of my relatives. Many of them offered sympathies and encouragement. Some of them still believed Travis and I were going to work things out.

"It's Travis and you!" my aunt Victoria told me over the phone.

It *was* Travis and me. And somehow, even I couldn't believe that we were over. A huge part of me still stared at my phone or my door wistfully. Hoping that it would ring or somebody would knock and it would be him. We didn't really have to work things out. I just hoped we could talk to each other—didn't matter if we're yelling or not. I wished I could open him up. I wished he would just tell me what he felt—didn't matter if I felt insulted or hurt. I wished he would trust me to be strong or mature enough to hear the words he wanted to say.

*Green.*

Below the black swirls, I started a pattern in green, dark-hued at first, and then slowly brightening up as I progressed away from the dark colors. I smiled a little bit because the pattern reminded me so much of myself. I had come out of the black hole. The first months were really tough. I had lost count of the number of times I'd attempted to see a shrink just to get me out of my misery. But now, it was slowly progressing. Things were getting lighter and lighter.

I tried to stand on my own. For the first time in my life, I lived without the shadow of my guardian angel. I walked the streets knowing that I could get mugged or murdered, and no one would come to my rescue. No eyes were following me wherever I went, making sure I was safe.

Once in a while, I would dream about making love to Travis. It was as wonderful as the real thing. My body still craved him, still missed him. But my heart was too broken to hope that we could be together again.

When my physical wounds had healed, I began dancing again. I did it slowly at first. But it felt good, losing all my worries in the beat of the music, forgetting how to think and feel…just allowing my body to move.

I was starting to be strong on my own. I was dead scared at first. Because after Tom died, I was never on my own. Travis was *always* there. I could just be selfish and carefree. And he would always be there to pick me up.

I still couldn't believe what Travis had done to me. My family thought that the lost baby had taken a toll on our marriage. I didn't tell anybody, except for Sarah, the real reason why Travis and I had drifted apart. I couldn't. No matter what he did, I couldn't bear for my friends and family to hate him and think of him as a beast…because even I found it so hard to believe, even then. I still couldn't accept that the Travis who protected me with his life had taken advantage of me when I was too weak to defend myself.

*Yellow.*

I smudged an adequate amount of yellow on after the greens. It provided a lighter tone to my painting, which used to be so dark and sad.

I stared back at the canvas. It was a beautiful combination of black, blue, purple, red, green, and a touch of yellow. Tears rolled down my cheeks. All the other colors, except for yellow, represented a phase in my life that had lasted for the past couple of months. I felt like every dark and sad emotion I had ever felt was in that painting.

And then the yellow added so much brightness to the bleak mood that the painting had originally conveyed. I guessed that was my challenge now. To find the source of light that would give me hope…a hope that I could still find happiness in spite of losing the things that mattered most to me. The hope that I would still be able to smile, in spite of losing the one person whom I considered to be…my life.

# Chapter Thirty-One

One night, I got a call from Eric.

"Get your cute butt out of your apartment and let's go have fun!" he said.

I laughed. "Pick me up in thirty."

I smiled and then dialed Sarah's number. "Be here in twenty! We're going out."

A few minutes later, as I watched Eric's car stop in front of my apartment and Sarah walk up the steps to meet me, my heart warmed up. If I could translate this into my painting, I realized, Eric and Sarah would be my first strokes of *yellow*.

As we approached Eric's car, he frowned when he saw Sarah.

"What?" I asked him.

"I didn't know you were bringing your hump-every-stiff-pole friend."

Sarah stopped in her tracks and looked from me to him twice. And then she laughed innocently. "Oh, I'm sorry. Were you referring to yourself?" she asked Eric evenly.

Eric rolled his eyes. "Brianne, make sure she stays in the back. I don't want to totally wreck the passenger side of my car. It's too precious."

We got into his car, with me in the passenger seat and Sarah sitting behind me.

Yeah. Eric and Sarah didn't have anything in common. Except for the fact that they hated each other and they were getting more and more open about it. Oh, why did I think this was a great idea?

We went to a bar. They gave me shots and flavored vodka that came in neon test tubes. I thought it was kind of cool. But four test tubes later, I was completely floating on air, laughing my ass off.

The blond bartender was looking at me in a weird way, probably because I was laughing while looking at Sarah making out with some hot guy.

"I'm sorry, she's liberated," I told the bartender jokingly.

"Didn't you three come together? I thought that was her boyfriend." It took me a minute to understand what he said. I looked in Sarah's direction again. She was practically shoving her tongue down the guy's throat. His hands were on her ass, and he was kissing her back passionately. When they turned, I realized that the guy looked very much like Eric.

"Holy crap!" I said to myself. I had to blink plenty of times. And then I looked at the bartender and started laughing again.

"At least everybody's happy."

"Are you happy?" the bartender asked.

"Nope," I said, popping the P sound. "But I'll be okay," I said and ordered another shot of alcohol. "Test tube?"

It seems like all I did all night was laugh. When it was time to go, I insisted we all take a cab since Eric seemed drunk out of his wits, too. I wondered how he would feel if he realized he'd made out a dozen times with his worst enemy.

I felt like I was floating up toward my apartment. I threw my clothes on the floor, washed my face, brushed my teeth, and hit the bed wearing only my underwear.

I knew I was drunk out of my wits again. But it felt good. I'd had a blast with Sarah and Eric. Seeing them make out was weird, though, but really funny. I wondered if they would remember that in the morning.

I looked at the digital alarm clock on my bedside table. It was only one-fifteen in the morning. With a smile on my face, I felt myself drifting off to a place very familiar to me.

I saw a blond bartender in front of me.

"I'm sorry. My friend is...liberated!" I said to him, looking at Sarah, who had just rushed out with the other bartender.

"Many girls are these days!" he said, shaking his head. "How about you? Are you married? In a relationship? Or single?"

I laughed. "I'm engaged!" I replied.

"Where's the fiancé?" he asked.

"I don't know! Humping the stripper in the cake for all I care!"

"Are you sure you don't care?" he asked, laughing.

"Of course I do!" I said. "Do you think I would drink myself out of my skull if it was okay with me to think that he was with another woman right now?"

"Well, at least you're going to have him for yourself for the rest of your life."

I heaved a frustrated sigh. "I wanted to have him for myself when I said yes to his proposal. I didn't want him to touch any other woman."

"And maybe he hasn't!" a familiar voice said beside me. A figure seated himself in the empty seat to my right.

I stared at Travis. He had a mischievous grin on his face.

"Travis!" I felt embarrassed about what he had just heard. "I didn't..." I started taking back what I had said.

"Please do," he said. I stopped and stared back at him. "Please mean what you said."

"Wha-what are you doing here? It's your stag party," I said.

"It was. But somehow I couldn't get you out of my head. And I realized I had to come and find you. I wanted to see you, hear you laugh, more than I wanted to sit there with a bunch of immature guys cheering on half-naked girls!"

I was deeply touched by what he'd said to me. I smiled. And I couldn't help it. I lunged myself forward and I kissed him hard on the lips. Then I hugged him. He hugged me back.

"And here you are, drinking your brains out!" he said, laughing.

I stared up at him. "Take me to my room, Travis."

He stared back at me, studying my expression. "I should. You can barely walk."

He motioned for the bartender to get him the bill.

"I'll pay for it," I insisted, trying to reach for my bag. But Travis was already handing the guy his credit card.

I rested my head on his shoulder while he signed the credit card slip. I saw that he had just paid four hundred twenty-eight dollars and fifty cents for all the liquor that Sarah and I had consumed.

"I'll pay you back," I told him.

"Nonsense," he said. "Consider it my treat to you and Sarah."

"I got drunk too soon," I said, looking at the clock. "It's only one-twenty in the morning."

Travis put an arm around me and kissed my forehead as we walked back to my room.

At the door, I pulled him with me and stared at him naughtily.

He was grinning at me. "You, my love, are bold and brazen—you might not have this much courage when you're sober."

"Probably not!" I laughed. "But that would work to your advantage, wouldn't it?"

He laughed as he pushed me to sit on the bed. He bent down to take the sandals off my feet.

"No," he said. "I prefer that you be sober when I make love to you."

"But didn't you tell me you'd give me everything I wanted, Travis Cross?"

"I also promised to protect you from the beast inside me, remember?"

I stared at him. "Travis..." I said. Something about my voice made him stop to look at me. "I'm glad you weren't with the stripper tonight."

He smiled, bent forward, and gave me a gentle kiss on the lips.

"Do you really mean it? Were you really thinking about me?" I asked him.

He took a deep breath. "It seems I've been thinking about you every waking hour!" he groaned softly.

I smiled triumphantly. "Kiss me, Travis. *Kiss me.*"

He smiled and then gently he bent down and kissed me thoroughly...passionately. I pulled him toward the bed with me. He gently eased me up against the mattresses. He kissed the base of my neck, and I moaned softly. I wrapped my arms around his neck, igniting more of the passion inside me.

Then suddenly, he stopped. He smiled at me wearily. "Brianne...I have to stop."

"Don't stop, Travis!" I said, pulling him to me again.

"Brianne... I'm close to the edge! I may not be able to control myself after this!"

I groaned. "I'm sick and tired of you always controlling yourself, Travis! Always such a gentleman! I want you!"

There! I said it to him straight. I was drunk out of my wits, but that could also be the reason why I didn't feel ashamed of admitting to him how much I wanted him. He was the only one who'd ever made me feel like this. And right then, I was so tired of pretending I didn't feel anything for him...I was done watering this fire inside me that only he could ignite.

"Brianne..." he whispered.

I pulled him to me again and kissed him passionately.

"Dammit, Brianne!"

"The great Travis Cross has a weakness after all," I teased.

He stared down at me and then in a sober voice, he said, "You must know that my only weakness has always been you." And he kissed me again, giving in to the tide of passion enveloping both of us.

The next scene of our lovemaking was something I had already seen before. I had already had this dream before. Those vivid dreams of making love to Travis...reaching Nirvana with him.

"I love you, Travis!" I screamed, tears rolling down cheeks as I realized how I really felt about this man. At that moment, I truly let go. I was honest for once in my life.

Exhausted and happy, I felt him slip out of me. He held me for a while, and then I felt him drape the sheets over me to keep me warm. I was looking at the clock beside me with a smile on my face.

It was now two-thirty in the morning. I blinked once, twice. The clock still gave me the same vivid reading.

Finally...it dawned on me. In dreams, you don't have a sense of time. But now, I could read my digital clock well, and the number registered in my mind perfectly. That night that came back to me just now...it wasn't a dream...it was a memory.

I remembered him disappearing after that night. And the night before our wedding, he came to my room. I knew when he knocked on my door that he wanted to tell me something. That was it. He'd attempted to come clean before he married me...maybe he'd chickened out once he saw me and decided not to.

On our honeymoon, I remember him saying...

*My life. The reason why I live. The core of my existence...*

*There's one person I could live and die for...and I wanted to freeze that moment for eternity...because she screamed my name... she truly belonged to me...*

*It's too late when you realize your world revolves around one person...I thought it was my body craving hers, but that last time I was with her, I realized it was my heart screaming out for her...*

*She was the air that I breathed...I would go to hell and back for her...I would give everything just to see that look on her face again...*

*She told me she loved me..."*

In a way, Travis had already told me what happened that night. But since I couldn't remember it, I'd thought he was talking about somebody else. I remembered that when I heard him say those words, my heart had broken for him. Because I'd felt how in love he'd been...and how painful it was for him not to express what he truly felt. He felt guilty about taking me...even though I was actually the one who seduced him. He was right. He didn't mean to take advantage of me. I asked him to make love to me...begged him to let go of his control. And he did...

*Oh God! What have I done?*

I said some nasty words to Travis. I called him a liar. I told him that he'd taken advantage of me. That he'd *raped* me! How insulted he must have been! No wonder he didn't want to talk to me anymore.

He didn't tell me because he was such a gentleman. He couldn't tell me that I was the one who'd seduced him. I was the one who had begged him to go to bed. He wouldn't allow me to feel ashamed of myself. Instead, he let me fling insult after insult at him.

I had told him that he'd taken advantage of me while I was unconscious. I may have been drunk now, but I was very much aware of everything around me. I was not asleep now. Just like that night. When I dreamt of making love to Travis, I was...wide awake.

***

Sarah was in my apartment the next day. I was painting. What I was painting, I wasn't sure. But it was something abstract again. Just a swirl of hues and colors that reflected most of the turmoil I felt inside. All black, blue, and indigo.

"So you're telling me you were the one who orchestrated everything?" Sarah asked.

I nodded sadly. "Pretty much."

"Why didn't he tell you?"

I shrugged. "Because he was such a gentleman, he didn't want to tell me that I invited him to bed and begged him to have sex with me. He didn't want to humiliate me."

I wished Travis hadn't felt like he had to protect me all the time. Even from my own feelings. I wished I had trusted him enough to know that he always meant well for me and would never take advantage of me if things weren't beyond his control. I wished he'd trusted me enough to tell me what happened and to know that my love for him would make me believe him and understand the pain he'd been through all these years.

326

"What are you going to do now?"

"Nothing," I said sadly. "There's nothing I can do now. He wouldn't even speak to me. I tried calling him…he just won't pick up. The last time I spoke to him, we were saying our goodbyes."

"This is Travis, Brianne!"

"I know. And that makes it even worse. Because I couldn't imagine my Travis staying away from me like that…no matter how bad the situation was. But he was right. It was my fault. It was probably the first time after my brother's death that he bared his soul to another human being, and I accused him of many things. I called him a rapist. A beast! The gentleman he is, it would be far too insulting for him to be called those things. For everything that he's done to protect me almost all of my life, it would be lowering to be called a monster."

I put the brush down. I started organizing my paints and canvases. I opened the cabinet where I usually tucked away my finished canvases. When I was with Christian, he didn't like my paintings to be scattered all over the place. We bought a huge cabinet to hide away all my paintings. It'd been a while since I opened this. I realized I had at least ten finished paintings in here.

Sarah took one painting. It was another abstract.

"I don't really get it, but I like this. This is really, really good."

I stared at the painting she was holding. "I call this a rose."

She drew her brows together and looked at the painting closely. Then her face brightened. "There it is! There's really a rose here somewhere!" She looked at me. "You're really, really good!"

I looked at some more of my old paintings. There were loose papers and sketchbooks in the cabinet that I'd organized as well. I saw a rolled parchment tied with a black ribbon hidden in the farthest corner of the cabinet. I didn't remember this one. I turned it over and saw a red marking at the back of it.

*"A+. Good luck, Mr. Cross."*

I realized it was Mr. Atkins's handwriting. I remembered this now. This was Travis's artwork for Mr. Atkins. He'd asked me to hand it over to Travis when he didn't attend our class. I guessed I'd completely forgotten to give it to him.

I pulled off the ribbon and rolled over the canvas. It was painted in black and white. It took me a moment to realize what I was staring at.

"Is that you?" Sarah asked from behind me.

It was a face of a girl, her hair flowing over her face. But her eyes were clear, and her smile was bright. It was no mistake—it was me.

Tears welled up in my eyes.

"Yes. This is me. When I was a teenager."

"You painted it?"

"Travis did," I said in a broken voice. "Our art teacher asked us to paint...the...meaning of our lives."

Sarah didn't say anything for a while. I felt her put an arm around my shoulder and give me a gentle squeeze.

"He loved you...even when you were younger. You two...go very deep, and all the way back," Sarah said. "Have you really given up on him?"

I realized that many people in Travis's life had given up on him too easily. His parents thought having a kid was complicated and not good for their careers. They gave him up without trying hard to fit him into their lives. Instead, they kept him with nurses, nannies and kept him well-provided for without giving him the love he deserved. Because it was easier than trying to make their family work...easier than loving their son.

I got mad at him, and I made him feel I gave him up because of what he'd done...without even knowing that it was my fault in the first place.

Travis tried to unmask himself and to keep himself unprotected from me, only to get hurt again. He exposed his emotions and exposed himself to pain. It was easy enough for him to go back to being cold and ruthless once more. When I talked to him the last time, it didn't mean he didn't love me anymore. It only meant he'd put all his masks back on again to prevent himself from getting hurt.

The Travis who painted that portrait had me at the center of his life. He wouldn't give me up too easily...if only I could show him that I had not given up on him, either. If I could show him that I was sorry for all the things that I'd said...and that I'd forgiven him, too. That I was willing to start over.

I looked up at Sarah, a new ray of hope surging through me.

"I'm going to see him," I said. "I'm going to give it one more try, Sarah."

She smiled brightly and said, "That's the most sensible thing you've said in months, sugar!"

I sat in Travis's office, waiting for him. I was wearing a floral skirt and a white sleeveless top. I wanted to look good for him. I was hoping he still found me attractive enough to make him stop long enough to listen to what I had to say.

One hour.

Two hours.

Three hours.

I felt a tap on my cheek. I must have fallen asleep. I immediately straightened up on the couch and looked up. But it wasn't Travis. It was Karl. He was smiling at me apologetically.

"Where is he?" I asked him.

He shook his head. "He's not coming," he said. "He had this important meeting with his father. He had to fly to Dallas immediately. I'm sorry."

I smiled at Karl. I tried so hard to hold back my tears.

"Thanks, Karl. Could you tell him that I was here?"

He nodded.

"Will he be back tomorrow?"

"Maybe. In the evening," he replied.

I stayed with my mother in Manhattan. I was determined to see Travis. I knew it was not going to be easy. But I believed in what he'd told me. That he loved me. I still clung on to that and hoped it was true...it still *is* true.

I came back the next day. Karl was kind enough to let me sit in Travis's office again. He hadn't come back from Dallas yet, but when he did, Karl believed he would go to the office immediately.

I fiddled with my engagement and my wedding rings anxiously. I wondered if I still had the right to wear the engagement ring. It was his grandmother's.

*Well, aren't you here to confirm that you still can?* I thought to myself.

Karl approached me.

"Is he coming?"

He shook his head apologetically. "I'm afraid that he's been held back in Dallas. He may not return until tomorrow."

I smiled sadly. "Thank you, Karl."

I left Travis's office with a heavy heart. And yet, I smiled. I would keep trying. This was me. I was still his wife!

My mother didn't ask me what I was doing, and I was glad. Instead, she talked to me about the prospect of showcasing my paintings.

"You were born to do this. You're amazing! I want you to open your art to the public," she said.

I nodded. "That would be good. But I don't want to do it solo, Mom. Can you get some work of other artists? Some famous ones, and then I'll showcase mine in the same show."

She nodded. "That can be arranged." She smiled at me and then she gave me a hug. "You're a wonderful woman, Brianne. Never forget that."

I tried my best to smile at her. "Thanks, Mom."

Travis didn't want to see me. I knew because I tried every day after that, and still he made no effort to show up to his office because he knew I was there.

I went back to Connecticut in defeat. The pain in my heart was like nothing I had felt before. I was hurt when I thought Travis had betrayed me. The pain I felt now was ten times greater whenever I thought he did not want to see me anymore.

"Give him a bit of time," Eric told me one time. "He'll come around."

But I didn't know how much time I needed to give Travis. I tried calling him. His phone was either turned off or he wasn't picking up.

I kept myself busy with the gallery in Connecticut. My mother flew in and stayed with me for several weeks to sort out the exhibition we were going to launch. It would be my birthday celebration. I thought, with so much pain, that it was going to be my first birthday without Travis in my life. And a few months back, I thought it was going to be the first one I'd celebrate with him as my husband. It could also have been the first birthday that I would celebrate holding our little angel in my arms. It could have been the best birthday of my life. It could have been the happiest day ever.

But everything was upside down. My baby was gone even before I could tell him I loved him. My husband had caved in...and given up on me. And I was celebrating my birthday heartbroken about losing the two most important people in my life.

I found an article in a business magazine. It was about Cross Industries and how close it was to acquiring Cross Magnates. Travis was on fire. He was concentrating so much on his battles with his father. I guess he was more heartless than he had ever been before.

I stared at the picture of him. His face was cold. Ruthless. He was handsome as hell, but his face left no trace of boyishness or mischief anymore. The picture I was looking at was that of a devil not even trying to disguise himself as an angel.

He had his fingers intertwined in front of him. I realized with so much sadness that he was no longer wearing his wedding ring…our wedding ring. And I guessed that told me a lot of things because I was still wearing mine…including my engagement ring.

Sarah and Eric helped me a lot with my upcoming art show. We chose which paintings of mine would be showcased. I had to polish some of my work to make it really good for commercial viewing.

Somehow, Sarah and Eric were now civil to each other. They didn't try to bite each other's heads off or make nasty remarks to each other. God! I knew that relationship had no future. But still, I was curious about what had happened between them.

When Sarah was alone in one corner, I tried to speak to her about Eric. "Are you hooking up?"

"Nope. He's gay!"

"But you kissed him when we were all together at the bar! Did you have sex after?"

Sarah smiled at me naughtily. "Well, nothing better to boost a woman's ego than making a man out of a gay man."

My jaw dropped. "Shit, Sarah! That's Eric. He's dear to me! Are you playing with him?"

She shook her head. "Of course not. One-night thing. Don't worry, Brianne. I made sure he enjoyed it. He's not complaining."

My hand went to my temples. "You guys are giving me a headache!"

"What's wrong, sweetie?" Eric asked behind me.

I stared up at him and then at Sarah.

"We're cool. Don't worry about it, Brianne. One night I owned his ass!" Sarah said brightly.

Eric groaned. "And you promised never to speak about it!" He glared at her.

Sarah suddenly waved her hands over her head and started jumping. "It's hard to keep quiet about it when I'm ecstatic."

"Sarah please stop!" I said to her.

Sarah stopped and just laughed. Then she stared at Eric. Eric tried to look serious and then he started laughing, too.

"Yeah. I guess I don't entirely prefer men," he admitted. "Come, ladies. We deserve a little break. Dinner's on me."

On the eve of my birthday, my mother's Connecticut gallery was filled with my paintings. As I looked at them, I realized just how much my work showed a shadow of Travis in it. I saw just how much he'd inspired me to paint for almost half of my life.

The last piece I did was a replica of the painting he'd submitted to Mr. Atkins. I was proud that I was able to replicate his work to every little detail. But I made one major change at the last minute. When his portrait of me was smiling, my portrait of myself had a serious look on my face. There were no tears in my eyes, but I was able to convey the sad, dark, and intense expression that meant I was breaking and crying inside. My face reflected so much of the emotion I felt. My eyes lacked the luster that Travis showed in his portrait. My eyes were filled with sadness and every trace of a broken heart.

A lot of people came to my art show. I'd never seen the gallery this full before. There was a lot of interest in my pieces and my mother was ecstatic. She was extremely proud of me. In a way, I was happy. But I knew I wasn't complete. I wanted to share this moment with the man I loved. The man whose ring I was still wearing on my finger.

The exhibit did pretty well. A lot of brokers complimented me. Some people from the press said I was the next big thing. My father also arrived and I was glad that he and my mother didn't make a scene. Eric and Sarah helped me entertain everybody.

There was only one thing missing. And it was the most important piece of the puzzle. It was the person who mattered the most.

I wasn't able to stop myself. I dialed his number. I didn't know what I would say to him. But I just wanted to hear his voice...I just wanted to know there was still hope for us.

He didn't pick up. I tried over and over. I must have called him about ten times, but he didn't answer. Finally, when I called again, I got his voicemail. He'd turned his phone off.

I stared at his name on my cell. "Happy birthday, Brianne," I whispered to myself sadly.

# Chapter Thirty-Two

My mother was ecstatic about the turnout of my exhibition. My pieces were sold out.

"You were sold for fifty grand!" she told me excitedly.

"What?"

"Your portrait. The crying lady, as I like to call it, sold for fifty thousand bucks," she said. "There were three bidders. But the woman who bought it meant business. Upped the price to fifty grand to eliminate competition. The rest of your pieces sold for at least ten grand. You're going to be famous one day!"

I smiled. "That's great. But I'll get the details of the sale later, Mom. I'm gonna be late for my flight."

I decided to go to Manhattan again. Eric had agreed to come with me. I could tell he was worried about me, too.

My mother stared at me wearily. But she said, "Good luck."

I met Eric at the airport. "Are you worried about me, or are you here just to make sure I'm not going to make a fool of myself?"

"That too," he said, grinning, taking my bags, and leading me to the check-in counters.

Since Travis didn't want to see me in his office, I decided to try our…his apartment.

I just got out of the cab with Eric behind me when I saw Travis heading toward the entrance of his building.

"Travis!" I called to him. My heart was pounding in my chest. I think I wasn't even breathing.

He didn't seem to hear me. He turned to the beautiful blonde beside him, put a hand on her back and guided her inside the building. Karl seemed to hear me, though. He looked at me, and then he smiled apologetically. He gave me a slight nod, and he went inside to follow Travis.

I didn't know what I was going to feel. Angry, sad, humiliated, heartbroken…all those emotions inside seemed to be overpowering each other, trying to see which one would break me down first.

I felt the overpowering desire to settle this…once and for all. I thought he was just caving in. Trying to deal with our problems on his own. And then when he was ready, he would come to see me.

But who was that woman? If she was a business associate, then what the hell was she doing inside our apartment? That man was still my husband! If he wanted to screw other women, then he had to make sure he was man enough to face me…and finally end this! He couldn't keep running away from me and keep me hanging in the balance.

I ran toward the building, attempting to follow them, but immediately, I was stopped by security, even before I could take one step into the doorway. He was new. I hadn't seen him before.

"Do you have business coming here, ma'am?" he asked me in a polite voice.

"Travis Cross," I replied.

"What's your name, ma'am?" he asked.

"Brittany Montgomery."

He took his notes and flipped through the pages.

"I'm sorry, ma'am. I don't see your name here."

"What list is that?"

"The list of visitors allowed access to Mr. Cross's apartment without prior appointment," he replied. "No Montgomery."

"Must be an old list. I used to live here."

He shook his head. "I just got this copy last week. All tenants are asked to update the list at least every six months and whenever it is necessary."

"What about Cross? Brittany Cross."

He shook his head. "No. His visitor list is… actually empty." He replied.

"Are you a sibling or a relative?"

I shook my head. I was on the verge of tears now, but I tried to keep it together. "Thanks anyway," I said to him.

"You can give him a call now, and he can speak to us to let you in," the guy offered, obviously feeling a little sorry for me.

I shook my head. "Not necessary," I said. "Thank you."

"Ma'am, I'm really sorry. But we have strict policies in this building. Only tenants and visitors authorized by them are allowed inside. Actually, Mr. Cross does not allow anybody to come up without prior notice."

"I used to be a tenant here. Actually, I used to be his wife."

The guy was taken aback. "I'm really sorry. I will call my manager. Mr. Ferguson could fix this. I'm new here. It's the first time I've seen you. You can wait at the lobby while we sort it out."

I shook my head. Sure, Mr. Ferguson knew me. But it was pretty obvious Travis didn't want me in the apartment. "Thank you. You're very good at your job. But it's not necessary anymore. Goodbye."

I walked down the street blindly. Eric was walking beside me quietly. Tears kept rolling down my cheeks. I didn't know where I was going. I didn't know what I was feeling. I just wanted to get away from Travis's building.

We must have walked ten blocks before Eric finally pulled my hand.

"Stop!" he commanded. And when I stared at him, I thought I saw a trace of the Eric that I used to love. The one who was strong enough to be my man before he admitted to me he was something else. He hugged me to him. I cried on his shoulder.

"Don't you think you've been humiliated enough now?" he asked me, and I could hear a trace of anger in his voice.

I could not believe that Travis, who couldn't even make time to see me or answer my calls, had had the time to see another woman and bring her to our apartment! If he hadn't told me that he loved me, I would have understood. He was a player before I married him. But everything had changed...he was no longer that man. He had committed himself to me. And I was still his wife. He had still promised to take care of me...to make me happy. Why was he the cause of all my misery now?

I got that he was really angry and hurt...but had he really just erased me from his memory and simply not cared about how I felt anymore? Not even as a friend? And couldn't he just be honest enough to face me? To end our marriage himself? Was he waiting for me to do it? He didn't want to talk to me, and he also didn't want to be the one to let go?

For months, I'd waited for him. Karl surely must have mentioned how many times I'd come to his office. I was pretty sure Karl had told him. That's why he'd avoided his office whenever I was there. I'd called him more than a hundred times since I decided to fix things between us. He made no effort to answer or to call back. He didn't even remember me on my birthday. I'd called him. Because I was hoping he remembered and he could at least talk to me on that day. But he didn't pick up before he finally turned off his phone.

Now, I saw that he was bringing another woman into our apartment. But could I really blame him? After all I'd said to him? After I'd called him a monster? After I'd showed him I had no faith or trust in him? After I'd lost his baby? After I'd become useless as a woman? After he knew perfectly well that I couldn't give him the heir that he desperately wanted and needed anymore?

Realization crept through me like an assassin seeing the opportune moment for the kill. I'd hurt Travis. I'd called him words that seemed unforgivable. I didn't trust him, when that was all he had asked from me. He'd taken all his masks off and made himself vulnerable to me, thinking that I would believe in him more than anything else, but I failed him. I made him choose between saving my life and risking our baby's. He lost his heir because my body was…sick. And now…I couldn't even give him the one thing that could make him complete…and whole. The one thing that could save him…his own family, his own child.

How could he want me? He had no future with me. He'd spent more than half of his life doing what my brother asked him to do. He gave up his own happiness and his own life because his life was tied to mine. And I realized now…I couldn't do that to him anymore. I loved him too much.

Maybe they were right. Sometimes, you can't fix relationships. And the best option that you have…is to let go. Set the other person free, and let him find the happiness that he deserves.

Suddenly, my heart felt lighter and heavier at the same time. I was okay now. For months, I lived without the shadow of Travis. And I was fine. I was able to stand up on my own. My first art exhibition was successful. It raked in cash that would sustain me until my next show. It also generated a lot of publicity and profit for my mother's gallery.

My health was restored. I had finished all my therapies, although the doctors still offered no guarantees of conception. My chances of conceiving still ranged from slim to none. Maybe that was the way it was supposed to be. Maybe the guy who was really meant for me was one who only needed a wife. Not a child.

Maybe I would find someone…maybe not. But whatever my fate became, I would not tie it to Travis's. It was time he found his own and lived his life the way he wanted it. Not because of any promise he made to me or my brother. We were done manipulating his life and his choices now. This time…he should be free to choose on his own, and not even Tom would hold it against him, wherever he was.

I looked up at Eric. "I'm going home, Eric."

He nodded. "You can go home or to Antarctica for all I care! You can go wherever you want, honey. Just get out of here!" he said, using the old term of endearment he used to use with me.

I told Eric that I would be fine traveling without him. In fact, I preferred to be alone. I didn't go back to Connecticut. Instead, I decided to take the next flight to South Carolina.

One last time, I needed some clarity. I needed to let go of Travis…not physically. But in my heart. I needed to accept that it was over. I should be the one to let him go.

I realized I hadn't slept in almost twenty-four hours. I couldn't. My heart was so heavy. Funny, because it had broken into pieces. I barely had time to put my bags in my old room. I decided to take a walk.

The weather was bad and I had forgotten to bring a jacket. I walked the old streets I used to walk when I was younger. The streets I walked with Travis and Tom when I was barely a teenager…back when my family was whole and complete.

I caught a chill as the cold wind blew. The leaves and branches swayed in protest around me. There was a storm coming. It was only midday, and yet the clouds in the sky were heavy, making the whole surroundings very dark. As if it were twilight.

I loved Travis. This was probably the most difficult breakup that I would ever have to get through. It was especially hard because it was with him. Before, he was always there to help me get up…to hold me through the night as I cried my heart out. But now, I felt completely alone and broken.

I wanted to fix things between us. If we would end, I didn't want us to end like this. But now, I realized maybe there was no hope. Even if we fixed things now, there was the fact that I'd lost our baby, and that I may not be able to give him an heir anymore. A slim chance was almost equivalent to not having a chance at all. And maybe Travis knew that, too. Maybe it was better that we set each other free. After all, he'd told me that I should find a man who wouldn't care for a child...even if *I* did.

I didn't know where my feet were taking me. I walked the streets without a destination in mind. I was just lost in my own thoughts, oblivious of the fact that I felt very cold, and I hadn't slept properly in a while. I was unaware of the fatigue that was starting to envelop me.

I walked for a whole hour and then I realized where I was. Tombstones lay before me. I realized my feet had taken me to where my brother was.

I walked the rows of tombstones before I finally reached the end where my brother rested.

I stared at his name, carved on the stone.

*Thomas Antoine Montgomery*
*Forever young...*

Tears immediately rolled down my cheeks. I remembered staying here after the funeral. Long after everybody was gone. I was only a little girl, and I cried like a baby as I stared at my older brother's tombstone, as if it were a nightmare I couldn't wake up from.

It was raining that day, too. But I didn't care that I was alone and that I would get wet. I kept crying, silently calling my brother's name.

I remembered the arm that had wrapped around my shoulders then.

I looked up and saw Travis staring down at me, his eyes wet with tears, too, but he was trying his best to be strong. He hugged me to him.

*"Ssshhh..."* he'd said to me. *"Everything's going to be okay. I promise I will take care of you for as long as I live,"* he said. Then he turned toward Tom's grave. *"I will protect her with my life, bro. You don't have to worry. She will never be alone for as long as I am alive."*

I felt him kiss the top of my head. And that was the first time after Tom died that I'd actually felt a ray of hope.

And now, sixteen years later, I stood in front of Tom, crying the same way I'd cried that day, but this time, I was completely alone.

"Tom..." I whispered. "I hope you can hear me now," I sobbed. "I want to let you know that I'm mad at you!"

I couldn't stop sobbing like a little girl.

"Why did you have to leave me?" I asked. "You're so unfair...when you left, Mom and Dad chose to mourn in their own worlds...I was left behind! I lost our whole family the day you left…and then…you asked Travis to take care of me. You…threw us together, Tom. For a long while, all we had was each other. Didn't you know that we're only human? That we could end up falling in love with each other? Was that part of your plan? Was that what you wanted? Were you happy when I married Travis? Were you happy when I fell madly in love with him? If you were, then your heart must be breaking, too…because mine has shattered into a million pieces…I lost my best friend, my guardian angel, my protector…the one guy who could make me complete…"

There was lightning followed by a loud bellow of thunder. I almost got scared. It was dark in the graveyard now. But I was too busy crying to be really afraid. I figured I couldn't be in much worse shape than I was in now.

The rain poured, and it poured hard. I looked up at the heavens and thought, Thomas must be crying for me right now. As if he were answering my questions. His heart was broken, too.

"I need to release him from the things you made him promise before you died. I need to release him from any obligation, any tie that you bound him with," I said in between tears. "He needs to live his own life, without tying his own fate to mine, Tom. We haven't been fair to him. I'm not going to run after him anymore. I'm not going to chase him. I will set him free of the vows he made to me when we got married. I knew that he made those promises because it was his obligation to do so. But it's not his obligation to keep me safe and happy anymore. I will set him free. And I'm not going to allow him to hurt me again, or to turn me way. He's free of me from now on."

The words I spoke hurt me physically. And now, more than ever, I wished there was someone here who would hold me and tell me that everything was going to be okay.

I don't know how long I stood there under the rain. I was soaked and cold. I could feel the numbing of my fingers slowly. I was shivering, but still I refused to turn back home, to take cover. Tears were streaming down my cheeks, mixing with the drops of heavy rain.

Then suddenly, the world started spinning. If I'd cared, I would have panicked. I knew that fatigue had won this time. And then everything started to turn dark…darker than it already was…

\*\*\*

I was walking back home after the rain. I felt warm already. My clothes were dry. I don't know why, but I felt very comfortable.

Suddenly, I realized that I wasn't alone. Somebody was walking beside me. He was just as tall as I was. He was not muscular. He was wearing our school jacket, his strawberry-blond hair almost covering his eyes. He looked at me, and I recognized those familiar gray eyes, which were so much like mine. He smiled at me.

Tears filled my eyes. It'd been so long since I last saw him.

"Tom…" I whispered.

He smiled at me. "Everything is going to be okay, Brianne."

At that instant, I thought I'd died. Right there in the graveyard. I must have fainted there, and nobody found me. Or I must have hit my head.

"Are you taking me with you?" I asked Tom. And somehow I realized that wouldn't be so bad.

He shook his head.

"I love you, Brianne," he said to me. "I promise you, you will be happy for the rest of your life."

And he started walking faster than me. I tried to keep up with him, but somehow his strides were always longer than mine and I couldn't keep up.

"Tom, wait for me!"

He turned toward me again and shook his head. "I'm always waiting. But you're going to live a long, happy life, Brianne."

"No! I can't be happy! You saw what happened to me! I will never be happy anymore!"

He just gave me a sly smile. Then he shook his head. "I promise you, you will be. Wake up now, Brianne. And send my love to Travis, too."

"Tom!" I called. But somehow, I was frozen in place. I couldn't move my feet. I watched Thomas walk farther and farther away from me.

"No, Tom! Don't leave me!"

He turned one last time and gave me a grin and a salute, and then he faded into the light.

"Tom!" I screamed.

I blinked, and then suddenly everything around me changed. I was no longer in the street. I felt comfortably warm, and I was lying down on something soft, with my head resting on something firm, warm and...familiar.

I started to get up, but strong arms were wrapped around me, keeping me still, preventing me from pulling away.

"Sssshhh..." I heard a soft, soothing voice whisper against my ear.

# Chapter Thirty-Three

I tried to breathe steadily. I opened my eyes slowly, almost afraid of what I would see before me. My dream about Tom had seemed so real, I thought I had died and he'd come to get me. I wouldn't have minded that. I missed him. Now, more than ever, I missed the brother who had always brought the sunshine with him. God knows I needed a ray of sunshine in my life right now.

But he wasn't real. He was a dream. And in my dream, he promised I would live a long and happy life. So I couldn't be dead. I was still breathing.

When reality finally dawned on me, I realized that I was in a huge, dark room. There was light coming from the fireplace. A storm was still raging outside. A bolt of lightning would sometimes illuminate the room, followed by a bellow of thunder. I shivered even though I felt warm. I almost felt scared. And then I remembered that I wasn't alone.

I gently pulled away from the person holding me. The room that I was in was very unfamiliar to me. I hadn't been there before.

I looked up to see the face of the person who was comforting me, making me feel warm and safe. The fire coming from the fireplace and the lightning outside gave very little light in the room. But it was enough for me recognize his face.

My heart pounded in my chest, and I forgot to breathe. I should have known. The warmth of his arms around me, the comfort that his body provided, and the intoxicating scent of his skin were all too familiar to me. So familiar, yet he seemed so unreal. He was so close, and yet he felt so far away.

"Travis..." I whispered his name. The feel of it on my lips brought up so many of the emotions I had been bottling up inside me. Pain. Anger. Love.

He didn't say anything. He stared at me for a while, and then he pressed his palm against my forehead, feeling my temperature.

I pushed farther away from him. This time, he let me go, allowing me to put some distance between us. I sat up on the bed.

"Take it easy, Brianne," he finally said to me.

I found that I was dressed in one of his pajama bottoms and shirts. They were too big for me, but they were enough to keep me comfortably warm.

I looked around the room. It was massive, with a matching couch and coffee table beside the fireplace. Were we in a hotel room again? How did I get here? And what was Travis doing here with me?

"Where are we?" I asked, trying to keep my voice steady.

"In my room. In my grandparents' house," he replied.

"How…how did I get here?"

"You fainted yesterday," he answered. "I was just right behind you. What were you doing bathing in the storm?"

I shook my head. I remembered flying home and walking toward Tom's resting place. I remembered what I told Tom in the graveyard. I was setting Travis free…not only of the promises he'd made me, but also of the promises that he'd made my brother.

"I need to go home," I said.

Travis took a deep breath. "You *are* home," he said. His voice lacked the trace of anger or coldness. It was steady, and somehow there was a trace of anxiety.

I raised a brow at him.

"Remember, you're still married to me. This is your home, too," he said in a low voice.

I shook my head. "Not for long, Travis," I said to him. "I'm sorry for all the trouble." I took a deep breath and willed all my strength to be able to speak the next words that came out of my mouth. "You're free of your promises to me or to Tom now. You can live your life as you please. It's time you made your choices without considering any vow or promise you made my brother or me all these years. We haven't been fair to you. It's time to set you free."

I slowly stood up from the bed.

"I'm not going to bother you anymore," I said to him. "I will consult with a lawyer and file a divorce. Don't worry—I will not take anything from you. I'm keeping my part of the bargain. I don't want your money."

He didn't say anything. I had my back on him while I was saying those words. I was afraid to look at him. I was scared that I would lose my courage if I looked into his eyes.

"Th-thank you for everything you've done for me, Travis," I said. "I want you to know, I will not hold any grudge against you...after all this ends."

I bit my lip to keep from crying. "And I h-hope...someday...we can still be...friends...but I cannot keep holding you hostage to your promises, to your guilt, or your conscience...and likewise, I can't allow myself to be hurt by you anymore...I think it has to end. Here. Now."

There was silence. Tears welled up in my eyes, but I willed myself to be strong. I didn't want him to see me cry. This was harder than I thought. But I knew that I was stronger than I gave myself credit for. I stood up on my own two feet those months that Travis wasn't with me. I would be okay. And I'd always wish for Travis to be happy.

When I finally looked up at him, I found that he was sitting on the bed, his back on me. He was looking down at the floor, lost in his own thoughts, taking in every word that I'd just said to him.

I took a deep breath. "I was at Tom's grave...to tell him that I was setting you free...of the promises that you made him before he died. You've fulfilled more than that already...it's time to let go, Travis. It's time to move on. It's time to unbind your fate from mine...so you can live your own life, the way you want it...the way you were supposed to live it." God! I didn't know where I'd gotten the courage to say those things without breaking down on his bedroom floor.

Then I remembered seeing Tom again...after many years. He was just as happy, just as positive as he was when he was alive. And he promised me that things were going to be okay. That I would be happy. I guessed I could hold on to that hope. After all, Tom was also one guy who could keep promises.

I stared at Travis's finely sculpted back. He just sat there. He didn't move...didn't say a word.

After a couple minutes of silence, I turned to look at the couch, trying to see if my clothes and shoes were somewhere in the room.

I heard Travis's sharp intake of breath. Then finally, he said in a sober voice, "You released me of my promises to take care of you...but don't you remember? You promised to take care of me, too."

I bit my lip. I remembered making that promise, too. But with Travis shutting me out of his world, I guessed that was impossible to keep. We were too broken. I'd hurt him deeply. I didn't trust him completely when I thought I trusted him with my life. He hurt me terribly when I thought he'd betrayed my trust and when he said hurtful words to me. He risked our baby's life, when I would have given everything to keep it safe. I wouldn't be able to give him the family he wanted when I knew it was the only thing that could save him. I'd tried to fix us...but he didn't give me a fighting chance.

How else could I keep my promise to save him? To take care of him? I know they were impossible now.

Finally, he stood up from the bed and faced me. His face was as dark as it was broken. "You can go now, Brianne," he said in a low, sober voice. "But I promise you, no matter where you go, no matter where you run...I will find you. And you know that when I make a promise...I will die to keep it." He took a deep breath. "Because while you released me from the vows I made to Tom, I will *never* release you from the promises that you made to me...if that's the only way to keep you...to make you mine forever."

Tears welled up in my eyes. I didn't try to hide them from him this time. I shook my head. "But you don't want to keep me forever, Travis."

Anger, pain, and desperation crossed his face. "Dammit, I do!" In a few strides, he was in front of me, snatching me to him, enveloping me in his warm embrace...crushing me against his bare chest.

"I...tried to see you. I called you about a hundred times," I said to him. "You didn't even want to see me or talk to me."

He gave out a sigh of frustration but kept me prisoner in his arms. "I was afraid, Brianne!" he said. "I was afraid of what you were going to say to me...I wasn't strong enough to hear you say the words you are saying to me now. No matter how much I pictured a happy ending for us, I couldn't see you ever forgiving me. I knew you were going to ask me to set you free. I couldn't think of any other reason why you would want to speak to me...except to say the words you just said to me now. I couldn't hear them. I couldn't hear you say that it was over...so I avoided you instead. I stayed out of the country most of the time, because I was afraid that divorce papers were on their way. And I couldn't face it."

"But...that's not why I wanted to talk to you, Travis."

There was silence for a while. Travis kept his arms tight around me, refusing to let me go even for just a moment. Then he asked, "What were you going to say to me then?"

"I was…going to tell you that I remembered everything that happened that night. That I was sorry for hurting you, for calling you a beast! That…I wanted to try again." Tears rolled down my cheeks, soaking Travis's chest. "But I realized…in the end, it was better to let you go."

I felt him shake his head. "Even if you let me go…*I* won't let *you* go!" he said in a rough voice. "Remember I told you that you are the air that I breathe!?"

"You avoided me these past few months. And you breathed just the same."

"No," he said. "I died the moment I walked out the door of your apartment…that day you told me you were pregnant."

I savored the feel of Travis's arms around me. I felt home…I felt safe again. But I realized that, just the same, this did not change anything between us.

"We said hurtful words to each other…that destroyed us forever," I said.

He shook his head. "No. It could never destroy us, Brianne. We're stronger than you give us credit for."

"How can it not destroy us, Travis?" I asked. "I called you a rapist, a beast! I accused you of raping me to get an heir to win your battles with your father."

"And I forgive you. I know now that you didn't mean those words. You were angry and hurt. And you were right—I did betray you…I should have told you what had happened between us before we got married. Damn! I shouldn't even have left you in the room that night. I should have waited for you to wake up."

He was right. He should have waited for me to wake up. But I understood now why he didn't. He'd promised me over and over that he would protect me from himself. I was conscious that night, but I wasn't entirely myself. He couldn't forgive himself for letting go of his control. He felt angry with himself for slipping…even though I prevented him from making the right choice.

I remembered the most hurtful words he'd said to me that day while we were fighting. "You said…you shouldn't have married me at all! You felt this was a mistake."

He laughed bitterly. "No. That's not what I meant at all. Marrying you was probably one of the few things I did right," he said. "When I said that, I meant I shouldn't have married you without laying all the

347

cards on the table. I felt like I'd cheated you. I should have told you before the wedding…that we'd made love…that you'd told me you loved me…and that I loved you too. And when I married you, I no longer intended just to buy you time to find the man you were going to spend the rest of your life with…because I intended to let you spend the rest of it with me. You should have known all that before you married me…I should have left you with a choice.

"I knew you could still choose to marry me after knowing what I really felt…and what my new conditions were. But I realized that when you were sober, you hadn't even figured out how you really felt about me. So I also knew there was a fifty percent chance that you would choose not to marry me at all. And I didn't want to take that chance. So I chose not to tell you about that night. I married you…without telling you what you were binding yourself to." He paused for a moment and then he said, "I felt that I had started our marriage with lies…and treachery. I was a manipulative man, Brianne…and I felt ashamed because I felt I'd manipulated you to get what I wanted…into the ending that only I might end up winning."

I listened to his every word, trying to accept the apology behind them. His arms tightened around me once again. "But without all those complications in the way, Brianne…I would marry you over and over again. I'm sorry if I made it sound like I didn't want to marry you at all. I think I've wanted to marry you since your sixteenth birthday…after I took you out on our first date. I've always known I wanted you…but I always told myself I was forbidden to have you. Maybe all these years, I was hoping you wouldn't find another guy to settle down with. Because I knew that when the time came for you to call in my promise…it might be the only chance for us to belong together. And that night we made love, I realized why I was waiting for you…taking care of you all these years…why you meant the whole world to me…why for years you'd been the meaning of my life. It wasn't just because of my promises to your brother, Brianne."

I closed my eyes and more tears slid down my cheeks. Yesterday, I would have been jumping up and down to have Travis say those words to me. But today, I realized the intensity of the damage in our relationship. Apart from the night I thought he had betrayed me, a lot of things had happened that could put a wedge between us forever. And I couldn't take him back now…and risk losing him again in the future. I was stronger now, but I wouldn't be able to recover from this the second time around. "I lost your child, Travis. You gave it up," I said. "I wouldn't have risked his life. I would have fought."

"I know," he replied. "But the choice was left up to me. And it killed me to make that decision. I loved you both. I knew you would fight for our baby's life. But I chose to fight for yours." I could hear the tears in his voice. He took a couple of deep breaths, trying to keep his voice steady. "It tore me apart to make that choice, Brianne," he said. "That reduced me to the cold, ruthless devil I was before I married you. Because I would have to live with myself, knowing I had sacrificed our child...but I couldn't bear to lose you, too...to not see you again...not see you smile again...even if I couldn't have you...I still wouldn't be able to live in a world where you did not exist. And I know you won't be able to forgive me for that. But I'm really sorry, Brianne. I just love you too damn much—I just won't live without you...regardless of whether we are together or not."

I remembered waking up in the hospital that day. I wasn't prepared for the pain that would greet me. I thought about our little angel once in a while. He would have been a couple of months old by now. I always wondered what he would have looked like and how he would be when he grew up. The biggest pain of losing a baby is confronting the hundreds of questions about what could have been if he or she had survived. Knowing that you will never know breaks your heart every time you think about it.

And I knew...just like losing Tom, the only other person who felt the exact same pain I felt when I lost my baby was Travis. And knowing him...he would deal with his pain on his own. I understood now why he ran away from me. Why he was not at the hospital when I woke up, even though I knew he'd held me during the times I was unconscious. He was broken because we'd lost our child. He was angry because it was his decision to risk it. He couldn't face me because he knew I was blaming him for all of it.

I heard his sharp intake of breath. "We cannot be over, Brianne..." he said in a desperate voice.

"Th-there was a woman...you were with a woman, the last time I saw you."

He pulled away from me. I stared up to look into his eyes. I found that his cheeks had been streaming with tears. He gave me a broken expression.

"What woman?"

I took a deep breath. "The one you were with when I went to your apartment."

He thought for a while and then finally, he remembered. "Blonde?"

I nodded. He smiled at me. "That was Sarah Atkins," he said. "For your information, she's fifty years old, and I don't fancy older women. She's almost like a mother to me. She's our old art teacher, Mr. Atkins's, sister. She's been my art broker for years."

"Art broker?"

He nodded. "Sometimes I buy paintings. If she has a good find that's worth buying, I buy it. This time, I asked her to check something out for me, and she came to deliver what I asked her to buy."

"There was no other woman?" I asked.

He smiled at me wistfully. "I promised you I would never cheat on you, Brianne. You still are my wife, remember?"

Tears kept streaming down my face. I was having new hope again. Hope that all is not lost. Hope that there was a chance Travis and I could get through this.

"Do you want to see what I asked her to buy?"

He didn't wait for me to answer. He motioned his hand near the couch where a painting in a golden frame was sitting. It was still partially wrapped, but I recognized that painting. It was mine. The one I'd replicated from his work in high school.

"How...how did you..." I stared at Travis.

"I didn't miss any of your dances. Did you really think I would miss your art show? I asked Ms. Atkins to photograph all your pieces so I could see your work, and see which ones I wanted to buy," he replied. "When I saw this..." He stopped and took a deep breath. "This completely tore me apart, Brianne. And it made me realize what I needed to do. It made me realize that it was time for me to find the courage to face you...because regardless of what you would say to me...it would not change the ending I wanted."

He gently pushed me so I could sit on the bed. He kneeled in front of me. "I realized that no matter how many times you ask me...I cannot stop fighting fate for you." Tears rolled down his cheeks, and in his eyes, I saw that his soul was torn and broken, too. "We cannot be over, Brianne. We can never be...I won't let it."

I struggled to find my voice. "Travis…you must remember…I…may not be able to conceive anymore. And I know you have dreams of having…kids. Lots of them."

He chuckled bitterly. "I'm not going to have them with another woman, Brianne. The doctor said thirty percent, remember? We'll work through that percentage. We'll keep trying. And if we can't be blessed with one, then we can look at other options. But I would rather be childless with you…than be the father of some other woman's children." He shook his head. "I already chose you over my heir once, Brianne. I will still make that choice now. And I will make that choice over and over again."

He held my face between his palms. I couldn't stop crying.

"You told me once that you were tired, Travis."

He shook his head. "I said I was tired of not getting it right…every time, I only wanted to do what you and Tom asked of me. But somehow…in the end, I always lost, I always ended up eating my heart out. Tom asked me to take care of you, and I ended up feeling something for you. You asked me to take your innocence from you…I was stupid enough to agree…not knowing that I would end up craving you like a drug!

"You asked me to marry you…as your safety guy, and I ended up not ever wanting to let you go. You asked me to make love to you that night, and I ended up realizing I was madly in love with you, that I had been in love with you all those years. I was tired of doing you all those favors and risking losing you forever. I'm not saying I was tired of taking care of you, Brianne. I will never be. I will put my masks down for you a hundred times over…but I'm tired of being afraid of losing you. I need assurance that I never will…that you're mine forever. That's all I ask."

I pulled his hands away from my face and rested them on my lap. I realized that he was wearing his wedding ring again.

"You're wearing your wedding ring again!"

"I never took it off."

"I saw a picture of you recently, in a magazine. You weren't wearing your wedding ring there."

"That was taken months before we got married," he said. "If they took a picture of me now, after we've been apart, I'd be in a much worse shape than I was in that picture."

I stared at him. I could not believe what I'd been hearing. And slowly, I was beginning to trust again. To believe in Travis...to believe in Tom.

*Is this what you meant, Tom? That I would live a long and happy life? With Travis?*

He pulled me gently by the nape of the neck and kissed my forehead. "You see? You can let me go all you want. But nothing is going to change because I choose not to let *you* go. And if I have to spend the rest of my life chasing you, running after you...then so be it. As long as in the end, I know you and I will be together."

"Travis..." I stared up at him. "Have you forgiven me? For what I did to you? All that I said to you?"

He smiled. "Forgiven. Forgotten," he said. "If you forgive me for hurting you, for avoiding you...for saying words that I know must have hurt you...if you give me another chance, I'll spend the rest of our lives making up for it all...I'll spend the rest of my life making you happy..."

"There's nothing to make up for, Travis," I said and this time, the tears I cried were tears of happiness.

He pulled me to him. "God, I love you, Brianne!" he said. "I love you so much; I died the moment I thought I lost you! And I swear to God, I'm never going to lose you again!"

"I love you, too, Travis! And I will never doubt your intentions, or your love ever again."

He pulled away from me and smiled. Then gently he leaned his face forward and kissed me on the lips. He kissed me gently, and then more passionately.

He pushed me down the bed and continued kissing me. He kissed me as if he couldn't believe he was doing that...as if he couldn't believe he could still do that.

We were lost in our passion. When he finally joined with me, we were both crying. We held each other, as if we both couldn't believe we were back in each other's arms...as if we had both just woken up from a very bad dream.

"I love you, Mrs. Cross. Very much!" he whispered to me, in a voice that made me cry even more.

"I love you, too!"

Even after we'd both reached our peaks, Travis didn't let go of me. He kept kissing me, nuzzling my neck, tracing my lips with his tongue. Moreover, he kept whispering how much he loved me.

When he finally pulled out of me, he lay on the bed and gathered me in his arms.

"God, I missed you, love!" he whispered. "I think I only realize now just how empty I have been. And just how broken my soul really was."

"Me too," I whispered. "It's like you have to live again, to realize that you've died...and now is your second chance at life."

"I'm not going to waste it anymore," he said. "I want to treasure every single moment of my life with you." He took a deep breath. "I have been...an empty soul for so long, Brianne. I did not have the warmth, concern, and love of a family. Is it too much to ask for those things now? From you?"

I propped up on my elbow so I could look at him in the eyes. I shook my head. "It's never too much to ask for those, Travis. And of course! As much as I can, I will give you those things...I will nurture this little family that we have."

He pulled my head to him so he could give me a kiss on the cheek. Then he leaned his forehead against mine. "Thank you, love."

"Thank you, too, Travis," I said. "Because you've made me whole again."

He smiled, and the boyishness returned to his face again. "Thank you...because you've made me live again."

I lay on his shoulder, both his arms wrapped around me.

"How did you know I was here?" I asked.

"Eric. Karl told me he saw you with him. So when I finally made the decision to stop running...I called him. He told me that you had just boarded the flight home. I went to your house. When I found that you weren't there, I knew there could only be one place you would be. And I was glad I'd found you just in time. You could have hit your head or fainted with no one to find you."

I sighed. "At that moment, I didn't really care."

Travis squeezed my shoulders, and I felt him kiss my forehead. But he didn't say anything. I knew that he was sorry for making me feel the way I did. But it didn't matter now.

"Travis…yesterday, I went to your apartment. I called you. You didn't see me or hear me. I wasn't allowed to enter your building. Did you ban me or something?"

He tightened his embrace of me again. "Of course not. I'm sorry. I introduced you to Mr. Ferguson. But the building underwent management changes and shuffled some of their staff. I was asked to update my tenant list to prevent any hassles like that. Back then, I was dead to the world…I just didn't get around doing the things that I was supposed to be paying attention to. I'm sorry, Brianne. But next time you come to the building…you won't be questioned anymore. Brianne Cross will be on the list…as one of the owners of an apartment in that building."

I sighed contentedly. After so many months of pain…after feeling almost numb, I never thought I would feel this happy again. I knew…only one man could make me feel this way.

Travis kissed me passionately. He turned so that he was on top of me again.

"Travis!" I laughed. "We just…"

"Sorry, love. I told you I'd make up for everything. This included! And I've got months I need to make up for!" My laughter died as he covered my mouth with passionate kisses again.

# Chapter Thirty-Four

It was against Travis's will, but I insisted on a hot bath. He joined me in the tub, and it was a glorious feeling. Until then, I still couldn't believe that Travis and I were back together...back in each other's arms. I didn't need to lose him again. That finally, we'd laid down all our cards on the table, and taken off all our masks. We were starting afresh, and nothing could come between us again.

I dressed in one of his pajama bottoms and shirts, which were too big for me. I had to tie the shirt in the waist area as it was big enough to be a dress.

Travis's room was huge. It had a royal bed in the center, the headboard and edges of which had elegant gold carvings. The couch set had matching carvings, and the fabric on them was lush and luxurious.

"Would you like to have dinner here, or downstairs? Or perhaps you'd like to go out?"

"I'd like to see the house, if that's okay with you," I replied. "I haven't been here before."

He took my hand in his and led me out the door.

The whole house was massive. Like their lake house, it was covered mostly in glass. The chandeliers were elegant and looked very expensive. I could tell that the house was years old. Probably older than Travis. But it was rich and luxurious. More like a manor or a small castle than a house. It had about eight bedrooms, two living rooms, a library, a game room, and a huge nursery.

"Is this the house you grew up in?"

"I can't tell which house I really grew up in," he replied. "This was my grandparents' house. I have many happy memories here from when my grandmother was alive. My grandfather died a month after she did." He took a deep breath. "They were so in love with each other. Even in their old age, I remember how happy they were. When my grandmother died, my grandfather was devastated. Then one day, he told me, 'I will be happy again, son. Soon, I will be with my love again.' He died after a few days. I remembered being so sad…but then again, I knew that he was happier. Because they're together again."

I couldn't help crying. Travis's grandparents' love story was so touching.

"Hey…" Travis said, pulling me into his arms. "Why are you crying?"

I giggled. "That story was sweet."

"I know," he said. "I was only ten then. It's been a while since I thought about that. Maybe I used to believe in love because I witnessed that through my grandparents. Then my parents shattered whatever hopes and beliefs I had." He looked down at me. "Thank you for making me believe in that again, Brianne. I know that love like what my grandparents had really exists…because I found one just like theirs."

I smiled and then I reached up to kiss him. "I love you."

"I love you more."

We checked out each of the bedrooms. They were all only a little smaller than Travis's bedroom, but still about twice the size of my bedroom in Connecticut.

"When was the last time you were here?" I asked.

"I don't remember," he replied. "It's been a long while. I found out that my grandparents left me this house when I turned nineteen. If I had known that earlier, I would have moved out of my father's house sooner. Here, I'm safe from him and his bodyguards."

"But you're safe from him now, aren't you?" I asked.

He looked at me wearily. "I am. Because I'm his son. But I'm afraid of what he might do if he finds out just how important you are to me."

I hugged him. "You know you can stop, Travis," I said. "I know you don't need the money anymore. I'm a simple woman with simple needs. Don't you have enough money…to quit this war? Leave your father be?"

He took a deep breath. Then he pulled away from me slightly so he could look me in the eyes. "Are you asking me to?"

I took a deep breath. "I want you to be happy, Travis. To concentrate on your own happiness, on your own life, instead of your father's destruction. It's not worth it. You deserve to live your life…for yourself."

He didn't say anything. He just gave me a hug. Then I heard him take a deep breath and kiss my forehead.

He led me to the dining room. There was a long table in the center. Maids were standing close by. They greeted us warmly. The table was set for two.

"Hungry?" he asked.

I nodded. "Yeah. Actually, I am."

After dinner, Travis decided to show me the outside of the house. At the door, I saw a familiar old woman. She was much older now. But I still recognized her.

"Mrs. Beets!" I reached forward and gave her a hug.

"Madam." She smiled.

"Do you live here now?"

"Wherever the Master needs me, madam," she said. "I'm happy that you are our Mistress now. I know you will take care of him."

"I will." I smiled at her. I knew I meant that.

The garden was massive, beautifully landscaped and adorned with roses. There was a gazebo where luncheons and private dinners could be held. They also had a pool and a huge yard where kids could play football.

I realized, as I toured the house, that I could picture our kids playing here. I could picture us having family dinners in the gazebo, the kids playing football with their father, or the entire family swimming in the pool.

I sighed sadly. If only I could give Travis kids...if only there weren't something wrong with me.

"Are you okay, love?" Travis asked, forcing me to look into his eyes.

I smiled at him but he knew me better.

"Brianne...this is me," he said gently. "You never used to hide anything from me."

He was right. He used to know every single one of my pains. He could read me like a book. After all that we had been through, he deserved my honesty.

"I was just thinking that it's so beautiful here," I said. "This...would be a good place to grow up in."

He smiled. "Would you like us to live here?"

"Yes...if only...we could have kids."

He hugged me. "We will have kids, love," he said. "We will keep trying. There are plenty of options now. Medically, we could try two or three options. If nothing works, we can always adopt. There are plenty of kids out there looking for a family. Like the two of us…when we were young. We were two kids desperately wanting to belong to a family again. We had each other. We were all the family we needed. If we can't have kids of our own, then we will adopt."

I gave him a hug. "I'm really sorry, Travis," I said to him.

"Don't be," he said. "It isn't your fault. And we still have a chance. Right now, I'm just so happy that we're back together. That I don't have any risk of losing you anymore."

I reached up and kissed him.

"Thank you," I whispered. "Thank you for accepting me…in spite of my…condition."

He pulled away from me so he could look into my eyes. "Don't you ever think that you're less of a person…or a woman…just because you have lesser chances of conceiving, Brianne. And don't ever think I would love you any less because of that. I don't, and I won't."

He wiped the tears from my cheeks.

"Our chances of having a baby are more than you give it credit for, love. I know you never missed any of your doctor's appointments. And your recent tests were getting better results."

"But still no guarantees," I replied.

"But our chances are increasing."

I nodded. Then I stared back at him. "Wait a minute. How do you know all that?"

He stared at me for a while and then he smiled. "I get all the results of your tests and your gynecological reports are sent to me."

"That's illegal."

"I'm your husband, Brianne. I have a right to know what's happening to you, too." He stared at me deeply and then he leaned forward and gave me a gentle kiss on the lips. "I don't have to always be physically with you to keep my promises to keep you safe. I did that for more than a decade before we got engaged. Come on, don't you know me by now?" There was laughter in his eyes.

I pinched him playfully. He laughed and hugged me to him tightly.

"And there I was thinking you'd stopped loving me," I whispered.

I felt him shake his head. "Never," he said. "I could and would never stop loving you, Brianne."

We stayed in the gazebo for a while. The moon was shining above us.

"So do you want to live here?" he asked.

"Yes. I think I like it here. It would be the best place to raise our kids. You have happy childhood memories here. I grew up in this city, too. Education for the kids is good. It's closer to Tom and to your grandparents…it's a drive away from the lake house, if we want to spend a weekend there," I said to him.

"Well, I don't really mind where I live as long as I'm with you."

I smiled at him. "But we need to renovate some things. I hope your grandparents won't mind. We need to repaint many of the rooms. I think we need more chandeliers. I want this house to be full of light…full of life. We're done being sad, Travis."

He chuckled. "I think you're right. And I think my grandparents will be very happy. I think Grandma would be very pleased it is you wearing her engagement ring now." He kissed the top of my head. "Do you think Tom will be pleased with this?"

"Yes," I said, remembering my dream. "He…sends you his love."

Travis pulled away from me to look at me in the eyes. "Brianne…"

"I saw him, Travis," I said. "In my dreams. Before I woke up here. He told me that I was going to live a long and happy life. And he told me to send you his love."

Tears welled up in Travis's eyes again. He pulled me to him in a tight hug. I heard him take a deep breath. Then I heard him whisper, "Thanks, bro."

# Chapter Thirty-Five

I was looking at the fantastic view of New York from Cross Magnates' glass wall. My pulse was hammering, and I felt that familiar heavy lump in my chest. A surge of emotions was raging inside me. I recognized the strongest of them all. *Pain.* I smiled to myself. I welcomed it. It was my very old friend.

But I had to let it go. Along with its best friend—*Anger.* For years, these two had kept me company all throughout my miserable nights. But I didn't need them now. My entire life had changed. My days were no longer cold and my nights were no longer lonely. Now, I had sunshine and warmth. Pain and anger need not be my company.

I had joy and love.

I had Brianne.

My heart swelled at the mere thought of her name. I remembered many years ago when I was just ten years old and my best friend introduced me to the cutest girl I'd ever seen. She was wearing a white sleeveless top and a pair of lime green shorts. Her long hair was braided on both sides of her face. She had a pair of green hoop earrings. Her face was emotionless when her brother introduced us. I extended my hand to hers.

"*Cherie,*" I greeted her, not letting my friend realize that I was somehow star-struck with his sister.

The girl raised a brow and then turned her back on me. *Feisty,* I thought to myself. And I think I liked her even more after that.

I grew closer and closer to her family. She grew more and more beautiful to me. But Tom was more than a friend to me. He became a brother. And I knew there was this Bro Code shit that said you weren't supposed to screw your best friend's sister. Well...not that I want to 'screw' Brianne. She was not the type of girl you just had fun with. She was special. Everything I wanted in a girl was rolled into *her.* And that was probably the only thing I didn't like about my friendship with her brother.

"Seriously, dude, your sister is gorgeous..." I decided to test the waters with Tom one day. He didn't go out much. Who knew? Maybe he hadn't heard of the Bro Code before.

"Shut up!" Tom scolded me. "Stay away from my sister, Travis. She's not like one of your girls. She's off-limits! Especially to you."

I heaved a sigh of disappointment. "I know. Kills me," I murmured to myself and hoped Tom didn't hear.

One night, she came home from a party. She was so scared that her parents would be disappointed in her. I pulled her to my room. I was teasing her. It was the first time I held her in my arms and leaned my body against hers. And I wished I hadn't! She was soft like velvet. She smelled of strawberries. And she trembled against my touch.

When I grazed my nose against the base of her neck, I felt her knees buckle. I was pretty sure she would fall flat on the floor if I wasn't holding her. She was sensitive on that part. *Damn!* I didn't have to know that.

I reminded myself over and over. *Forbidden.* But I would give my life just to have a taste...a moment. Her hatred toward me provided me with comfort. The way she repelled me kept me at bay, provided a reminder that I couldn't have her no matter how much I wanted her.

The day she rode in my car on the way to the lake house, I could feel her presence charge the air around me, her scent fill my senses, intoxicating me. She fell asleep beside me and I could see the goosebumps on her arm. I had to fight to keep my eyes on the road.

Tom was driving behind me with their parents. He was driving very slowly. He didn't like to drive even half a mile over the speed limit. And I was getting sleepy driving so slowly. Brianne was feeling cold beside me, but she was sleeping like an angel.

I stepped on the pedal and drove way ahead of Tom. I knew it would take time for him to catch up with me. When I rounded a street, I stopped on the side of the road. This gave me time to recline Brianne's seat and to drape a jacket over her to make her feel warmer. I pushed a lock of hair away from her face and I watched her as she slept. If peace had a face, it would look like this, I was sure. From the rearview mirror, I saw Tom approaching. I reluctantly tore my gaze away from Brianne's sleeping form and started to drive again, this time at Tom's very slow pace.

Later, he asked me why I'd sped up, and as an excuse, I told him that I needed an adrenaline rush because his driving was sending me to dreamland. Now, I find it quite ironic that Tom would die in a car crash just a few weeks after that trip.

I thought I was numb with pain all my life. Both physical and emotional. I didn't have a happy home and I didn't give a shit anymore. But that last time I spoke to my best friend, I realized what pain really was.

He was physically damaged, and he knew it. Guilt was gnawing my insides, and I thought I would throw up blood on the floor. And more than that, I wanted to kill my old man for causing all this.

"It's not your fault...Travis," Tom had said to me. "Do. Not. Blame. Yourself." I gathered that he was trying to be firm...trying to be the big brother, as always.

Tears welled up in my eyes then. I was on the verge of breaking down. My carefully built cold façade was crumbling. I loved this guy! He was my brother. He was the only one who looked out for me those last few years.

"I want you to promise not to tell my family about this, Travis."

My eyes widened in protest. I shook my head. "No, Tom. I will take responsibility! I was stubborn. I was stupid!"

He slowly shook his head. "They will need you, Travis. We both know I'm gone." He struggled to take a deep breath. "My sister will need you. And I can't let her hate you. If she knew what happened, she would get mad at you. And you won't be able to do what I'm going to ask you to do."

I stared at him. "And what is that?"

He took another deep breath and tried to compose his sentences. "My parents have been pretending to be okay...for a while. I'm not stupid. My father is having...an affair. One day...they will drift apart. It's only a matter of time. Brianne can't be alone. She will need someone...to be there for her...to look out for her...the way I would...if I could. Promise me you will take care of her, bro. Promise me...you will always be there for her. You will do what I would have done. You will take my place in her life. Make sure that she will never be alone...after I'm gone... and for the rest of her life."

"Tom...for years you told me to stay away from her!" I protested. "Man...I'm not a saint! And now...are you saying I need to intertwine my life with hers?"

He took a deep breath. "No, I'm saying you take care of her without ever seeing her again!" I couldn't believe he'd still managed

363

to go for sarcasm. I raised a brow at him. Tom heaved another sigh. "Yes, Travis. I want you to make me a lifetime promise. Make sure that Brianne is safe…and taken care of."

"Tom…I don't know if I can do that. I can barely look out for myself," I said in a weak voice.

He shook his head. "I may be older than you, but you're the 'adult' between the two of us, remember?" Right! He had to remind me that I was emancipated and could do whatever I wanted to do. My emancipation didn't make me feel lucky or privileged. It had always made me feel…abandoned. "No one would be able to take care of Brianne better than you. I know you, Travis. And I know you care about her more than you show. I know you can…and will do this."

Then he raised his pinky at me. Tears welled up in my eyes, and I tried my best not to cry…not in front of him. I hooked my pinky with his.

In spite of myself, I remembered how difficult it was for me to do what he asked me to do. How difficult it would be for me to take his place… as Brianne's big brother. Because I never saw Brianne as a sister. "Tom…are you also asking me to promise you not to… want her?"

He stared at me for a moment. Then he sighed, "Try your best to control yourself, okay?"

I was disappointed. In a way, I wanted him to give me his blessing. For sure he knew how I'd felt for Brianne throughout those years.

"And if I can't?" I asked quietly.

He didn't answer. We were interrupted by the doctors. When I got up to leave the room, I looked back at him, and I thought I saw a smile on his face. Back then, I didn't know what he was smiling about. I dismissed it and thought that he was forbidding me to go after what I felt for his sister. But it all made sense to me now, and I felt my heart swell with gratitude and joy.

Tom wanted Brianne and me to be together. That's why he'd asked me to make him a lifetime promise. He knew I loved his sister and could take care of her better than any guy. But I was young and reckless then. She was too beautiful and innocent. We had a lot of years ahead of us. We had so much to learn from life. If I'd gone for Brianne then, we wouldn't have made it this far. Tom wanted us to love each other as friends first…and nurture that relationship over the years…to strengthen us. He wanted us to be together…at the right time. So no matter what storm came our way later, we'd survive through it. Our love would be deeply rooted.

And he was right. Brianne and I had been through a lot. But it never even crossed my mind to give her up. I dismissed what I felt for her because I thought Tom wouldn't want that. But in the end, I was only human. And I went after the one thing I wanted in my life. The one thing I had been depriving myself of for years. The one thing I knew would make me complete.

Now, I felt none of the guilt. I knew that if Tom were alive, he would be the happiest person on Earth because his sister and his best friend were together…bound not just by marriage…but by deep friendship and everlasting love.

And now…I had our whole lives to look forward to. Brianne was so sad that we couldn't have a baby, but I would not allow her to feel she wasn't enough for me. Because she was. She had always been.

And today…I would prove that to her. I was done wearing a mask in front of her. I was done running away from her every time I got scared that I would hurt her…or lose her. I made a promise to myself that I would trust her and our love. I knew that she would fight for me, the same way that I would always fight fate for her. Brianne and I were a single unit now. She would be there for me like I would always be there for her. She would be strong for me, the way I was always trying to be strong for her.

She had given herself fully to me. I had to do the same to her. And because of that, I had to do what had to be done. So I could be free of my past. So I could finally give my whole self to her…me minus the pain, anger, and hatred. Brianne deserved nothing less than joy and love.

I heard the door open behind me, followed by a series of footsteps. I didn't turn around immediately. I tried to control the emotions raging inside me. He couldn't know what I was thinking about and what I was feeling. More than anything, he couldn't know what made me change my mind…and who lived there inside the confines of my heart. The more I shielded her from him, the safer she was going to be. I never trusted him, my whole life. I was not going to start now. But that didn't mean I would keep fighting this war. I was done. Brianne was right. I needed to walk away.

When I turned around to face the man I loathed the most, my face was the same way it had always been—stoic.

He sat on the leather chair directly opposite from where I was standing.

His face was weary. There were dark circles under his eyes, as if he hadn't slept in days. He looked down at the papers in front of him, pretending to read something, but I knew better. He was trying to compose his lines, preparing to swallow his pride. He was left without an option but to sell to me. He needed the money. I had it. He needed me. But he didn't know how to say it. Moreover, he was wondering how the boy he had abused over the years had managed to take him out of his game.

He opened his mouth to speak.

"Save it," I said in stone-cold voice. I took the stack of papers in front of me and handed it to Karl. Karl took it to him.

"Those are your loans. I paid off all the interests and restructured them. That buys you at least four years to get your act together," I said as he schemed through the papers in front of him.

Karl handed him another set of papers. "In there you will find the transfer papers. I sold off twenty percent of my shares to your company to external shareholders. You will find the transfer of the remaining fifteen percent to your name."

He scanned through all the papers, as if he was unable to believe what he was seeing.

Then finally, he stared at me. "And you will keep only five percent?"

I shook my head. "Oh no," I replied. "I want nothing to do with your company anymore. I transferred it to the name of an orphanage, so they will get a percentage of your annual profits. I figured you could use good publicity to dig you out of the hole you were in."

He narrowed his eyes at me. "Why would you do this?"

I had taken a deep breath before I answered. "I don't want anything to do with you or your company. So long as you stay away from me and anything that has to do with me." Then I motioned to Karl. It was time to go.

I walked past the old man and his hounds without another word.

"She made you do this, didn't she?" he said just before I reached the door. When I took in what he'd said, I felt my blood boil inside me and all the hairs on my body rise up. "She is an exquisite woman."

I turned back to him. My face was not stoic at all.

He smiled slowly. "I met my daughter-in-law. That's why I was late for our meeting."

In a few strides, I was on him, holding him by the collar.

"Travis!" Karl screamed. My father's bodyguards were on me, pulling me away from my father, preventing me from murdering him with my bare hands.

Surprisingly, he remained calm. He looked at his bodyguards. "Leave us," he said in a commanding voice.

The two men hesitated at first but walked out of the room when he gave them a reassuring nod. Karl walked out of the room, too.

I stood opposite him, with balled fists and blazing eyes.

"Relax, son," he said. "I didn't do anything. She's safe and alive." I raised a brow at him. He sighed and sat back in his chair. "I have known about the Montgomerys ever since you were ten, Travis. Don't take me for a fool. I know how important Thomas was to you, and now, don't even think I don't know how much you love his sister. You've always been in love with her. And now, she's your wife. Nothing about you escapes my radar."

I was a little surprised about what he said, but I kept myself from moving toward him. I was afraid I would not be able to stop myself from committing murder once I was less than a foot away.

"Today, I went to her mother's art gallery," he said. "I was wondering when you would introduce us. I figured you never would."

"You're damn right about that!" I muttered.

"She was gracious even though she was aware of how broken our relationship was. From the first minute of meeting her, I understood why you would fall for her charms. She compliments you in many ways. She is what you needed..." He took a deep breath. "After all the things I put you through."

That didn't come as a surprise to me. It came as a shock!

When he looked at me again, I thought I saw tears in his eyes. "Travis...to say that I have been a terrible father is probably an understatement," he said. "I broke you in so many ways. And I am sorry, son." He took a deep breath and tried to compose his sentences while I stood there, open-mouthed. "I was set to give you my company today. You've earned it. All your life, it seems I have been preparing you to be worthy of taking over my company...everything that I have worked for. You've exceeded my expectations...far beyond my

367

imagination. You are an outstanding man…any father would be proud to have a son like you. I made you tough and ruthless…which made you successful in business. But unlike me…you have a heart…and soul. And I know I have your wife to thank for that. And that's why I went to see her. I wanted to meet the woman that made my son who he is now…which is more than what a father could ever ask for."

I stood there looking at him as if he had just lost his mind.

"I pushed you and trained you to be tough and wise…the only way I knew…the way I was trained by my father. But you became a better man than I was," he said. "Your wife taught you how to use your heart." He took a deep breath. "I know you will never forgive me for all that I have done to you. But I vow…I will no longer try to destroy you or damage you in any way. I promise you that. And if forgiveness brings us together…I will be forever thankful."

We stood there for the next five minutes. I was trying to process what he said. For years, I had waited for my old man to change. What had happened to him now? Was he dying? I wouldn't have been surprised if he was and that was why he was doing this. I just found it so hard to believe that he would do this…just because he was…truly sorry.

I backed away from him, un-balled my fists and put them in my pockets.

"I don't know if I can ever forgive you," I said quietly. "But I only ask one thing from you now."

He looked up at me…his eyes hopeful. "Anything, son."

I took a deep breath. In a cold, sober voice I said, "Stay away from my wife!" My voice was low, but the venom and threat it carried was enough to make him stare back at me in surprise.

I raised a brow at him. He studied my expression for a moment and realized that I was dead serious. He took a deep breath and said, "No harm from me will come her way, I promise you that. In fact, I will do everything in my power to keep her safe…if she's the only thing that will keep you sane…if she's my only hope for your forgiveness."

"I won't let you use her!" I growled.

He smiled confidently, to my surprise. "I don't have to. I am sure that with her by your side, you will learn to believe how truly sorry I am for everything that I did to you."

I narrowed my eyes at him. "Why…why are you doing this?"

He sighed. "I...I have cancer, son." He said. "I have...a few years ahead of me. I am working to fix my relationships...rectify all the damage that I have done. Starting with you. I stayed away from Brianne these years. I didn't touch her no matter how important she was to you, and even though I know that getting to her would get through your thick skull the fastest...I let her be. I figured...I had been so tough, and our family had been so broken...you deserved something good in your life. Somebody who could still make you feel loved."

"Do you think that makes me feel grateful? Or sympathetic toward you?" I asked, keeping my face stoic once again.

He stared at me thoughtfully. "I don't expect anything from you. I know I don't deserve it. But I hope you can...give me a chance. And when the time comes, make me a part of your...children's lives."

I raised a brow at him. "Brianne is...we can't have kids," I said bluntly. "And I'm okay with that. In a way, I find comfort in knowing that *your* genes need not be passed on. It stops with me."

I don't know if I imagined it. But I thought I saw sadness in the man's eyes. Well, did he honestly think I could forgive him or trust him that easily? The damage he did to my soul was far too deep. If I didn't have Brianne in my life, I would have been as soulless as he was.

He took a deep breath and stared at me with eyes so similar to mine. "I will accept your offer, only for one reason," he said. "To turn this company around...back to its former glory. I will not leave it in ruins. And in the end, I will give it back to you. You are still my heir, Travis. You cannot change that. So when I go...you have to take this company...this is, after all, my legacy. And you can choose whatever you want to do with it. But it is yours, son...whether you like it or not."

I stared back at him. I tried to assess whether he was serious. Whether he really was trying to change. Had his cancer changed him? Was he truly sorry for all the monstrous things he'd put me through in my life?

"What kind of cancer do you have?" I asked.

He took a deep breath. "Liver. But that's the least of your concerns. I have the best medical team on my case. My main goal now...is to fix whatever damage I might leave behind once my treatments fail."

"You mean you're cleaning up your mess?"

He sighed and nodded. "Yes. And I'm starting with you."

I gave him a hard look. Something inside my chest seemed to be tugging at me, poking me from inside… annoying me to no end. I didn't want to feel anything for this man. He'd done nothing but hurt me and break me all my life. And I could not trust him.

I took a deep breath. "Good luck with that," I muttered, and then I spun on my heel. Before I left, I turned back to him again. "And I mean it. I will stay out of your way from now on. Stay out of mine. And leave my wife out of the picture. You said she was the only one who kept my soul anchored to my body. You're right. You won't like me at all when she's not in my life." And I left.

I kept my silence all throughout the ride home. My emotions were raging inside me. I could still feel pain and anger. But now…something else was there. Something I couldn't place or name. And I didn't like that feeling at all…especially not for my old man, who was the cause of all my troubles…one of the reasons why Tom was taken away from Brianne and me.

When I reached home, I found Brianne standing on the balcony. She was holding a glass of juice, and she was looking out at the view, lost in her thoughts.

"Brianne," I called her. She didn't turn around as if she didn't hear me at all. "Brianne!" I called a little louder.

She spun around, almost startled to hear me. "Travis."

I assessed her expression. Did she look scared? Did her meeting with my father terrify her? Did he threaten her?

But she smiled, placed the glass on the table, and immediately hugged me. I breathed in the scent of her. Her touch warmed me every single time—no woman had ever done that to me.

Then she looked up at me, wearing a nervous expression on her face. I already knew what she was nervous about.

"Your father…came to the gallery," she said. "He…spoke to me."

I nodded. "What exactly did he say to you?"

She shrugged. "He just said it was lovely to finally meet me. He thanked me for always being there for you. And he gave me…this." She pulled away from me, pointing at the box that was sitting on the table.

It was a large wooden box. She opened it to show me its contents. I'd already known what that was. It was a whole set of diamond and

370

sapphire jewelry that had been in my father's family for at least four generations, passed on to the women their men chose to marry. The last person who'd worn it was my grandmother...the mother of my father. I'd always wondered why my father never gave it to my mom. But I guessed they hadn't stay married long enough for my mother to get her chance to wear the Cross family heirlooms. This had to stay inside the family no matter what.

So my father didn't think my mother deserved this treasure...but Brianne did? I knew she did, but it was a big step coming from my old man.

I smiled at Brianne. But she knew me better now. I knew the questions that she would soon ask.

"The Cross family heirloom," I said, "has been passed on to the brides of the Cross family for generations. My grandmother wore it last. It skipped my mother. But now...I think it's my father's way of telling you that you're worthy of being the keeper of this treasure now."

Tears welled up in her eyes. And for the life of me, I couldn't believe it either, but I felt like crying, too. I closed my eyes and slowly tried to process these new emotions sweeping through me.

My father broke me in unimaginable ways. He'd taken my childhood away from me; he'd never shown me an ounce of respect or love. But now, he was starting to fix things between the two of us. I promised Brianne we would leave all of it behind. Could I really accept him and give him a chance? Could I really forgive him for the numerous ways he'd tried to take my life away from me?

Brianne reached up and touched her lips to mine. I leaned my forehead against hers. When I pulled back and stared into her teary eyes, I saw love, faith, encouragement...hope.

And I realized...I knew what I needed to do.

# Epilogue

My hands were shaking. I didn't really realize how nervous I'd been until now. My heart was pounding inside my chest. And the pain I felt was nothing like I'd felt before.

*I can do this. I can't do this. No! I can do this!*

Pain slowly built up in my abdomen again, and I knew that from there, it could only get worse. I closed my eyes and tried not to scream.

"Let's check again," I heard a female's voice say, and I didn't even know who she was speaking with. Then I felt something down there. A finger, a hand, I don't know. And then an unexplainable pain.

"Son of a gun!" I shouted, and I crushed the fingers I was holding. I could only imagine the pain I was inflicting on that person right now, and I was beyond caring. I would do anything to share even half of my agony.

Instead of cursing or writhing in pain, I felt the person beside me lean forward to give me a kiss on the forehead.

"I love you, *cherie*," I heard Travis's familiar voice in my ear.

I looked up at him, and I saw tears shining in his eyes. I saw love. He gave me an encouraging smile. I knew that he felt my pain. And he would do anything to share it with me, too, if that was possible at all.

"Not yet," the nurse said, after checking me. "A couple more minutes."

I squeezed Travis's hand. "Where's Anthony?" In spite of my pain, I couldn't help worrying about our little boy.

"He's with his grandfather," he replied. "He couldn't stop crying—he was worrying about you. Dad had to take him to the toy shop."

I smiled at that. Travis's father spoiled his grandchild. It warmed my heart to think about the memories of the past few months. Maybe remembering all those wonderful things would take my mind off the constant pain I felt in all parts of my body.

Anthony came into our lives just over a year ago. He was the cutest three-year-old, with dark blond hair and beautiful gray eyes. We

373

found him in an orphanage. Both his parents had died in a car crash, and they left him with nothing, not even guardians who would be willing to take care of him. The minute I laid eyes on him, my heart swelled, and for the first time, I felt those motherly instincts kick in. I felt this need to take care of him...protect him and nurture him. When I looked at Travis, I knew he immediately understood what I was feeling.

He did all we could so we could bring Anthony home. He was ours the very first moment we saw him. Having him in our lives made Travis realize what a father-son relationship really meant.

Travis gave up his shares of his father's company and finally ended the battle between them. Before that, his father found out he has liver cancer and might not last long without a transplant.

Travis's father didn't have many friends or relatives. He was at the hospital with only his bodyguards for company. When I showed up at his hospital suite one day, he was surprised at first. He found it hard to believe that I would even bother to visit him. But after we got past the awkwardness, he started appreciating having another person in the room who wasn't on his payroll.

I didn't tell Travis that I was visiting his father. But I knew that he knew. We'd been married for almost two years, and he still hadn't stopped making it his business to keep me safe, twenty-four seven. He knew where I'd been going in the afternoons when I was not at home painting, or at the studio dancing, or at my mother's gallery helping out. I'd been making his old man feel that in spite of the things he'd done in his life, he still had family.

"Thank you, Brianne," Mr. Cross whispered. "My son is very lucky to have you."

I smiled at him and gave his hand a squeeze. "I'm sure forgiveness will come for you someday."

He smiled weakly. "I'm getting worse. And not on the priority list for a transplant. We both know I might not even live long enough to see that day happen."

Just then the door opened, and I was startled to see Travis enter the room. He gave his father a hard look. Then he handed his nurse a piece of paper. The nurse passed the paper to his father. His father read it, and then he looked up at Travis with a wild expression on his face, his eyes almost teary.

Travis took a deep breath. "I'm not going to do it for you...I'm going to do it for her," he said, pointing at me. Then he turned to me. "I'll wait for you outside." Then he left.

His father was speechless. Then tears rolled down his cheeks. He handed me the piece of paper that Travis had given him. My heart caught in my throat. Just as I suspected, it was his compatibility test for liver donation. Travis was his father's perfect match. He was going to donate a part of himself to extend his father's life and give him a fighting chance.

I smiled at my father-in-law. He smiled back at me in spite of his tears. "I will forever owe you my life, Brianne," he whispered. "Thank you."

I shook my head. "When you get through all this, please promise me you will do all that you can to fix your relationship with him. The fact that he's doing this...it means he's already forgiven you."

The old man nodded and reached out to give my hand a squeeze.

Travis was leaning against the wall beside the door of his father's room. He was looking down at the floor, his face cold and serious.

I reached out for his hand. He looked at me. "I have to do it, Brianne," he said. "I'm the only chance he has."

I nodded. Tears streamed down my cheeks. "I understand."

"I just want to do it. Then we'll move on. I don't want the burden of my relationship with him to be in the way of me giving myself to you and to Anthony completely."

I reached out and hugged him. "I know. I just want you to promise one thing to me."

He gave me a squeeze. "Anything, love."

I took a deep breath. "Just come back to us, alive and well."

I felt him smile through my hair. "I promise," he whispered.

After a week, we were back in the hospital for the operation. I was scared as hell. I almost asked Travis to change his mind about what he was going to do. But I knew he would fight for us. I knew he would wake up and he would recover well. I wouldn't accept any other possibility or ending.

Just before they brought him to the operating room, he smiled at me. "I will see you in a while," he said.

"You'd better," I said, tears rolling down my cheeks. I hugged him.

"Daddy, can we play ball?" Anthony asked, peering up at his father's bed.

Travis smiled at him. "Sure. Daddy just needs to do something for Grandpa. And then we'll play ball."

The child's eyes brightened. "Can grandpa play with us, too?"

It took a while for Travis to respond. Then he nodded. "Sure, kiddo. I'll make sure he will be able to."

I wiped the tears that were rolling down my cheeks. I didn't want my son to see or feel how worried or scared I was.

Travis stared at me. He smiled and pulled me to him. "Don't cry. I'm tougher than you give me credit for," he teased.

I giggled. "You better make sure of that, because I don't want to go nursery shopping alone in a few months."

He immediately pulled away from me and looked into my eyes. "You want to adopt again?" he asked. Then his eyes went to Anthony, who was now happily playing with his toy train on the couch. "He would make a good big brother. Maybe we could get a girl this time."

I smiled up at him. "Yes he would. But no, we're not adopting."

He looked at me questioningly. I sighed and reached for something in my bag. It was a plastic pen-type stick with a small window in the middle. The window showed something that could not be mistaken for something else—a clear blue plus sign.

"Looks like those fertility treatments were working just fine after all," I whispered to him.

It took him a moment to recover. He was just staring at the plastic stick in my hand. When he finally looked at me, his eyes were shining with tears again. He pulled me to him and crushed his lips to mine. Then he leaned his forehead against mine.

"I love you, Brianne," he said. "As if I needed one more reason to fight for my life. You and Anthony were enough. But now...this. I love you, Mrs. Cross. I love you so damn much! You always have a way of making things perfect for me when I thought they already were."

I giggled against his lips. "So do you."

After that operation, Travis recovered at record speed. His father's body accepted his liver quite well. Now...his father is cancer-free, and trying his best to make amends with his son, starting with his grandchild. He never saw Anthony as being adopted. He was very good to him the moment I introduced them to each other.

Travis didn't travel for business all throughout the duration of my pregnancy. He was always there, conducting most of his businesses from home. He shared as much of the burden of the pregnancy as he could. It was hard enough to carry one baby—just imagine carrying two.

A sharp pain in my abdomen took me back to reality, stopping me from reminiscing about the past few months of my perfect life with the man who made me the happiest.

The doctor checked me again, and I cursed at her for like the hundredth time.

She smiled. "It's time."

Travis gave me another kiss on the lips. He held my hand in his. "I'm right here, love. I won't leave you. We can do this."

A few short breaths, a loud wail, a thousand curses, a dozen unsuccessful attempts to push, and then the doctor said, "Give it your best, sweetheart, and it will all be over soon."

It was my choice to go for natural childbirth. Travis was not so much a fan of it. He wanted it to be as painless as possible for me. But right now, hell! I couldn't remember why I'd opted for this in the first place!

I took one long breath, and then I screamed at the top of my lungs, "Son of a..." I wasn't able to continue that curse. I heard a cry that seemed like music to my ears. I looked up at Travis, and his eyes were transfixed on something in front of me, as if he was looking at the most beautiful thing in the world.

"Here's your baby boy," somebody said, and they showed Travis something wrapped in a blue blanket. Everything was still hazy, I was still drugged with the pain. And the contractions in my abdomen didn't even feel slightly less painful.

"Okay, sweetheart. I need you to give me another push," my doctor said, and I could only assume she was talking to me.

Travis turned back to me. "Sweetheart, one more, okay? Last time."

I glared at him. "Easy...for you to say!" I cursed when I felt another huge contraction and I couldn't help the urge to push.

"Dammit, Travis!" I screamed.

And I heard another cry. Instantly, all the pain I'd previously felt was gone. The contraction pains were immediately wiped out as if they never happened at all.

I took the time to catch my breath. I felt Travis's lips on mine and I tasted his tears. When he pulled away from me, he was crying.

"You did well, Brianne," he whispered. "Thank you. I love you so much!"

They brought the baby to him. "A healthy baby girl," the nurse said.

Travis reached to touch her toes. "Hey, little princess," he whispered, and I knew just how happy he felt at that moment. I knew, because if there was one person who felt exactly the same way he did, it was me.

A few hours later, I was back in our room, cleaned up and dressed in a fresh hospital gown. I closed my eyes and took a nap. When I opened my eyes again, I found that I was in a different room. Or maybe it was the same room, only it looked different. There were flowers everywhere, and a lot of balloons, both pink and blue.

I heard Anthony squealing somewhere.

"She's awake, Daddy!" he said.

I looked up and found Travis looking down at me. "Good morning."

"It's already morning?"

He laughed. "Yes. You were out pretty much the whole night. I didn't wake you up. You deserved it." He leaned forward and kissed my lips. "After all, you have given me the greatest gifts I could ever ask for...aside from Anthony and yourself."

I smiled. "Labor pains...not a joke, Travis. I'm serious."

"I know," he said, raising his fingers to my eye level. "You have a hell of a grip," he laughed.

"That was not even half of what I felt during those times," I said.

Travis leaned forward to kiss me again. Longer this time. When he pulled away, I looked around the room. The huge VIP hospital suite had been transformed into some sort of flower and balloon heaven. It was absolutely beautiful.

"You did this?" I asked.

"Yeah. Figured you would like it. It was the least I could do."

"It's beautiful," I smiled.

"I helped, too, Mommy," Anthony said, standing on tiptoes beside my bed.

I smiled at him. "I know you did, sweetheart. Thank you." I turned to Travis. "So who was here?" I asked.

"Everybody. Your mom, your dad, my father, and my mother...Sarah, Eric."

"Where are they now?"

"Down at the nursery," Travis replied. "Drooling over two very cute *mini-mes*."

When Travis said *'mini-mes,'* he wasn't kidding. The nurses finally brought my babies to the room. Our parents and friends had decided to have lunch outside together to give Travis and me some alone time with our new babies. Anthony fell sound asleep on the couch. Travis decided to let his nanny go on lunch break, too. I knew he wanted a little private time just for us, as one family.

"Thomas James. We'll call him TJ," Travis said, touching the cheek of our new baby boy. He had black hair, and I could almost tell that his eyes would be blue, just like Travis's.

I looked up at him. *Thomas James.* That's what he'd decided to name our boy. I couldn't help the tears that slipped from my eyes.

"And the girl?" I asked, looking at our black-haired princess.

"I figured you could pick a name for her," Travis said. "I will call her Princess no matter what name you choose."

"Therese Anne," I said. "And I'll call her Thea."

Travis smiled. "My Princess Thea."

Tears of happiness rolled down my cheeks as I held both my babies in front of me. I felt Travis's arm around my waist and he gently pulled me to lean on him.

"I have something for you," he whispered.

"What?"

He reached for his jacket pocket and handed me a black box wrapped in a white ribbon. I recognized the name. One of the famous makers of fine jewelry in the world.

I opened the box and found a startling screw-type bangle, adorned with white, blue, and pink diamonds, which are quite rare.

"Travis," I whispered. I was absolutely lost at the beauty of the jewelry. Travis turned it over so I could see the words engraved inside the bangle.

*Travis & Brianne...til eternity.*

I smiled. Tears welled up in my eyes again. It was absolutely beautiful.

"What's this for? It's not even my birthday," I said to him.

He took the bracelet from me and placed it on my wrist. Then he put the screw in place. He pulled a small screwdriver from the box and screwed the jewelry in place, so it wouldn't be removed from my wrist at all.

"This is my thank-you gift to you. For giving me three little angels. The white diamonds are for Anthony. The blue diamonds are for TJ. And the pink diamonds are for Thea," he said, his eyes almost teary. "This is a love bangle. I'm keeping the screwdriver, so only I will be able to remove it." Then he looked at me. "So you will always remember that you and I will always belong together."

Tears rolled down my cheeks. I couldn't say anything. I was overwhelmed by his words. I reached up and gave him a kiss on the lips.

"I love you, Brianne," he said to me.

"I love you, too, Travis," I said when I could finally speak.

"I love you more," he said.

I giggled. "How can you be sure of that?"

"Because I'm sure no one has ever felt this much love for another before," he replied.

I lay in his arms, all warm and happy. It was perfect. It was bliss. I used to be a kid, mourning the loss of my brother and struggling to keep it together, trying to always see the silver lining even though fate had dealt me a cruel hand more than a couple of times. But Tom was right. He promised me I would never be alone in my life, and I have never been. Travis had always been there for me. Tom promised, too, that I would live a long and happy life. And I am sure he is right. I have a long and happy life ahead of me.

With Travis by my side, we would raise Anthony, TJ, and Thea with all the love and comfort in the world. We would teach them how to love and look out for each other, how to love and value family. We would teach them all the good things in life, and how to live life completely. We would teach them how to laugh and have fun, as well as how to be tough and strong. And we would tell them about their Uncle—Tom—the angel who's always looking out for all of us in heaven.

"Travis…"

"Yes, my love?"

"Do you think Tom is happy?"

"Yes," he said. "I know he is. I know he's happy you ended up with me. I know he trusted me more than he trusted anybody." I looked up at him. His eyes were dancing, although they were almost wet with tears. "I'm thinking now he would feel...better me than some random guy who would just break your heart, right?"

I laughed. "Yes. I'm very happy it is you, too," I said, and I knew Tom was smiling down at both of us in heaven now. I knew that when he asked Travis to take care of me, he'd meant for us to be together like this.

I raised my head up and closed my eyes. In my thoughts, I spoke to him. *Thank you, Tom. Thank you for asking Travis to take care of me...*

# About the Author

Jerilee Kaye was born under the sign of Leo in the year 1979.

She graduated with a Bachelor's Degree in Legal Management, and with post-graduate qualifications in the fields of Product Management, Project Management and Procurement.

She is currently managing a global vendor portfolio for a multinational company based in Dubai.

She is married to her first love, Sam, who has been her boyfriend since the age of 16. They are blessed with a beautiful five year old daughter, MarQuise.

When she's not buried under stacks of paper at work, or engrossed with her writing, Jerilee Kaye spends some down time playing golf, kicking her husband's butt on a judo match, and learning to play the piano.

‹

# Other books by this author

Knight in Shining Suit:
*Get up. Get Even. Get a better man.*

Coming Soon:

All the Wrong Reasons

Wingless and Beautiful

# Connect with Jerilee Kaye

Send Jerilee Kaye a shout out, feedback, comment, suggestion, photo, snapshot or screenshot of your copy of Intertwined through:

Email:        jerilee.kaye@yahoo.com
Twitter:      @iamjerileekaye
Facebook:     www.facebook.com/jerileekaye
Web:          www.jerileekaye.com

Printed in Great Britain
by Amazon

51797759R00218